PERIL AT THORNYWILDE

Jonni Rich

Peril at Thornywilde

Jonni Rich

Published by:
Southeast Media Productions
Carlisle Pennsylvania, USA
www.semediapro.com

ACKNOWLEDGMENTS

Rosie, her interest in my work is inspirational.

Mary Lou, for her constant support.

Jodi, my editor, for making the story better with her excellent editor's eye.

To all my family and friends for their encouragement and love.

To Terry, my son.

Chapter 1

Dublin, Ireland, 1835

*L*ovely, lovely Dublin!

Lady Mariana Alice Belmont bounced forward on the dingy coach seat. The early morning overcast sky had cleared - a good omen. Shafts of golden sunlight glinted off the hundreds and hundreds of chimneys emitting wispy swirls of white smoke spiraling upward. Catching the stabilizing straps as the carriage bowled rounded a corner, Mariana gasped at the sight of the impressive stone mansions along this wide residential square.

A number of pedestrians hurried along. Gentlemen in fitted frock coats, maids with shopping baskets out to the shops for daily fare, nurses trundling carriages, all scurrying along on important tasks.

Mariana closed her eyes. *I'm now a part of this bustle.*

She leaned back against the seat, scarcely believing she was in Dublin. Then, tightness corded her chest. Would her father welcome her? Had she taken a foolish risk as Aunt Portia warned? Had His Lordship Charles Alexander Belmont, fifth earl of Thornywilde, issued a direct invitation at Christmastime last? She'd trusted her own audacity believing the invitation true. Her father, a busy man, spent precious little time at Thornywilde Castle. Less time with his only child, Mariana.

He meant it, she whispered, scowling thoughtfully. Life's opportunities must be seized, else they burned away, vanishing like the morning mists.

The carriage lurched to a stop mid-way the square before the most impressive mansion of all, in size certainly. Though not in upkeep. Italianate terraces surrounded the structure.

Overhead, iron balconies claimed the upper stories. Ivy enshrouded the walls. Two great stone lions lounged beside the balustrades addressing the front door. She frowned. She'd never visited her father's Dublin townhouse before. It boded ill—this air of neglect about the place. A brooding mansion, she thought, if structures could brood.

The stone fence encircling the garden gave the property the appearance of a fortress. Bedraggled whorls of ivy dangled from the fence. Not clipped as neatly as it could have been. Not as neatly as the other front gardens along the square. On closer inspection, it appeared no one had lived in the house for a very long time—if ever. A wave of self-doubt tightened Mariana's chest.

What if her father were away in London or even on the continent? What if he'd not meant her to come at all? Her courage wavered. For a moment, panic griped her. *No!* That was not true. Her father *had* invited her. Her lips pressed tightly, she recalled Aunt Portia's warning.

"My nephew, Charles's, invitation was a loose invitation at best—if at all. He does not mean you to go to Dublin; trust me."

"Yes, he meant it," Mariana had vouched that day to her aunt, squelching back the troubling, tiny fingers of doubt. Later alone, as she thought on the matter, she had admitted to herself his word or two at Christmastime as he'd rushed through the swirling snow to his carriage, could have been vague. "I look forward to seeing you in the spring, Mariana," he'd called over his shoulder.

"And, I, as well, Father," she'd shouted against the wind. She'd stood shivering, aware that her words were swept away on the winter's wind.

She had determined he shouldn't forget, and she'd written dutifully reminding him of her impending arrival. True, he hadn't answered her letters, but he seldom wrote, being a mercurial man. Still, he must know she planned to come.

The coach stopped. The exhausted team of fours neighed and snorted. The driver climbed down from the box; his florid face appeared at the door, as he pulled down the step. "Be careful, m'lady," he cautioned, his cheeks red from the wind, his eyes watery from a recent pinch of snuff. He was an older man with thin gray hair brushing his high collar and a matching thatch of gray whiskers.

He'd exhibited great patience on the road when the carriage threw a wheel. He'd treated her kindly and respectfully when her maid, Abbie, left her at the last village to return to Thornywilde as Mariana had planned. A lady traveling alone, though not unheard of, did cause raised eyebrows.

Mariana collected her valise and the packet of books at her side, and slid forward. Alighting, the wind struck her face sharper than she'd imagined. She fastened her cloak at her throat against the gusty blast. On the curbing, she stood, watching the driver fetch her trunk down from the boot. The wind whipped his bottle-green waistcoat behind him as he struggled with the trunk's weight.

She glanced anxiously toward her father's townhouse. The mansion's upper level windows loomed dark, not sparkling and shiny as those across the square. She forced a cheerful thought; at least, here, there were no ancient turrets or dungeons for torturing enemies like the horrors remaining at Thornywilde Castle from olden ages. What could you expect from a twelfth century monstrosity?

A brief memory skittered through her brain. As a girl, she and her friend, Kathleen, had chased up and down the turret's rough stone stairs, venturing even into the dungeons below with the rusting remains of brutal torture machinations . . . she and Kathleen pretending they were damsels in distress.

Her trunk clunked onto the curbing. Next, the driver plunked her hatboxes atop the trunk. All the baggage out, the man blew on his hands, emitting a funnel of fog in the cold. "Is none to meet ye, miss?" he asked.

"Uh. . ."

At that moment, the mansion's front door sprang open. A man descended the short flight of stone steps to the street. He reminded Mariana of one of France's ballet dancers in his tight breeches and white poet's shirt. She'd never seen a French ballet dancer other than pictures in a book, but this man was the perfect replica of those pictures. Stopping at the curb, he frowned up at the driver, who'd clambered onto the box, reins in hand.

"Why the bloody coach?" the man demanded of the driver.

Frowning, the driver shook the reins. "'Twas arranged, sir." He bobbed his hat and the carriage rattled away.

His scowl deepening, the tall, well-built man turned to Mariana. "Why the bloody coach? We won't reimburse you, you know."

Her breath caught sharply. How dare *he!* Despite his rude, shocking words, his eyes captivated her—eyes as blue as the Irish Sea, and at this moment, as stormy. Holding his gaze, while recovering from his coarse remark, Mariana found the presence of mind to reply tartly. "Nor do I expect you to reimburse my fare, sirra." Since, obviously, he worked for her father, she'd see him reprimanded. A footman, no less, and one with cheek.

The man appeared much younger than she first thought. He glared at her and shook his head, his untidy fair hair escaping the black velvet at the nape of his neck. His uncombed hair and rumpled shirt seemed to fit the general air of neglect about the townhouse.

Obnoxious servants! A trial! Her knees trembling, she whirled her cape around her shoulders, started up the walk, turning on her heel when the man didn't follow.

He stood at the curb gaping oddly at her baggage.

She shook her umbrella toward her leather-bound trunk. "Would you bring my things inside? Or is that too great an imposition to ask?" An odd and lazy footman, if indeed, he were a footman. No other servants emerged from the house. Accustomed to her share of duties at Thornywilde, she retraced her steps, gathered her hatboxes, and marched forward, her heels clicking on the cobbled stones. Great-Aunt Portia had reared no molly-coddle.

The footman hoisted her trunk onto his shoulders, his face red, he staggered toward the door. "We've costumes enough here for you girls," he muttered. "Or, are you one of those too conceited to trust a master's selections?"

You girls! Costumes! Conceited? What madness! She glanced down at her best wool skirt. "I'm in the habit of providing my own clothing." Was Sir Charles Belmont's house so fine that his own daughter should be accosted at the street's curbing and be expected to don special finery before entering? *Finery does not define a virtuous young woman.* One of Aunt Portia's pronouncements.

Muscled arms rippled through the man's thin shirt as he ascended the steps ahead of her. Stopping at the door, he wheeled, and ground out the words. "Would you get the bloody door or is your arm broken?"

"Well!" she sputtered. Then, viewing his wobbling legs, the teetering trunk, and his challenged patience, she scurried ahead to open the door. God forbid he'd drop the blasted thing on her head. The door open, she stood aside, her head high.

"Ladies first," he barked. "I can't stand here until doomsday with this beastly thing. What have you inside, boulders?"

Her cheeks burned. Grabbing the hat boxes, she stormed into the vestibule. He followed, slamming the door closed with his foot. As quick as lightning, he locked the front door.

Thud! The trunk hit the parquet floor. A cloud of dust rose in its wake. The footman took a deep breath. Quickly, Mariana glanced around her surroundings in the dim light. The hall's magnificence quite took her breath away even in the uncertain light. No ancient stone castle like Thornywilde; this was a modern townhouse with grand proportions. In spite of its grandeur, the musty scent of long-closed spaces drifted about her. To her right, her shadowy image floated in an enormous mirror over an ornate commode. "Why . . . why it could be lovely," she said half-aloud.

"We haven't all day," announced the man, staring at her with an even more impudent gaze than before, if that were possible. He approached her, standing close, and blatantly began circling her, looking up and down at her body as though assessing her.

She gripped the umbrella tighter. A step nearer, and she'd give him why-for with the brolly's sharp metal tip.

Instead, he stopped pacing and frowned, perplexed.

No more perplexed than I, she thought.

"The best light has past," he finally said, clamping his hands on his narrow hips. "What took you so long?"

Surely, he'd taken leave of his senses. That being her truest observation, and since he may be a mad man, she decided it best to answer him civilly. "There was trouble along the road. The carriage threw a wheel."

He interrupted. "Enough of that drivel."

Saint's teeth, she muttered under her breath, He was a regular rascal! "Where is everyone?" she demanded. She couldn't ignore this man's reprehensible behaviour much longer. Especially now that she suspected her father had no idea she meant to arrive this very day. Not only was her father *not* in residence, he'd not been here for some time judging from the dust in the entrance hall.

Saint's teeth! What had she done coming here?

The odd servant began speaking. "If it's luxuries you're expecting, m'lady, there's none to oblige." He placed galling emphasis on *m'lady*.

"I require very little coddling," Mariana returned coldly, her eyes gradually adjusting to the gloom. "And, where pray is the master, His Lordship, Charles Belmont?"

The man slapped his thigh. "You are a piece of work, my lovely . . . you ask for the master, no less." Engaging in an even heartier laugh, he plopped down atop her trunk, howling until tears flowed from his eyes. Then, with alarming quickness, he vaulted up, circling her again, staring appraisingly. "I don't know," he mused in an under-breath, his thumb and forefinger supporting his chin.

She tightened her grip on the umbrella. "You don't know what? That I'm unexpected?"

"You're expected all right," he hooted, "though late, and a regular minx. Ahhh," he continued, before she could summon a fitting reprimand. "Your bosom will be difficult to disguise. The viscountess, Lady Vesta Chasteen, is a flat-chested woman." He spoke with slow deliberation.

Mariana gasped. "How dare you say such a thing to me! I demand to see His Lordship immediately."

He scowled. "Sorry, lovey, he's away in the country." Gesturing toward the end of the hall where darkness lay gloomier than India ink, he grinned wickedly. "The servants are on holiday. I'm in residence with the cook. Be a good girl and don't give me any trouble, and I shan't give you any. We have work to do, as you well know."

Work? Whatever could he mean? She faced him squarely, determined to hold her ground and at the same time mask her nervousness until she could escape this mad man. "Call the cook at once!"

Her father's odd servant didn't budge. His wide mouth bore a half-smile—no, an impudent grin.

She repeated more forcefully. "I demand you call the cook. And, bring my things to my room immediately." Her head high, she stooped, clutched the hatboxes, then started toward the impressive staircase rising from the center of the hall. She paused at the first step. She had no idea where to go once she ascended these stairs, *where was her room?*

Her trunk upon his shoulders, the man brushed past her, teetering up the stairs ahead of her. "You're an odd one," he said through clenched teeth.

She odd! He *was* the daft one. A sinking cold hit the pit of her stomach. If he spoke the truth and she was alone in this enormous house with only him and a cook, she'd best not rile him further. Somehow, her arrival had set his teeth on edge, yet, at the same time, he seemed to have expected her. Perhaps there was a cook and perhaps not. Perhaps her father was in the country, and perhaps not. She didn't know what to think.

As she followed him upstairs, she noted he was decently, if casually dressed. His breeches were of fine cloth, their cut and fit expensive. The blousy shirt, fashioned of the sheerest cotton. In fact, his costume seemed above that of a footman. Her brain reeling, she wondered—what if this person bearing her trunk was an intruder and a trespasser. Should she bolt downstairs and run toward the front door? No, he'd locked the door from keys at his waist.

Think clearly, Mariana, think clearly.

Again, she stared at his heaving backside in the tight breeches. He must be a person of some quality, but who was he? He'd not denied knowing her father. He'd said her father was away in the country. He'd employed a sort of civility by begging she enter the house before him even though he carried her monstrous trunk. Very slight civility by any standard.

She took a deep breath, before exhaling shakily as the upper landing came into view. She'd not shrink from him, she decided. She'd faced fiercer sorts of men at

Thornywilde when riding her sweet mare, Hera, about the estates. Her practice of riding alone disapproved of by both her father and Aunt Portia. She'd even had the nerve once when a mere girl to accost Old Madge, the mushroom gatherer, who was reputedly a witch, and lived in the wilds. Her friend, Kathleen, had ridden with her that day. Despite Kathleen's misgivings (for Kathleen was easily frightened), Lady Mariana Alice Belmont proved herself no coward.

She and the footman reached the first landing. He motioned her down the hall to her right. She decided that once inside whatever chamber he led her to, she'd demand the cook, bolt the door, and wait until that person arrived.

She'd have this woman summon her father. If, indeed her father was away, the woman would tell her where to find him. She'd take a coach there at once. What if there was no cook? *You mustn't think in that fashion,* she chided herself. She'd deal with that problem should it arise.

Stopping before a closed door, the footman banged the heavy trunk down. Selecting a key from the chain about his waist, he unlocked the door and gestured her inside. "See that cupboard against the far wall. Open it. No matter what you've brought, wear the white silk. The Josephine," he said with a grin.

She stepped inside the room. It appeared to be a salon. The long narrow space had settees in burgundy velvet, a number of fancy tables on spindly legs, and dark, old-fashioned paintings crowding along the walls. The cupboard he spoke of stood between two windows overlooking the square below. She turned. "This is a salon. Haven't I a private chamber?"

His forehead crinkling in surprise, he angled a level look. "What's all the fuss for private chambers? Usually, you girls aren't so particular." With a mischievous nod, he beckoned, "If 'tis luxury you want, my lovey, you may enjoy it for a day. You don't seem a bad sort, just impudent. Follow me."

Lifting the trunk, he started down the hall. She had no choice except to follow. He stopped before another door, dropped the trunk, selected the proper key, unlocked the door, and pushed it open.

With a puckish grin enhancing the attractive planes of his face, his blue eyes danced. "Don't disturb this room. And, don't lift even one trinket. It's all catalogued." He shoved her trunk inside. "Go back and fetch the white silk from the salon," he repeated, "and don't keep me waiting."

"Why . . . of all the gall!" she spluttered.

He leaned against the doorjamb, crossed his arms over his chest, and gestured expansively about the room. "I mean not one trinket taken or moved," he repeated.

"The key," she demanded, whirling to face him.

"What key?"

"I may be from the country, but I assure you I demand my privacy." *Saint's teeth,* she swore silently. The moment she saw her father, this rogue would be discharged.

His muscular thighs strained against his tight breeches as he bowed offering her the key. "I shouldna do this but you're so cheeky, I cannot refuse."

The brassiness of the blighted man!

He dropped the key into her outstretched hand. "If you pilfer this key and pass it along to your henchman, I'll hunt you throughout Dublin and see you at Spiller's Island Gaol. Now, hurry. I haven't all day. Here, we work for a living."

What was this about work? Twice he mentioned work. Best not to question him. "Send the cook to me at once," she demanded, aware her voice had never before sounded so shrill. Nor had her senses ever been so accosted as by this most . . . this most disdainful man. *Saint's teeth!* But he was a handsome rogue.

He continued lounging in the doorway, one foot crossed in front of the other. "I suppose you haven't eaten, as well," he said. "However, your kind above all others should know a hollow jaw makes for a woman's good looks."

He turned to leave. Mariana rushed to close the door. He hurtled ahead of her and slammed the door closed. She heard him whistling as he swaggered down the hall.

Turning the key in the lock, she plopped down atop the trunk and tried to collect her thoughts. What could she expect next? For one thing, she would not go to the . . . the salon and change into some white silk gown . . . not if . . . not if mad King William himself so ordered.

As her anger cooled, she became aware of her surroundings. This enormous room wasn't dusty and grim like the grand entrance hall, nor cold and formal like the salon with the cupboard. This room sparkled with apricot and maize upholstery. Gilt decorated the delicate white furniture. Bright green bed hangings anchored the bed like some welcoming island amidst a golden sea. Very definitely, this accomodation was meant for a fine lady. Dare she think her father had ordered it prepared for her?

Moments later, a bold knock sounded at the door. If the man meant to return and further torment her, she wouldn't allow him entrance. "Go away," she shouted in her harshest tone.

"It's Liza, the cook, miss."

The umbrella in hand, Mariana moved to the door, cracked it a fraction, and peered out. Instead of the man, a short, round woman of indeterminate age stood in the hall.

"Miss," the woman scolded. "Mr. O'Geary knows better than to bring the working classes in here. Ye're to go at once to the salon down the hall. Then to the studio on the third floor." A scowl of contempt accompanied the woman's annoyed instructions.

"I saw the salon," objected Mariana. "It isn't satisfactory. I preferred a suite." Was everyone in her father's townhouse daft?

Liza squinted sharply. "Ye can't stay in here. It itn't allowed." Anxious and hesitating, the woman appeared at a loss for words. After long moments, she found her tongue. "He said ye were hungry. I brought tea and buns to the salon. Follow me."

Mariana didn't budge. Why the assumption she was of the working classes? Very clearly, she expected to work in the future. She meant someday to open a girls' school if ever she got the chance. However, these people didn't know that. Certainly not this woman. Not even her father. "You are the cook?" Mariana asked.

Liza took a deep, raspy breath, her patience wearing thin. "That I am, Miss." She looked as though she wished to boot Mariana down the hall to the salon. "It's enough ye've disturbed me work and yet ye still tarry in here." The cook spied the key that Mariana had laid on the table near the door.

"Awwwwh," she screeched, seizing the key, dropping it into her apron pocket, then clutching the pocket closed with her rough hand. "Ye're a bedchamber sneak come to steal our keys to make wax impressions for your accomplices," she hissed in fear. "He said ye were out of the ordinary. Ye're in the house to do us 'arm." Accordingly, she backed away from Mariana, and opened her mouth to scream.

Lunging, Mariana clapped her hand over the woman's mouth. "I'm neither a thief nor a thief's accomplice," she whispered harshly in the woman's ear. "I am Lady Mariana Belmont, the master's daughter. I've just come down from Thornywilde at my father's invitation."

JONNI RICH

Chapter 2

iza squirmed. "Don't scream," warned Mariana. She didn't want to alarm the man who'd led her upstairs. "I mean you no harm." She withdrew her hand. At least the woman didn't scream.

Instead, Liza's eyes rounded in shock and she blinked. She blinked again as if she couldn't understand what was happening.

"I apologize for putting my hands on your person," Mariana said gently. "It was a reflex." Why explain further? One did not explain to servants.

Liza caught her breath harshly. She clasped the apron pocket containing the key. "There may be a mite of resemblance betwixt ye and the likeness in 'Is Lordship's chambers," she admitted, as if ceding a battle victory. Her eyes narrowed shrewdly. "If ye be who ye say ye are, tell me the name of 'er ladyship in charge at Thornywilde."

"Lady Portia Craven, my father's aunt and my great-aunt."

Liza nodded. "I suppose that 'in't common knowledge in Dublin."

"Of course, it isn't." After the wearying trip, dealing with the upstart footman, and now this brash cook, Mariana realized she *was* hungry. She'd missed breakfast due to the accident with the carriage and the great deal of time repairing the wheel. Some miles later, they'd stopped at an inn that served weak tea, and rancid biscuits.

Mariana drew herself up. "I am hungry. There were difficulties on the road. If I might have tea, perhaps a bun or two. . ."

Liza nodded. "If ye'll follow me, miss . . . er . . . yer ladyship. The tea and buns is in the salon."

"Where is my father?" Mariana asked, preceding Liza down the hall to the salon.

"He's with his fiancée."

Stopping mid-stride, surprise sharp, Mariana turned. "His fiancée! I'd no idea he planned to wed." The words tumbled out before she could stop them. What must the cook think if she, Lord Belmont's daughter, had no knowledge of her own father's engagement?

A fiancée! Mariana continued on to the the salon, grateful the cook followed unaware of her stunned expression. Yet, an engagement was not out of the realm of possibilities, for her father could be backstairs at times. A known fact, he kept his life private from his daughter and his aunt.

Mariana's thoughts ran to Aunt Portia's explanations for her nephew's shortcomings.

"He's an artist at heart," Aunt Portia had said, as if that excused his peculiarities. "Artists are unpredictable personalities." Which was true. Her father had had a penchant for painting as a very young man. One or two of his earlier works hung at Thornywilde. Mariana attributed those paintings to her father's youthfulness, and certainly no indication of his life in the business world.

They reached the salon. Liza stopped, rounded on Mariana with a suspicious expression. *Would the woman ever believe her,* Mariana thought wearily.

"Iffin, ye're Lord Belmont's daughter," Liza began, "ye'd know of his fiancée."

A logical question, however Mariana was tired of logic. "How dare you question me," she replied coldly. "Open the door, please."

Liza pushed the salon door open. Mariana swept inside. Perhaps further explanation may satisfy the cook. Too, she was truly grateful the woman was in the house. "Obviously my father's and my posts haven't connected. The mails are unpredictable this rainy spring."

"Yes, m'lady."

Liza went to the table holding the tea service and buns. She turned a cup upright in its saucer, and began laying out frosted buns on a porcelain dish. She then began puttering about the room.

Mariana had given her situation some thought. "May I inquire as to where my . . . uh . . . father's fiancée resides?" Were it nearby, she'd change her traveling gown to something more suitable and take a carriage there. To delay here could make awkward matters even worse.

Liza said. "The master is at Lady Chasteen's country house in KinKerry. Some thirty miles from Dublin. He's expected here Monday next, as are the other servants."

"I see." Mariana judged KinKerry to be a day's journey from Dublin. A day's journey, were she fortunate enough to engage a coach on such short notice. A journey not possible this day with the day more than half spent. If he'd not expected her here at his townhouse, she could hardly imagine his reaction should she barge into his fiancée's country home?

Mariana sipped the tea. She took a pinch of one of the rich biscuits. Obviously, the cook didn't completely believe Mariana's claims, nor trust her completely, for she kept a discreet distance going through the motions of setting the room aright.

"Would ye be wantin' more tea, m'lady?"

"No, thank you." Despite the cook's nervous activity, Mariana was aware that Liza watched her closely. The tea consumed, Mariana stood.

Liza hurriedly began stacking the soiled dishes on the tray.

"Pray who is the rude footman who met my carriage?"

Liza dropped a fragile cup, shards clattering across the polished floor.

"The man who brought my trunk inside, then?"

"Oh, Mr. O'Geary, ye mean."

"Yes. Who is he?"

A guarded look crossed the cook's face. "He's no footman, yer ladyship. He's yer father's art protégé. Oh, dear," Liza lamented. "He thinks ye're one of the models come to sit for Her Ladyship's engagement portrait. I daresay he'll be most upset when he learns ye're His Lordship's daughter, and not one of the modeling girls from the art academy." Liza turned up her nose in distaste. "Loose lot, those girls are. Going about half-naked before grown men."

More news. Her father employed an art protégé? He'd continued his hobby. How very interesting and how very secretive. A fiancée. A protégé. What else about him did she not know?

The broken glass cleared away, Liza lifted the tray with the stacked dishes. "Would ye have me to inform Mr. O'Geary there's been a terrible mistake about ye're not being one of the modeling gels, Your Ladyship?"

"No," Mariana said quickly, the germ of a daring plan forming in her mind. The art protégé needed comeuppance. "I should like you *not* to inform Mr. O'Geary that I'm His Lordship's daughter. I shall do that myself. Where may I find him?"

"But . . . Miss . . . er, m'lady."

For reply, Mariana smiled broadly at Liza.

Chapter 3

*L*iza gave directions to the art studio on the third floor of the townhouse. Not waiting for more of Liza's objections, Mariana strode to the cupboard between the windows and thumbed through the gowns and accessories. Finery of every sort filled the mahogany cabinet. Silks arrayed in colors of the rainbow. Rich velvets. Furs, many, many furs, even a rare white-fur shawl she recognized as coming from Russia. Sables, ranging in colors from rich browns to black.

She dug amongst the gowns. He said to wear the white silk. Which white silk? There were numbers of them. She pulled out a be-ruffled white silk ball-gown with mutton sleeves and tiny jet bows and buttons at the throat. *Too girlish,* Mariana decided, a flush creeping up her neck at Mr. O'Gearys' remark about her bosom.

The next white silk was a ballgown with an awkward voluminous skirt. The gown one a wallflower damsel would wear pressed against the wall fearing any man who dared approach her. Another white gown sported gaudy peach beading down the bodice and front of the skirt. Not that one, either. Nor the white silk dress with matching sacque. Too matronly.

"But, m'lady. . .," protested Liza, obviously disturbed.

"You shan't be held responsible," Mariana said, thinking of her little maid, Abbie, at Thornywilde, if placed in such a situation. At Thornywilde and here, as well, servants obeyed those in charge—their betters. "Ah. This must be the one," she exclaimed. The empire-cut, white-silk gown with a daring neckline was very Josephine. The gown's simple lines would flatter a woman's figure. The Empress, Josephine had bewitched Napoleon in such a gown.

"This is the one," Mariana said to Liza, who cowered at the door holding the laden tray.

"Well . . . yes, miss. It 'tis. But . . . ye shouldn't. . ."

Ignoring Liza's protests, Mariana examined the gown's daring décolletage. She pulled down a white fur circlet with ermine tails; a wise choice for the drafty house. "Bring these to the bedroom."

Liza slipped the tray onto a hall table and gathered the gown and fur circlet, muttering below her breath. "Ye shouldn't, miss—Mr. O'Geary believes ye're a modeling girl." Marina swept past the mumbling maid and into the golden room to change.

The cook wrung her hands. "Ye shouldn't be in 'ere," she wailed, beside herself.

"Really, Liza, that is quite enough," ordered Mariana.

"Yer Ladyship, I mean no disrespect. 'Is Lordship ordered this suite made up for Her Ladyship, Lady Chasteen. The drapers left only yestere'en."

Mariana stiffened. It behooved one to show control in difficult situations. "You say this is my father's fiancée's room?"

The cook nodded.

Mariana replied. "Very good. I shall occupy it until my father and his fiancée return."

"But, m'lady. . ." A furtive glance about the room, Liza said, crestfallen. "I'll assist you, m'lady . . . Lady Mariana."

"That's very kind of you."

Mariana donned the gown, and turned before the pier mirror. She'd never worn anything this costly or daring - or this lovely.

Should she?

Yes! Mr. O'Geary needed a lesson.

Mariana followed Liza's directions to the set of stairs at the end of a long, dark hall, the quickest way to the artist's studio. The stairs, dark and narrow with risers very close together, bade her lift the gown's trailing skirts to avoid tripping over the train.

Liza said the studio lay midway this third-floor hall.

Someone occupied the described room, for the door stood open, light spilling from within. Her heart hammering against her ribs, Mariana inched toward the studio. A jaunty whistle sounded from inside - Mr. O'Geary, about his work. She paused at the threshhold, lifted her head, took a deep breath and entered, clutching the fur circlet tightly across her breasts.

Mr. O'Geary looked up from his cluttered work table. "Ah, prima donna, you're here." He bowed from the waist mockingly.

"Indeed, I am." Her first impulse, run, though her misgivings fled at his haughty manner. The cocksure man annoyed her. He must be taught a lesson. Temperamental, she wagered, as described most artists.

"Well, don't just stand there. The chair, your majesty." He pointed to a raised section of flooring across the western side of the room upon which stood the most elegant chair Mariana had ever seen. A throne, perhaps, from some punjabs' court.

"Take a seat. The dais," he ordered impatiently.

She'd had little direct experience with men, except one long ago experience with a gentleman who'd proved to her that even gentlemen weren't always gentlemen. Mr. O'Geary, a commoner, had no claim to being a gentleman. He certainly did not act gentlemanly. In fact, he set her teeth on edge, while at the same time, setting her heart aflutter.

She proceeded to the dais, the gown's abominable train trailing underfoot. Once flounced on the throne-chair, she wrapped the fur circlet higher beneath her chin. Too angry to be embarrassed, she sat and glared at Mr. O'Geary.

"My modest lovey," he began in exasperation striding toward her, "is this your first time?"

"How dare you, . . ."

He unlatched the circlet's ties one loop at a time and withdrew it from her shoulders. "Now, the fan." He selected a frond of white blowsy feathers she'd not noticed and placed it in her right hand. "Just, so," he said in concentration. He positioned her arm.

Standing back, his chin in his hand, he announced. "Perfect." From the easel he gave an exasperated look. "You look like thunder. A pleasant expression please. You're safely here, you're fed. I bowed to your whim and allowed you in the best room in the house."

"But . . ." she spluttered.

"Please, don't shift your arse even one degree until I tell you so."

"Saint's teeth! You blithering idiot!"

His startled blue eyes shot fire. "What did you say?"

Heat rose in her face. She mustn't give away the charade. Not yet. She doubted he'd believe her. "Foolish of me, sirra. Pray continue," she managed through gritted teeth.

Shaking his head, he returned to work, but not before she glimpsed his most engaging slight smile. A pity her father must disengage him the moment he returned from his fiancée's country estate.

The long afternoon dragged on. Finally, Mr. O'Geary ended the session—much to Mariana's relief. She'd grown stiff holding the exaggerated position for hours. There seemed no simple way or perfect time to admit her identity. Perhaps she shouldn't just yet. Of course not. Tomorrow morning at breakfast would be a better time; a new day, a new revelation.

Mr. O'Geary began cleaning his brushes. She sat on the dais in the chair relieved she'd decided to delay the truth until the morning. What if Liza told him? So much the better, it would support her truth, and hopefully cause Mr. O'Geary even more discomfort. Too, it may prove Mariana an even greater coward. A risk she must take.

He scowled. "You're free to go," he said. "Don't pinch the gown. Put it back in the wardrobe as you found it."

"I would never. . ." She quelled the angry sparks this man brought out in her. "Of course, gov'nur," she said. "I'd never pinch such a lovely gown, though I think it becomes me more than the original owner." She slipped from the chair and bounded toward the door. He called out. "Wait."

Pivoting, she simpered, "Sirra?" How she wished to strike his grinning face.

Swaggering to the door, he blocked her exit. Her heart thudded. She deserved whatever he meant to deal out. The ermine wrap fell to the floor. His strong arms encircled her waist. He pulled her against his body. With clutched fists she struck his rock-hard chest, aghast he would accost her in such a primitive fashion.

He grabbed her left hand pinning it behind her back. Her right hand he captured in his own, bracing it rigidly against his side.

"You mustn't. . ."

With fascinating control, he embraced her like unto the strongest vice. His lips descended upon hers, not grappling—but with mastery. She squirmed. She would have kicked him but he was much too fast or expectant of that move, for he forced the length of his body against hers, sinew against sinew, pinning her against the wall.

She could not move, nor could she scream, for the pressure of his mouth—his lips alarmingly exploring hers. Not a crushing exploration but a slow, sensual probing of the curves of her mouth, the corners, and the tender middle absorbing the fullness of her lips. By degrees, she stopped struggling. Aware she'd stopped fighting, he released her and laughed.

She leaned against the wall, heat suffusing her. A deliquesce state possessed her limbs. Staggering forward, she would have fallen over the gowns' train lest he hadn't caught her. "How dare you laugh at me!"

"Ah, lass, you're sweeter than the nectar of a thousand flowers. And, you so surprised me, I laughed in wonderment, not laughing at you."

His hooded eyes held enchanted fascination. She had affected him powerfully. As he had summoned her most intimate longings. Longings denied this long time. "So, you say," she retorted saucily, gathering her senses.

"A laugh is a laugh, sirra. A laugh for which you'll soon be sorry."

"Your name, lovey," he asked, his voice breaking the witchery between them. "What did you say your name was?"

Grasping the fur circlet from the floor, she called as she fled. "I didn't."

* * *

The following morning, Liza brought a breakfast tray to the golden bedroom. The aroma of fresh-baked bread and sausages piqued Mariana's appetite. "How kind of you," she said. *Oh,* she thought on a sigh; no opportunity to confess her identity to Mr. O'Geary over the breakfast table. Just as well, she'd dress for another sitting and go to his studio. She'd tell him then. Then, make arrangements to go to her father.

Liza settled the tray on the bedside table and poured a cup of steaming, dark-brown tea. "Tis necessary, m'lady to bring your tray. What with His Lordship away and staff, too, the dining room is closed. There'll be a full scouring of the rooms before they return. Cream or lemon, m'lady?"

"Cream. I'll add it myself."

"Yes, m'lady."

"Tell me," Mariana began. "Will Mr. O'Geary be painting today?" She meant to do the honorable thing and confess her identity to the man. In fact, she'd endured a sleepless night worrying about what now seemed a tawdry trick. A trick with certain repercussions if not remedied. What would her father think of her audacity?

Liza crossed the room and opened the curtains. "Mr. O'Geary is gone, m'lady. "We ne'er know when to expect him. He comes and goes of his own accord. He were gone this morning."

Mariana sipped her tea. What if her father saw Mr. O'Geary before she had a chance to explain? The thought chilled her. How very unfortunate she hadn't righted her foolish prank.

Liza left the room.

Marina tried to think clearly through her mounting panic. Why should Mr. O'Geary mention a mere model to her father? A man like Mr. O'Geary, would never tell he'd stolen a kiss from a tart. The true problem—what if Liza chose to reveal the farce to His Lordship. The cook struck Mariana as one wont to carry tales. Mariana sighed, and spread quince jelly on her thick bread. What an awful mess she'd made of things.

* * *

It seemed a folly to go to KinKerry unbiddden. Instead, she wrote to her father telling him she was in Dublin, and she would await his pleasure, should he want her to travel to KinKerry or remain in Dublin.

The next week passed with only Liza and Mariana in residence at the townhouse. The spring weather turned colder, cloudy, and drizzly. The house became oppressive. On Wednesday a group of cleaning women arrived from the city to refurbish the main rooms of the townhouse.

The charwoman in charge, a tall person of stocky build, with masses of untidy, gray hair, and a sharp tongue, worked along with her two assistants. The twosome accompanying the older woman were talkative and obsessed with prattling endlessly about how to placate the fairies.

Mariana spent as much time outdoors in order to avoid these cleaners. Most of her forays were around the ragged garden in a huge mackinaw, floppy hat, and stout boots. Instead of the weather clearing, it became drearier, wet, with heavy rain almost everyday.

The house stultifying, the gardens muddy and slippery, she took a coach into Dublin to explore the city. This became a daily practice. Some days, she walked into the city proper. It wasn't too far and she needed the exercise. She hadn't left Thornywilde penniless; however, she must take care how she spent what she had.

The cleaning women finished their work Friday afternoon. On Saturday morning, a harsh, wintry wind assaulted Mariana as she stepped outside. She planned to walk into the city and should she tire, she'd hire a coach to return to the townhouse. She needed a turn about the city square even though her company were strangers about their errands. Too, she liked browsing through the shops. So many lovely things to see. Far more pretty things here than in Thornywilde's nearest village, Lough Gendelough.

Mariana stopped in at an apparel store Liza recommended and purchased a thick rain-proof cloak with attached hood.

She felt herself attractive and warm in the new wool. Thus, her walks about the city began in earnest. Anything to escape the house. The city fascinated her. She stopped in a tea shop and ordered strong coffee. Then, took a long walk across the bridge over the River Liffey. She strolled about the college next, admiring the building holding in its midst eager young minds pursuing higher learning. She longed to further her Latin studies. A better education would bring her closer to opening a girls' school in her village.

She walked along to the customhouse with its carved adornments. This particular day, the weather grew worse. With reluctance, she returned to the townhouse.

On Sunday, she attended church services with Liza, who directed Mariana to her father's pew. There she encountered many curious stares, but managed to escape before being questioned too closely. She overheard Liza explain that she was His Lordship's daughter.

The Sunday passed slowly. The only difference, the townhouse claimed cleaner rooms, and the pungent scent of oil polish.

Mid-afternoon, a page delivered a letter to Liza. The letter from His Lordship instructed the cook to prepare for his return on Monday. Tomorrow. Odd, he had not written to her, Mariana thought. She wondered about the letters she'd written him each day since arriving at the townhouse. Letters given to Liza to post. Had the cook posted them? Too, it struck her singularly that Liza could read and write.

Late afternoon, the staff returned. An upstairs, girl, Hermoine, and a man of service in butler's livery. The man gave his name as Gibson. A charwoman, Tilda. They each greeted her respectively trying to mask their inquisitive stares.

* * *

Monday morning the gong rang announcing breakfast. "Is Lordship will be arriving today," Liza announced as Mariana came downstairs. "Breakfast is set out in the dining room, m'lady."

Indeed, how festive the room appeared. Silver serving dishes lined the sideboard, interspersed with vases of fresh flowers; mostly early jonquils, sprigs of greenery, and a few hot-house roses. Mariana sat at the long mahogany dining table, enjoying her pot of strong brown tea and buttered toast.

At every sound she expected her father's arrival. He did not arrive during breakfast, nor at mid-day. Monday passed without his arrival.

Tuesday morning breakfast was again placed on the dining room sideboard. Mariana took her place at the table and added cream to her tea. She looked up to see Gibson scurrying past in the hall.

Liza brought a dish of stewed fruit.

"What is it?" Mariana asked

"A carriage, m'lady." Liza placed the dish on the sideboard. The cook's words were lost as a great pounding sounded upon the front door.

Mariana pushed back her chair, stood, and hurried into the great hall in time to see Gibson open the door to a footman in gray and silver livery. A handsome carriage stood out front, its driver resplendent in a scarlet uniform with masses of gold braid. Another footman in the same gray and silver pulled down the coach step. *Father,* she whispered, her heart hammering. She prayed for a warm reception from him.

What?

His Lordship did not emerge from the carriage. Instead, the footman assisted a tall woman, fashionably dressed in green and yellow silk, down the coach steps. A stylish woman! This imperial person surely was her father's intended, Lady Vesta Chasteen.

Glancing at her reflection in the hall mirror, Mariana lamented her appearance. Why hadn't she taken more pains with her toilette? Upon arising she'd pulled her hair into a silly net. A few wispy tendrils now escaped. Quickly, she ran her hands around the net, capturing most of the errant hair. She smoothed her plain skirt, regretting she'd chosen the dowdy old thing. No time to mend her appearance, for the stylish person was now being escorted to the door. As a last stab at decoration, Mariana grasped a few of the pansies from the hall table arrangement, tucking them into her weskit.

Summoning every shred of dignity she possessed, Mariana rushed into the drawing room to await this visitor.

"Lady Vesta Chasteen," announced Gibson.

Mariana moved to the door and extended her hand. "How very pleasant. Do come in and have a seat."

Lady Chasteen drifted into the drawing room with slow strides. She had very dark eyes, titian red hair and a haughty bearing. Her demeanor and her height intimidated Mariana. Dread of dreads, Mariana thought. Where was her father? His absence flooded her with worry. Was he on the continent? Had he fallen ill?

"How good of you to come," managed Mariana. She gestured to two chairs before the hearth. "Please take a chair. How good of you to come."

Gibson had lain the fire to cheer the chill surroundings. "Thank you, my dear." Lady Chasteen glided forward, selecting the most comfortable chair near the blazing fire. Mariana struggled against her nervousness. It was obvious Lady Vesta knew her way around Charles Belmont's townhouse.

"So, you have come to Dublin," Her Ladyship said with a touch of irony.

"Yes . . . uh . . .," stammered Mariana. "Has my father accompanied you?" A foolish question since obviously he had not.

"Your father is a busy man. It was impossible for him to break away from business. Thus, I'm here." Lady Chasteen smiled magnanimously, though not sincerely, in Mariana's opinion.

Puzzled, Mariana suspected her father had read her letters after all. How else would Her Ladyship know she'd come to the city?

Gibson came to the door. "What is it?" Lady Vesta asked before Mariana had a chance to speak.

"Liza will send in a tea tray."

"Thank you, Gibson," purred Lady Vesta. "Splendid." Idily withdrawing saffron-colored, leather gloves, Lady Vesta continued to Gibson. "The fire is lovely. It's a beastly cold morning." She turned to Mariana. "Liza took the liberty of sending word to KinKerry that you had arrived. How unfortunate the other servants were on holiday. Of course, had your father known your plans beforehand, other arrangements would have been made."

"But -" Mariana began, then fell silent. No need to repeat what she'd believed an invitation. "I did long to see him. I wrote . . ." Mariana took a deep breath, before exhaling with a forced smile. Caution urged—why explain she'd written to him at KinKerry as well as Liza. Mischief may be afoot if her letters were intercepted and withheld. Instead, she said. "I'm honored you've come. It's good to meet you. I had no idea...." Mariana's voice trailed. She mustn't blurt she'd no idea her father intended to wed. Instead, she said. "I had no idea to expect you today."

"Indeed? Has Thomas arrived?" The woman seemed almost puckish.

Mariana blinked. *Thomas?* Saint's teeth, not Mr. Thomas O'Geary! Of course, Lady Vesta meant Mr. O'Geary. Mr. O'Geary, the painter, painting Her Ladyship's engagement portrait. The painting for which Mariana had posed. Heat suffused Mariana's neck. Not only from embarrassment for modeling, but for the kiss, and not so much for the kiss itself. But for her response to it. Pray it wasn't evident that she'd thought of little else except the handsome painter after he'd left her father's house.

"Why, no, m'lady, I haven't seen him since the day I arrived."

Thank goodness Liza arrived with the tea tray. Mariana poured, her hand shaking.

"There's a nasty chill in this room despite the fire," complained Lady Chasteen. Where is that lazy Hermoine?" she asked Liza. "Poor soul," she continued to Liza. "You must attend to everything."

Liza curtsied and left the room, a smile on her broad face.

With Hermoine, the upstairs girl, Gibson, the man of service, and the scullery maid who did the kitchen rough work, a great deal or responsibility lay on Liza. Still, it seemed odd Lady Vesta should patronize the cook.

Gibson came and attended the fire. The fire mended, and the room considerably warmer, Her Ladyship continued. "My trip from KinKerry was a horror. I shall find it necessary to rest shortly." She had the most annoying voice, high-pitched and strident.

Mariana stiffened. The golden room! Pray Liza had removed her trappings before this woman ventured upstairs. "My father," Mariana began, "No ill fortune with my father's business, I pray." She knew his weakness for drink that flagged his health.

Her Ladyship smiled a practiced false smile. "Dear, dear Charles. I explained he is at KinKerry with his secretary pressing him with work. It's true he suffered a slight twinge of dysentery earlier, but that's long over. Trusting you will understand, he regretted he must remain at my estate for the present. He will join us as soon as possible." Her Ladyship gave Mariana an arch stare as if challenging her to question the subject further.

Chapter 4

he tea and sweetmeats did little to settle Mariana's nerves. She wondered how much longer Lady Vesta would continue their unpleasant exchange in the drawing room. She hadn't long to wonder. Though, the subject broached shocked her.

Lady Vesta placed her cup on the tea tray. "I heard you've recently visited Cork. Your mother's estate," began Lady Vesta.

Frowning, Mariana recalled writing her father she intended going to Cork. Evidently, he had read some of her mail, or his secretary had. Her visit to Cork occurred months before. Certainly nothing to concern this woman. "I go to Cork occasionally," she said. Anywhere to escape the tedium of Thornywilde. "There's a competent overseer in charge and several houses on the family lands. The manor house is leased." An extremely uncomfortable feeling settled in the pit of Mariana's stomach.

"You will inherit those properties when you marry," Lady Chasteen said. "The very moment the vows are exchanged," she continued. The woman's fathomless, dark eyes revealed nothing. Yet, Mariana detected a hint of greed.

"That is correct," Mariana replied, surprised her father had had occasion to discuss his dead wife's will with his fiancée.

Lady Vesta continued. "If you remain a spinster, your mother's estate will come to you on your thirtieth birthday."

At three and twenty Mariana felt well on her way to spinsterhood. "It is a delicate subject," Mariana said firmly. How very forward of her father's fiancée! To not only know the where-to-fors of her future stepdaughter's inheritance but to blatantly speak of such.

"I shock you," Her Ladyship said, laughing.

"Not as shocking as insensitive," Mariana said truthfully. "About my father's illness, you said he had dysentery."

"Tut, tut. Your precious father will be fine. He'll join you soon. I assure you of that." The woman's black eyes beamed hard on Mariana. "Before you form an unbecoming opinion of me, I feel you have the right to know the truth. Dear Charles promises many things. He does not always fulfill these promises. That is his significant flaw. Despite that, he's a charming suitor and a doting fiancé."

"And a dear father," put in Mariana forcefully, the sentiment coming directly from her heart. She ignored Her Ladyship's cold stare. What a shrewish creature this woman seemed. A woman with a hidden agenda. Had her father taken the time to know Lady Vesta well? Or, had drink blurred his judgment? Mariana studied Lady Vesta from lowered lashes.

She resolved to refrain from absolute judgment of either Lady Vesta or her father until she viewed them together. Perhaps the woman's curtness was a ploy to alienate her fiance's only child. Some women chose to not be bound to stepchildren. Some women despised stepchildren, even grown ones, as they could become an unwelcome burden.

Her Ladyship need not worry. Mariana had plans to continue her studies and open the girls' school she'd dreamed about. Even if it appeared she must wait until her thirtieth year for inherited funds. A school for gentle young women whom proper society frowned upon. Young women with a background similar to her own.

Mariana wished the unpleasant visit over. Surely Lady Vesta meant to retire soon. Instead, Her Ladyship fixed Mariana with a quizzing stare. "Why do you not hold your head up straight? You lean to the side when you speak. It is offsetting."

Stunned, Mariana stared at the woman. "I wasn't aware I'd not held my head straight—ma'am—er—Your Ladyship." What a difficult woman! Mariana's lofty thoughts of withholding judgment began to dissipate like a fine day assaulted by thunderclouds.

Aunt Portia's advice came to mind. Aunt Portia swore that the most awkward social moments could be endured, even overcome by adopting perfect manners.

Mariana stood, pulling the bellcord. "It's lovely you are here," she said firmly, "but I have matters to see about."

"Indeed," returned Her Ladyship. "And, how soon you've acquired pressing matters here."

This woman had no right to criticize or belittle her. Mariana couldn't hold her tongue. "You may jest about me that I'm not accustomed to presiding over a great house such as this one, and you are right. However, I assure you, I take what duties I've assumed here seriously. Too, I recognize rudeness when it strikes me in the face. You have no cause to talk down to me, ridicule my inexperience, or even criticize my posture."

Her Ladyship's eyes widened in mock surprise. "Ah, a spirit. There may be hope for you yet. Don't get so ruffled, my little hen. I meant no affront. And, seriously, a lady always sits erect, holds her head erect. It is a sign of good breeding." Lady Vesta yawned. "I find Dublin a bog. I confess I am overtired. However, there is one thing more. You may as well learn it from me. Your father has other weaknesses besides broken promises – drink, and gambling. But we'll discuss this another time."

Lady Vesta stood, drew her wrap about her, left the drawing room and started toward the stairs without further word.

Liza motioned to Mariana once Her Ladyship moved out of sight. "Hermoine has moved your things to the bedchamber across the back of the house. You'll find it airy and large with a dressing room."

* * *

Next morning Mariana awoke in the unfamiliar room to wind tossing the branches against the windows. She slipped from bed and peered out. The view from this chamber did not overlook the street but showed the back garden. A garden even more unkempt than the front garden. Overhead leaden skies dulled the gloomy morning. Not a pleasant day for a walk. Too, her obligation remained in the house with the guest, Her Ladyship. How tedious, Mariana thought not looking forward to Lady Vesta's company. What if Mr. O'Geary came today to resume work on the engagement portrait?

She dressed quickly in a teal skirt with a matching waist, both trimmed in black Spanish lace. She added a soft yellow shawl, and the set of pink cameos that had belonged to her mother.

Downstairs, the dining room table had been set for one. Mariana took her place, relieved and puzzled. Where was her father's fiancée?

Liza hurried in with a pot of tea, which she placed on the table before Mariana along with a tray of scones and pots of jams. "Will Her Ladyship join me?"

"No, m'lady. She ne'er comes down in the morning but takes a tray in her rooms. I'll bring in the sausages and eggs. Will this be all, m'lady?"

"Yes, thank you, Liza. This is lovely," Mariana replied, pouring her tea, then buttering a scone.

True to Liza's word, Lady Vesta did not come downstairs, though Mariana lingered a bit longer at the table, giving the woman every chance to make an appearance. Breakfast over, she went upstairs to write to Aunt Portia. She sealed the letter and waited for the hot wax to harden before placing it in a packet. From now on she'd walk into the city to post her letters and not place them on the hall credenza, as was the townhouse practice.

Outside, the wind whipped dark clouds across the leaden sky. It did not rain. She pulled her coat closer and walked the short distance to post the letter. Since it was but a short walk to the shops, she went on and browsed through the stores. She purchased two French novels, a card of lace for a new gown, and a packet of note paper decorated with lavender roses.

She arrived back at the townhouse before luncheon. A peek in the dining room showed no table settings, and drawn curtains. Mariana went down into the kitchen where Liza presided over a number of bubbling pots and sizzling pans. A joint of meat sputtered on a spit over a fire banked to glowing coals.

"Yes, Lady Mariana?" Liza asked, looking up, frowning.

"I hadn't thought to disturb you," Mariana said sincerely.

"'Tis no bother, Your Ladyship. As Gibson said you was out, I thought you'd take lunch at some of the tea-shops as you've done before. I'll send up a tray. As I told you, m'lady, Lady Vesta in't one for formal dining unless His Lordship is with her."

"I hadn't meant to rush you."

"'Tis no rush, Lady Mariana," answered Liza. "There's a bellcord in your room. No need troublin' yourself comin' down 'ere. Hermoine will answer. The kitchen stairs is steep and the ceiling dangerous low at the first landin'."

"Of course."

A short time later, Tilda from the kitchen brought the luncheon tray. Nice brown tea, a small pitcher of milk, fresh scones, fig jam, thin slivers of ham on crusty bread, and a rice pudding with raisins.

After lunch, Mariana went to the drawing room, then the library. No sign of Lady Vesta. She actually felt relieved at not finding the woman. A very odd person indeed, to spend her time upstairs in her rooms.

Mariana went upstairs and began reading one of the French novels. She read most of the book, a scathing romance that brought a blush to her cheeks as she recalled the kiss Mr. O'Geary had stolen, believing her a modeling girl from the academy. His mistake, however, had not diminished her exquisite pleasure recalling the kiss.

She vowed to apologize and beg his forgiveness the first moment she saw him. At times her boldness surprised her. Really, she must behave more ladylike. Her freedom at Thornywilde enabled a certain degree of hoydenism. Dublin was not Thornywildle.

Late that afternoon, Hermoine brought a tea tray. "Will you be needin' 'elp dressing for dinner?" she asked.

"Yes, I shall." She'd brought only one gown suitable for a formal evening, a thick gray muslin with a blue waist sash and matching blue bows along the bodice. The hem of the gown had four rows of stiff ruffles. The sleeves were admirable and of the latest style with the leg-o-mutton cut moved halfway down her slender arms.

The tight waist, wide sash, and saucily placed bows accentuated her bust. The gown was difficult to manage on her own. She meant to take a great deal of trouble with her toilette since Lady Vesta was here. Surely the woman intended coming down to dinner.

At the appointed time, Hermoine came, helped Mariana dress, and took great pains with Mariana's hair, putting it up in an impressive upsweep. Satisfied with her appearance, Mariana started downstairs.

She met Tilda on the stairs bringing up a tray.

"Oh, Lady Mariana," the girl said. "'Tis your supper tray I'm bringing up."

"I see," Mariana began. Was her father's fiancée not dining downstairs—again? "Lady Vesta-"

"-is gone, Your Ladyship," Liza answered, coming up beside Tilda.

"Gone?" Mariana felt the fool for her blurted response, but the word left her lips.

"'Tis her way," Liza said with a shrug by way of explanation. "If you prefer, there's a fire in the breakfast room. I've laid the table there. That is, if you prefer."

"That would be lovely," Mariana replied. She'd grown restless spending the day in her room.

Mariana went back for her shawl, the corridors being drafty. *How ridiculous,* she thought. Taking such pains with my dress proved for naught.

The meal over, Hermoine built up a fire in the dressing room off Mariana's main bedroom. The maid closed the heavy Flemish drapes surrounding the blue, French bathtub. Gibson brought up bucket after bucket of hot water while Mariana waited behind a screen. She needed a soothing bath after this strange day where nothing went as expected.

"That will be all," Mariana said to Hermoine, once she was dressed in her warm nightgown with its embroidered, matching dressing gown. She sat before the bedroom fire, her thoughts plaguing her. Such a strange house. Such peculiar goings on. Her father in another village.

Was he ill or too busy at business to come to Dublin? His fiancée appearing unannounced, then leaving unannounced. Whatever did it all mean? Why had Lady Vesta gone to the trouble and distance of traveling to Dublin from KinKerry? A messenger could've sent word of her father's business pressures without Lady Chasteen enduring the rigors of a trip. Odd, as well, Lady Vesta seemed to expect Mr. O'Geary.

Mariana went to the dressing table and began taking down her hair. She stared at her stark reflection in the mirror. She missed Thornywilde and Aunt Portia. She missed her friend, Kathleen. The unusual goings-on at the Dublin townhouse were the sort of things Kathleen would understand and help explain. Kathleen, with her more experienced social life.

In bed, Mariana pulled the counterpane under her chin, and watched the fire die. The wind set up a howl, drowning out the fire's crackling, dying embers. Rain slapped the casement windows. The candle on the bedside table sputtered. *What should I do? Go home to Thornywilde? Go to KinKerry to see about my father?*

Mariana sighed. Kathleen would know exactly what I should do!

Kathleen, a quiet girl, never had Mariana's energy. Though very different, Mariana and her red-haired friend had become inseparable. She recalled one rainy Saturday after first term was out for the holidays, when Aunt Portia had allowed Mariana to visit Kathleen at Shannon Hall, the Stephenson manor house. Gannett, Thornywilde's handyman, had driven Mariana in the rig.

Upon arrival, Kathleen wished to stay indoors, read, and paint, for she was a great homebody even on fine days. Mariana wheedled and coaxed until Kathleen relented, and they had the stableman saddle two horses.

The rain slackened to fine mist as they rode over the estate. The damp curled Kathleen's hair into a frizzy tangle. They rode farther into the woods than they'd ever ridden before. Kathleen begged to turn back. Ahead, lay the cottage of Old Madge—a witch, a healer, a midwife, depending on whom you asked.

Those who called on Old Madge did so under cover of darkness or stealth. Many in the village sought the woman's herbs for various ailments and conditions. Fine carriages from some of the great houses traveled there, the servants sent, white of face, and eager to leave.

Kathleen reined her horse to a stop. She gestured at the gray stone cottage below the hill.

"We're not to go there."

"We aren't," Mariana explained. "We're only riding to the edge of the wood to see what the old hag does out here all alone." Mariana had overheard Thornywilde's servants saying that Old Madge's isolation was of the devil.

"I'm not riding down there," Kathleen protested, shaking her head.

"Just a bit farther," Mariana coaxed. "She can't see us from here for the trees."

A thick copse surrounded the little cottage. Smoke curling from the stone chimney indicated the old woman at home.

Before Mariana goaded her steed forward, brush rustled behind them. Old Madge stepped into the small clearing, her blue eyes glittering. "What, ho, be ye doin' 'ere trampling my fine 'shrooms beneath your horse's hooves?" The woman held a tattered wicker basket containing various leaves, roots and berries.

35

Kathleen went a sickly pale color intensified by her flaming, red hair.

"We didn't know you had mushrooms here," Mariana said, grateful her voice hadn't trembled.

Old Madge glared. "I know you," she said to Mariana.

"I'm sure you do not know us," Kathleen shot back, finding her courage. "For we've never been here before." The redhaired girl glanced at her friend for support. Instead of reassuring Kathleen, Mariana lifted her chin and spoke to the old gnome.

"I know you, as well. You bring babies." It was a bold statement, for Mariana knew little of bringing babies except what she overheard from the servants.

Old Madge shook her finger at Mariana. "There was two," she muttered, her pale eyes narrowing.

"Come along, it's starting to rain harder," Kathleen shouted over her shoulder to Mariana, as she wheeled her horse. The animal cantered up the hill. Mariana couldn't very well remain in the odd woman's company, nor did she wish to. Tossing her head at Old Madge, she put her horse into a run to catch up with Kathleen. Foolish old woman, Mariana thought. There was two. Anyone with a grain of sense could see there were two—she and Kathleen.

Memories, Mariana thought, plumping her pillow, her focus coming to the present. She listened to the wind. She really must sleep. The day had taxed her in every way. With a small sigh, and not a bit of envy, she thought of Kathleen's life today. Kathleen, settled in her married life with a husband and two small children.

Lough Glendelough, Thornywilde's village, became drab after Kathleen's marriage. She and her husband had settled in the north on a family estate. An estate many miles from the village.

Marriage, Mariana thought, her eyes wide in the darkened room, lit only by the glowing fire. She'd met no one worthy of marriage, in her opinion. How could she make a suitable match with the rumors about her background? She wondered if Lady Vesta had heard the rumors. Even Aunt Portia had given up her matchmaking attempts.

"She has a good heart," Aunt Portia had explained to her lady friends at Thornywilde for tea. "I must leave her to her ways." Kindly spoken, but with slight misgivings.

It matters not, sighed Mariana. No prospects for marriage. Her dream was to open a girls' school. True, this day she hadn't funds, but she would receive her mothers' legacy upon her thirtieth birthday.

The thing to do - go to KinKerry and see her father. She did not trust Lady Vesta.

Chapter 5

London
Ten days later

he slight middle-aged lawyer raked his hand nervously through his scant, gray hair as he awaited Lady Vesta's interview. She'd kept him waiting in the unheated receiving room the better part of an hour.

The footman appeared at the door. "Follow me, sir."

He trailed the footman and went into Lady Vesta's library. "My dear lady." He bowed.

She did not rise from her chair behind the carved desk, but half-frowning, indicated the chair before the desk. He sat down, grateful for the cheery fire warming and brightening the room. His hands were cold from the unheated receiving room. "I beg your pardon, m'lady." The solicitor pulled a square of embroidered linen from his jacket pocket to mop his bulbous nose.

How irksome he is, thought Lady Vesta, but useful on occasion. "May I see your dispatches? I am pressed for time."

"Yes—uh—yes, of course." Opening the case balanced on his knees, he selected a sheaf of papers bound with brown ribbon. He placed the neat bundle on the desk before her. "You'll be perhaps disappointed."

Smiling falteringly, he continued, "No birth records exist for Lady Mariana Alice Belmont in Lough Glendelough village." Hastening, he explained. "Not an uncommon happenstance with country births and village registrars."

Lady Vesta glared at him. "Did you check in Dublin? Lady Catherine and His Lordship, both peers, surely registered the birth of their only heir.

The notice likely went to Dublin and the records were never transferred to the village registrar."

"Yes, m'lady, I sought information in Dublin with the same result." He cleared his throat and smiled slyly. "I learned from those of the villagers willing to talk for a small sum that lady Catherine contracted milk-leg after the birth and never regained her health. She died five days after giving birth. His Lordship, distraught over his wife's death left Thornywilde. Through the years, he returns infrequently. At lambings, for instance."

Lady Vesta held her hand up for silence as she perused the documents. Her eyes averted, she thought swiftly. An unregistered birth meant many things. However, not certain evidence Mariana was a bastard. "This is not satisfactory," she said, looking up. "You must look further into the matter."

"With your kind permission, of course."

"By all means." Lady Vesta noted the official signatures and proper seals on the documents.

Shifting in his chair, the solicitor adopted an apologetic air. "There is one other thing. A rumor. A rumor repeated from more than one person. Lough Glendelough is a backward village. It hardly seems to have moved into the nineteenth century."

Her Ladyship leaned forward. "Go on."

"This . . . uh . . . rumor." He cleared his throat again.

"Do continue."

"It is said that a very winsome upstairs maid, Ena Guthre, some distant relation of Lady Catherine, served as her lady's personal maid after Lady Catherine married Sir Charles. The Guthre woman left Thornywilde in shame after delivering a healthy baby some say was His Lordship's bastard. This occurred about the same time His Lordship's sickly wife delivered a stillborn. Gossips say the maid's baby was brought to Lady Catherine to appease the dying woman. Many believe Lady Mariana Belmont is the Guthre woman's bastard."

Lady Vesta's brows arched. "A maid's infant substituted for the dead heir?"

"It would appear so, m'lady." The solicitor fidgeted, blinking rapidly. "Rumor, it is. But, the oddity of it all is this Ena Guthre left Thornywilde with a baby."

"If Lady Catherine delivered a stillborn, it's hardly likely a dead child could spring back to life," said Lady Vesta. "Who then is Lady Mariana Alice Belmont?" The contempt in Lady Vesta's voice caused the solicitor an audible wince.

"Uh . . . that's not known, Your Ladyship." He smiled cunningly. "Any child from the village or even of a surrounding village could've been brought to Thornywilde. One babe at birth looks the same as another. Money may have greased a palm. A baby brought in. A baby reared as the heir. It's very possible."

Possible, indeed, mused Vesta. Mariana may be illegitimate, or at best adopted. Little wonder Sir Charles did not allow his daughter to come out in a London season. One thing puzzled, however, what service became a substitute heir after his wife's death? "What became of the babe the Guthre woman carried away? Was that child the true Mariana?" she asked the solicitor.

"The matter is unclear, Your Ladyship. These are rumors—rumors I encountered on more than one occasion. They may be no more than that—simply rumors. However, perhaps His Lordship wanted an heir. An heir to inherit Thornywilde."

"That's quite preposterous!" Lady Vesta countered heatedly. "His Lordship was a very young man when Lady Catherine died. He could have sired any number of heirs had he chosen to remarry."

"Very true, Your Ladyship," agreed the solicitor, "however, why would he not have selected a son if Lady Mariana is no true heir. Why choose a girl?"

The solicitor struck a nerve. Why had Charles allowed this child to carry his name and reside at his ancestral home, and stand to inherit Thornywilde with its vast ancient estate? Charles has as many secrets as I, she thought.

Lady Vesta sat up straighter, and glared archly at the little man. Until she knew for certain Mariana was a bastard, she must hold her peace. This bastard child or true child stood to inherit all of Lady Catherine's holdings, as well as Thornywilde. How could Charles allow that? Unless, Mariana was . . . *his* bastard child. But the maid left with her infant. She must locate this illusive maid at once.

She turned to the solicitor. "You found no grave marked or unmarked for a stillborn from Thornywilde?"

"No, Your Ladyship. Nor any record of an infant's death occurring at Thornywilde."

Lady Vesta frowned. "You must investigate further. Also, locate this Ena Guthre at once. If I'm not in London when you complete your search, my secretary will tell you where to contact me."

The solicitor pushed his briefcase closed, the heavy locks clicking.

"You may wait for your fee. Cedric" she called. Cedric, the footman entered. "See this gentleman to the receiving room to await my secretary."

Once the tiresome man left the house, Her Ladyship watched him through the library window. He crossed the square and hailed a coach. She meant to personally peruse the village church records when she accompanied Charles to Thornywilde. No good to question Lady Portia. That woman bore her no love. Until then, Lady Mariana Alice Belmont would remain Charles's questionable heir.

She left the library for the back parlor and rang for tea. She sat alone over the tea service ruminating. *A bastard brought up as the heir.* A bastard without claim to legal adoption. Pure and simple, the chit now residing in Dublin must never inherit. She would force Charles's hand when the proper time came. Until then, the news the solicitor reported perplexed her. Rumours of a stillborn. Rumors of a substitute infant. No proof. Only rumors. No infant's grave.

Was it possible Charles became so prostrated with grief over his wife's death until he neglected his legal child? Perhaps a substitute baby had been brought in without Charles's knowledge? She'd heard Charles and Catherine's marriage was a true love match. Why then, neglect the child of his beloved? There were many things about Charles she didn't understand. Nor was he a forthcoming man. He avoided personal questions with great charm and his endearing personality.

Too, this substitute baby business could be lies. Lies. Fireside tales. Fancies. Rumors were often false. On the other hand, the slightest rumor often held a germ of truth.

She rang for the maid. "Hot water. The tea is cold," she ordered irritably. Cedric brought in the day's posts. Bills. Her debtors hounded her day and night. Once the marriage occurred, she could pledge Charles's holdings with her own. Blast his delicate health. At this moment, he lay at KinKerry suffering from gout and left weak after dysentary. All, delaying the marriage.

Chapter 6

London

The following morning, Lady Vesta glanced at the clock. Now nine-thirty. Callers would begin arriving by ten o'clock. Mostly ladies called at this early hour. She must present a polished, pleasant image. She called to her maid to assist in changing her gown and touching up her coiffure. "Must you shake so much powder in my hair?" she grumbled to the maid.

"Pardon, m'lady."

The appointment with the solicitor left her unsettled and angry. Rumors, he provided rumors. He'd proved useful, though, in other matters for his ability to turn a questionable deal in her favor.

"The carriages are arriving, m'lady," announced Cedric, the footman, ever elegant and polished in appearance and manners.

"You had the fire made up in the large drawing room?"

"Yes, m'lady." Cedric bowed and departed.

Lady Vesta sighed once her maid left the room. These early callers, mostly women, bored her. However, one must keep up appearances and remain in societys' upper bosom. The men callers waited until the late afternoon to make their rounds when sherry accompanied the tea and delicacies. Smoothing her gown a last time, Vesta went down into the drawing room. She'd asked her son, John, to greet the callers. She didn't see him. Where was he?

"The chief Magistrate's wife, Mrs. Theodiosa Sully, and her niece, Lady Armentrout," announced the butler.

"My dears, how delightful to see you," simpered Lady Vesta—noting Theodosia's unbecoming gown and her bad skin violently over-red this morning. As if the poor woman had devoured a tub of strawberries. "How lovely you look."

The chief magistrate's wife's annoying habit of breathing heavily as though she'd been running sounded in Vesta's ear as they embraced. Lady Vesta turned to Lady Armentrout. "And, you dear, dear Cassandra, how lovely to see you. My dears, do take the wing chairs near the fire. It's beastly cold this morning. What an abominable spring we're having."

"You're so divinely kind," exclaimed the magistrate's wife. Go Cassie," she whispered, turning to her stick-thin niece, "before someone else claims the cozy spot.

"Now, Vesta," Theodosia continued, once Cassandra moved from earshot. "I must have your opinion about silks I've had imported for the upcoming season. Becoming colors, that sort of thing. You're always wonderfully dressed. I so admire your style, my dear Vesta."

"You're far too flattering and far too kind," said Lady Vesta. "Ah, here's Cedric with the tea. Darling, do enjoy yourself."

Hurrying to greet her other callers, Lady Vesta managed to keep clear of tiresome Theodosia and her plain niece. A glance in the woman's direction and Theodosia beckoned. Lady Vesta smiled, and rolled her eyes, indicating she was too tied up with other guests to sit and enjoy her favorites.

Carriages came and went. Callers arrived and departed with other houses to visit. True to form, Theodosia and Cassandra remained until the very end of morning callers. And, where was John? He'd made a brief appearance earlier. She'd observed him leaving the drawing room with Miss Grissom. Miss Grissom, a fast young lady, in Vesta's opinion.

Perhaps no one noticed John's departure with her.

The magistrate's wife stood. She and Cassandra approached Vesta, intent on a further word. "We've hardly had a moment for conversation," Theodosia said enviously, eyeing the silver tray filled with calling cards. "I really must beg your opinion." She drew two swaths off silk from her reticule - a royal blue and a garish red. Which color is most flattering? On me, that is. I dote on your opinions."

"The blue silk, dear," Lady Vesta said absently, her new shoes pinching, and her temper festering by John's absence. "Blue is becoming to you. Its delicate hue brings springtime to your fair cheeks."

"Lady Vesta, you are too kind. And, so knowledgeable." Theodosia laughed, showing bad teeth. The woman's affectation bordered on a giggle. She tucked the swaths of silk into her bag and glanced slyly around the room. "Where is your son? I had hoped to see him. Cassandra, too, prayed he would stay longer."

"He made an appearance," Her Ladyship replied. She'd like to know his whereabouts, as well. "I daresay he was called away. He's sitting for his portrait with a very temperamental artist."

He'd escorted Miss Grissom into the conservatory what seemed hours ago. "John will hate he missed you, both," Lady Vesta replied. "He's quite fond of you. I shall tell him first thing you asked about him."

"Oooooh, how kind of you." The magistrate's wife beamed and chortled. The silly posturing put her several chins to jiggling. "I wanted to introduce him to Cassandra. They've not met since they were children."

"Really, Aunt," murmured Cassandra.

"I thought I saw Miss Grissom," said Theodosia. "Didn't you see her?" She asked her niece.

Cassandra flushed. "Perhaps. I'm not certain."

Once the irritating twosome left, Lady Vesta fled to her private drawing room, fearing her feet would ache for the rest of her life pinched as they were in her Parisian slippers. She'd noticed the considerable number of engraved cards in the silver salver. She'd had a most impressive morning. The cream of London society.

Once inside her personal salon, she rang for her maid. "Bring my gray felt slippers and send John to me at once."

Almost a half-hour later, she heard John's step in the hall. He sauntered into the room and flung himself down in a soft chair. "Close the door," she ordered. There are things we must discuss." Her tone rang grittily as she struggled to mask her anger at her son's lack of judgment.

His surly expression didn't help matters. Shortsighted as usual, John had escorted young Penelope Grissom into the conservatory in the presence of numerous callers. His foolishness with Miss Grissom could prove disastrous. He'd dallied there until Penelope's mother had been forced to summon the pair.

Then, he'd not shown the courtesy of greeting the other guests but sulked off to his rooms. A faux pas to be chattered about in a dozen or more houses during afternoon visits. However, she must do battle over the larger issue—her upcoming plans for him and Lady Mariana Belmont.

"You're displeased, mother," John began. "Let me explain-"

She glared at her son, handsome as a Sistine Chapel cherub - but lacking in reason and logic. The temptation to goad him churned in her throat, but she contained her tongue. "No explanation will suffice. The crux of the matter is if the simpering Penelope demands an engagement. Anything can be said to have happened in a flowery bower."

He blanched white. "Engagement?" He all but shrieked. Ah, he had the ability to understand the situation if not the wisdom to manipulate similar situations to his benefit.

He sat up straighter, shaking his head back and forth like a naughty schoolboy caught at a prank. "Penny . . . er . . . Penelope offered her gloved hand and I refused."

Lady Vesta waved him quiet. "Who witnessed you refusing her glove, and why did this chivalrous refusal take half the morning?"

"Mother, I need no witness. My word is my bond."

Groaning inwardly, she wished for a glass of port to wash John's stupidity from her brain. "We haven't time to discuss Penelope. Thomas O'Geary arrives in London tomorrow."

"My portrait!" exclaimed John. "It's to be completed at last?"

Vain, vain John. How like his father, her deceased husband, Sir Hugo, dubbed Sir Cuckoo behind his back. "How should I know?" retorted Her Ladyship. "Artists are temperamental."

John crossed his long legs, tented his thin, white fingers beneath his chin. "My portrait should be completed," he complained petulantly. "I'm tired of waiting for it."

Frowning at her son, she explained. "Mr. O'Geary is a perfectionist. He cannot be rushed. Now, listen. I've had word from Charles. His gout has improved. He leaves KinKerry, perhaps this very morning for Dublin."

"I thought he was prostrate with gout and that other obnoxious malady, and expected to croak off for good."

"Really, John, you're impossible. He's ill, but improving. I've heard he still manages to dally at cards. A few days ago, he had a disastrous turn of luck. By the grace of God, he lost but he hadn't pledged Thornywilde and the north holdings. I have sent word by the morning post that he is to go to Dublin. I will join him there."

John propped his highly polished boot upon the sofa cushion. "Mother, you wicked, wicked girl. You fixed the game again, didn't you? You wanted him to lose so you could rescue him."

John, on rare occasions showed cunning about matters and stratagems one didn't openly discuss with one's son.

Leveling a severe gaze at him, she lowered her voice. "There is a matter of graver importance. As you know, Charles has a daughter, Lady Mariana. This daughter is in Dublin at his townhouse," she told John. "I had opportunity to read a letter she wrote to Charles. She has some ridiculous fancy to study languages and open a school."

John broke into laughter. "God forbid! You, a mother, after all this time. You're taking this girl under your wing?"

"Would you listen," admonished Her Ladyship. "This daughter puts a very different light upon my upcoming marriage to Charles." She didn't tell John that Charles had neglected informing her he had a daughter. She'd depended on her spies for the information.

"You're breaking off the engagement?" questioned John.

"In a word, no. You are to see to the daughter."

John snickered, wriggling his blond mustache. "What am I to do? Take a stone and crush the life from His Lordship's darling daughter? Push her into the sea from a cliff? Smother her with kisses?"

"You are to marry her."

Chapter 7

London

he pale February sun sank across the Thames as Thomas plowed through soot-tinged ice and slush in the gutters. He passed gentlemen in greatcoats and ladies swathed in fur-lined capes hurrying along the London street.

At one corner, he halted, barely missing a carriage stopping suddenly in front of him to disgorge a laughing foursome. Early diners, he thought, or last-minute shoppers. All bound for pleasantries.

His appointment, certainly not pleasant, he thought grimly. He'd left Ackerman's where he'd posed for a quick charcoal sketch by an artist-apprentice. A spur of the moment act. His Lordship's instructions never varied when the elusive painter, Italia, released works. Italia, a friend of Sir Charles, and the most elusive painter in the world, who kept his identity a secret.

"He has reasons for remaing anonymous," His Lordship had explained. "We are old acquaintances. I am nothing if not loyal to my friends." Loyalty, Thomas understood. He did not understand Italia's methods of delivering his masterpieces to those who'd purchased them in advance—sight unseen.

Thomas checked the time. He must hurry. He was to meet the unpleasant woman, Ena Guthre, whom Sir Charles chose to deliver the paintings to London. They met each time of delivery at the same London pub.

The pub was an out-of-the way establishment. Always heavily attended with customers, it brought anonymity to the transaction. He paid the woman, Mrs. Guthre, who then sent the camouflaged paintings to his room in the city.

The following morning, Thomas would deliver the paintings to an old jeweler, Mr. Canady, in London's jewelry district. Thomas understood Mr. Canady was a lifelong friend of both Sir Charles and Italia. Once His Lordship confided that Martin Canady had at one time been his art teacher when he was a very young student in Cork. Odd, as well, once Mr. Canady asked about Ena Guthre when Thomas delivered the paintings.

Thomas enjoyed His Lordship's trust. Not only for being in His Lordship's confidence, but for Sir Charles's generous help taking him on as an artist apprentice. His Lordship's help in the artistic world had brought Thomas a measure of success that otherwise he couldn't have achieved so quickly. It was not his place to question the unpleasant Guthre woman or the mysterious Italia.

Thomas hurried along Harley Street to meet Ena Guthre. The woman reminded him of a person of fallen estate. After this night's work, Thomas had an appointment later the following day with Lady Vesta. His work with her, or rather her son, Sir John Desmond, to complete the son's portrait.

Thomas did not like Lady Vesta, and disliked her offspring even more. However, commissions were commissions. He couldn't afford prejudices as His Lordship's protégé.

He arrived at the pub early for the appointment, and took a table in the room's far corner where shadows surrounded him and he could watch the door. He hadn't long to wait before the Guthre woman appeared in the low-ceilinged pub's doorway. He recognized her at once though she wore a veil. Tall and of imperial bearing, she scanned the room for him. He noticed she wore a gray gown and mantle, not too shabby, not fashionable, either.

She spotted him and approached. "Good evening, sir."

"Madam," he responded, stood, pulled out a chair for her. She settled at the oaken table, black with age. After smoothing her skirts, she lifted the veil. Her face always alarmed him. Perhaps once attractive, she appeared haggard and older than her years. She watched him, her expression cold and calculating. He noticed her woolen skirts were damp about the hem, as though she'd walked a great distance, though he knew she usually arrived by cart.

The responsibility lay upon her to send the paintings to his lodging house. His job - to pay her. He often wondered what would happen if she took the payment and didn't deliver the paintings. Apparently, His Lordship and Italia trusted her.

"The packages," he asked, "arrived satisfactorily?"

She smirked. "They await now at your lodgings as usual. Why do you ask? Do you not trust me?"

"How many, madam?" He kept a tight smile, refusing to spar with her.

"'Tis two this time."

Thomas frowned. "Only two. Mr. Canady has buyers for four." Thomas's heart felt heavy. His Lordship mentioned four canvasses. "Are you sure?" he demanded sharply.

"You doubt me?"

"I pray not," returned Thomas threateningly. If she pinched two paintings and sold them, pocketing the money, the responsibility lay not at his door. His gaze softened viewing the woman's obvious weariness. Each time they met, it seemed she'd traveled quite a distance from her village to London. "Forgive me, madam, have you eaten?"

"I have not. The lad is outside, too."

"Call him in, and we'll sup."

She left, returning with a boy of six or seven, her grandson. He would be a winsome lad if his curly, fair thatch was combed and his jacket not so rumpled.

Thomas ordered shepherd's pie and salt-crust bread all around. When the waiter brought the steaming bowls, the boy fell upon his as though his life depended upon sopping the bowl clean.

The widow's gaze narrowed. "I must have the money." She bore an unsavory expression as he slipped the bag of coin under the table, which she instantly secreted in her skirts.

"Shall I count it?" she said, cocking her head at a saucy angle.

Thomas shrugged. "If you're comfortable emptying the bag in this bawdy place, go ahead."

She decided against counting the money—a wise decision, he thought. The boy finished eating, and the widow, as well. He escorted them to the curbing outside the pub and hailed a for-hire carriage.

"Tim, boy, wave goodbye to Mr. O'Geary," Mrs. Guthre said, as some notion of protocol occurred to her. A carriage approached and stopped.

The boy turned and grinned. "Goodbye, gov'nor, sir."

Thomas laughed. "And, a cheery goodbye to you, Timothy. Mind you learn your lessons."

"Aye sire."

The coach drew away, splashing muddy water upon the curbing.

He'd completed the first leg of the transaction. His head down against the wind, he made his way to his rented rooms. The landlady opened her door to him. "Aye, Mr. O'Geary. Your parcels, sir," the landlady said indicating two large, square packages leaning against the hall-tree. "The same as always."

"Thank you, my obliging friend." He handed her a packet of coins. Once inside his room, Thomas tore away the brown paper and cord, then the wad padding. Seascapes. The painter, who signed his work, Italia, favored the sea. Thomas stood the pictures against the far wall, studying them. Clearly, the artist's influence and subtle brushstrokes came from studying with the Italian masters, though both seascapes depicted what appeared the wild Irish Sea. One at sunrise. One at sunset, possibly near Cork. However, Cork was mere speculation. Lovely work, though. Brilliant! Thomas couldn't take his eyes from the paintings.

Thomas had tried his hand at landscapes, and seascapes; however, portraits proved more lucrative. He hadn't the means yet to travel abroad, study, and support himself, while he trained under a master. One day, he would. His Lordship's kind mentoring kept Thomas's dream alive.

His Lordship dabbled at painting, he loved art, and his interest in Thomas's work helped Thomas secure appointments for the portraits. Thomas had gained a growing reputation. Carefully, he re-wrapped the paintings in their wad and brown paper and slipped them under the bed until delivering them to Mr. Canady the following morning.

The next morning, he rose early, washed and shaved. He had breakfast downstairs at the landlady's table. She prided herself on setting a good table, and serving a fine English breakfast.

Setting out early for Mr. Canady's shop in the jewelry district, he found the establishment not yet open for business. He went to the back door off the alley and knocked.

Canady himself opened the door. The stooped, little man wore the weary expression of one often indoors in good weather and bad. He wore gray breeches and a fresh white shirt, which served to inhance his sallow complexion. His yellow weskit further drained the color from his sunken cheeks. His black frockcoat lay across a chair in the tiny office where he led Thomas.

"Only two?" Canady questioned viewing the packages.

"Two, but brilliant."

Frowning, Mr. Canady shook his head. "We've buyers for four. A dilemma. How can I decide between the buyers?" he muttered, taking the paintings, and slipped them into a closet. He took a key from his waistcoat pocket and locked the closet door. "I'll have a look at them after hours. Though, I've no eye for art anymore. There was a day when I earned my living teaching art. But that was many years ago."

Thomas laughed. "But you must admit you taught one student well. Italia's work is stunningly brilliant!"

"Aye, who said I taught Italia? Only a blind man could miss the man's superb talent. I regret he was no student of mine."

* * *

During the afternoon, light sleet peppered the cobblestones as Thomas hailed a hansom for the more fashionable section of London. What a capricious spring, he thought—as cold as winter. Lady Vesta's butler met him at her townhouse door. "Good morning, Mr. O'Geary. Her Ladyship is indisposed and Sir John is out with companions. Your studio is readied. I have a fire laid."

"You're most kind." Thomas made his way to the third floor where Her Ladyship had improvised a studio. Nothing as fine as His Lordship's Dublin studio, but adequate. Removing his blue frockcoat, he donned a smock, and began laying out supplies. Sir John Desmond was often tardy for sittings.

Just as well, Thomas thought, after an appraising look at the portrait in progress. He needed time to paint out some of the pink in John's cheeks. The young man, puffy-cheeked naturally, appeared to be sporting two bright apples beneath black currant eyes. John, a foppish youth, had unusual coloring, white blond hair, black eyes, and ruddy skin. He gave evidence of some Danish forbearer. Once the cheeks were corrected, Thomas worked on the pair of spaniels at John's feet from a sketch he'd brought.

He'd worked intently for hours unaware of the time. A knock at the studio door surprised him. The maid opened the door a bit. "Lady Vesta regrets she cannot lunch with you. Cook has set food out in the dining room."

Downstairs, he ate alone, which he much preferred. After lunch, he set to work again.

Steps sounded in the hall and John burst in, attired in riding kit. An undercurrent of excitement accompanied the young man, his cheeks redder than ever. He'd no sooner taken his seat than he began peppering Thomas with questions.

"Have you met His Lordship's daughter, Lady Mariana?"

Thomas nodded. "I have." Liza had informed him that the young woman he mistook for an artist's model was indeed His Lordship's daughter, lady Mariana Belmont. He'd lain awake many a night wondering why she'd played a model. Of course, he knew why.

He'd treated her badly the day she arrived at the townhouse. But, how could she fault him? He had expected a model. No one knew His Lordship's daughter was due to arrive. Now, speaking to John Desmond, Thomas felt the heat rise in his neck.

For some reason he felt protective of Lady Mariana despite her foolhardy prank. He'd not forgotten that kiss, either. He could never forget the kiss. Nor, could he betray the lovely creature who'd meant only to play a prank on him. A prank that he deserved.

Sir John laughed. "I've heard she bleats like a sheep and has viper's teeth. What think you?"

Obviously, John Desmond had partaken of his share of spirits this early in the day. How could Thomas defend His Lordship's daughter? Especially with the passionate kiss foremost in his mind. For reasons of simple chivalry, he couldn't allow Her Ladyship's son to dismiss the young girl as some unattractive person. Nor could he appear above his rank with Sir John. In the spirit of sheer fabrication, he said. "The young lady is quite reserved in her manner." He paused before adding. "Rigorous in her studies."

"Folly, man, I haven't asked about her blasted habits, but, her face and her form." John Desmond's degrading tone rankled until Thomas could scarcely bear to answer. All the while, a miserable foreboding troubled him.

"Well, speak, Thomas O'Geary. Or has the cat chewed off your tongue?"

A surge of anger filled Thomas's breast at the arrogant young man. Measuring his words, Thomas said carefully. "Lady Mariana is an upstanding young lady, both charming in countenance and stature." He would say no more even if John proceeded to pull at his tongue with pliers.

Thankfully, he was spared further questions for a group of John's friends barged into the studio. They begged John to ride through Hyde Park with them. Though John protested he'd just returned from a ride, he went off anyway. With relief, Thomas bade him goodbye.

* * *

Lady Vesta requested Thomas's presence for dinner that evening. He arrived promptly. She presided at the dining table, her emeralds and diamonds glittering by candlelight. There were only the two of them this evening, though Thomas observed a third place set.

"I expect Sir John presently," she said.

He nodded.

"Thomas," she began, in a badgering tone as a footman served the soup. "This elusive master painter Sir Charles sponsors—Italia, I believe. Is there anything new from his brush?"

If he lied, she'd learn of his falsehood through her network of acquaintances and spies. Thomas, always cautious in her presence, suspected her of being meddlesome and a saboteur. "There are rumors," he replied truthfully. "I have heard the works are sold—abroad—before he sets brush to canvas." He took a sip of the green turtle soup. Excellent, as always.

"France," she lamented. "The French are to have our precious Irish Sea on their fussy papered walls. Who is the dealer?"

He must tread carefully now for His Lordship specifically demanded that his and Mr. Canady's involvement with Italia remain a secret. "My dear lady, if I am correct and I am not certain I am, a middleman receives the paintings from Italia, and he then dispatches them to individuals." That was not the whole truth, but he prayed it would appease her curiosity. "I do not know who sells the art."

"Oh, tut, tut, Thomas, do you expect me to believe that? You artists are a select group. Surely, you know the dealer's identity and where I can purchase one of the pictures. I intensely dislike being placed on a waiting list."

"At present, I regret I am as much in the dark as you." Thomas smiled uneasily. After dinner, he bade Her Ladyship and Sir John goodbye, and fled the house. Pulling his hat low, he hailed a carriage, regretting Sir John's portrait needed more work.

* * *

The following morning Thomas worked on Sir John's portrait. He was invited for dinner. He'd worked all day in the studio, and longed to end the day, go to his lodgings and rest. Instead, now he must take a carriage to his rooms, bathe, and dress before returning to the townhouse.

A nasty drizzle with the bite of salt-air assailed him when he stepped out of her townhouse. He had trouble finding a carriage. The bitter weather left the streets mostly deserted. It was the hour when commerce ended, and all of London's citizens seemed in a great rush to get home. Once in his room, he bathed and dressed. On his way downstairs, the landlady met him in the hall.

She asked with a beaming smile. "You'll be dining with Her Ladyship this evening, or would you share steak and roast turnips at my table?"

"Ah, madam, your cookery is finer than anything Lady Chasteen's chefs could possibly prepare. But I'm expected there."

Outside, he hailed a carriage. He didn't like the looks of the night sky with low-hanging black clouds. He was certain they were in for more bad weather. A few ice-laden drops fell as he exited the hansom at Her Ladyship's brightly lit townhouse.

Dinner passed with much the same prattle as the evening before. Her Ladyship badgering him about Italia's identity, and Sir John, moody and withdrawn.

The wind rattled the French doors at the far end of the dining room. When the meal ended, Thomas prepared to have Her Ladyship summon a carriage for him. Before he spoke, the butler entered the room bearing a silver tray upon which lay a letter.

"My apologies, m'lady, this was delivered as most urgent," the butler said. "The courier awaits your reply."

Frowning, she broke the red wax seal, which Thomas recognized as His Lordship's crest. Under the pretense of eating the last of his sponge and berries, he kept his attention riveted on her. She uttered an almost imperceptible gasp, which she quickly masked, then assumed her usual superior air. Folding the letter, she tucked it into her satin sleeve. "There will be no reply," she said to the butler.

"Very good, m'lady." The butler, an astute elderly man, the epitome of refinement, bowed slightly. He withdrew through the archway and into the hall, his steps resounding on the polished parquet floor.

"It has become a beastly night," Her Ladyship said, gesturing toward the windows. Thomas wondered if her statement was a *double entente,* comprising the letter's contents as well as the foul weather.

"Bad news?" John asked, staring at his mother.

Ignoring his question, she said. "Dear John, shall we retire to the library?"

John rose and pulled out her chair.

"You will join us for coffee, Thomas." She took her son's arm. He escorted her into the library. Thomas followed with trepidation for she seemed in a strange mood after reading the letter. Admittedly, he was curious about the correspondence for it had a profound effect on Her Ladyship.

She settled on the sofa, two fat pugs at her feet. "Maman," John said, "you act as though your head is to be severed and stuck on a pike." He nudged the pugs with the toe of his boot. "Are we to grovel like Romulus and Remus here before you disclose the letter's contents?" It was clear that he'd had his limit of spirits for in the warm room, his red cheeks were rosier than ever and his black eyes pits of festering rancor.

Her Ladyship gave John a cold look. "When do I ever disclose my private communications, my dear boy?" She turned to Thomas. "I'm certain our dinner guest is as curious as you, John. Tell me, Thomas, did you recognize Charles's seal?"

Thomas hated the flush crawling up his neck. She was a cunning woman, and little escaped her. "I could not help but notice. Is he well?"

"He is a busy man," she replied, with an annoyed expression. Before she commented further, the footman entered the room with the coffee service. Her attention drawn to the steaming cups and seed cake, she looked up, smiling at Thomas. "I confess I'm agog with curiosity to see my portrait. Have you brought it along with you?" Her slight overbite accentuated her teeth's dullness contrasted with the clear jewels at her neck and ears. She was an attractive woman who'd been regaled a beauty in her first youth, and though she'd aged well, and despite her trim figure, there were times in certain light when she appeared plain and unsightly. This evening she appeared particularly grim.

"You'll see your likeness soon," Thomas promised. "Perhaps during your stay in Dublin." He spoke as innocently as possible, but he caught the quick twitch in her expression, as she perceived his duplicity. She was a master of such, and she caught his. He suspected the letter was about her trip to Dublin, and something about the trip had not gone as she expected.

"That will not be possible. My stop in Dublin, if I go there at all, will be of the shortest duration. I must go to KinKerry for a pressing business matter."

Sir John fixed his mother with a sharp gaze. "What business, *maman?*"

"Do be realistic, dear . . . I never discuss business before guests. Mr. O'Geary, our wonderful artist, is our guest this evening. And, fortunate, we are. Half of London would beg to have such a renowned portraiture artist present in their home." She lifted her cup to Thomas. "To you, my good man."

"M'lady, you flatter me beyond what I deserve."

"Tut, tut. Your reputation has caught the attention of His Majesty. I wouldn't be surprised if you received a royal commission very soon."

"How kind you are, m'lady." She was up to something. Exactly what, Thomas couldn't fathom.

The storm broke at last, snarling outside the windows. Two footmen rushed into the library with extra candelabra which they proceeded to light and place around the room. The brighter light showed Sir John sulking by the fire. The pugs had begun to snore after Her Ladyship had stuffed them with remnants of seed cake.

These weren't realistic people. Thomas had tried to please them with his work, though in both cases, the flattering likenesses that stared back from the canvasses barely resembled the mother and son. The adulteration he performed with his brush caused Thomas a pang of conscience, for he longed for purity and realism in his work. He longed for purity and realism like Italia's seascapes he'd delivered to Mr. Canady, the jeweler.

Thomas couldn't deny being flattered by Lady Vesta's suggestion that he might secure a court commission. Her contacts were viable, and she wielded a great deal of power among influential people. A royal commission would set him for life. He contained his excitement for he suspected she might be baiting him for some unknown reason.

"John, dear, you are uncommonly quiet." Lady Vesta spoke with such force the pugs roused and began to chase each other around the room. "How did your sitting go today?"

Sir John, who'd been staring into the fire, turned to his mother. "Better than yesterday when I longed to ride. Wonderful weather then. Only a cold wind. The sleet over by mid-morning. In the park, I enjoyed clear skies, new grass, bulbs sending up bud and bloom." John turned to Thomas. "Will you complete my portrait before you leave London?"

Thomas chose his words carefully. He wasn't without sympathy for the young man who seemed at times a pawn of his scheming mother. He said with a sincere smile. "A good painting, like a good wine, cannot be rushed."

"There's your answer, John," Her Ladyship said, with a brittle laugh. "You're still fermenting." Before John could reply, Her Ladyship turned to Thomas. "Tell me, what do you think of Sir Charles's daughter?"

"Lady Mariana?" He thought fast before answering her. Why ask him? He a commoner, and Mariana of the peerage. Why the question? Why John's earlier questions? What were these two up to? "She is lovely and intelligent," he said truthfully.

A sharp flicker passed in Her Ladyship's dark eyes.

"There's gossip about her birth," John put in, sitting up with interest, the first he'd shown all evening.

Her Ladyship shot John a disquieting stare. "Twaddle talk, dearest. You mustn't put stock in idle gossip." She addressed Thomas. "What say you?"

"About what?" Thomas ventured, truly puzzled. He dared not comment about Mariana's birth. He knew nothing of that. He'd wondered why His Lordship had never told him that he had a daughter in the country at Thornywilde.

Wishing desperately to defend Mariana against this woman and her son, he dared not make any comments that Her Ladyship could pick apart. He adopted what he prayed was a benign air. "She seems very much her father's daughter."

It seemed odd since Lady Vesta and His Lordship planned to wed, that she'd allow her son the privilege of besmirching her intended's daughter. More disturbing than that Thomas detected a spirit of ill will toward Lady Mariana from both Lady Vesta and her son.

Chapter 8

Dublin

*H*ermoine met Mariana in the hall with the post. It arrived late. "M'lady, here's a letter for you. *The Belmont seal.*

With trembling fingers, Mariana broke through the red wax lion's head, and the three lilies. What had her father replied? She'd written asking permission to visit him at KinKerry.

Your Ladyship, Lady Mariana Alice Belmont.

At this present time, do not travel to KinKerry. I am much improved, though advised by the physicians to avoid untoward excitement. It is my express wish that you remain in Dublin until further notice to return to Thornywilde.

Your beloved father and servant,

Lord Charles Belmont.

Mariana read the brief letter twice, then three times. *How odd*—not travel to KinKerry, and the suggestion of returning to Thornywilde. No mention when he'd arrive in Dublin.

She suspected her father's secretary had written the brief message. Folding the letter, she slipped it into her pocket then went to the kitchen in search of Liza.

"Yes, m'lady?" Rushed, and apparently out of sorts, Liza bobbed respectfully.

"Why were you so certain His Lordship would arrive today?"

"Tis his way," Liza replied. Her usual tiresome answer whenever she avoided a question. Indeed, preparations were underway for a sumptuous meal.

"I have had word he's to remain in KinKerry," Mariana said. Lady Vesta and Liza seemed on close terms. Maybe the cook knew other plans.

Liza bobbed—an affirmative acquiescence—then frowned at Tilda's bent form tending the joint roasting over the spit. "Gel, mind ye'll have the joint dry. Baste it at once."

So much for information from staff.

* * *

The gong sounded for dinner. One place was laid at the dining table. Mariana ate alone. *What a peculiar household,* she mused as Liza brought in the coffee tray, cheeses and biscuits. "M'lady, will you take your coffee here or in the library? The fire is made up there."

"Here is fine." Liza's pale face, shaking hands, and troubled countenance concerned Mariana. Clearly, Liza was upset. Mariana, after only a half-cup of coffee, rose and went to the kitchen. She found Liza wringing her hands.

"What's wrong?"

"Oh, m'lady, I'm not to worry you, but 'tis a waste. I've gone to a great deal of trouble preparing this meal. The joint will keep but the soup will fail . . . 'tis made with cream."

Mariana sought to soothe the upset cook by engaging one of Aunt Portia's solutions for too much food. "Perhaps someone nearby could use a good meal?"

The idea struck like a major chord upon Liza's troubled countenance. "'Tis such a family I know," she said, brightening at once. "My own dear niece, sick as she is, and her good husband fallen on hard times. With leave, Lady Mariana, directly after I wash up, I'll take the remnants there. Tilda will go with me as the hour is late."

"That's a wonderful and most practical idea," Mariana replied.

While reading in the library, Mariana heard the cart leave—the two women on their way to Liza's niece's house. She put the book aside. Difficult to concentrate with a gnawing sense of unrest troubling her. Everything was so very confusing. Her father's instructions for her to remain in Dublin . . . her fear he'd suffered a setback.

Dark fell early. The library fire had burned down to glowing coals and ashes. Liza and Tilda had not returned. The downstairs rooms seemed especially lonely. Wrapping her shawl around her shoulders, Mariana made her way upstairs.

Hermoine turned down her bed, laid out her robe and slippers. She attended Mariana as she made ready for bed. Hermoine removed the ruby pendant necklace from Mariana's neck and laid it in the velvet-lined, jewelry box. Moving behind Mariana at the dressing table, Hermoine began removing the hairpins.

Mariana shook her hair free. "It isn't necessary that you stay," she said. "I can manage."

"Yes, m'lady." Hermoine curtsied, then closed the door gently. Her footsteps sounded in the quiet house as she went down the hall.

Mariana brushed her hair. She jumped at every small sound. Finally, she lit two candles to dispel the gloom and settled to read in the easy chair by the window. The odd noises in the house were her imagination, of course. She couldn't concentrate on the book, a French novel.

She slid into bed, drew the bed curtains and plumped her pillow when the certainty someone was in the room had her scrambling up, and reaching for one of the guttering candles. She strode across the cold floor, peered into every corner and under the bed. Nothing. No one.

Back in bed, her conscious state lingered at the forefront of that final doze before oblivion overtook the body. She heard a singing voice. Coming fully awake, she realized it had been a dream. Awoken now, she slipped from bed, went to the window casement, and peered out. There were no stars, only a sliver of moon. The hall clock had long since struck midnight.

Mariana stood, her face pressed against the glass, looking at the street below, masked in darkness. In the distance the yellow lamps of a carriage moved toward the house. The carriage stopped below. Disembarking forms moved ghostly-like toward the house. Liza and Tilda had returned.

Relieved they were in the house, Mariana crawled back into bed. It seemed she'd just fallen asleep when Hermoine's distraught face loomed over her. The maid had pushed back the bed curtains. She held Mariana's wrapper and slippers. "Lady Mariana. Lady Mariana. You must rise."

Foggy from interrupted sleep, Mariana sat up in bed and pushed her hair over her shoulder. The corners of the room were yet dark while gray light seeped in between the curtains. The maid had stirred the fire and a tray with hot tea waited on the bedside table.

"Why have you woken me so early?"

Hermoine's face creased more. "You haven't heard the row?"

"What row? What are you talking about?" Slipping the wrapper about her shoulders, Mariana swung her feet over the side of the bed and into her slippers. She took the cup that Hermoine pushed toward her, and laced it with cream. "Now, what pray, are you trying to tell me?"

The distraught maid gestured toward the floor. "Them downstairs."

"You're making no sense at all."

"They've not gone to bed since they arrived this long night," Hermoine said, wringing her hands. She really was a tiresome creature.

"Who's not gone to bed, Liza and Tilda?"

"No, m'lady, Her Ladyship, your father, and the son. Neither have Liza nor I caught a wink. Liza thinks you should come down at once and see if you can unravel the terrible muddle they're all in."

Her father was home! Dressing quickly, Mariana gulped the remainder of the tea that had gone lukewarm. She pulled her hair into a velvet snood, and started downstairs. As she approached the library, loud voices rose and fell from within. A man and a woman spoke, their conversation undiscernible. Then silence. Mariana knocked. No one bade her enter. She pushed the door open, and paused on the threshold.

Her father sat on the leather settle by the fire, his head in his hands while Her Ladyship faced him, perched on a straight chair. A younger man with blond hair so pale it appeared white leaned against the mantel. The young man looked up and smiled at Mariana.

"I believe the bone of contention has made its appearance." His lazy drawl communicated he found everything amusing.

His Lordship stiffened, and peered at Mariana through bleary eyes. How terribly, terribly tired and how terribly terribly old he appeared. "Mariana." He held out his hand. "You're here."

She ran and knelt at his feet, clasping his hands in hers. "Father, dear father, you're here at last. Are you unwell?" He motioned her to stand. She did so as he with great effort clamored to his feet. How disheveled and scattered he looked with his hair tousled, his eyes puffy and his riding clothes untidy and damp as though he'd seen foul weather.

After a quick embrace and a dutiful kiss on the forehead, he took her hand, drawing her to sit down beside him on the settle. "My dear, we were discussing your future."

Her future? Dread knotted Mariana's stomach. Hermoine declared there'd been a row. Surely, not over her studies. Her father knew she'd inherit when she turned thirty. She'd written to him about her plans for a girls' school. Any money he advanced would be repaid. Mariana glanced at Lady Vesta. She maintained an icy façade while the blond man smiled laconically.

It was some long moments before her father spoke. "It's impossible..." his voice trailed.

"You're not well," Mariana cried. "Oh, dear, you're ill, terribly ill."

"Ah, yes . . . it isn't about that."

Lady Vesta cut in icily. "Your father is trying to tell you this notion of language studies is out of the question. Quite out of the question. Tell her, Charles." Her Ladyship's voice carried an edge as sharp as a blade.

His Lordship lifted his head as though it were a great weight. "It's true," he confessed. "My fortune has suffered reversal. You and Sir John Desmond must travel to Thornywilde this very day. This Dublin townhouse has been let. The tenants arrive on the morrow." He then recited a sketchy account of his financial affairs which made no sense to Mariana.

Who was Sir John Desmond? "Father, it's not necessary to trouble this Sir John with my troubles or travels. I'm quite capable of traveling alone. The distance is short—merely one night on the road. If that isn't satisfactory perhaps you could send to Thornywilde for Gannett to accompany me, or Abbie."

She'd missed the kindly faces at Thornywilde, Gannett Hooks, the man of all trades, his wife, Betsy, the cook, and little Abbie, Mariana's personal maid. And, most of all, dear Aunt Portia.

"That's out of the question," her father said. "There isn't time for such arrangements."

Her Ladyship craned her neck, staring at Mariana. "You should be grateful my son is willing to accompany you. The roads are no place for a gentlewoman."

"Yes," the blond man chimed from his stance before the mantel. "I am most select to whom I offer my services." Again, he laughed.

Sir Charles looked up from staring at the floor. "Mariana, it's best." He sounded pathetically like a lost child. "You understand I'm poorer now and though a robber could scarcely gain a half-chest of silver if he kidnapped you, I cannot chance any evil or harm befalling you. You must travel with Sir John."

He allowed no further discussion. Though the traveling arrangements were highly unsatisfactory to her, Mariana dared not burden her father with her bitter disappointment. She found both his intended wife and her son vexing and troubling people—though she'd viewed Her Ladyship's son only a few minutes. Mariana chose to not voice further complaints.

They went in to a solemn breakfast. After breakfast, a flurry of packing ensued with Hermoine promising to send whatever Mariana left behind by carrier.

The cellar boy was sent to fetch a carriage. A short time later a coach arrived with drapers who'd come to measure the windows for the new tenant's draperies.

At the last minute, her father decided that Hermoine would travel with Mariana and Sir John as far as Lough Glendelough, the village before Thornywilde.

Arrangements made, trunks hastily packed, they made their way to the curb—ensconced beneath umbrellas as a nasty drizzle fell. When the coach arrived, Sir John took Mariana's arm and escorted her aboard. Obviously, he was accustomed to giving orders for he shouted up to the driver. "The maid will take her seat on the box with you, my good man."

Preposterous, Mariana thought. Hermoine was a frail woman who didn't need frigid air in her lungs as already the cold and damp had her coughing. "I prefer she ride inside with me," Mariana insisted.

Sir John's black eyes flashed. "There's no room. Your book boxes are stacked everywhere."

"They can be rearranged," Mariana said firmly.

He shrugged. "If you like."

Hermoine looked beseechingly at Mariana not wanting to cause trouble. "'Tis no trouble, miss, the box is fine. I rather like to take the air."

"No," Mariana insisted, stepping into the coach. The only space to sit was a narrow section of the forward seat. Hardly room for the pompous Sir John and the maid.

"But, m'lady, I want to sit on the box."

"For a short distance, then," Mariana relented.

"Sirra," she called up to the driver. "A moment while I rearrange things." She slammed the coach door in John's startled face and began stacking her belongings, forcing him into the seat across from her.

All boarded, the driver cracked the whip, and the coach lurched forward, the team's hooves clicking smartly across the cobbled streets.

Mariana stole a final glimpse at her father. He stood at the curbing waving, the umbrella masking his face. Would she ever see Dublin again? Or her father?

The coach traveled at a smart pace. Mariana took out a book for she found John's presence disquieting. Each time she looked up, she found him watching her—a peculiar look in his dark eyes as though he plotted some mischief. Worse than that, he seemed amused by a private joke.

Every nerve in her body screamed caution. Caution she'd learned with a certain debonair captain at Kathleen's birthday ball. A captain who'd followed her onto the terrace that warm night forcing a kiss upon her, a kiss so forceful he ripped her gown, revealing her chemise. She'd fled in disgrace.

A flush reddened her neck as she thought of the kiss she'd shared with Thomas O'Geary. His muscular body pressed to hers, the strength of his embrace, the intimate plundering of his mouth. Quickly, she thrust the memory away.

At some point she must confess to her father about that encounter, and how she'd deceived Mr. O'Geary. What if Thomas told him first about her foolish prank? No, he wouldn't, she thought. He couldn't. Not if he were a gentleman. *He isn't a gentleman,* she thought, he's an artist.

"Half-penny for your thoughts."

Sir John's remark drew her to the present. "Ah, yes," she said. She didn't trust Her Ladyship's son and she didn't know why. It was unchristian to dislike another person for mere rudeness. Many people were rude. She sensed she must guard her every step around Sir John Desmond.

She tried laughing lightly. It rang false in her ears. "I'm afraid my poor thoughts aren't worth even a half-penny." She turned, staring out the coach window.

As they passed the Custom House on the River Liffey, Mariana almost wept at the sight of the stone River Gods. She'd learned they represented the fourteen rivers of Ireland. The edifices protected and kept Ireland's waterways safe and pure.

Likely, she'd never see Dublin again since her father had suffered financial reverses. In her short time in the city, she'd come to love Dublin. So exciting and stimulating. So different from her village and Thornywilde.

Sir John crossed one leg over the other, advantageously displaying his fine leather boots buffed to a mirror finish. "Tell me about yourself," he said.

Annoyed, she put down the Latin grammar she'd held before her face. "There's little to tell."

"You like to read, or is that dull grammar a ploy to hold me at bay?"

Her face reddened. "At bay, sir, I don't understand." She understood well enough to sense he believed he held some special claim on her.

Smiling, he leaned forward at which moment the coach lurched, catapulting him onto her lap whether by design or accident, she wasn't certain. In addition, a box of books tumbled to the floor, rolling about their feet like a crate of apples.

"See, even the road chastises you for ignoring me." He straightened, making a fuss of removing books from around her feet, even smoothing her skirt over her kid slippers.

"My garment is fine, thank you," she said when she felt his hand brush her ankle. "If you're so eager to help, you may retrieve the books that have rolled away."

Pushing a number of books aside with his foot, he said as he righted his jabot. "We shall let the maid see to them once we stop for the night."

The coach hit another patch of bad road. Mariana put the Latin grammar before her face to deflect his further attempts at conversation.

They arrived at Lough Glendalough after dark. A large number of coaches, drays and carts crowded the inn's yard. If they had changed teams they could've pressed on and reached Thornywilde before morning, but the coach was engaged only as far as Lough Glendelough.

A thin young groom approached to take the team. Sir John stepped down, holding the door for Mariana. Lifting her skirt, she alighted. Hermoine already down from the box, seemed no worse for the ride. "Shall I see about your books and baggage, m'lady?" she asked. "Since you go on to Thornywilde in the morning."

"Bring the small valise. The rest can wait until the morning." Not waiting for Sir John, Mariana preceded him into the inn, Hermoine behind her.

The innkeeper didn't appear a pleasant fellow. He eyed Mariana with a scowl. "How many in your party, madam?"

Sir John pushed past Mariana. "You address Lady Mariana Belmont of Thornywilde. I represent this party. I am Sir John Desmond. My mother, Lady Vesta Chasteen made arrangements in advance." John Desmond looked down his long nose. "You should have her script."

Scratching his head, the innkeeper ran his finger down a ledger page. "That would be two large bedrooms, not attached, and a private dining hall?" He spoke without looking up.

"Indeed so." John gave Mariana a triumphant look.

"Alas, that cannot be," the innkeeper said, shaking his head. "We're filled to running into the road. So much so all male guests must lodge in the annex behind this building."

"Preposterous!" John shouted.

The innkeeper, a stooped man with a sharp gaze, and accustomed to the foibles of letting rooms held his ground. "Sir, the Duke of Elderwood and his Lady have unexpectedly graced the inn. They travel with a large company of kin. You can understand my dilemma. You will enjoy every comfort in the annex."

Sir John Desmond's color blazed. "Lady Chasteen of KinKerry sent her script in advance. You would set aside her wishes when she so intimately represents the crown in England."

"The crown," the man repeated in Irish lilt as if unimpressed by England's sovereign. "Ah, yes, promissory scripts, they were." The innkeeper leaned over the desk, leered, withdrawing a handful of coins from the till, jingling them like a wizened monkey dancing for its organ grinder. "The duke paid with gold. I cannot refuse gold for script. The owner would have my hide, sir."

"Blast and damn!"

The innkeeper pursed his lips. "Sir, the lady and her attendant will enjoy a small but neat space over the main part of the inn. Your accommodations will be quite satisfactory, as well. A private dining hall is out of the question. Lo, the porter comes to escort the ladies."

Mariana gave Sir John a jaunty wave as she and Hermoine followed the porter up the stairs to their rooms. She prayed she'd seen the last of Sir John Desmond until the morning.

That was not the case, for she'd no sooner removed her traveling cloak and bathed her face than he sent word by the same porter that she was to join him downstairs for dinner in the main dining room.

Once the porter left, Mariana instructed Hermoine. "You will go down and thank His Lordship for his hospitality. Also, tell him I have an excruciating headache. I cannot possibly abide entertainment or food this evening."

The unpleasant man dismissed, Mariana fell into bed and slept soundly.

Up early the next morning, Mariana bade Hermoine goodbye. Again, she arranged her baggage forcing Sir John opposite her. He appeared a sausage squeezed on both sides by packing boxes.

The coach thundered out of the inn yard on the way to Thornywilde Castle.

Sir John smiled at her. "I see, Lady Mariana, you have survived your aching head." A thread of disdain colored his voice.

"Yes. Thank you, sir. It's kind of you to inquire." He said nothing more. At least he had the good manners to not pursue the subject of her headache. This morning he seemed preoccupied with private thoughts, which pleased Mariana.

Though she loathed engaging Sir John in conversation, she longed to know his plans once they reached Thornywilde. She hoped he'd return to Dublin on the next coach. As they neared the estate, Mariana could no longer quell her curiosity. "I expect you'll return to Dublin once I'm safely at Thornywilde." She failed keeping a slight tinge of sarcasm from her voice.

Turning his attention from the window, he looked at her. She couldn't deny he was somewhat attractive in a polished way. "Return to Dublin? By no means. I intend to relish your countryside's fresh air and the hunt. I hear birds thrive up here."

Alarmed, she cried. "You mean to stay until the autumn?" Field birds were more plentiful then.

"We shall see, shan't we?" He turned back to the window with a chilling chuckle.

Fresh air would suit him, for his peculiar coloring made him appear ghostly white. His very red cheeks appeared redder, and his very black eyes blacker, by contrast with his white blond hair.

They rode in silence. Her spirits lifted when she recognized familiar parts of the road. At last, the coach drew up the long path to the castle. Aunt Portia stood outside the door. The frail little creature had donned her best cashmere shawl. She resembled a small beaming carving as she stood before the massive oak door.

Disembarking, Mariana ignored Sir John's hand on her arm and ran to her aunt. "I'm so glad to see you. There's much I must tell you."

Aunt Portia hugged her. "My dear, dear Mariana. The sight of you fills these old eyes with true delight."

Once Aunt Portia released Mariana, she turned to Sir John. "You must be Sir John Desmond. Welcome to Thornywilde."

John didn't embrace the older woman, instead bowed stiffly, and taking her gnarled hand, kissed it solemnly.

They all filed into the back drawing room, Aunt Portia's favorite sanctuary. The familiar old room seemed welcoming after the Dublin townhouse. A peat fire glowed on the hearth, the pale sun streaming in through the tall windows. "Dublin," Aunt Portia said, with a sigh. "It's a lovely place. Far too log since I've gone there. There was once a time when I traveled quite extensively. However, you are most welcome here," she said to Sir John. "You are to make Thornywilde your home as long as you please."

"You're very kind, Lady Portia."

Impeccable manners. Well schooled, Mariana thought about John Desmond. The question troubling her, why was John here? Indeed, not to hunt birds. He seemed deceptive though she couldn't place her finger upon an exact imposition. Her father's failed circumstances made her no catch for a gentleman. If she married at once, she'd inherit her mother's estate—whatever the value of those holdings. Otherwise, she'd not inherit for seven years. In a subtle way, Sir John gave her the impression he had a claim on her. Nothing could be further from the truth. He had no claim. He would never have a claim.

* * *

The following morning after her arrival at Thornywilde, the capricious early spring weather took a decidedly frigid turn. Frost lay over the fields. A bitter East wind swept about the old castle rendering the ancient stones as cold and frozen as though hewn from ice.

Gannett scuttled about tending roaring fires in Aunt Portia's drawing room, the morning room, and the library.

Days like this taxed Mariana's restless spirit. She longed to get out of the house and ride. Especially in the hills. Her spirits soared in the uninhabited spaces devoid of other humans where she could be herself, think her thoughts, and dream her dreams.

To her surprise, John did not come down for breakfast. The dining room table had been set for two, the sideboard resplendent, displaying a sumptuous array of sausages and eggs.

Aunt Portia had seen that every amenity awaited their illustrious guest. This annoyed Mariana for she didn't feel Lady Chasteen's son worthy of special accommodations. *It's only a breakfast* she reminded herself. She became further irritated when she saw Gannett trekking upstairs laden with a tray for the lay-a-bed.

After breakfast, she hurried upstairs, and pulled on her riding kit. The leather breeches, the greatcoat and her wide-brimmed hat. John Desmond could sleep the day away. She'd not sit around and wait for the desultory task of amusing the man.

Abbie popped into Mariana's bedroom bearing an armload of fresh linen. She stopped, a shocked expression on her elfin face. "You're riding out, Lady Mariana?"

"Yes, as you can plainly see. Send word to the stablehand that I want my Hera saddled." As an afterthought, she added. "Have cook pack a light lunch. I shan't be in a hurry to return."

"But-"

"No, buts about it, Abbie. Hurry yourself."

Chapter 9

*T*he wind flapped Mariana's hat. Reining Hera to a full stop, she tied the leather hat strings beneath her chin. The day brightened gradually, if still cold. No vista would suit her today except a run up Cormac Hill, and then a wild ride down through the ravine below. Cormac Hill, the farthest point of Thornywilde holdings. The point her father instructed her to never ride alone, because the familiar tenant farms, and cottages lay far behind. She'd have no protection if a highwayman approached her. The dreaded Ribbonmen also banded together, raiding cattle from those they knew supported the English throne, and the English Church.

His Lordship, Charles Belmont of Thornywilde, being a staunch loyalist, was firm in his support of the English crown. He was fair to his tenants, and treated them well. Hence, despite being a loyalist, he was well liked in Ireland.

The Ribbonmen were not a new movement. They'd emerged from earlier groups under other names. At first, the Ribbonmen's plunderings seemed noble in a way. A means to recover unfair taxes the English imposed upon all in Ireland, the poor and the rich, to support the Church of England. Of late, however, the motives of these marauders had become more virulent and evil in nature. To stand against them or identify one of them meant swift death. Their atrocities, instead of being noble, became criminal.

Mariana had misgivings that she'd ridden so far. But, the view from Cormac Hill drew her onward. Hera seemed eager to run, too. The intelligent horse sensed her beloved mistress had been away for far too long. Both needed the freedom of a wild ride.

The wind bore unusual keening noises; it whistled amongst the crags as Mariana rode higher up Cormac Hill. Other noises imploded on her senses. *Aye, what were those noises?* Panic gripped her. She heard thundering hooves and bawling stock. Mariana's heart stood still. The melee could mean only one thing. Ribbonmen at work. Warned by instinct, and fearful of what lay in the gorge below, she drew Hera to a stop before reaching the summit. Tethering Hera to a scrub tree, Mariana slipped through the rough heather and gorse to peer below.

They didn't see her. There was at least a dozen of them - the Ribbonmen! All intent on herding the thrashing hooves through a narrow gap at the far end of the ravine. Foam scattered on the stiff wind from the terrified cattle's mouths as they thrashed about.

The Ribbonmen hated English rule and wreaked havoc in every Irish village they could infiltrate. They slipped through the ravines and gorse like phantoms, destroyed cattle, and burned crops - anything to abort the excessive taxes to the English crown. The group had become as much a terror to the Irish countrymen as to the English soldiers.

Mariana, flat on her belly, feared her fate if they saw her. She squirmed to the edge of the overhanging ledge, keeping her head well down and behind the heather. None of the Ribbonmen looked up. Intent on their raid, they drove the cattle through the gap.

A Ribbonman, surely the leader, leapt from his horse. His sheepskin vest dripping with blood, he drew his sword. What was he doing? Rock outcropping on the ledge blocked her vision from the section of gorge directly below her. Dare she lean closer? Standing back, the man shouted an auld Gaelic curse. She knew enough of the old language to know the meaning of the words. *To your death and to your hell!*

She raised her head and gasped. She'd not seen the policemen at first. Three of them. Dead all! The tall Ribbonman did the unthinkable. As a final insult, he slit the dead men's throats with his sword.

Covering her eyes, she prayed. *God preserve the souls of these dead men.* She didn't look up until she heard the last hoof beat bearing the marauders away down the ravine. They rode north.

After what seemed ages, and with a ball of nausea filling her throat, Mariana slithered back to Hera. Hera gently nuzzled her trembling hand. Before Mariana could stand and mount the mare, the retching started, spilling her stomach's contents onto the grass. Once the heaving subsided, she pushed up and sat with her back against a large, sheltering stone until she could think clearly. She must do something. What? The men below were dead. Her help to them, useless.

Already the sun dipped low into the west. Night on these lonely mountains posed many dangers. Why had she ignored her father's warnings? He forbade her to ride alone here on the wildest part of the estate. She'd done so anyway. She couldn't remedy that foolish mistake now.

She must ride to the Constabulary headquarters in Lough Glendelough, some four miles east. The authorities would know what to do. Hera nuzzled her shoulder. "Yes, luv," Mariana whispered. "'Tis a journey we must yet take. Four miles, luv."

God help her. Furze scattered beneath Hera's hooves as Mariana goaded the mare. In the west, the sun sank lower and lower over Wicklow Mountains. Keening wind whipped her hair across her face.

If only she hadn't ridden out this day, she'd never have witnessed the horror in the ravine. She would now be safely at Thornywilde, her feet beside the hearth, warm tea and a lovely slice of Irish bread in her hand. Her embroidery at her side. Her beloved books on the table. Too late now.

The wind rose in intensity. She rode like a madwoman. When it seemed she could ride no farther, Lough Glendelough's cobbled streets appeared in the distance. Slowing Hera, she reined the mare to a stop. The horse's sides heaved like a pair of twin bellows. "Steady, sweet girl. Catch your breath, luv."

It was some minutes before she urged Hera ahead. The village seemed deserted, as most of the shops had closed for the day. The cold, blustery weather had most people inside by their fires. The scent of boiling cabbage and sausages filled the late evening air.

She reached the constabulary paddock. The white stone building stood just ahead. In the paddock yard, she saw an officer she recognized, Duty Officer Liam Ross. Seeing her ride up, Ross glanced askance at her. She knew she looked a fright - her leather breeches, her voluminous coat, the hat pulled low, her long hair, free of pins, streaming about her face. "Officer Ross, it's me, Lady Mariana Belmont. A terrible thing has happened!" Her head spun. She feared she'd faint.

Liam rushed toward her. "Lady Mariana, what's happened?"

In her shocked state, she watched him stare at her soiled riding attire, her disheveled hair, and surely her expression of horror.

"I would speak to the Chief Constable. At once."

Liam helped her to the ground. Her knees buckled. She struggled to stand.

"Quick man," he shouted to a junior officer, "Lead this horse to the mews. This young woman is prone to faint on me."

The officer ran quickly, taking Hera's reins.

His arms supporting Mariana, Liam pushed open the headquarters' door and led her down a drafty passage. Men's voices drifted from what must be a canteen farther down the hall. Pausing before a door, Ross opened it. "In here, Lady Mariana."

Mariana stepped inside a clean, square room with yellow light spilling from a lamp on a lampstand. The scent of sage-laced, scrubbing soap filled the air. A cozy room, but sparsely furnished. The office faced west where the sun had now disappeared below Wicklow Mountains leaving faint, pinkish tints streaking across the dark sky. Warmth from the stove in the corner took the edge off her cold face.

Liam pulled out a chair for her. She dropped into it. She'd scarce had time to gather her wits or take a deep breath before Chief Constable Jagger stepped into the room. An Englishman sent to this village to keep the peace, Jagger was a big man with sharp, dark eyes. He held a cup of steaming tea for it appeared he'd just come from the canteen. "What trouble, Lady Mariana?" It was a question with tangible perception. His cunning eyes missed nothing as he assessed her appearance. He turned to Officer Liam. "Fetch her a cup of tea. Bring a blanket. This woman appears to have been long in the elements."

"What happened, Your Ladyship?" Jagger asked, turning back to Mariana.

She took a deep breath, exhaled on a ragged sigh. "I'd gone riding earlier. I stopped atop Cormac Hill giving my mare a rest. I saw cattle being driven through the northern gorge. I saw Ribbonmen!" Her voice failed. "God help them..., there were three dead policemen."

"What dead policeman?" Jagger barked.

Officer Liam Ross returned with the blanket and tea.

"Close the door, Liam," Jagger commanded. "You may stay," he said to the officer. Jagger turned his dark eyes on Mariana. "Continue, Your Ladyship."

Mariana didn't answer at once. She draped the blanket around her cold legs, cradling the warm cup of tea in trembling hands. When it appeared she'd drop the cup, Liam took it and placed it on the chief's desk.

She began, barely above a whisper. "The men lay in the deepest part of the ravine below Cormac Hill. All wore blue uniforms."

Jagger swore. "How many Ribbonmen?"

"I should say a dozen, though perhaps that's not accurate. It was such a scene of horror and fast moving men, cattle and horses, I couldn't be sure."

"Did you recognize any of the Ribbonmen?"

"No. They wore sheepskins and had blackened their faces with bog peat." To say she believed she recognized any of them would be a fabrication. She shuddered, recalling the leader's wild oath. *To your death and to your hell!*

"Were you alone on Cormac Hill?" Jagger's tone condemned her foolishness for riding without escort in the wilds. He also stared at her riding breeches, long coat and her hat, now on the floor at her feet.

"I was. I'd ridden farther than I intended before I realized it." Foolhardy of her to put herself in jeopardy to avoid Lady Vesta's son. But that was the truth of the long ride. It was also none of Jagger's business.

The Chief Constable continued glaring at her, his eyes so dark she saw no pupils. "Nothing more you can tell me."

"The leader was tall," she added. "It happened so fast, it's difficult to remember." She put her hands to her lips. "I think . . . I think the policemen were dead when the leader cut their throats. They were on the ground and not moving." She dropped her head and pushed her hands beside her temples, the horrifying picture filling her mind's eye.

"It'll be all right, m'lady," Officer Liam muttered softly.

Chief Constable Jagger, a man without a soft edge had no comforting words. "You are Lady Mariana Belmont, are you not?"

"Yes," she said.

He knew she was of the gentry, even if there were rumors about her birth. The tight, hard line of Jagger's lips relaxed slightly. She knew he feared offending her father. Lord Belmont, a true loyalist, had Jagger's admiration.

When Mariana met his gaze, she found the Chief Constable surveying her skeptically. The scurrilous expression faded at once. "You were alone? In the hills?" He'd said that before.

The implication stung. No lady rode alone—especially in the wild hills. She had sought the desolate countryside to bring blessed relief from Thornywilde's oppressiveness with John Desmond there. Her father cautioned her to keep to well-known paths and in sight of their barony's tenants. He wouldn't have approved of this day's ride. She'd gone against her father's sound advice and put herself in harms way, if one of the Ribbonmen had seen her.

This stone-faced, police officer would never understand her need for freedom.

"A well-traveled path would have served you," Jagger said coldly.

"Indeed," she agreed.

The estate tenants had never bothered her, though she realized she couldn't totally trust them. Some of them may be Ribbonmen. That is how the Ribbonmen operated, docile men by day at their jobs and rebels on their raids. She recalled her father's warnings about the raiders. *At best, they are servants, though they serve the barony as free men. We do not know their hearts or true loyalties.*

Many of the tenants serving the barony were descendants of generations that had served Thornywilde and were honorable people. Yet, in these troubled times, no one knew where true loyalties lay.

"Where is your father?" asked the Chief Constable.

"KinKerry. We expect him soon," replied Mariana, imagining her father's dismay once he learned what she'd experienced. By now, Gannett, Thornywilde's handyman, must be out on the hills searching for her.

The Chief Constable stood, whispering something to Liam. Liam left the room. A few minutes later another officer came into Jagger's office. Mariana recognized him as Officer Whitcomb, the officer directly beneath Jagger. Both Jagger and Whitcomb stepped out into the hall, partially closing the door after them. Their voices rose and fell. Then, the sounds of running feet as other officers were summoned.

A few minutes later Jagger rejoined her. She was frantically pushing stray hairpins into her disheveled hair.

"You've suffered a great shock, Lady Mariana. I've had Officer Ross order a coach. I'm personally escorting you to Thornywilde. If we're fortunate, none of the Ribbonmen saw you on Cormac Hill. Until we know for sure, your eyewitness account must be kept secret."

She nodded. "Thank you. I must get home. Our old handyman is surely out looking for me."

A team and coach were brought around. Mariana followed Jagger out into the courtyard. A young officer sat upon the coach box. Hera whinnied—a pathetic sight, the spirited mare hitched to the rear of the coach like a broken nag. Mariana went to her, stroking her soft nose. "Luv, 'tis an insult to be tethered like a common steed. I'll make it up to you."

Instead of joining her in the coach, Jagger mounted a handsome black stallion a junior officer had led into the courtyard. Once Mariana settled in the coach, Jagger gave the command to move out. He rode ahead.

They reached Thornywilde hours after sunset. Gannett and a dozen or more of tenants stood along the road bearing flaming torches. Gannett hurried up to the police coach. "Lady Mariana, you're safe." Old Gannett appeared to have tears in his eyes. He gestured into the dark distance. "We rode the hills and found no sign of you nor Hera. Thank God, you're safe."

A murmur of approval from the clutch of barony tenants confirmed Gannett's relief.

Mariana didn't see Sir John among the searchers. "Of course, I'm all right," she said to Gannett. "I rode too far. I . . . lost my way. I should have known better. You didn't tell Aunt Portia, did you?"

Gannett wiped his forehead with a strip of linen. "She was abed when we left. I felt it best not to mention you missing just then. The shock, you know." Gannett paused, a questioning and confused expression filling his honest face. He glanced up at Jagger, who still sat astride the prancing stallion.

If Gannett had questions about the police escort, he knew his station and didn't voice them. However, low murmurs rumbled through the company of tenants knotted along the road. Mariana wondered how many were aware of the day's raid, and the murders.

The torches held by the men along the road shed flickering tongues of light, casting the familiar surroundings into an illusory landscape. Spooked or annoyed by the crowd or the torches, Jagger's mount neighed and pranced in a half-circle.

Gannett, in a moment of rare bravado, called up to Jagger. "'Tis a good thing, Chief Constable, sir, that you were there when Lady Mariana lost her way." His voice sounded shrill and troubled. "For 'tis been an ill day for Thornywilde. The tenants lost stock this day. Both cattle and horses. Some want to take up arms against the Ribbonmen."

Loud murmurings arose from the gathered tenants. Their discord sent a shock of alarm up Mariana's spine. These men were farmers and herdsmen, not warriors. She felt their losses keenly, and knew many a babe would go without warm clothes or decent food. Like many avengers, the Ribbonmen destroyed their own kind, as well as their enemies. Instead of righting wrongs, they wreaked far greater harm.

The Chief Constable's voice rang out like a shot, his gaze hard on the assembled crowd. "Stopping thievery is best left to the police." He turned to Mariana. "When His Lordship returns, I'll speak with him at once." Tipping his hat, he said. "I'll call at a later time when your aunt is available." His steed pranced wildly. "Wagoneer, return to Lough Glendelough."

Chapter 10

O nce in the house, Abbie came to Mariana at once. She stared at her mistress. "Did Hera throw you?"

"No. I lost my way."

"Lady Portia thinks you need a gentler horse."

Ignoring Abbie's concerns, Mariana pulled her wrapper from the cupboard. She gestured to the back of her riding waist. "Would you help me with these buttons?"

Abbie gasped. "There's dirt and grass stains on your waist and the chemise beneath. That wicked beast pitched you. God's breath, you're taking the chills, m'lady."

Mariana trembled, reliving the horror of the afternoon. She had no chill, suffering instead from what she'd witnessed below Cormac Hill. Had she not ridden to the hill, the police officers's remains could have lain in the deep crevice for days.

"A simple accident," she said sharply, deterring Abbie's questions. "It was cold in the hills, and the heather and gorse slick with rain and wet. I expect we'll see ice by morning." Shuddering, she recalled the three dead officers and the Ribbonman who'd leapt from his horse, slitting the men's throats. Clinging to the bedpost, she closed her eyes until the spell of dizziness passed. "I'd like my bath now."

Abbie, her cap bobbing, scurried toward the door. "I fear that wretched Hera will be the death of you, m'lady. You oughta find a gentler horse, not that fancy prancing demon."

"Abbie!" Mariana warned.

The maid scuttled downstairs.

Once the French tub was filled with warm water and fragrant oil, Mariana sank into its depths to her chin. Despite the warm room and the warm water, her trembling continued. She sank lower into the tub, water sluicing into her ears obliterating the sound of the hissing fire beyond the tub's velvet curtains. And, for the briefest moment, blocking out the Ribbonmen's screams, flaying horses, and dumb cattle lowing in alarm. If only she could drown the afternoon's memories.

Abbie waited just outside the dressing room door, Mariana's gown and peignoir ready. "Shall I brush your hair, m'lady?"

Mariana nodded. "Where is Sir John? I failed to see him when I arrived."

Abbie paused the brushing, her brow furrowed. "'E left Thornywilde shortly after you. That was before luncheon. Going into the village, I think. 'E hasn't returned."

* * *

Late the next morning, Mariana had the stableman saddle Hera. She must keep her nerve and not allow the events of the day before keep her from enjoying her mare. Only, today, no wild ride in the hills, but a short turn through the acres and acres of wooded park east of the great house.

The brisk ride did her good. She returned to the house in a better frame of mind. She was ready to begin her duties, establishing menus with Mrs. Hooks, allotting personal linens to Abbie, her usual activities at Thornywilde.

Her duties performed, Mariana climbed up to the old turret room, relishing time alone. She was especially glad that John Desmond hadn't returned. Though, she wondered who he knew in Lough Glendelough. He'd been gone long enough to have ridden farther than that village.

She settled on the old-fashioned windowseat facing the western section of the estate. She loved the view of the hills from this side of the house, the groves of Plane and Larch trees. She'd brought two French novels, one with the pictures of the male ballet dancer she'd found extremely alluring in the past. Looking at the pictures, her cheeks flamed as she remembered the kiss in the artist's studio in Dublin.

By faith! Surely Mr. O'Geary wouldn't repeat her wayward behavior to her father. If her father suspected such behavior had occurred, Mariana felt certain that Mr. O'Geary would be dismissed from his position as her father's protégé. The longer she perused the pictures of the ballet dancers, the more certain she became that Mr. O'Geary, in person, was far more attractive than these provocative pictures. She mustn't think of the man or the kiss. But instead of absolving the memory, she envisioned it the more—the soft but demanding pressure that encompassed her entire being. God's breath, what wanton need he had incited.

Never before had she experienced such sensations—such elation driving her senses—such sensual promises she didn't fully understand. She had responded to the man's demanding lips though feebly her mind told her to push him away, to repel the pleasure he promised. Had she truly tried to back away from him? She couldn't remember clearly.

Perhaps she had for a brief second at the very first contact. The slightest moment before she'd succumbed to the invitation he offered.

Her body had contended with her will, the endeavor hopeless, until she stopped struggling and accepted his kiss. That she was capable of such battle between will and flesh shocked her. Especially since her flesh betrayed her.

It would never happen again.

Should she pen Mr. O'Geary and request an apology? On second thought, that may not be wise. A letter could be intercepted and misinterpreted. She thought of Lady Vesta. How that unappealing woman would love to discredit her. Why, Mariana didn't know.

Unable to concentrate, she closed the French novel with a thump. Leaving the turret room, she made her way down the winding stone stairs to the second level.

She'd no sooner entered the drawing room when a carriage drew up and stopped.

Oh, no! The familiar silver and gray footmen's uniforms. Lady Vesta Chasteen's coach! The coach door opened. A man stepped down. At first, Mariana thought it was her father. No. Grasping the velvet draperies, she shrank back as Thomas O'Geary took Lady Vesta's arm and escorted her to the door.

Abbie's quick steps hurried past to admit the visitors. Aunt Portia walked regally behind the little maid. At the sight of Mariana in the doorway, Aunt Portia stopped. "Mariana, I've been looking for you."

Drawing herself up, Mariana said breathlessly. "I'm here, Aunt, why the . . . uh . . . fuss?"

"Fuss, indeed. Her Ladyship and your father's protégé have arrived. I've searched the house over for you. Rather, Abbie has done so. The message came a half-hour before their arrival. I feared you'd gone off on that abominable horse of yours."

If only she were riding Hera rather than standing in the drawing room waiting to welcome Her Ladyship and Thomas O'Geary.

"As you can plainly see I'm not in the hills with Hera," Mariana said, linking her arm in her aunt's. She drew the older woman into the drawing room to receive their guests formally.

Anxious, but determined not to cower, Mariana wondered why Mr. O'Geary had come to Thornywilde. Foremost, why was he in the company of her father's fiancée? Where was her father? And where was Sir John Desmond?

The artist and Lady Vesta's mutual laughter rang down the hall as they approached the drawing room. Judging from Lady Vesta's fawning familiarity with the handsome young painter, perhaps his arrival with her was more than artist and subject. In any event, Mariana meant to put him in his place should he have the audacity to betray her. Commoner that he was. How dare he even glance at her!

"My dear, dear Mariana," Lady Vesta gushed, "May I take the priviledge of presenting your father's understudy. That is what it's called, isn't it?" She gave Thomas a simpering smile, "Your relationship with dear, dear Charles?"

"M'lady." Thomas O'Geary bowed, smiling benignly at Mariana. "How honored I am to see His Lordship's daughter. My highest regards, Lady Mariana."

"Mr. O'Geary," Mariana said primly. By the fates, if Mr. O'Geary in the slightest manner had indicated he'd met her before and under such embarrasing circumstances, she'd see him thrown from the house. Gannett would see to that, though just how she'd coerce the old caretaker's help in this delicate matter proved vague.

However, Mr. O'Geary had not given away her indiscretion in the slightest. Still, wary, she moved woodenly as Aunt Portia offered seats to the guests. At once, Aunt Portia and Mr. O'Geary entered into lively conversation. Mariana couldn't overhear much that passed between them for Lady Vesta's remarks.

"You seem surprised by our arrival," Lady Vesta said almost mockingly. "I sent word. I regret I hadn't the opportunity to alert you sooner. Do forgive me, dear Lady Portia," Lady Vesta gushed to Portia. "Things seen to move so fast these days."

"It's lovely having you at Thornywilde, my dear. It's our pleasure, isn't it, Mariana?"

Though Mariana didn't agree with her aunt, she smiled and said. "Most definitely. A charming and pleasant surprise," Mariana avoided meeting Mr. O'Geary's eyes. "Where is my father?"

"He will join us as soon as possible. He's a very busy man." Lady Vesta turned to Portia. "You did receive my message, did you not?"

The older woman nodded. "We did," she said, a warning glance at Mariana. "A very short time ago, the couriers being what they are in the country. You both must be famished from the road." Aunt Portia clapped her hands. "Abbie, have Mrs. Hooks prepare tea. A tray, as well."

Abbie scurried away.

Lady Vesta, who'd taken a comfortable chair near the fire was in the process of removing pale-green kid gloves. The woman seemed partial to Italian leather.

"You must wonder why His Lordship's protégé has accompanied me here. Kindly, accompanied me," Lady Vesta said after a beguiling smile at Thomas. Mr. O'Geary didn't appear as enthralled with Lady Vesta as she pretended.

"I'm pleased to meet the young man I've heard so much about," Aunt Portia said kindly. "Do sit, and make yourself comfortable." Thomas had stood in the center of the room during the verbal exchanges. Mariana thought he appeared uncomfortable.

Aunt Portia, delighted with guests of any kind, beamed at Thomas. "How very chivalrous of you accompanying Lady Vesta here to Thornywilde. We are civilized people in Lough Glendelough, though we can lay claim to the occasional highwayman or two."

Thomas laughed appropriately and took the chair Lady Portia indicated.

Mariana met his clear, blue gaze. *By the saints!* Was that a twinkle in his eyes? "I'm sure Mr. O'Geary will find our hospitality to his liking," she said coldly—her first shock over seeing him past. To his credit and her great relief, he entered again into conversation with Aunt Portia.

Her aunt, a tireless follower of politics, began a litany of questions. She stayed well informed with her delivery of London newspapers and periodicals. "How are things in London? With the king and parliament?"

"King William is busy, as usual. The poor man is uncertain whether he's a Whig or a Tory."

"And, he's no friend to Ireland just now," Aunt Portia supplied. "Riling the Catholics up when they outnumber us Protestants." Aunt Portia spoke firmly for she was a staunch Protestant in a country with so many Catholics. "Our country is in turmoil. Cattle thefts, burning cottages and the like. All for forcing the English tithe upon our Catholic citizens. The tithe is personal and should be handled by a man's conscience, not by forced decree."

"The Irish situation is grave, Your Ladyship," Thomas admitted. "We look for a better day. As you know, England has a turbulent history of making and enforcing religious decrees."

"Sadly, but true," Portia admitted. "If Silly Billy has his way, he'll ship us all to Australia."

Thomas laughed. "No, Your Ladyship, it isn't as dire as that. And, your loyalties are on the right side of the coin."

They continued discussing political affairs.

Grateful for the distraction, Mariana, stole a glance at Thomas, her lips burning from the memory of the kiss in her father's studio. Even with her limited experience with men, she suspected that Mr. O'Geary himself likely thought of nothing else at this moment. Gallant of him to spare her embarrassment. Making a great task of arranging her skirts, and avoiding Mr. O'Geary's gaze, she sat quietly.

Lady Vesta, who'd listened to the conversation around her without comment, suddenly blurted to Portia. "And, where indeed is my son?"

Aunt Portia smiled. "He's out. I believe he has friends in the village."

"You are quite right, though not friends exactly in Lough Glendelough, but a neighboring estate. A young man he was with at school and the young man's twin sister." Lady Vesta gave Mariana a measuring stare. "The young woman dotes on him."

JONNI RICH

Chapter 11

The drawing room gathering over, Thomas breathed a sigh of relief. He'd suffered mixed feelings when he'd received His Lordship's instructions to escort Lady Vesta to Thornywilde. He'd both dreaded and anticipated seeing Lady Mariana again. His Lordship's message bore promise that, he, Thomas, would see a great deal of Mariana in the future.

My dear Thomas,

I find I must remain longer at KinKerry under the physician's further care. You will escort Lady Vesta to Thornywilde. While there, find materials and workmen ready to outfit an artist's studio. The architect has instructions to fashion the studio after the one at my Dublin townhouse.

Lord Charles Belmont

Thomas passed the afternoon in a cabriolet with Lady Portia, riding over the extensive estate. He found the older woman charming company. However, he'd much preferred Mariana had joined them. She'd declined. He decided Mariana was even lovelier in person than the picture of her he'd cherished in his memory. What were her thoughts of him? Difficult to know. She certainly wasn't the playful, saucy, girl who'd masqueraded as a model. How could Sir John Desmond ramble off and leave Mariana's company? Especially as John expressed interest in her in London.

Now, the dinner hour was upon them. Thomas dressed carefully. He had no valet. His income was increasing, and it appeared very soon he could afford some of the amenities a gentleman enjoyed.

He went downstairs, his pulse quickening at the sight of Mariana standing near the sideboard, her lovely face in profile. She'd changed into a peach-colored, gossamer silk gown, the shimmery fabric reflecting her high color. Her luxuriant light-brown hair was artfully arranged.

"My dear Mr. O'Geary," Lady Portia said graciously, indicating his place at the well-appointed table. Manners at Thornywilde seemed more relaxed than with the formal procession of taking the ladies in to dinner.

Still, he couldn't resist offering Lady Mariana his arm. "Lady Mariana," he gestured. She gave him a slightly irritated look, then allowed him to escort her to the table. Bowing to Lady Portia and Lady Vesta, he took his place beside Lady Vesta.

Removing her napkin in such a way as to touch his hand, Lady Vesta simpered. "You seem in remarkable spirits tonight, Thomas. Your color is most high."

"You find it so, m'lady," he said in what he prayed an innocent tone. "The bracing country air, and our charmings hostesses."

"Indeed," Lady Vesta responded.

The serving girl brought the soup. Grateful for the diversion, Thomas turned his attention to the soup bowl before him. On the road, he'd thought of nothing except how to greet Lady Mariana. After all, they'd shared a passionate kiss. He hadn't imagined that. She'd responded delightfully. He'd decided to take his cue from her reaction to him. He would never betray or embarrass her. It was obvious she wanted matters to appear as if they'd never met beforehand. Indeed, they'd not met as Thomas O'Geary and Lady Mariana Belmont, but as Thomas the portraiture artist and a model sent from the modeling academy.

Lady Vesta, her mouth twisting in disgust, said. "I hear there was a raid on Thornywilde estate—those dreaded Ribbonmen. Such abominable creatures. I'm thankful John is away and not exposed to such barbarism."

"A tragedy, and unfortunate," agreed Lady Portia. "No need to worry, my dear. The attack occurred on the estate's farthermost reaches. There's no danger here at the castle." She sighed. "Our political times need much improvement."

Thornywilde's dining room became exceedingly warm to Thomas as he listened to Lady Vesta and Lady Portia. The women's lively discussions gave him time to compose his emotions, especially after Lady Vesta's remark about his high color. Try as he might, he couldn't prevent his gaze from the lovely creature sitting across the table. Each time he glanced at Mariana, the memory of the shared kiss leapt to his mind. Surely, she thought of it, as well. How vividly the memory tortured him now. He almost choked on a bite of beef as he recalled how perfectly Lady Mariana had fit into his arms. How willingly she'd offered her lips to his.

He'd had no reason to suspect she was not a model from the art academy—though a very, inexperienced model that he'd taken compassion on. He'd meant to inquire further about her but he'd not had the opportunity. He'd not known Mariana's true identity until Liza informed him.

Liza's disclosure grieved him for it distanced Mariana from him— their different social status. She, of the peerage, and he a commoner. True, there were instances where that gulf had been conquered. However, those rare alliances were the exception and not the rule.

Most daunting of all, she was the daughter of his mentor, Lord Belmont. He, Thomas O'Geary, couldn't behave as crass as to ignore that truth.

Now, thrown into the very company of the lovely prize he'd sought in his dreams, he could scarce disguise his emotions. Alas, though she sat but a short distance away, she ignored him as though he were some blighted monster.

At first opportunity, he'd speak to her, express his apologies. He owed her that much.

Chapter 12

Mariana could not believe her father had commissioned Thomas O'Geary to remodel one of the estate summer houses into an artist's studio. Thomas's duties would be engaging an architect, overseeing carpentry crews, and outfitting the structure with artist's supplies. It was obvious her father trusted Thomas's imagination and taste. The downside of this noble project—Thomas would be at Thornywilde constantly.

Life at Thornywilde settled into its familiar routines. To her great relief, Mariana saw little of him. He rose early and retired late. Also, he took his breakfast in the small breakfast room off the servant's dining room, his luncheon sent out to the summer house, and his dinner usually a late tray brought up by Gannett.

She welcomed going down to breakfast and enjoyed eating alone. This particular morning, Sir John sat at the table.

He'd obviously eaten, and lingered over coffee. He looked up when she entered the room. "Ah, the beautiful mistress of the manor deigns to favor me with her company." He stood, bowed, and held out her chair. "What have I done to merit this pleasure? Tell me, and I'll do such every day of my life."

"Good morning, John," she said icily. She'd much prefer Thomas O'Geary's company than Sir John Desmond's.

John took the chair across from her and smote his breast with his riding gloves. "You break my heart, you cruel creature. Nevertheless, I forgive you. Come have your wicked mare saddled and ride over to Shannon Hall with me. Squire Patrick wants to discuss the hunting party plans. You know it's a small group, quite intimate."

Squire Patrick Stephenson, Kathleen's father, Thornywilde's nearest neighbor, and a dear friend included Mariana and Lady Portia in all gatherings at Shannon Hall. It annoyed Mariana that John had made a friend of Patrick Stephenson. She shuddered inwardly at the thought of attending a hunting party in John Desmond's company. How loathesome John managed to make the word intimate sound.

"Riding to Shannon Hall is out of the question today," she said firmly. "Kind of you to include me," she added with a touch of sarcasm.

He stood. "You break my heart, you cruel creature. If I can't convince you to accompany me, I'll go alone." He rolled his eyes in a mock expression of heartbreak.

A bitterroot taste filled Mariana's mouth as John sauntered from the dining room. What confusion his presence caused at Thornywilde. Patrick's hunt was not the small intimate affair that John intimated. It was an annual gathering that included a great number of young people, as well as neighboring peers. There was a ball afterwards. Quite a festive occasion.

Mariana had attended the affair every year, especially the hunt. She and Kathleen were excellent shots. Patrick allowed them to take places at the stands, farther along the field away from the men. After Kathleen had married and moved away, she'd returned every year to Shannon Hall for the hunt and ball. Mariana looked forward to these affairs since it enabled the two old friends to visit and catch up with each other's lives.

"My Kathleen won't be here, this year," Patrick had said when he'd called at Thornywilde weeks before. "She's expecting another wee one."

That made three babes, Mariana thought, gladdened at Kathleen's new life, which served to bring her own life in sharper contrast. She, with no prospects. She'd decided not to attend this year's festivities at Shannon Hall. It would be no fun without Kathleen. Now, to make Aunt Portia understand.

Sir John, present the day Patrick had called, had rounded on Patrick. "You may expect Lady Mariana and me. Lady Portia, as well. It will be my express delight to accompany them."

The older man had appeared not to acknowledge John's statement for he was busy talking to Aunt Portia. Their engrossing conversation - the damage the heavy spring rains wreaked on the crops deemed for their livestock. The Ribbonmen becoming more and more threatening.

Once Patrick took leave, Mariana cornered John. "You may go if you like. I'm not. I'll explain to Patrick."

"How very inconsiderate of you," John had taunted. "But of course, you'll go."

"No," she said, considering the matter settled.

Now, he dared bring it up again. After breakfast, she went upstairs and changed into her leather breeches and floppy hat. Feeling defiant, she had Hera saddled and left for an extended ride. She rode for hours. She let the mare rest, then took a turn through the wooded park. When she returned to the stable, John met her. He stopped her in the stable.

"Why are you avoiding me?" he demanded.

The stone barn's dim light made his presence threatening. She looked around for a groomsman. The man was coming down the wide aisle, loops of harness in his hands. "Allo, yer ladyship."

"Good day." Mariana called, following the groom into the stall as the man made ready to unsaddle Hera.

John stepped into the narrow stall, easing beside her.

"Er — Allo, Your Lordship," said the groom.

"Would you leave us," John said to the groom.

The man retreated from the stall.

"You didn't answer my question," John said, turning to Mariana. He stood very near her skittish mare.

Couldn't the dolt see the effect he had on Hera? "Calm, down Hera," soothed Mariana. "Would you move aside?" She didn't temper her anger.

John's face reddened and his lips tightened. "It isn't courteous to speak to your houseguest in that tone. I am your guest, you know."

"How can I forget it? You're underfoot at every turn. Really, John, you're testing my patience. You're my father's houseguest—not mine." She flung the words in the heat of the moment, regretting her temper at once. John turned livid. He closed the distance between them in the narrow stall, pulling her into his arms, crushing his lips upon hers.

She beat him with her fists, and lifted her foot to kick him. Alas, her foot caught in the draping folds of her riding cloak. She stumbled. She'd have fallen if he hadn't caught her. "Take your hands off me! How dare you insult me?"

"I'm simply helping you up."

Breathing hard, she pushed past John to the stall door. He didn't try to stop her.

She wheeled as she stepped into the dim main hall. "You really are odious!" Stomping out of the barn, she fled across the paddock to the house.

Aunt Portia met her in the great hall. "Really, Mariana, you must stop wearing that unsuitable outfit. We have guests in the house. You could be mistaken for a man. I forbid you to leave the house in such dress. And, why for heaven's sake have you straw all over your coat?"

"An unfortunate incident, Aunt Portia," Mariana said. "You are right, of course, I should dress more appropriately." It occurred to her that perhaps her unorthodox dress had emboldened John Desmod to approach her as he had in the barn.

"I'm glad you see reason, my dear." Aunt Portia continued. "Thomas will take meals with us in future."

* * *

That evening at dinner, Mariana, acutely aware of Thomas, hated the flush climbing her neck as she sensed his attention upon her. All because of her regrettable foolish prank.

The only redeeming note at this uncomfortable meal was Lady Vesta's absence. She'd traveled to KinKerry some days before leaving Mariana anxious of news about her father's condition.

The serving girl passed a platter of succulent roasted fowl. John took a sizable portion, then pulled a puckish face. "About the hunt, Lady Mariana. Patrick is one of your father's oldest friends. He'll be insulted if you're not there. What will Kathleen think? I understand you two are dearest friends."

How dare he continue to bait her! Especially after what happened in the stable. Aware Aunt Portia watched with shrewd eyes, Mariana fought back her flare of anger.

"Kathleen won't be there," she replied. "She's expecting another baby. And, basking in her loving husband's attention, and seeing to her home and her children. All the things a happy young wife enjoys."

"Nevertheless, you shall go to Patrick's," said John, as though he wielded authority over her.

"I simply cannot," Mariana returned, holding her ground. She deserved better than Sir John's company.

Were Sir John a true gentleman, he would cease badgering her. Instead, once he learned Aunt Portia favored Mariana's attendance at Patrick's, he became relentless. Not only was he not a true gentleman—he proved devious.

Wretched young man that he was, he'd taken the liberty of informing Patrick of Mariana's refusal to attend the hunt and ball. Patrick had then sent a formal note to Aunt Portia demanding to know how he'd offended Lady Mariana. Patrick's note settled matters with Aunt Portia. Mariana would travel to Shannon Hall and be happy to do so.

"I'll explain to Patrick why I shan't go," Mariana said gently.

"But of course, you'll go," Aunt Portia said. Her firm expression left no room to question her decision.

* * *

Mariana was expected to travel to Shannon Hall the day before the actual hunt. Instead of preparing to go, she sat dawdling in her room with her third cup of tea. She'd written note after note to Patrick expressing her regrets. The notes lay crumpled at her feet. She took up the pen to write yet another excuse, when a soft knock sounded at the door. It was Abbie.

"What is it, Abbie?"

"Lady Portia begs you come to her room. It's important."

Further pressure, Mariana thought, rising slowly.

Aunt Portia sat in her comfortable chair at the foot of her canopied bed. Soft light drenched the light walls and gleaming oak furniture. Her aunt wore a soft wrapper with a white fur collar. A string of gleaming pearls accentuated the peach wrapper, reflecting cheerfully upon Portia's porcelain complexion.

"Yes, Aunt," Mariana said, closing the door behind her, and taking a seat on the brocade stool near her aunt's feet.

"Her Ladyship has arrived." Aunt Portia said.

"My father. Is my father with her?"

"No. He remains at KinKerry. Lady Vesta says he's much improved, but not able to travel just yet."

In Lady Vesta's questionable company, her father seemed always unwell—ill even. "I don't understand this extended illness," Mariana lamented.

"Her physicians are excellent," Aunt Poria said, the pronounced jowls of her aging face trembling.

Needing her elderly kinswoman on her side, but doubting they'd agree about Lady Vesta, Mariana chose her words carefully. "I'm grateful you haven't pressured me about going to Patrick's," she said.

Her aunt sighed "I'm respecting your decision, though I think it's unwise and foolhardy to risk offending Patrick."

"I'll make the proper apologies, Aunt Portia. I promise."

"See that you do, and swiftly."

"So Lady Vesta has returned." Mariana lowered her head a moment. How to make her aunt understand the suspicions she harbored about Sir John and his mother. While Aunt Portia hadn't expressed a dislike of Lady Vesta or John, Mariana sensed her aunt had reservations about the dreadful couple.

"Dear Aunt," Mariana began. "Don't allow Lady Vesta or Sir John to work our emotions to their advantage. There's much I haven't told you."

Aunt Portia stiffened. Two bright, red spots bled through her powdered cheeks. "You've had opportunity aplenty. Be quick. Explain what you mean. I'll abide no ill-will under this roof. Sir John has a-ready ridden to Shannon Hall."

Her pulse quickening, Mariana tried to explain. "I've had little opportunity to speak to you privately for Sir John has dogged my every step. Agree with me, Aunt, please."

A swift expression swept through Aunt Portia's pale eyes ceding Mariana's point—however, it vanished as quickly as it appeared. "I doubt the dogging as you call it. I fear John seldom can find you." The older woman spoke archly, and she spoke the truth. "You've made your company scarce for him. I don't understand why, Mariana."

"I scarcely know him," returned Mariana quickly. "He and his mother talk in corners and I fear they plot against me." She recalled John's hand brushing her ankle in the coach—by design and not by accident. Remembrance of the moment made her skin crawl. The morning in the stable when he'd forced a kiss. He'd approached her at other odd moments when no one was around. Always with a lecherous grin and eager hands. These encounters weren't accidental. "It is always thus___"

Aunt Portia gestured her quiet. "You're a lovely young girl, Mariana. I can't blame Sir John for being taken with you or for Her Ladyship wanting to foster a union between you and her son."

This was not going well. The thought of Her Ladyship and John in the house like two spiders treading a treacherous web chilled Mariana. It may not be possible to sway Aunt Portia's thoughts just now. Nevertheless, Mariana gave it a final try. "How can you suggest a union, Aunt? You know I'm not a wealthy catch. Not after my father's losses. And, I'm scarcely a young girl at three and twenty. I'm well on my way to spinsterhood. Her Ladyship has little to gain by forcing me into a marriage of convenience with John."

"Mariana, Mariana, how you go on. It's your tongue you must guard. You're a very pretty young lady of a good family."

The last remark stirred Mariana's deepest fears. "You know as well as I that rumors fly about me. That I'm the by-blow child, the bastard daughter."

Craaack! Aunt Portia's cane struck the floor. "Preposterous!" she cried, her voice rising, the pearls swinging precariously against the wrapper. "Have I brought you up to wilt in the face of groundless gossip?"

Mariana grasped her aunt's hands. "Please listen to me. The fear I experience is real. It isn't imagined. I fear worse than marriage from Her Ladyship and her son. Their intentions seem darker and frankly they frighten me."

Shaking her head sympathetically, Aunt Portia patted Mariana's hand. "My dear, you're an imaginable girl. You've suffered fanciful delusions all your life. Surely, Sir John views you as a virtuous young lady. He has been most attentive." Portia stroked Mariana's hand as she spoke. "You can't believe either he or his mother wish you harm. Now, calm yourself. I'll explain to Her Ladyship that you're not receiving guests just now. I'll allow no more talk of you going to Patrick's hunt." Aunt Portia stood. "However, I expect concessions from you. I expect you to come to the drawing room at six o'clock and have a cordial tea with Lady Vesta and myself. Surely you can manage that with all your fears, imagined or otherwise."

"But, Aunt -"

"No excuses!" Aunt Portia's features tightened in anger. There were times she exhibited a temper. "You are much too sheltered at Thornywilde. It's my fault. I've changed my mind. Tomorrow, you will join Sir John at Patrick's. You'll see what a grand time you'll have. A week at the lodge with others your age will do wonders for you. Write a note to Patrick, and Gannett will deliver it. Now, be a good girl, rest and get your wits about you, then dress for tea later. I've been very lenient allowing you to remain here and not go to Shannon Hall until the morning."

Mariana acquiesced. She must leave the battle for another time. Aunt Portia had summoned her merely to inform her that Lady Vesta had arrived, not for a combat of wills over going to Patrick's or not. Managing a weak attempt at a smile, Mariana stood.

"One other thing," began Aunt Portia. "I've noticed Mr. O'Geary's attention toward you, as well as your reaction to him. Can there be anything between the two of you? Did anything happen in Dublin that I should know about?"

"Aunt, how imaginative you are!"

Aunt Portia met Mariana's gaze with a shrewd glance. "'Twas merely my watchful tendancy. I am the eyes and ears of both your father and your mother, my dear."

Mariana had never doubted Aunt Portia's devotion. Her kindly great-aunt had guided her life these three and twenty years. Surely the sharp older woman hadn't guessed the kiss. The kiss intended for another - a model from the art academy.

"There is one other thing," Aunt Portia said musingly. She sat back down.

Mariana settled on the edge of the bed. "What is this you speak of?"

"I will admit I'm old-fashioned. You recall I've told you I remember the days of Buachailli Bana, or the Whiteboys or Rightboys who plundered the land against the church and landowners, causing many labourers and tenants to lose their jobs. Those were hard times. Their terrible raids were at night. The men wore white to distinguish themselves beneath their torches. But, that was long ago—some of the events a great deal before my lifetime. Especially the Whiteboys. Now, we have the Ribbonmen riding in the night pillaging and stealing from landowners like your father, who has turned from tillage to livestock, and who's been forced to raise rents. Thornywilde people are suffering, the tenants, our cottiers, our labourers, our farmers. With the lands put to pasture, there are no great fields to sow and harvest." Aunt Portia smiled weakly and shook her head. "I hate all this. I hate the fear these Ribbonmen cause. If you have fears, Mariana, you should focus them on these men destroying our way of life." Aunt Portia seemed on the verge of tears. She remained quiet a long moment, then said, "How I go on. I'm afraid it's *a sign of old age."*

"Darling, you're the farthest thing from old."

Aunt Portia smiled, and took Mariana's hand. "There's more I want to say to you."

"I had a long talk with Inspector Jagger. You needn't look so shocked, Mariana. I know all you've withheld from me. Inspector Jagger is concerned for your welfare, as am I. Since your father is away, the inspector confided in me. The others in the house know nothing of your unfortunate incident. However, as a future precation, you're not to ride alone. I have instructed Mr. O'Geary to accompany you when you ride, even in our wood. We have no assurance the Ribbonman leader didn't see you. They are of the peasants and they meld back into their daily lives once their raids are over. We have no idea of their identity. Perhaps some of our own people protesting the higher rents."

"I asssure you I was not seen," Mariana protested. "And, forgive me for not telling you."

"Mariana, what you went through took great courage."

"But . . . really, Aunt, Mr. O'Geary accompanying me? He's here to see to the artist studio, not look after me."

"Not another word, Mariana, either Mr. O'Geary will accompany you or Sir John. You may choose."

"Certainly Mr. O'Geary," Mariana returned heatedly.

The discussion ended.

The Ribbonmen! Mariana caught her breath. She'd put the horrible event on Cormac Hill from her mind. Now, Inspector Jagger had spoken to her aunt.

Chapter 13

*M*ariana returned to her room to rest before going downstairs for tea with her aunt and Lady Vesta. Since her aunt demanded she go to Shannon Hall, and she'd half-way agreed, another project she'd toyed with filled her imagination. A daring plan. A trip. But not a trip to Shannon Hall. She'd planned it all out in her mind. All she needed was a catalyst to prod her forward. Aunt Portia's temper had fired Mariana's resolve. Two could show spirit.

She'd dawdled far too long. She hurried to the armoire and withdrew a knapsack. She placed a stack of carefully folded clothes into the knapsack. Next morning before the household stirred, she and Abbie would ride to KinKerry to see about her father. She didn't trust Lady Vesta's platitudes. Nor did she trust the few letters he'd sent for they were written by his secretary.

"The green silk, m'lady?" Abbie asked, as she assisted Mariana.

"Yes, the green gown."

Abbie helped her into her linen shift. The maid then slid the chemise and corset over Mariana's head and arranged her stays, pushing her breasts up. "M'lady, your hair is lovely today," Abbie said, arranging Mariana's ringlets in the latest fashion.

Surveying herself in the mirror, Mariana experienced a moment's unease—a vague sensation. The green gown, of course! She'd worn a similar green gown once years before when she'd taken a walk in the estate's park—the thick wood east of the castle. She'd been forbidden to walk there for it was rumored that Ribbonmen frequented the wood.

That day she'd chosen to walk rather than ride Hera as she usually did.

As she walked down a secluded lane, a coach rolled slowly up the private road. That in itself unusual, for coaches didn't enter the private roads unless they were coming to the main house. The coach drew to a stop. The moment the coach stopped, her father stepped from a copse of trees across the lane. He'd been waiting for the carriage.

The coach door opened. Her father assisted a woman down. The woman's face was obscured by her large bonnet. She seemed nervous. Her simple country woolens indicated her station as beneath her father's. They walked a short distance from the coach and nearer to Mariana. Startled, Mariana stepped behind heavier foliage.

It would have been awkward and embarrassing to make her presence known, especially as her father and Aunt Portia had forbidden these solitary walks. Nor dare she move farther away, for they would hear leaves and bramble crackling beneath her feet.

"M'lord," the woman began in an agitated tone. "I don't know how long I can continue this task."

Her father stared at the woman sternly. "You must. Why do you think I pay you if not for loyalty and tight lips?"

Mariana pressed her hand over her mouth lest an exclamation escape. This seemed a private conversation and one not for her ears. The woman sighed, her back to Mariana, so close Mariana could have reached out and touched her cloak.

At once, the woman turned and stared into the wood past Mariana's head. She had a hard face. A face that had seen trouble. Pivoting quickly, the woman beat her fists against her father's chest. Taken aback, Mariana gasped, expelling surprised breath through trembling fingers.

"You pay me because you cannot afford not to," the woman cried, her voice rising with each word. "Who but me would do your dirty work?"

Grasping the woman's arms, her father tightened his grip as the stranger struggled to free herself. "Say too much and you'll regret it. You know it's dangerous to come here."

The woman twisted, wrenching her arms free. Again, the woman turned her gaze into the wood. Madness filled her pained face. Madness and evil. "Don't be a fool," she rasped. Then, she wept.

"Come now," her father said in a cajoling tone. "It can't be as bad as all that."

"My obligations have increased," the woman said. "My daughter has gone to the continent and I now care for my little grandson. There's none to help me. Those in the village watch me. I'm ostracized you know."

"Your lot is difficult, I agree," said her father flatly. "However, your debt to Thornywilde will never be paid."

"You are far too generous, sirrah." She spoke in a mimicking tone.

"As for your ostracism," her father continued, "you have only yourself to blame. There were other options."

The driver started the coach forward, stopping near. Mariana caught only a snipppet of the departing conversation.

Her father drew a money pouch from his waistcoat and handed it to the woman. "I will expect delivery as usual. Do you understand? If you cross me, I'll have your head."

"What choice have I?" she spat bitterly. After a malevolent glance at her father, the woman boarded the coach and it sped away.

Mariana never saw the person again, nor did she learn the meaning of the meeting. She dared not question either her father or Aunt Portia. Eavesdropping, however innocent, would be difficult to explain. Too, walking alone so far from the estate could bring trouble upon them all. With the livestock thefts, an angry tenant might view harming her as an opportunity to settle scores with her father.

Whatever secrets existed between her father and this woman, they seemed best buried. Mariana never spoke of the occurrence to anyone. She had wondered if the cruel appearing woman was her mother. The green silk gown brought the memory to mind. Too late now to change the gown for the mantel clock chimed the quarter hour.

* * *

The hall clock struck six as Mariana started downstairs to the drawing room for tea. Neither her aunt nor Her Ladyship were present. *Ironic, that I'm early,* she thought.

The drawing room, lovely in the late afternoon with a soft southern breeze threading through the tall windows, promised a true spring.

I will go to my father, she pledged, growing giddy at her plans.

109

"My dear, how grave you look."

Mariana hadn't heard her aunt come into the room. "A reflective, moment, that's all."

"Reflections over what?" demanded Lady Vesta entering the drawing room in a stylish maroon silk and glittering diamond brooches. Diamond bracelets adorned her wrists.

"It's nothing, Lady Vesta," said Mariana.

"Indeed." Her Ladyship planted a kiss on Portia's cheek. "How charming the drawing room is this evening. It does give one the impression of yesteryear."

It's shabby enough, thought Mariana, the woman reminding her of a brilliant serpent slithering through grass.

Lady Vesta always had further words. "My dear, you have absolutely blossomed here. Your color is high, and, your eyes dance as if you've plotted some mischief. Tell me your secret."

It was as if the woman had power to peer into Mariana's brain. Forcing a smile, Mariana said. "Thornywilde agrees with me."

"Indeed," Her Ladyship observed appraisingly.

Mrs. Hooks brought in the tea tray and delicacies. Aunt Portia poured out. Mariana caught Lady Vesta's sharp gaze at moments she didn't think Mariana was looking. How disconcerting being watched. Arranging her bracelets, Her Ladyship took her tea. "I understand Thornywilde once boasted the finest racehorses in Ireland," she said to Aunt Portia.

Her cup raised to her lips, Aunt Portia replied. "A truth, yes. For many, many years. However, Charles's interest in the horses wasn't as keen as his forbearers."

Nor had he the means, thought Mariana, to keep a king's stable. Too, he'd left the estate in the hands of overseers who weren't always the most diligent employees. He'd meant well, she was sure. "Speaking of my father," she said, directing her comment to Her Ladyship. "When may we expect him?" Lady Vesta craned her long neck around. Her eyes dark as coals, she peered hard at Mariana. "Charles led me to believe your relationship didn't merit daily communications."

"Sad but true," interrupted Aunt Portia. Mariana stared at her aunt. "Charles has spent much time away," continued Portia. "However, my niece and her father harbor utmost devotion for each other though there isn't daily communication."

Lady Vesta smiled glacially. "As they should."

An unpleasant truth settled in Mariana's brain. If her father needed this woman for her money, how desperate he must be. How base. "Why didn't he come to Thornywilde to convalesce? After all, you are here." The last statement hung in Mariana's throat. She forced it out.

Aunt Portia's sharp glance warned Mariana to hold her tongue. "No cause for alarm, dear niece. Vesta has explained that Charles prefers her doctors rather than our country ones hereabouts. I've written him a message of good cheer. You must pen one, as well, and we'll send them on tomorrow's early post coach."

More than good cheer messages would travel on that post coach if things went as Mariana planned. She and Abbie would board the coach at Lough Glendelough, then ride north to KinKerry.

Leaning forward lazily, Lady Vesta selected one of Mrs. Hooks's tarts. "Your father wishes to continue his treatment in KinKerry," she said to Mariana. "It's his decision. He's aware the realm's finest doctors practice there. You need not vex yourself. He'll join us soon." She spoke in a tone of dismissal

Mrs. Hooks brought more hot water for fresh tea.

"These are delicious tartlets," Her Ladyship said to the cook. "I beg you, please. My cook must have this recipe."

"'Tis a simple dough," Mrs. Hooks said, beaming.

The cook began to share the ingredients for her tartlets and their method of preparation.

Once Mrs. Hooks withdrew, Her Ladyship turned her shoulder toward Mariana. "I envy you young people and your marvelous energy. My John quite misses your charming company at Patrick's. You should've joined him. How can you bear to miss a grand ball?" she asked suspiciously.

"My sentiments, as well," commented Aunt Portia. "She will go in the morning."

Mariana managed a repartee. "How kind of you to imply that Sir John misses me. However, Patrick always has a house full of charming young people."

"He's such a dear boy," Lady Vesta continued, ignoring Mariana's comment. "He will make some fortunate young woman a devoted husband."

That blatant hint chilled Mariana. Aware of her aunt's discerning gaze, Mariana carefully chose her next words. "Your son's future is an admirable consideration and worthy of your most ardent interest."

Lady Vesta laughed.

Chapter 14

$\mathcal{T}$he early morning brought damp and cold. Darkness shrouded the grounds, casting the familiar outbuildings in vapory images as Mariana and Abbie crept toward the stables.

The nippy air bade Mariana draw her cloak closer. Abbie trotted behind her. The heavy iron bolt fastening the stable door felt like ice in Mariana's hands. As the creaking door opened, a stable-keeper leapt from his straw mattress.

"Who goes there?" he demanded, rising and rubbing his eyes.

Relieved that the voice came from a mere lad and not the usual stable-master, Mariana replied. "It's I, Lady Mariana, and her maid." She stepped into the arc of light from the boy's lantern. "Be quick. Saddle my mare and a suitable horse for Abbie."

Before the cocks crowed at Thornywilde, Mariana and Abbie passed down the lane and onto the road leading to Lough Glendelough.

Abbie, afraid of horses, didn't like riding. "M'lady, if we're to take the coach in the village, we're going the wrong way."

This shorter, more precarious route through the hills meant they wouldn't be seen by anyone on the main road. Her head to one side, Mariana looked back. "Keep up. We'll hire a coach past Lough Glendelough. It's quicker this way." She nudged Hera forward. They rode in silence until darkness bled into soft gray. More than once, Mariana suspected they were being followed. Pulling her cloak tighter, she glanced over her shoulder. No one there, except Abbie. Yet, Mariana had been certain she'd glimpsed a shadowy figure following, riding a distance behind them. However, the early gray light portrayed familiar objects uncertainly. A boulder resembled a hut, a tree a man. She couldn't trust her eyes.

She glanced back again. A moving shadow flashed. Certain now that they were being followed, Mariana rode faster. If an unwanted rider followed, it meant several things, and none pleasant. A marauder out to rob them—an evil rogue who'd think little of ravishing or killing them. Or one of the poachers about his devious work before full dawn.

"M'lady, I'll fall." Abbie's voice carried thin and tinny on the wind. They entered a hilly stretch of trail where no trees concealed them. They were quite a distance above the road below. Hera's hooves sent tufts of grass scudding downward. How vulnerable they were. The precarious ground forced Mariana to slow Hera. Abbie chose that moment to hurry the bay alongside Mariana. "M'lady, we must turn back. Lady Portia will sound the alarm once Gannett finds the horses gone."

Abbie's truth rankled. "'Tis none of your affair," said Mariana sharply. "She will think I've gone to Shannon Hall early. That's all. You are doing as I bid. Any blame rests on my head. Besides," she said, lowering her voice. "We have a greater problem. I think we're being followed. There's a cave ahead." Mariana gouged Hera to a run.

Abbie, screaming, dropped the reins, lost her footing, and tumbled to the ground, her horse galloping away. Reining Hera to a sudden stop, Mariana dismounted. Abbie didn't appear hurt. She sat on the ground pulling at her bonnet strings.

The rider who'd followed them galloped into view. Mariana stared in disbelief. *Thomas O'Geary!* "How dare you follow me!"

Thomas reined Excalibur, his black stallion, to a stop, jumped down with easy fluid motion. He hurried to Abbie, who sat in a pathetic heap. "Are you all right, lass?"

"I . . . I . . . I think so, sir." With Thomas's help, Abbie tested both legs, then settled on a grassy knoll, a picture of utter dispair. Mariana fumed. Why had she brought the girl in the first place? She knew Abbie's excitable temperment. Abbie started crying.

"Are you trying to kill her?" Thomas asked Mariana.

"It's obvious she isn't harmed," Mariana retorted, the biting wind whipping her cloak from her shoulders. Thomas smoothed her cloak, his fingers lingering on the rough wool beneath her chin. His person, his shining hair, his liquid eyes enveloped Mariana's senses. She caught his hand, removing it from her cloak. "I can see to my garment."

What sort of wanton was she? One kiss and she behaved like the most fallen woman. Had not the rumbling of a cart on the road below arrested her attention, she feared she'd collapse in Thomas's arms.

114

She looked down the hillside to the road below. Gannett manned the cart.

"Is all of Thornywilde outward bound this morning?" She scowled at Thomas.

"Allo, allo," Gannett called from the road. Alighting, tethering the team to a stubby tree, he started up the hill on foot. At the summit, out of breath, he nodded at Thomas. "I followed, sir, as you said." Doffing his cap, he dropped his gaze at the sight of Mariana. "Your Ladyship."

Mariana brought her clasped hands to her face. For all her plotting, she'd proved herself to possess a gnat's brains. "I suppose both Aunt Portia and Lady Vesta have a full account of my plans." The trip to KinKerry now proved impossible.

Thomas roared with laughter. "It isn't as bad as that. I arranged an invention of my own on your behalf. I advised your aunt you decided to spend some time at Shannon Hall. Lady Portia was most grateful. She requested I ride with you."

"How very devious of you," Mariana said half-aloud. He'd managed her awkward plan brilliantly. Now, what had he in store for her? After a sly glance, she dropped her gaze. "It will serve me well to keep a sharp eye and a sharper ear upon you at all times."

"Perhaps you shouldn't allow me out of your sight," Thomas replied, jokingly.

Rubbish, she thought.

"My ploy will get you to KinKerry then back by way of Shannon Hall," he said. "Despite the deception, everyone at Thornywilde will remain in good spirits, and be none the wiser." As if sensing her mounting irritation, he held his tongue.

She didn't cut across his words. "How did you know I was bound for KinKerry?"

A quick glance at Abbie answered her question.

"Abbie!" Mariana scolded.

"Lay no blame to her, m'lady. I overheard her speaking to one of the dairy maids."

Gannett, who'd stood aside, beckoned to Thomas. The two men conferred in low tones.

Gannett then busied himself capturing Abbie's runaway bay docilely nibbling grass nearby.

Thomas spoke. "It's decided. Gannett will take Abbie to her sister in Lough Glendelough until we return."

"We?" Mariana questioned.

"You and I, Your Ladyship." He bowed. If only she hadn't seen the twinkle in his eyes.

"You've interfered with my trip, plan to send my maid away, and leave me stranded on a hillside with a blatant lie to my dear aunt. What help is that, Thomas O'Geary?"

He shrugged. "The best I could manage on such short notice. You've missed the post coach anyway."

Turning to Abbie, Thomas ordered. "You'll tell your sister you're visiting for a few days. Say nothing of Lady Mariana's trip if you value your tongue in your head. I'll see Her Ladyship safely to KinKerry and back. Is that understood?"

Abbie nodded. She and Gannett trailed down the hill to the cart below.

Mariana swallowed the knot in her throat, then wheeled toward Thomas. "Would you ruin my reputation? Traveling alone with a man isn't done."

"I'm not *any* man, Lady Mariana," he said gently. "I am your friend and your protector. You have nothing to fear from me. In fact, I'm a protecter ordered by your aunt, since you have a penchant for wild rides."

Mariana turned to mount her horse, when the soft earth near the ledges' overhang gave way beneath Hera's impatient hooves. Waving her arms for balance lest she fall, Mariana grasped Thomas's outstretched hand. He pulled her to safety. Shuddering, she inhaled his spicy scent. Her fingers slipped along his arms unwillingly, testing their sinewy strength.

Strength and heat radiated through Thomas's rough woolen coat. She couldn't help herself. She leaned closer. His thumb and forefinger beneath her chin, he lifted her head to meet his gaze. She couldn't actually say he lifted her head, or if she stood on tiptoe to meet his lips.

The meeting of their lips soared like wildfire set to dry fields. His tongue tasted the delicate corners of her mouth. She trembled, opening her mouth. His tongue invaded slightly and outlined the edges of her teeth. Daringly, she followed his lead and explored beyond his lips. With a sudden jolt of embarrassment, she pushed back from the tight circle of his arms. He didn't stop her. Nor did he offer an apology.

"That shouldn't have happened," she said shakily. Humiliated and angered by her own deceptive senses, she ran toward Hera.

He'd been as affected as she. "Forgive me," he said, coming behind her. He held out his hand in a gesture of truce. "I didn't mean that to happen."

"Nor did I," she cried harshly. "We must go." She wasn't sorry. Not sorry at all. She should be contrite for kissing a man in such a solitary place. Her degradation should condemn her. She didn't feel degraded. What was wrong with her? Was she like the women the servants spoke of who, once they tasted carnal love, became shameless? God help her. And, this man her father's protégé.

She meant to love no man, but to pursue her studies and when she came into her majority; she would take her mother's legacy and open a girls' school. It had been her dream for as long as she could remember. A kiss in the wilds wasn't love. *Love?* Whatever made her think of love?

Nudging Hera's flanks with her boots, Mariana set the spirited mare into a run. The way became steeper and rougher as the sun climbed higher. Mariana recognized the section of wood. It was here she and Kathleen had ridden long ago, encountering Old Madge, the woman who gathered mushrooms. Her father was fond of Old Madge's 'shrooms, as the old woman called them, and each Christmas when he remembered Thornywilde's tenants with bountiful baskets of food—he remembered Old Madge, as well.

"I know this wood," she said to Thomas, when the rough way forced them to ride slower.

"It's beautiful," he replied.

"It is," she agreed.

He chose a path that was unfamiliar to her. She prayed he knew the way. They rode in silence. The sun had peaked above before he signaled to stop. They reined atop a high hill, a clear view of the valley below.

"We'll stop at the cottage there," he said, pointing downward to a crude hut with out-flung, stone walls. A curl of grayish-white smoke traced upward from the chimney.

"That cottage belongs to Old Madge," she said. "Why are we here? Are we traveling in circles?"

"No circles, m'lady. We're farther north this way from Thornywilde. The horses need rest."

Without another word, Thomas started down the hill first, Mariana following. Halting below in the hut's yard, Thomas alighted. "Wait a moment," he said. He dismounted, strode to the door and knocked. The stooped woman, as ancient as Mariana remembered, opened the door and motioned him inside.

Mariana waited, mounted on Hera.

After a short interval, Thomas came out. He helped her dismount. "Go on inside."

"But," she protested. "Old Madge? Is it safe?"

"I wouldn't take you anywhere that wasn't safe." He left her standing in the yard as he led their horses to a narrow paddock beside the cottage.

The hut's front door opened again, the old woman stepping onto the crude, stone stoop. "Don't be a-feared, dearie. Old Madge will do ye no harm." Mariana dared not look directly into the woman's face, but nodded and started inside.

It took a moment for her eyes to adjust to the hut's gloom. A lone candle burned on a rough table against the back wall. A peat fire glowed on the hearth. Old Madge, short enough to be a dwarf, grinned. She was toothless.

Onions, fastened on long strings, hung from the low ceiling. A kettle holding something savory bubbled on a hook angled in the hearth. Various drying grasses and flowers filled a cupboard.

"Make me 'umble 'ome your own," Old Madge said, taking a basket from a peg on the wall. "I gather me lovely 'shrooms. I pack them nice and moist in damp moss."

"You know who I am?" Mariana asked.

"I do. Ye're 'er of Thornywilde." Nodding and smiling to herself, Old Madge left the cottage.

Thomas entered as the gnomish woman departed. Loosening his clothing at the neck, he stretched out on the bare floor, his cloak pillowed beneath his head. Almost instantly, he began to snore.

Mariana helped herself to water from a pewter tankard, stepped over Thomas's prone body, and sat down in the corner, for there were no chairs save a couple of low stools cluttered with odd containers. Enveloped in her cloak, she settled on the stone floor, angst gnawing at her conscience. What conclusions would Aunt Portia draw from her niece's astonishing actions? Soon Thomas's snoring and the fire's warmth lulled her into a relaxed state. She must have dozed, for she startled fully awake - confused. Thomas, his eyes wide, assessing her, sat on one of the stools eating toasted bread.

She scrambled up, straightening her riding habit. "You let me sleep," she admonished.

"'Tis time we started," he said. "Eat this bread and butter first."

"Where's Old Madge?" Mariana asked, looking around.

"Gone to tend her goats. She left a rucksack of mushrooms for Thornywilde." Standing, he laid some coins on the table, and strode outside where the horses waited.

"I feel silly that I fell asleep," she said, following him into the yard.

"Nothing to feel silly about. It was a hard ride."

"How do you know Old Madge," she asked once they were on their way.

He answered pleasantly. "I lived in Lough Glendelough for a time when I was a wee boy. My father was a Dublin merchant. We spent summers here and further north in Furrah Down."

Perhaps she'd seen him as a child in Lough Glendelough, she thought. Not likely, as she'd been sheltered at Thornywilde. After leaving the village school, her studies had continued at Shannon Hall with Kathleen.

Chapter 15

*H*er worry increased the farther they rode. She'd never ridden this far into the hills, even when she had seen the Ribbonmen. Though the trip was for a serious reason, she found herself wishing she'd not undertaken the trip at all. The bands of Ribbonmen lurked everywhere. Bandits, robbers, the like.

Thomas, not one for idle chatter, rode hard, the wind at his back. What would they find in KinKerry once they arrived at Lady Vesta's estate?

By early evening, they reached KinKerry, a small village teeming with inhabitants. The area's rich potato fields, wool and linen industries made KinKerry a prosperous town. The pubs they passed were full, and the merchants manning stalls were beginning to shut down for the night.

Stabling their horses at a livery, Thomas rented a coach and team. After securing directions, they rode northeast to Lady Vesta's estate.

Dark had fallen when they reached the great house. The only light there was a faint glimmer threading through the massive windows, indicating someone was in residence.

"An imposing place," Mariana said as Thomas drove the small carriage near the door. She glanced uneasily at the stone and pale brick structure. The place reminded her of a fortress. Her ill father lay somewhere inside.

No groom appeared to take the carriage and team. Thomas tethered the horses to the stone balustrade and together, they approached the wide door. He rapped the knocker.

Hounds bellowed inside. Moments later, a serving woman in a cambric apron opened the door. "'Tis no visitors we're expecting," she said crisply, a lamp in her hand.

"I'm Thomas O'Geary. This is Lady Mariana Belmont, His Lordship's daughter. We're here to see His Lordship."

The woman opened her mouth to speak, then apparently thinking better of it, ushered them inside. "You'll find His Lordship in the bedroom at the top of the stairs." She followed them as they ascended the stairs.

At the bedroom door, the housekeeper moved in front of Mariana, knocking at the door softly. "M'lord, you have visitors. Your daughter and a gentleman."

A muffled voice bade them enter.

Mariana stepped inside first. It took a moment to adjust to the room's dim light. A lone candle burned on the bedside table, and a shaded lamp sat across the room. Her father lay in a large curtained bed with the curtains partially open. A number of medicine bottles and a clock cluttered the bedside table along with the candle.

"Who's there?" her father asked, struggling to sit up. He was encumbered by what appeared to be dozens of feather pillows. He stared brightly, but didn't speak. He appeared to have trouble orienting himself to the notion of visitors.

Mariana rushed to his bedside. "Father, it's me, Mariana. Can you hear me?"

"He's had his sleeping draught, m'lady," the woman explained.

Charles's eyelids fluttered. He squinted. "It *is* you, Mariana. I see you now. I suffer such stomach pain. This dysentery," he mumbled, wincing, and lying back, closing his eyes.

"Where are the doctors, sir?" asked Thomas, moving nearer to the bed.

At Thomas's voice, Charles pushed up from the pillows. "Thomas, is that you?"

"It is, my lord"

"And, Mariana, why are you not at Thornywilde?" He sounded very confused.

"You shall go there," Mariana said. "At once."

Sighing, Charles lay back. "Ah, going home, t'would be prudent. I've not seen the physicians this day. Nor the day before."

The housekeeper moved near the bed, then shrank at Mariana's glare. "Her Ladyship wishes. . ."

"Gather his things at once," Marina ordered. She had the ominous feeling neither she nor her father should remain one minute longer than necessary under Lady Vesta Chasteen's roof. The housekeeper complied, and within the half-hour, Mariana, Thomas and her father were ensconced in the carriage bound for Lough Glendelough. First, they stopped in KinKerry and retrieved their mounts, which they tethered to the back of the carriage. Thomas paid a hefty sum for the carriage rental and for a groom to retrieve it from Lough Glendelough.

They made better time traveling the main road, reaching the inn shortly before dawn. It was the same inn where Mariana and Hermoine had stopped when John Desmond escorted them to Thornywilde. A message was dispatched at once to Gannett. Exhausted, they took to their beds.

The following morning, Mariana rose early. She found Thomas in the main dining room. "How is my father?" she asked.

"He seemed better than last night," Thomas said. "He ate most of the food I carried up, and only complained that he was sleepy. I left him to rest until we're ready to travel on to Thornywilde. I've had a lad from the inn go and fetch Abbie. When she arrives, the two of you must go on to Shannon Hall and visit Patrick."

Mariana had become accustomed to Thomas's commanding ways. She understood why her father had taken him on as a protégé. He was truly a resourceful and helpful man. By degrees, she'd come to respect his strength of character. It was herself that she didn't like nor respect. Her wanton self, who'd practically run into Thomas's arms.

"I shall be a pitiful sight at Shannon Hall with its festivities, and me with no fine gowns."

Thomas smiled conspiratorially. "You've no worry. I instructed Abbie. She and Gannett will see to your finery."

By the grace of God their ploy worked. Mariana arrived at Shannon Hall dusty from the ride, and nervous about Patrick's greeting since she'd not attended the ball. Too, she felt a great conspirator—in truth she was. Patrick had grown quite wealthy as county squire and had acquired hundreds of acres of prime lands—lands rented to tenants.

His manservant met Mariana at the door. "Lady Mariana, this way."

Seated in the smaller drawing room reserved for relatives and close friends, Mariana awaited Patrick. She hadn't long to wait. His quick step soon sounded in the hall.

"My dear Mariana." He bowed, then took her hand briefly. Devotion beamed from his creased smile and kind eyes. "We did so miss you, my dear. The festivities weren't the same without you."

"I regret I couldn't be here," she said demurely, praying he wouldn't pry further.

"If you wished to see your houseguest, Sir John, I'm afraid he's departed for Thornywilde."

"No . . . no, I'm not seeking him." She answered quickly. Too quickly, for Patrick's sharp gaze discerned her annoyance mentioning John Desmond.

Wisely, Patrick changed the subject. "'Tis a sad thing ye missed the lovely ball. But 'tis like the old days, you arriving without announcement. These old eyes are glad indeed to see ye."

Quite obviously, Patrick awaited an explanation for her visit. She took a deep breath, exhaling slowly. Why not tell the truth, not the truth about rescuing her father, but truth about John. "I can speak plainly to you. I'm afraid I don't like Sir John's attentions toward me."

Patrick nodded knowingly. "Like that, is it?"

"Yes."

"Well, lassie, ye did the right thing by not coming to the ball."

Chapter 16

The alibi now sealed at Shannon Hall, Mariana arrived at Thornywilde and slipped upstairs undetected. She undressed, and stretched onto her bed to settle her nerves. She gave Abbie strict orders not to be disturbed. She'd no sooner drifted off when a sharp knock of wood on wood sounded at the door. It must be Aunt Portia with her cane. "Come in."

She'd barely time to sit up on the side of the bed before Aunt Portia entered. The older woman pulled up a chair and rapped her cane on the floor before sitting down. "Young lady, I demand to know why you've allowed Thomas to take matters into his hands. Have you no care for your father's health? He's brought Charles here this very day, with your permission! He says your father is very ill."

Mariana hesitated. How much Aunt Portia knew of the dark adventure had yet to be known. Mariana dared not betray Thomas, nor herself, for that matter. "It *was* my idea to have my father brought home, and not Mr. O'Geary's."

Her aunt didn't comment, but faced Mariana with a steely gaze. "Why was I not informed of this?"

Without time to think, Mariana blurted. "It's for his health. I wanted him home to see about him." She couldn't say *because I don't trust Lady Vesta.* Not yet—not until she had a clearer understanding of Aunt Portia's true feelings toward her father's fiancée.

"I suppose I should keep you under lock and key now you've become so willful," her aunt said with a snort.

"Perhaps," Mariana conceded, slipping up from bed, drawing on her dressing gown. Keeping her head lowered, she tied the gown's ribbons, avoiding her aunt's skeptical gaze. Her cheeks burned at the memory of the hillside kiss. She couldn't fault Thomas for the kiss for she'd not tried to stop him. In fact, she'd encouraged the kiss with sensual eagerness.

What must he think of her? If he thought less of her character, he'd not shown such, for he'd proven himself trustworthy the long way to KinKerry and back.

With a quick smile, Mariana looked up, "It won't happen again, Aunt. I promise I'll come to you first before I undertake what you'd consider my rash actions."

A faint smile warmed Portia's features. "These are troubling times. We are dealing with many difficult subtleties. I must say I'm glad Vesta is visiting her friends." Portia paused. "I have no idea how she'll react once she learns Charles is here."

Mariana went to her dressing table and began brushing her hair.

"Shouldn't your maid see to dressing your hair?"

"Of course." Mariana pulled the bellcord.

* * *

Charles's room hadn't the appearance of a sickroom. Vases of fresh flowers from the conservatory freshened the still air. Snowy linens graced the massive tester bed. Charles, in a maroon silk dressing gown, sat before the bedroom fire. Fire that would soon be banked against the forthcoming night. Mariana sat near him with her embroidery. Lady Vesta's presence unnerved her. Had the woman's housekeeper told her that both Mariana and Thomas arrived in KinKerry and ferreted Charles to Thornywilde?

The village doctor, in attendance, finished his examination of Sir Charles. The man adjusted his pince-nez. "You're improving nicely," he said. "The country air agrees with you."

Sir Charles shot a triumphant glance at his fiancée hovering beside his chair, and to Mariana. Mariana caught a quick flicker of disapproval on Lady Vesta's face, then an even quicker smile—a forced smile. "Dearest," she said to Sir Charles, taking both his hands in hers, and pressing a kiss upon them. "The fact you're recovering is the most important thing."

"Tell me," Mariana said to the doctor, who'd closed his bag and now reached for his coat. "Is he strong enough to come downstairs? I know he's tired of this room."

"That I am," her father agreed heartily. "Bored, actually with the sickbed in general."

"But-" Lady Vesta began.

"I think a change of scenery would be the best tonic for you, Sir Charles. Of course, you mustn't overdo," cautioned the doctor. "Your constitution is still weak. But, perhaps, a trip to the dining room will pique your appetite."

"Well said, old chap." Charles beamed like a school-boy at term's end.

But His Lordship didn't come down to dinner that evening. He felt tired. Nor the next evening, since a grand dinner was planned in his honor three days hence. Charles vowed to join the family around the table then.

For the upcoming occasion, Mrs. Hooks sent to the village for an extra serving girl and two scullery maids. A flurry of last-minute housecleaning ensued.

The evening of Charles's debut downstairs arrived. The dining room had been heated, and Mrs. Hooks, with the extra help, set a festive table. Thornywilde's delicate porcelain rested atop intricate Irish lace. Flickering tapers in three ornate candelabra splashed yellow light across urns of fresh flowers from the greenhouse.

"It's lovely," Mariana exclaimed to Aunt Portia, who joined her. Aunt Portia wore a dark blue woolen dress with draping lace collars. Her face was serene, indicating she'd rested well during her afternoon nap.

"I'm so happy father is joining us."

"He's much improved," her aunt said after their trip to the kitchen, where they'd admired Mrs. Hooks's fine meal. The hired serving girl seemed more of a woman than a girl. Familiar, too, in a vague way. Though most of the villagers resembled each other in dress and mannerisms. Gannett struck the gong announcing dinner. One of the old ways observed at Thornywilde.

Sir John and Thomas filed into the dining room deep in conversation. Mariana gave a start of surprise at the sight of her father leaning upon Lady Vesta's arm. His pale countenance disturbed her. How very ill he appeared. Gannett, acting as footman, took His Lordship's arm, assisting him to the head of the table. Charles began a lively conversation with Thomas.

John Desmond escorted Aunt Portia to the foot of the table, then assisted his mother to His Lordship's right. Mariana sat to her father's left. John pulled out the chair beside Mariana - his nearness was disturbing.

Thomas sat across the table from Mariana, his visage partially blocked by an enormous marble vase of yellow and white roses. Grateful for the overpowering flowers, she kept her gaze averted lest Thomas see the giddy effect he had on her. He had the advantage.

Tonight, he talked nonstop. "...miniatures," he continued to Charles. "I've never seen such splendid work."

The serving woman brought around the wine. "None," Mariana demurred softly, setting her wine glass bowl down.

"...Indeed, Sir," continued Thomas to Sir Charles. "I was able to acquire a few of the miniatures. In my opinion, the best of the lot before they went to auction. As usual, Mr. Canady has buyers when such prizes come into his possession."

"Ah, Martin Canady," Charles said, turning to Lady Vesta. "I've told you of my old boyhood tutor. The fencing master's son."

"Numerous times," she replied without interest.

"One day I'll take you to meet him. You'll find him a fine fellow," said Sir Charles without noting Vesta's look of pained boredom.

"Is Mr. Canady an artist?" John asked. A portion of his blond forelock escaped its pomade as he leaned forward seizing Charles's attention.

"He has dabbled," Charles explained. "When he was much younger, he tried watercolors. His form was not very strong. A very good teacher, though."

"It would've been a fine collection if he'd had the foresight to preserve his earlier work," tittered Aunt Portia. Her statement brought all eyes upon her. She flushed slightly. "That is . . . in . . . my very amateurish opinion."

Mariana's father had held great affinity for artists all his life. Aunt Portia had said he was a dreamer as a young man. Were artists dreamers? Mariana didn't know. She knew they must view the world differently - capturing people, scenes and objects in a way that others overlooked. She glanced across the table and looked down quickly as she met Thomas's gaze.

How dare he look at her so boldly! Kisses! She blamed kisses for her present discomfort. She didn't want to think of kisses. The mention of Mr. Canady had sent her imagination swirling. Any person from her father's past intrigued her. She'd ask Aunt Portia about Mr. Canady at first opportunity. There were so many strangers in Charles's life. The woman in the wood. He'd given her a pouch of money. Money for what? Some debt he owed the woman?

"My bright-eyed friend, what must I do to capture your attention?"

John! He'd been speaking to her. "You look lovely tonight," he whispered against her ear. The fetid scent of liquor tainted his breath. He'd imbibed much this day.

John Desmond was the last person on her mind. "How observant you are," she said coldly.

"Tell me," he badgered almost under his breath, "what was it like riding through the hills with Mr. O'Geary? Did the churl violate you in some manner?"

Thomas hadn't overheard John since he and her father were again discussing miniatures.

Mariana kept her voice low, but firm. "Don't be absurd."

Apparently, John delighted in her flustered manner. He kept whispering nonsense in her ear forcing her to turn from him which put her in full view of Thomas.

She scarcely tasted the delicious meal Mrs. Hooks and the hired staff had prepared. As the wonderful beef joint and wild mushroom pastry passed, she took small helpings, along with the jellied duck with artichokes. She'd looked forward to this meal with her father, only to have it spoiled by odious John Desmond. It seemed dinner would never end with him breathing down her neck.

Her father took a generous portion of the beef and mushroom pastry, a favorite of his.

Lady Vesta seized her father's knife and fork. "Charles, I must cut your beef." She proceeded to cut the beef in portions suitable for a nursery child's plate. She held a forkful of beef out to Charles. To Mariana's astonishment, he ate it.

Her Ladyship then began spoon-feeding the mushroom pastry to him.

"I'm not an invalid, dearest," Charles protested after several bites. The weak protest fell on deaf ears. She continued to feed him. That he allowed the display shocked Mariana. She couldn't eat another bite.

John leaned closer, his lemon verbena scent overpowering. "See what you're missing by locking your heart as tightly as a miser's vault."

Glancing up, Mariana caught sight of Thomas's stricken expression. Surely, he couldn't believe she was taken in by John's sentimental sop. How confusing. What difference to her what Thomas thought?

Aunt Portia saved the awkward moment. "Sir John, you're going shooting at Patrick's, I understand."

Kind, accepting Patrick Stephenson, Mariana thought. He saw only good in his fellow man, continuing to befriend John Desmond.

"Yes," John replied to Lady Portia. "Mariana is invited, as well. In fact, everyone at Thornywilde is expected."

"That's out of the question," Mariana said quickly. "Not with father needing looking after."

"Come, come," said her father laughing. "I'm not such an invalid as that. Of course, you'll go. It'll do you good to be around other young people. Patrick knows how to plan a shoot and parties afterwards. There will be entertainment for the ladies, as well."

Sitting up straighter, John pulled a delighted face. "My sentiments exactly, Sir."

The meal progressed. The serving woman brought in an assortment of vegetables. John leaned into Mariana as he pushed back his chair. She pretended not to notice.

"If you'll excuse me, Lady Portia, Your Lordship," he said, rising and going to the sideboard. "I forget Thornywilde isn't London. No footmen here to see to a gentleman's thirst."

A flush crept up Mariana's neck. What crass, drunken rudeness! She opened her mouth to reprimand John when she caught Aunt Portia's warning gaze. Her father, in conversation with his fiancée, seemed not to have noticed.

Thomas leaned around the flower arrangement "Are you all right?" he asked softly.

She nodded.

John stumbled near His Lordship on his way to the sideboard. "M'lord, with your permission, I would freshen my glass at the sideboard. Are you up for a whiskey?"

"Thank you, no," Lord Charles replied. "The bell, Portia, summon Mrs. Hooks. The gentleman would have service."

"Nonsense," the younger man slurred.

Mariana glanced at Thomas. "I asked, are you all right?"

"For the moment, yes," she whispered. "The only thing unbearable is enduring the remainder of this meal."

John fumbled among the flagons at the sideboard.

"We'll get to London this next season, Charles," said Her Ladyship. "The theatre is brilliant." As she spoke, she scraped the last of the mushroom pastry from the serving platter onto Charles's plate. "You must eat a bit more, dear Charles," she coaxed. "Your health requires it."

To Mariana's relief, the server brought in the entremets with fruit compote, and then cheeses signaling the meal's end. She couldn't wait to escape to her room.

Her father grew tired. He summoned Gannett. "Gannett, my good man, would you assist me upstairs?" He gazed around at everyone at the table. "I've enjoyed the fine company and delicious meal, but it's time I rested."

Once Gannett left the room with her father, Mariana said, "I've developed a frightful headache. Please, excuse me."

Aunt Portia raised an eyebrow. She hesitated, then said to Mariana. "I shall expect you in the library for coffee."

Mariana rushed upstairs and to her father's room. His door stood closed. She'd look in on him later. What an unnerving dinner, she thought, once in her room. She simply couldn't manage coffee with Aunt Portia and Lady Vesta, no matter her aunt expected her.

How could her father indulge Lady Vesta's bizarre ways? He'd not seemed himself at dinner—allowing the woman to spoon feed him. On the morrow, she'd go to the village, call on the doctor and speak frankly about her father's condition. She'd settled in her easy chair when a knock sounded at the door, and Abbie entered.

"What is it?"

"It's Lady Portia. She wants you at once."

Mariana found her aunt sitting on the side of her bed, a cloth around her forehead. "Whatever is wrong?"

"Almost the moment I went into the library, I couldn't drink the coffee." Portia gestured to the white cloth on her head. "I called Mrs. Hooks for a remedy. I had an attack of the dysentery. Not a severe attack, only discomfort. She's given me a tonic just now."

Mariana knew Gannett's wife was famous for her remedies. "Are you better?"

"Somewhat. Only, Mrs. Hooks told me Gannett had a bilious spell, too. He fell ill after helping your father upstairs. Have you felt ill, my dear?"

Mariana frowned. "No. I found the jellied duck too rich and ate but little of it. I've noticed no ill effects." Truly, she hadn't eaten much of anything after her irritation with John and his mother. Her aunt appeared more drawn by the minute. "You look as though you might faint. Let me help you into bed and call Mrs. Hooks."

Aunt Porta looked up. "Not necessary, if you'll help me to bed. Frankly, I'm worried," she continued. "Your father seems well and yet he doesn't seem well. Despite Her Ladyship's constant assurances that he's fine, I think otherwise."

"I agree," Mariana said. "I plan speaking to the doctor in the morning. Without Lady Vesta's presence."

"Such may not be necessary," Aunt Portia said. "I've sent one of the stablehands to fetch the doctor. He's on his way. He can see about Charles when he arrives."

Chapter 17

Mariana flew to her father's room once she was certain that Aunt Portia felt better from Mrs. Hook's remedies. He lay prone on the bed and appeared much worse than earlier at dinner. Worse, even, than the night in KinKerry when Mariana and Thomas brought him to Thornywilde. Lady Vesta was with him. She sat in a high-back chair on Charles's left. John stood in the shadows behind his mother.

The room smelled pleasantly of herbs—Mrs. Hooks remedies.

Mrs. Hooks, busy bathing His Lordship's forehead, stepped aside with Mariana.

"Lady Mariana, 'tis worse than my poor Gannett's touch of sickness after supper," whispered the cook. "And, Lady Portia. The doctor is coming." The good woman took the basin and departed the room.

What was keeping the doctor? The mantel clock ticked as Mariana paced back and forth awaiting the sound of the doctor's carriage.

"You may as well see about Lady Portia," said Lady Vesta. "John will come for you the moment the doctor arrives."

Since her father appeared to be resting and not retching, Mariana took the woman's advice. She had no desire to sit with her or her son.

She was grateful Mrs. Hooks's remedy had eased her aunt's symptoms. Aunt Portia stroked her hand. "How is Charles?"

"Resting. I'll go to him when the doctor comes."

Aunt Portia sighed. "Oh, dear," she mumbled. "I hold only one thing against Charles," she said. "His practice of keeping secrets. Catherine wanted it that way."

Coming to attention at once, Mariana frowned. "I don't understand." Had Mrs. Hooks's tonics loosened her tongue? Aunt Portia seldom if ever mentioned Mariana's mother. "I've kept silent too long," continued Portia.

"It's difficult to speak, but I must, since your father plans to marry Lady Vesta. Most men forget the past when they take a new wife. The new wife wants every memory of the former wife buried and forgotten."

The fire's glow brightened her aunt's face. Mariana scarce dared to breathe lest her aunt lose her train of thought. *The ugly rumors . . . bastard . . . by-blow child.* The past flooded Mariana's mind.

Aunt Portia shuddered. "Life is short," she said. "I should've spoken long before now." A far away expression on her face, she spoke to the crackling fire. "Ena Guthre came here as your mother's lady-in-waiting." She stopped herself. "No, that isn't right. It began long before that. Before your mother married your father. Catherine and Ena were distant cousins by marriage. When your father was a young man, he frequented Cork with his tutors and his art instructor, Martin Canady. Charles loved to paint the sea. Mr. Canady reveled in his young student's talent. Ena, a forward girl, struck up a friendship with the budding artist and Mr. Canady. She made it her business to follow them everywhere. She was winsome in those days, and the two young men didn't find her annoying like one would assume."

Noises sounded below. The doctor had arrived. "We will discuss this later," Aunt Portia said, coming to herself.

Charles began a violent vomiting session as Mariana entered his room. "Would you all step aside," ordered the doctor.

Mariana slipped around to the far side of his bed and clasped her father's hand. He looked up at her with a tortured expression.

"Summon the housekeeper to bring fresh clothing and sheets," ordered the doctor. When it seemed the horrible vomiting could go on no longer, the doctor administered a draught. "I've given him a sedative. He should rest. I'd stay the night but I'm delivering a baby in the village."

Mariana ignored Lady Vesta, responding, "We'll look after him."

The doctor nodded. "By all means, send for me in the event of any drastic change. I'd send for a midwife for the birth, but this is a first baby and the young mother is terrified. The wait could be long." He turned to Mrs. Hooks. "My good woman, take up a portion of the stomach's bile. I would inspect it."

Once the doctor took his leave, Her Ladyship wheeled toward Mariana. "Why should we all weary ourselves? My son and I will look after Charles. You may retire."

"I'm staying," Mariana said firmly, taking a step nearer her father's bed. She smoothed the counterpane, grateful the sedative was working. He seemed to be dropping off to sleep. "You may do as you wish," she said to Lady Vesta. "Both you and John."

Mrs. Hooks stepped forward. "I fear it'll be a long night. No need for all of you to weary yourself. If Lady Mariana stays, I'll watch with her."

Mrs. Hooks's practical solution took some of the haughtiness from Lady Vesta's manner. "You may go, John," she said to her son. "I'll stay a short while longer."

John retired from the room.

"Then, I'll see to things in the kitchen and come back," Mrs. Hooks said.

Mariana drew her wrapper around her shoulders. She did not intend to engage Lady Vesta in conversation.

"The sedative is working," Lady Vesta said. In the next breath, she asked. "Why are you against our marriage?"

Mariana refused playing into the woman's hands. "Why are you for it? I cannot believe you love my father."

Her Ladyship's eyes took on a hard glint. Her lips pinched, she said. "What do you know of love, you chit. Look at you. You're well past your prime. What gentleman would take you as his wife?"

Heat suffused Mariana's neck, creeping up to her face. How dare the wretched woman spout her malice over her father's sickbed? "I know truth when I see it," Mariana said, struggling to keep her voice low and calm. "Truth comes from living among honest folk. You ring false." She rose from her chair, went to her father's side, straightening his coverlet.

"Since you insist upon playing the martyr, I shall leave you to it," spat Lady Vesta. The woman swept through the door at maximum speed, her silk skirts snapping about her ankles.

Mrs. Hooks came through the door as the other woman rushed past. "Is Her Ladyship ill, too?"

"She's a troublesome person," Mariana replied, "and obviously unaware how her actions affect others. How's Gannett?"

"Some better, m'lady. He's sleeping. He's resting well enough," she said.

135

The night wore on. Mariana settled in an easy chair huddled under a blanket. Mrs. Hooks rose and went to her father's bed. Mariana did the same, seeing he slept. In the very early hours of morning, his breathing sounded shallower, then more labored. Mariana removed some of the quilts around him. He didn't rouse, but slept on.

Shortly before four a.m., the doctor arrived again. "The young mother is delivered," he said. Before I go home, I wanted to check on Sir Charles. The doctor went to the bed and took Charles' hand. "My God, he's dead."

Chapter 18

*T*he days that followed her father's death passed in a blur of grief and sorrow; the vicar's visits, the wake and the burial dominated Mariana's emotions.

A fortnight after His Lordship Sir Charles Belmont, fifth earl of Thornywilde, lay in his crypt in the churchyard, the doctor called in at the castle. He asked for Mariana. She joined him in the library. The doctor appeared grave and concerned. "Had anyone else eaten mushrooms the evening your father took ill?"

"We told you some in the household fell ill. You remember you left draught for Gannett, our man of service, and Aunt Portia suffered mild discomfort."

"I suspected at the time that M'lord's condition was mushroom poisoning, before I had his stomach contents tested. A good thing I had the maid save the stomach specimen. I was right. The laboratory at Dublin confirmed my suspicions."

Mariana felt faint. "Mrs. Hooks prepared the pastry," she said, her voice trailing. "But, surely . . . you aren't suggesting-? There must be some mistake."

"I'm not suggesting foul play," the doctor said kindly. "Your father's weakened condition caused the tainted mushrooms to deal more harshly with him than the others."

Tainted mushrooms! Old Madge! Thomas brought mushrooms to the castle when they returned from KinKerry. Mrs. Hooks made the pastry with them. Were those mushrooms poisonous? They couldn't be. Old Madge gathered them. She knew the good from the bad.

Angry tears welled in Mariana's eyes as she recalled Lady Vesta forcing her father to eat more and more of the mushroom pastry. Had the woman known the mushrooms were bad?

The library door opened and Lady Vesta burst into the room. Her black widow's weeds relieved by a single diamond clasp at her throat. "Why didn't you tell me the doctor was here," she snapped to Mariana.

"My dear Lady Vesta," explained the doctor, "I came to inform Lady Mariana that His Lordship grew ill from tainted mushrooms due to his weakened constitution."

"You are certain?" Lady Vesta demanded overloudly.

"There's no mistake about tainted mushrooms in His Lordship's system? I had his stomach contents tested at King's Hospital. His weakened state rendered him more susceptible to the poison. That's why the others hadn't as violent a reaction."

Lady Vesta's face became a picture of excitable anger. She blurted. "I blame Thomas O'Geary. He brought the bad mushrooms here. Not only that, he risked Charles' life trucking him here in a carriage like . . . like . . . like a side of beef."

Mariana gasped. How dare Her Ladyship make such damning remarks! "You cannot suggest such a thing. The trip proved restorative to him," Mariana cried, heat threading her cheeks. "And, no one in this house deliberately fed my father bad mushrooms. Everyone ate mushrooms that evening. Aunt Portia grew ill, as well as Gannett."

Mariana recalled Lady Vesta and John hadn't fallen sick from the food. Were they aware the pastry was bad and avoided it?

"And, why not you?" Her Ladyship questioned snidely.

"I don't eat mushrooms. I've never liked them."

"That's right," Aunt Portia affirmed, who'd stepped into the room. Mariana had no idea what her aunt had overheard. "Oh, dear, this is dreadful-"

Her Ladyship shook her finger at Mariana. "You think yourself clever. You know Thomas O'Geary brought tainted mushroom into this house . . . mushrooms the cook prepared. I dare anyone here to deny it."

Mariana fought for control. "Yes, Thomas brought mushrooms," Mariana said firmly. "But other mushrooms could've been used in the pastry. Shall we call the cook?" The doctor nodded without real interest. Lady Vesta shook the bellcord vehemently. Mrs. Hooks arrived in short time. Mariana explained the conundrum.

Looking at the doctor, her face white and drawn, Mrs. Hooks said solemnly. "They were the very mushrooms Mr. O'Geary brought. They were good 'uns. I saw to 'em me-self."

"Putrid bilious mushrooms!" shrieked Lady Vesta. "Murder. It was murder!"

Chapter 19

*L*ady Vesta's accusations were ascribed to overwrought nerves. The doctor left a compound for her. Before going upstairs, she hissed at Mariana, "This is not the last of this."

Later that afternoon a carriage arrived at the castle. Mariana saw Gannett admit a stranger up to the house, a man, short in stature with wispy, gray hair, and wearing an untidy greatcoat. He carried an old-fashioned leather portfolio.

Gannett stopped Mariana in the hall. "Lady Vesta's barrister to see her."

"Has anyone notified her?"

"Yes, m'lady," Abbie said. "She's waiting in the library."

The interview in the library took hours.

"What do you imagine she wants with a solicitor," Mariana asked her aunt.

* * *

Later that afternoon, Mariana sat in Aunt Portia's back drawing room. What a sad room, she thought, with its black crepe swathing the mirrors, and great black bands tied about the dark curtains. She noticed Aunt Portia had not started the clock—still set at the hour of His Lordship's passing.

Abbie came to the door. "Mr. O'Geary wishes to see you, Lady Mariana."

"What's this about?" she asked Thomas when he came into the room.

"I hadn't wanted to alarm you," he began, "but there's been a break-in and a theft in the artist studio. A number of things have been stolen. A valuable set of knives is gone. Knives a friend in India had made for me. They were inlaid with gold, and had precious stones in the hilt. Not only that, some canvases are cut. Windows are broken. It's a deliberate act. We must be vigilant here at the castle. Someone wants vengeance."

"Vengeance for what? What have we done?" asked Aunt Portia.

"I don't know," Thomas said truthfully.

"The only change is dear Charles's demise," continued the older woman. "I can't imagine this has anything to do with him. Unless," she said, turning to Mariana, "it's about your experience on Cormac Hill."

"That's ridiculous," Mariana said, glancing warily at Thomas. How much did he know about The Ribbonmen, and the dead policemen?

She hadn't long to wonder, for her aunt spoke up. "I've told Thomas about you seeing the Ribbonmen stealing Thornywilde's cattle."

"But-"

Portia waved Mariana's interruption away. "It's some retribution for that, I'm afraid. We must contact Inspector Jagger."

"It can't be as serious as that," protested Mariana. "Surely," she said to Thomas, "a few missing knives, a few ruined canvases. . ."

Chapter 20

*T*hree weeks hence:

The mushroom controversary did not reach pandemic proportions much to Lady Vesta's chagrin. Life at Thornywilde had settled into an uneasy routine, with both Lady Vesta and John staying on.

On Thursday morning, Mariana, accompanied by Abbie, rode into the village to shop. When they arrived back at the castle, a police carriage stood in the drive. Mrs. Hooks met them in the hall.

"Ye must go to the library at once," she said to Mariana.

"Of course. Whatever is wrong?"

"The inspector is 'ere. 'im from the village, Inspector Jagger."

Mariana suspected as much. Since the mushroom matter had died down, this visit could only be about the dead policeman, not the vandalism at the estate. Outside the closed library door, the murmur of voices carried into the hall. Taking a deep breath, Mariana knocked, then entered.

A sea of faces greeted her. Aunt Portia, Her Ladyship, John, and Thomas. Each countenance bore a grim expression. Though it was a cloudy afternoon, the library's blazing candles made the room appear as noonday. The dusty books, the stiff curtains—all seemed to choke her.

Aunt Portia, in an easy chair angled toward the fireplace, motioned Mariana to sit beside her. Her Ladyship and John occupied the horsehair settle. Thomas sat opposite Aunt Portia. What a dismal group they were.

Inspector Jagger, stood beside her father's desk. He frowned at her. "I will come directly to the point, m'lady."

"Please do."

Mariana had never particularly liked the English inspector. He cut an arrogant picture in the village. The night she reported the policemen's deaths he'd been curt and efficient. She couldn't fault him for that.

"There's been murder at Thornywilde," said the inspector in his clipped English accent.

"A murder!" Mariana exclaimed. Her muscles seemed to shrink in her body. "A murder?" she repeated. This wasn't about the Ribbonmen. "A murder...."

Jagger gestured to the east. "Ian Cluny, one of your tenant's sons. His body was discovered in the park."

"Our woodland park?"

"Yes, the wood beside this house."

The wood where she exercised Hera. "What has that to do with us? We don't know the comings and goings of our tenants and farmers. I'm sorry such a thing has happened and we'll minister to his family."

Aunt Portia nodded. "Best listen, my dear."

Ian Cluny. She knew the name well. Could he have been the Ribbonmen's leader on Cormac Hill? The one who stood over the dead policemen's bodies, plunging his sword into their still forms. Shuddering, she tried to compose herself. From the family's grim faces, she suspected they already knew the answer to her next question. "How was he killed?"

"Brutally, m'lady. Stabbed repeatedly with a sharp blade, then the corpse bludgeoned."

Shocked, she shook her head—her brain slack. "I'm sorry."

"Are you indeed?" said the inspector.

Inspector Jagger's expression frightened her. She glanced at each of the others. Why didn't they speak? "Why would you say such?"

Her Ladyship waffled up from the settle, striding imperially into the center of the room. Turning, she faced Mariana. "You may wonder about the inspector's presence. I summoned the authorities before I knew about the tenant's murder."

"Yes," John confirmed. "No one is to leave the house."

A shrewd look in his eyes, Jagger watched them all, allowing each to speak. Aunt Portia gasped, her black-jet earrings bobbing. Thomas frowned. Mrs. Hooks wilted against the door.

Finally, Mariana found her voice. "Why would you summon the inspector?" she asked Lady Vesta.

"Suspicions," blurted the woman. "From the first . . . I knew the authorities must investigate the double game here . . . the deceit . . . the evil intent." She dabbed at the corner of her eyes with a wispy lace handkerchief as John hurried to her side, taking her hand. "Maman, you mustn't weep. Truth will be done."

Truth? The room took on a surreal aura to Mariana.

"My dear lady," the Inspector began, speaking to Mariana, "we have received the doctor's toxicology report. His Lordship ingested lethal fungi. As did all of you. I understand you do not eat mushrooms."

"That is correct," Mariana replied.

"How very fortunate for you."

Everyone seemed frozen in place except Aunt Portia who slumped backwards in the oversized chair as limp as a rag doll without stuffings. Mariana knelt at her aunt's feet. "Abbie," she cried to Mrs. Hooks. "Have Abbie fetch the smelling salts!"

Apparently, Abbie had her face pressed to the library door for she ran with the drought in record time.

Aunt Portia hadn't actually fainted but lapsed into startled despair. She grasped Mariana's hands, whispering. "You haven't heard everything."

Lady Vesta charged up from the settle. She shot the inspector a malevolent stare. "There are particulars I demand you hear. Hear this moment while we are all present. I was Lord Belmont's fiancée. I demand justice for this deliberate act of murder by mushroom poisoning."

The inspector's gaze swept across each of them in turn.

Mariana wondered why the woman kept insisting someone murdered her father when the issue here plainly was a tenant's murder in Thornywilde's park. Lady Vesta knew nothing of the tenants. *Ludicrous! Ludicrous!*

Mariana directed her attention to the inspector. "The wood is intended for private use for us and our guests," she said. "It's immense. We can't supervise each parcel of the ground. We're all honorable people living decent lives. We'd never knowingly harm another soul."

Jagger nodded. "The cold body of Ian Cluny found in your wood defies your claim." The inspector moved toward the door. "Will everyone step into the hall? I will call you one by one." He cleared his throat. "A caution. You are not to discuss any of my questions among yourselves. Is that clear?"

As if Mariana wished to repeat anything she'd heard. She wondered about Lady Vesta's reasons for calling the inspector in the first place. Was the woman unhinged or merely evil?

"M'lady, will you be so kind as to remain. Without your son," Jagger said to Lady Vesta.

As they filed out, the door thudded solidly behind them. "My dear," Aunt Portia said to Mariana, "we'll retire to the back drawing room. Abbie, bring tea. We're in desperate need of refreshment."

"Whatever possessed Her Ladyship to complain about the mushrooms to the inspector?"

Aunt Portia sighed. "She believes someone maliciously poisoned Charles to kill him."

"That's ridiculous."

"Of course, it's ridiculous," Aunt Portia agreed. "And, the inspector must tread carefully. He has little respect for the peerage, but he fears repercussions from his superiors."

"Still, the timing," Mariana said bitterly. "It's unforgivable Her Ladyship would continue this witch-hunt, trying to accuse one of us with killing my father when the inspector is here about a murder."

"We mustn't forget the mushrooms may not have been a mere kitchen mistake."

Mariana couldn't believe her aunt's doubts. Mrs. Hooks's kitchen knowledge stood above reproach. "Too, Old Madge never made a mistake gathering mushrooms."

Abbie brought tea. They drank it in silence.

The inspector called Lady Portia next. Then, John Desmond. Afterwards, Thomas, then one by one, all the servants were summoned. Gannett emerged from the library, an expression of terror on his face.

Left for last, Mariana could only speculate what that meant. She dismissed the fact the inspector was here about Lady Vesta's wild belief that someone in the house had willfully poisoned her father. This must be about Ian Cluny's murder.

Jagger closed the library door after her. "M'lady, please take a chair."

Inspector Jagger moved behind the desk and sat down. Mariana took the chair nearest the desk. Ian Cluny could've been the Ribbonman below Cormac Hill—now the unfortunate man found stabbed and bludgeoned in Thornywilde's Park.

Jagger spoke first. "Have you spoken to anyone about the incident you saw on Cormac Hill?"

"No."

"Has your memory returned about the chief Ribbonman's identity?"

"No."

"The murdered man in the park was known to you?"

"I know of Ian Cluny - he is the son of one of my father's tenants."

"And, you will not identify him as the Ribbonman you saw."

"I cannot. Not with certainty."

"We will conduct a thorough investigation into this murder. No one is to leave Thornywilde."

"I understand."

The inspector peered sharply over his ornate pince-nez. "You realize there could be repercussions among the tenants and farmers with this man's body being found in Thornywilde's private park. As I cautioned you before, you could've been observed that day. Even the hills have eyes at times."

"We don't know those Ribbonmen were Thornywildle's tenants. They were disguised," she reminded the inspector.

"We don't know they weren't," he countered.

"Their own mothers couldn't recognize them," Mariana said. "Their faces were pasted with peat mud, and they wore shaggy clothing, like sheep's skin."

With a swaggering nod, Jagger suggested. "Ian Cluny was exceptionally tall. You described the Ribbonman leader as tall. Exceptionally tall."

She could only agree.

* * *

After the discovery of Ian Cluny's body, the estate settled into everyday life though uneasiness affected everyone. A frisson of trepidation lurked beneath the surface.

Three days after Inspector Jagger's visit, there occurred another daring raid. Herds of Thornywilde's cattle went missing. A mysterious fire destroyed one of the distant follies—a summer house His Lordship had favored. An effigy of the crown's tribute collector was burned there.

The afternoon after the fire, John came into Aunt Portia's back drawing room where Mariana and her aunt sat at their embroidery hoops.

"Patrick has invited us all to Shannon hall. Maman and I are going, and you, of course," he said to Mariana.

The needle pricked Mariana's finger. Blood spoiled the fine, white-linen piece. "I have no intention of visiting Shannon Hall. That's final," she said.

"How she enjoys tormenting me," bantered John to Lady Portia.

Placing her work aside, Lady Portia looked at her niece. "He's right, my dear. You are neglecting happy times. You should relish an opportunity to escape this cheerless house."

"And, you'll see to Inspector Jagger, should he appear," Mariana said, "And to a Ribbonman, should one of them set another fire?"

Aunt Portia's eyes snapped. "Should a Ribbonman set fire to the house itself, what could either of us do?"

"Exactly," put in John. "You worry too much, my dear. You're only a few hours away at Patrick's." John continued teasing. "If our handsome resident artist were going, I daresay you'd reconsider."

Heat suffused Mariana's neck—tellltale redness spreading across her cheeks. "No," she said plainly, "not even then."

"What's this about Thomas, dear?" Aunt Portia asked, looking up from her embroidery where she considered two shades of blue silk.

Chapter 21

he following Monday church bells from the village tolled the quarter hour. Lady Portia, and Mariana enjoyed tea in the drawing room. The toll of doom, Mariana thought absently, since Lady Vesta would soon return from her walk.

Abbie came to the door, her eyes wide.

"What is it?" Mariana asked.

"A stableman is come from Shannon Hall."

"Have him step forward," instructed Portia.

"A stableman?" Lady Vesta questioned archly, coming into the room, her shawl across her arms.

"Send the man in," said Aunt Portia.

This servant of Patrick's, a raw-boned man of middle years, broad of face, stepped forward and doffed his worn cap. "Your majesties-" he began, confused. Words seemed to fail him.

"I'm Lady Portia. What is your message?"

"M'lady, Sir John Desmond has been shot."

"Shot?" screamed Vesta, crumpling backwards. She'd have struck the floor if Mariana hadn't supported her.

"Go for Gannett," Mariana cried to Abbie. "Quickly!"

A great deal or scrambling ensued with Gannett finally settling Her Ladyship on the hall bench.

"Is he dead?" Her Ladyship demanded of the man in a strong voice for one so near prostration moments before.

Patrick's servant viewed the scene, fear etched across his face.

"Tell me exactly what happened!" Her Ladyship shrieked at the man, who stood squashing his hat in his fist.

"He ain't hardly dead, m'lady" the man managed.

At the word dead, Her Ladyship swooned again, her head slumping against the back of the bench, but not hard enough to inflict pain.

Abbie fanned her furiously with a palm frond fan.

Sputtering and sitting up, Lady Vesta ordered the man. "Well, go on!" The louder she spoke, the faster Abbie fanned.

"Am I the source of this drama?" They all turned. John Desmond stood in the open front door, his right arm supported by a linen sling. He swaggered forward. "A fool couldn't aim straight and I'm the brunt of his blunder." John spoke with a trace of pride as he sauntered down the hall.

He stopped and knelt before his mother. "Really, Maman, I'm perfectly fine. You can't believe a bad seed can go as quickly as that. Much too convenient, my dear." He leaned forward and kissed her on the forehead.

Lady Vesta swooned again, or pretended to, for she roused almost instantly. "Really, John," she admonished, her hand across her heart.

John, dismissed his mother's distress and turned to Mariana. "Dear Mariana," he rhapsodized. "Haven't you an ounce of sympathy for a wounded man?" He spoke as if they meant a great deal to each other.

All eyes on her, Mariana resisted a sharp retort. "I'm sorry that you're injured. Is it very bad?"

"The worst," John said. His exhibition of cow-eyes—inviting cow-eyes, appalling.

Stiffening, she silently vowed to not lead this man on, nor would she remain in the same room with him. Let him play his silly charade. "If you'll excuse me, I think it best you comfort your mother. She's had a terrible shock."

"An excellent suggestion," Aunt Portia said. "John, please help your mother upstairs. I'll send Mrs. Hooks with brandy."

John shrugged slightly as if his mother's drama were none of his concern. "Instead, dear Lady Portia, would you have brandy sent to the library? Have the maid see my mother upstairs." He cast Mariana a knowing look. "Please stay. I'd like to tell you how everything happened." He reached a persuasive hand toward her arm. She went rigid.

The others left the hall.

"We'll speak later," Mariana replied. "Your mishap could've had a dire outcome; I confess, it's quite enough excitement for me this moment." John stood close, blocking her exit from the hall.

Thomas came up the hall from the back of the house. Mariana was glad to see him. He stopped, "Is everything all right?" he asked, after a swift look at Mariana, and John's bandaged arm.

Willing her errant heart to beat normally, Mariana said, "I . . . uh . . . I thought you were busy in the studio."

"What she means to say is I've had a dreadful accident. Shot, exactly," John said, holding up his arm.

"My good man, I pray it was an accident."

"Exactly," Mariana said to Thomas.

"If you will excuse me," Thomas said.

"Wait. There's uh . . . something I must discuss." Mariana gestured to the drawing room door.

"I suppose you're bidding me *adieu*," John drawled. "What a pretty picture, you two make," he said. "Too bad you can't paint it, Thomas, fair maiden and stalwart man." John laughed. "Gad, man, have you been sailing, you're as brown as a sea captain. And, you dear Mariana, you're as red as a rose in full bloom."

Leaning his bandaged arm against the hall's paneled wall, Mariana realized his *terrible wound* was nothing more than a scratch.

With an exasperated sigh, she led Thomas into the drawing room and closed the door. She hadn't noticed that he held a large square parcel wrapped in brown paper.

"I met the post," he explained. "What did you want to see me about?"

She colored, then laughed softly. "A ploy," she said, realizing how very blue his eyes were. His skin *was* tanned from exposure to the sun as he worked on the studio. "Sir John suffered a shooting accident at Patricks. Nothing serious. I confess I used you-"

"Use me anytime," Thomas interrupted.

Jittery warmth spread throughout Mariana's body. How disconcerting, her physical reaction to this man. Kisses filled her mind— the kiss in the Dublin studio—the kiss on the mountainside as they traveled to KinKerry. "So, has the fire ruined the studio?"

"Pretty much. I want to see it rebuilt in honor of your father," he said.

Mariana could scarce keep her eyes off him. What a specimen of manhood he presented. Comparing the two men, Thomas and John, Thomas came out far the more attractive. His broad shoulders fitted well in his taupe-colored waistcoat—the coat hugging the outline of his body.

Chapter 22

*T*he next morning, after breakfast, Mariana sent Gannett to the stable to have Hera saddled and brought around. It was a lovely spring morning, crisp and cool, the very earth refreshed. From a distance, sheep's bells tinkled pleasantly in the air. The plentiful spring rains had turned trees and foliage brilliant green. The world seemed rejuvenated and idyllic.

The frisky mare trotted up to the carriage turn in front of the house, loosely held by Gannett's expert hand. "She knows ye're waiting, m'lady," Gannett said, moving the mounting block into the perfect position.

Mariana put her boot into the stirrup, lifted her body up, and slipped her knee around the ornate saddlehorn. She'd forgone the comfortable breeches, and wore her modest hunter green riding kit—a falcon's feather in her cap.

Hera, eager to be off, pranced in place. Mariana directed the mare down the stony path toward the village road. Once out of sight of the house, she reined Hera sharply eastward, and onto the path leading to the section of wood where Ian Cluny's body had been found.

She could scarce believe murder or ill will existed anywhere on the estate. Yet, a man had met his death some yards from where she now rode. Past the murder site, she guided Hera up to the path's highest point, a stony hill overlooking the glen below, and the Erin Rose Inn.

No! she whispered, bringing Hera to a jolting stop. The black police coach stood in front of the inn—its gold insignia glittering in the morning sun. An officer paced along the inn's sheltered portico. She recognized him by his sizable girth as Officer Whitcomb.

A knot of dread traced through Mariana's stomach. Her hands trembled. Why was Chief Inspector Jagger at the Erin Rose? To her knowledge, it wasn't a place he'd ever visited before. Within minutes,

Jagger emerged from the inn. Both men boarded the coach and set off in the direction of the village.

On impulse, Mariana nudged Hera down the steep hill toward the inn. She rode into the inn yard, dismounted, and handed the horse over to a stablehand.

Mr. Fitzwilliam, the inn owner, greeted her at the door. "Aye, Lady Mariana, 'tis wonderful to see you."

Mariana removed her gloves, gesturing to a table before the window. "I'll be having a spot of tea if you please, soda bread with your famous honey."

Fitzwilliam laughed. "I wouldn't be forgetting. The world could be ending and ye'd order me bread and me honey."

Mr. Fitzwillian returned a few minutes later with a tray laden with a steaming pot, bread and honey. "And, the lovely Lady Portia, how is that dear lady?"

Mariana steadied her hand, pouring the tea. "My aunt is well."

Mr. Fitzwilliam's broad face broke into a wide smile. "I can't ne'er forget you and Miss Kathleen coming here for the seisún. Aye, the loveliest two lassies in the county, and what dancers ye both were."

"We were mere girls out for a frolic. The old fun nights have ended," Mariana replied soberly, though she knew her eyes twinkled. "What with Kathleen married and expecting her third child." Steering the conversation to the inspector's visit, Mariana began. "I saw the police coach as I rode up. Is there more trouble hereabouts?"

"Aye. The inspector was here about poor Ian Cluny. The lad met a most foul death." Fitzwilliam continued after glancing around warily. "None too popular, the inspector is. English bred, you know."

"Cluny's murder is tragic," Mariana agreed. "I'm sure you've heard the gossip that my father died from eating tainted mushrooms. Some say they came from Old Madge."

Fitzwilliam's expression darkened, consternation visible upon his honest face. "I've heard the villagers talk, ye know. And, the inspector spoke about Old Madge. I told 'em I've known Old Madge since I were a wee lad. She makes no mistakes with 'shrooms. Neither she nor Mrs. Hooks, your cook up at Thornywilde. Neither would mistake a poisonous 'shroom for a sound one. None's more knowledgeable about 'shrooms than them two." Fitzwilliam blushed. He wiped his hands down the front of his starched apron. "Inspector Jagger forbade me to speak of anything he'd said. Ye won't be tattlin', will ye, lass?"

Mariana laughed. "No more than you tattled about Kathleen and I at the seisún."

"Aye, lass. Aye."

More customers came into the inn. Fitzwilliams bowed and moved to the other patrons. Mariana sipped her tea and nibbled at the fresh bread slathered with honey. It could've been paste in her mouth for her wondering who at Thornywilde the inspector suspected of murder. And, what murder—her father, or Cluny?

* * *

No member of the house disturbed the servants until past three. That being their private time. After lunch at Thornywilde, well past three o'clock, Mariana went down to the kitchen.

Mrs. Hooks, at the work table, prepared vegetables for the evening meal. "M'lady?" The cook pushed aside the bowl of parsnips she'd been dressing. "What can I help you with?"

Mariana smiled at the cook. "I have a few questions. Don't fear," she said, as alarm spread over Mrs. Hooks's face. "I know the inspector warned us not to speak about his questions to us, but what we say in confidence in our house is personal and has no bearing on the inspector's warnings."

Mrs. Hooks relaxed somewhat. But, not much judging from the firm set of her thin lips.

Mariana continued. "I've puzzled over and over about the mushrooms in the pastry the night my father grew gravely ill—were they from Old Madge as you said?"

"They were, m'lady. Fine as any, too, and I'd swear that on me dear mother's grave. None were tainted."

"You made the pastry days later," Mariana continued. "The mushrooms served that night couldn't have been the ones Mr. O'Geary brought when he came home with my father."

Mrs. Hooks thought a moment. "Ye're right, m'lady. Ye brought it back to me forgetful mind. It was this way. As Mr. O'Geary was going to the village that day to pick up some supplies for his studio, I sent 'im along to Old Madge's. He brought the 'shrooms. 'Twas the day before I made the pastry. Not the day he brought His Lordship 'ome. The house was in such a state—if I say so, meself—what with the temporary girls in the house. More in the way at times than help."

Thanking Mrs. Hooks, Mariana went up to the library. Gannett had made a fire. She closed the door, sighing. Mrs. Hooks's information helped little, for both mushroom supplies came from Old Madge and they were both delivered by Thomas.

Had he placed poisonous ones among the good? Preposterous. He'd never do that. However, someone could've mixed in poisonous ones with the sound. Who? Who wanted to kill her father?

She closed her eyes. Everyone had access to the pastry, and no one except her father had been dangerously affected. The doctor said his weakness caused the fatal reaction to the pastry. Perhaps his death wasn't murder. Her imagination could be playing tricks on her. That didn't excuse the fact that bad mushrooms had been in the pastry. Mrs. Hooks examined the mushrooms. Nor, could she be fooled. She knew the good from the bad.

Mariana tried to remember every event of that infamous meal. Mrs. Hooks had sent to the village for extra help. Help that was more in the way than help, the cook had said.

An air of excitement filled everyone because His Lordship would be at the table after his long illness. The serving woman brought in the pastry. Lady Vesta fed the dish to His Lordship. Her father tired and had to go upstairs.

Since, according to the doctor, her father died from bad mushrooms, they could've come innocently to the table with no intended victim. What if someone intended random victims? Indeed, Aunt Portia suffered some distress. As well as Gannett.

Anyone could've brought poisonous mushrooms into the house and slipped them among the good ones. If Mrs. Hooks had already prepared them, would she notice a few bad ones? Why had Lady Vesta cried murder?

Her feet to the fender for warmth from the glowing embers, Mariana sighed. So much she didn't understand. If only her father had confided in her through the years about matters troubling him—money, the estate's decline, his interest in the art world—even the long ago past, her mother and the rumors surrounding his only child's birth. Instead, he'd chosen secrecy. It was not a child's place to question him.

Was his kindness toward her extended from the guilt of knowing a harlot's child was substituted in place of his flesh and blood who'd died at birth? A merciful act to ease his dying wife's pain.

What of the mysterious woman she'd seen in the park that day long ago. Who was she? What was she to her father? It was all too confusing. Now, she would never know answers to questions that troubled her.

Chapter 23

hief Constable Jagger's swivel chair squeaked as he settled into it. He viewed his earlier doodlings—squiggly lines—on cream paper scattered across the oaken desk. He should be more careful. The squiggles represented money, privilege, power. Entities that ruled the world.

Taking up his pen, he printed the word A M B I T I O N in square letters. He put the sheet aside. Those fortunate enough to inherit money, privilege and power often lacked ambition. Many of the peerage failed miserably in life even with gilded advantages, or because of them.

Jagger had had ambition, though born without money, privilege, or power, he'd learned to use ambition to achieve his goals. His service in the British home office had garnered a promising future until he became embroiled in a nasty scandal. A murder occurred in the theatre district; the woman, an actress, stabbed to death in her dressing room. Fate's ill hand had placed him in front of the actress's closed dressing room door bearing a bouquet of pink roses. He'd admired the young woman and believed himself in love with her.

What happened next, happened quickly. Flinging the dressing room door open, a man sprinted past him. He'd not pursued the man—nor had he reason to involve himself in the peculiarities of those in the acting profession. Instead, he stepped inside the actress's room. The young woman lay on her back, one foot twisted beneath her still body. Blood dripped onto the dusty floor from a wound in her right temple. He'd knelt over her. Her life was gone. He'd placed the flowers at her side, gone into the hall and collapsed into a chair.

The police came. Recognizing him and his senior position in the forces, questions to him were for the moment delayed.

Later, the man seen running from the actress's room was identified as Lord Bramley. He was suspected of the murder. Murder of the young woman Jagger admired and loved. Lord Bramley had proved above the law. The police hushed up the murder for lack of evidence. Not for Jagger, though. He was of the law, but not above the law.

His superiors grilled him about his presence at the theatre that night. He admitted being there. He admitted buying the extravagant bouquet of roses. He admitted placing the roses near the dead girl's body. He admitted seeing a man flee the scene. No, he couldn't identify the man. It had happened too quickly.

Nasty articles appeared in *The Times*. Jagger's good name dragged throughout the sordid affair.

Commands came from Home Office. Publicity must be squelched. The regular police would take the case. Jagger's promising London career—over. There would be no advancement for him. In the end, dispatching him to Ireland as Lough Glendelough's chief inspector stopped the gossip. It wasn't long before a string of vicious murders dulled the public interest in the dead actress.

He should be thankful.

After taking the Lough Glendelough post, he lost weight. Sleep eluded him. The village became his salvation and his prison. Grateful he'd not been arrested and sent to the gallows for a crime he didn't commit, the ordeal had left him with a fervent hatred of the peerage. In his heart, he knew Lord Bramley had murdered the woman.

Now in this remote, insignificant village, the High Court Commissioner breathed down his neck again—about the police officers found murdered on Cormac Hill.

The Cormac Hill murders opened deep wounds. Wounds suggestive of Jagger's incompetence. Though he was not a suspect in the Cormac Hill affair, he realized his superiors judged him because of his entanglement with the London theatre district case.

Taking up the pen, cleaning the nib, he drew a furled ribbon on the cream page. Ribbonmen! They moved like thieves in the night. The killer or killers could be anyone in the village and surrounding areas.

Now a dead man, identified as Ian Cluny, had turned up in Thornywilde Park. He was the son of one of Thornywilde's farmers with a long association to the estate. He'd been a wild one, often in trouble with the law. Moreover, one sent to Australia with a group of criminals. No one admitted to knowing when he'd returned to Ireland.

Jagger crumpled the cream sheet. If the Cormac Hill murders and Ian Cluny's murder weren't enough to trouble him, Lady Vesta Chasteen's ill hand toiled over the smouldering cauldron.

She'd sent a letter to London's High Court accusing Jagger of derelict of duty by not arresting someone for the murder of His Lordship, Charles Belmont. The High Court Commissioner forwarded a copy of Her Ladyship's letter to Jagger's Dublin superior.

Once the screws were set under the Dublin superior, he sent a scathing letter to Jagger. The letter's gist - further investigation imperative in the mushroom poisoning. The poisoner must be brought to justice at once. Severely punished. His Dublin superior put Lady Vesta's demands above the three dead policemen and Ian Cluny's murder. The peerage again, he swore, thinking of Lord Bramley escaping the gallows because of his social position.

In separate post sent by special messenger, his superior had evidently come to his senses somewhat, for he demanded an immediate arrest in the case of the three dead police officers. Jagger's position hung in the balance.

Chapter 24

ariana went for a walk as Thomas started toward the house from the ruined studio. She fell in step with him. He was easy to talk to. "How goes the repair?"

"Some progress. Moving along, but slowly."

She noticed stains on his hands. He'd been painting again. "I see you're working by the paint on your hands."

He laughed. "A bit. Dabbling, really. I've set up a temporary studio. I'm really a portrait painter. But I'm sincerely trying to do justice to the hills here."

"Our hills should be grateful," she said. "Have you finished Lady Vesta's portrait?"

"Aye, hers and Sir John's."

"Why haven't we seen them?" she asked, wondering how the vain woman could resist flaunting a flattering portrait. John, as well.

"You'll see them soon enough. Her Ladyship has elaborate plans for their unveiling," Thomas said wryly.

She'd had words earlier with Lady Vesta.

Thomas picked up on her state of mind. "Are you troubled about anything?"

"Am I so easily read?"

"Perhaps not to everyone, but I confess, I see a troubled line across your forehead." He stopped walking, his gaze intent upon her.

They were now before the dining room terrace where the doors stood open, the curtains partially open.

"I know I can speak to you," Mariana began. She could trust him. He hadn't breathed a word of her scandalous behavior that day in Dublin. "I also know I can trust you. It's Lady Vesta. She vexes me on every hand.

She wants one of us convicted of murdering my father." She struggled against tears welling at the corners of her eyes.

Thomas took her hand. "Be careful. The woman can be a vixen."

"Do you think she tried to kill my father with the mushroom pastry?"

"What?" exclaimed Thomas? "I don't think so. Were she to attempt such a foul deed, she'd do so covertly. She'd need to cast blame on someone else."

"She has everyone in the house to blame," Mariana said ruefully.

Thomas continued. "Surely the bad mushrooms weren't deliberately planted in the pastry. Kitchen accidents occur everyday."

"But," Mariana objected. "Remember, she insisted my father eat every morsel of the pastry. She even scraped the dish and fed him the leavings."

"Odd behavior," Thomas agreed.

"Then, there's Sir John."

"What about Sir John?"

She said quickly. "He was at the table that night. He'd do anything his mother asked. Too, he was bumbling around the sideboard pouring whiskey. Could he have slipped bad mushrooms into the dish?" She sighed. "Foolish of me. John didn't have access to the pastry dish. He was only interested in getting drunker."

"Don't discredit him," Thomas said carefully. "The serving woman placed the pastry on the sideboard after we were served. I remember John going to the sideboard more than once pouring brandy, then whiskey."

Mariana shot him a swift look. "You're right. He did over-imbibe. His behavior became so odious, I refused looking at him." A flush burned her cheeks recalling John's unwanted attention. "I was grateful he left my side until I confess I didn't care how drunk he got. That's not Christian nor charitable, but it's true."

Thomas nodded, stepping closer to her.

"There's another thing that bothers me," she said. "Why is Inspector Jagger putting so much credence on Lady Vesta's accusations rather than trying to find Ian Cluny's murderer or even the person who murdered the three policemen."

"She's a powerful woman," Thomas said. "She gets what she wants."

Mariana glanced toward the terrace doors where a curtain moved. "I should go in now," she said. "We're being watched."

"Wait. There's something I must say. Be careful in the house. Things aren't what they seem."

Mariana nodded. "I sense danger, unrest, and evil." She laughed nervously "If only, I knew what."

Chapter 25

homas went into the house through the kitchen entrance. Gannett met him. "Mr. O'Geary, a message for you. Come this momen by post coach."

He recognized the jeweler's familiar seal. He sped upstairs to read the letter in private.

Dear Thomas,

A terrible thing has happened. Miss Guthre has not delivered Italia's last paintings, nor can I locate her anywhere. The buyers paid in advance. I haven't funds to reimburse them. I fear I will be arrested for theft unless Miss Guthre is found. Come at once.

Martin Canady

Crumpling the letter into his jacket pocket, Thomas fisted his hands. *The blasted woman!* He'd never trusted her. He'd worried about the secret he kept from Mariana earlier when he was talking to her. He'd meant to confess to her, but she told him they were being watched. It didn't seem the moment to break a secret to her. She didn't know her father was the famous painter, Italia. His Lordship had used the exhorbitant fees he received from his paintings to cover his gambling debts and keep his estates operating. He'd bound Thomas to silence.

Thomas knew there were two completed paintings entrusted to Ena Guthre. Paintings His Lordship had instructed the woman to deliver to Martin Canady personally. Had Guthre learned of His Lordship's death, and suspecting he was Italia, kept the pictures for her own use?

By now, Mr. Canady could be arrested and thrown in debtor's prison. If he sped, he may reach London in time to help Mr. Canady. With trembling hand, he dashed off a short reply to Martin, and a brief note to Mariana.

Martin Canady

Sir, have received your disturbing news. Enroute to London at once.
Thomas O'Geary

Dear Lady Mariana,
Word has come from London of an urgent nature. I will contact you as soon as possible. If Inspector Jagger wishes to reach me, he may contact me at Canady's Jewelry and Collectibles, South Strand, London.
Yours most respectfully,
Thomas O'Geary

Throwing a few items of clothing and Mr. Canady's letter into a bag, he pushed Mariana's note under her door, and started downstairs. Furious pounding sounded.

Gannett admitted Chief Constable Jagger into the great hall.

A gust of wind had accompanied the sour-faced police officer. "Mr. O'Geary," Jagger said, looking up, spotting Thomas paused on the landing. "The very person I wish to see."

"What can I do for you, sir?" Thomas said, coming downstairs.

The door opened a second time. Two police officers stepped inside.

"Seize him," Jagger commanded. The men sprang forward, pressing metal cuffs around Thomas's wrists.

"What's the meaning of this?"

"Time to speak later," Jagger replied in an unctuous tone.

With a startled cry, Mariana raced forward. "What's the meaning of this?"

"Step aside, Lady Mariana. Mr. O'Geary is arrested on suspicion of murder."

"Murder!" she gasped.

"Murder of whom?" Thomas demanded, his heart pounding.

"One Ian Cluny. Now move along, sir. To the coach with him," Jagger ordered his men.

"Cluny?" Thomas repeated, stumbling between the two Garda officers.

"It's a misunderstanding," Mariana cried.

Jagger's expression brooked no interference. The men led Thomas down the wide stone steps to the waiting police coach.

Mariana followed, stopping at the coach door as the men pushed Thomas inside. "It'll be resolved quickly," she reassured him.

"The letter," Thomas managed desperately. "You must read the letter. The valise." The coach curtain snapped closed.

Mariana spun to Jagger "Where are you taking him?"

"Spiller's Island Gaol."

"Dublin?"

"Of course, Dublin, Your Ladyship."

Chapter 26

"Sh, love, quiet yourself," whispered Aunt Portia, drawing a warm, herb-soaked cloth across Mariana's brow. "Gannett will send for our solicitor. 'Tis nothing any of us can do for the moment."

Mariana removed the herbed cloth. "I must see Jagger before we send for the barrister."

"You can't, my dear. I won't permit it."

Shadows filtered through the mullioned windows, tracing lacy dark images across the Arabian carpet.

Aunt Portia grasped Mariana's arm. "Dark will set in soon. The road isn't safe after dark."

"You needn't belabor the fact," Mariana admonished, going to the cupboard, pulling down her riding kit. "Send Abbie at once. I have time a-plenty to see Jagger at the headquarters before he leaves for the day. He's notoriously dedicated to his job. Rumors say he may very well sleep at his desk. If he has gone for the day, I know his house."

"But, you mustn't. You shouldn't," Aunt Porta pled. "It's unseemly. Thomas O'Geary is a fine man." Lady Portia frowned. "We'll give it a day or two if you wish, then we'll summon the barrister."

"No," Mariana said firmly.

Letters. Thomas spoke of letters. A valise. What valise? Mariana hurried downstairs. Thomas's packing case lay on the landing. She tore it open and plundered through his things until she found a letter from a Mr. Canady, and one addressed to the same party.

Martin Canady,

Sir, have received your disturbing news. Enroute to London at once.

Upstairs, she found his letter to her.

Dear Lady Mariana,

Word has come from London of an urgent nature. I will contact you as soon as possible. If Inspector Jagger wishes to reach me, he may contact me at Canady's Jewelry and Collectibles, South Strand, London.

Yours most respectfully,

Thomas O'Geary

What did Thomas mean—disturbing news?

The interview with Inspector Jagger did little to help Mariana or Thomas. It appeared a coach had already taken Thomas to the coast. Mariana returned to the house dejected and more troubled than ever.

She sank into the chair beside Aunt Portia. "There's little we can do here to help Thomas," she said. "He's on his way to Dublin. We must travel to Dublin and see the inspector's superior."

"Why Dublin?" questioned her aunt.

"Spillers Island Gaol. He's to be imprisoned there."

"That ghastly place!" she thundered. "I'll write letters to my solicitor at once."

"That'll be helpful," Mariana agreed.

* * *

The next two weeks passed with no news from Thomas, other than a correspondence from Portia's solicitor. It confirmed that Mr. O'Geary had been transported to Spiller's Island.

"We must do what we can," said Aunt Portia.

"We will," Mariana said. "We must."

Two weeks came and went after Thomas's arrest. Lady Portia's solicitor hadn't been helpful. He'd urged them to wait until further word from him. He assured them he was doing his best to aid Thomas.

The Monday of the third week, Mariana summoned Aunt Portia. "We can wait no longer. We must do something now."

"I know, my dear, I've not been idle, Mariana. I've been thinking. I have a special friend, Lady Rosamunde Carlisle, who resides in Dublin."

"What of this friend, this Lady Rosamunde Carlisle?"

"I've written to her. She'll accommodate us while we're in the city. We'll tell Lady Vesta that we're going for a visit. The events here have depressed us; we must seek some gaiety, or go mad."

"What an excellent idea."

Lady Portia smiled. "I thought you'd agree."

* * *

"Are you sure Lady Carlisle will welcome us?" Mariana asked for the third time as the coach bowled through Dublin's streets.

"There's no question of her hospitality," Portia replied. "Rosamunde and I are great friends. We've known one another from birth—a distant family connection. In our girlhood, we attended school together—a terribly exclusive finishing school for young ladies. Oh, dear," Aunt Portia reminisced, "we were regular hoydens in those days. It's a wonder we survived to womanhood. Rosamunde made a brilliant marriage. Both she and her husband, Algernon Carlisle, are charming people." Portia paused a moment, summoning up some obscure bit of information. "Unfortunately, they had no children. Though I recall they had a ward, a nephew of the husband, I think . . . either a nephew or a cousin. I suppose that fortunate young man will inherit handsomely when the time comes. Uh, er, there is a slight problem."

"What sight problem?"

"I haven't heard from Rosamunde. The posts are so very untrustworthy. But, she'll welcome us."

Aunt Portia's friends occupied a house large enough to be a castle, on Wexford-on-the-Quay, a block from King John's Street. The butler, a Mr. Sturbridge, greeted them. He recognized Portia's name, though he seemed uncertain about entertaining the two ladies for a period of time since they were unexpected houseguests. He led them to a front drawing room and disappeared into the depths of the house.

He returned in a more agreeable frame of mind. "Lady Craven, forgive me," he said, bowing to Portia. "I thought it prudent to speak with the housekeeper about an extended stay with the master and mistress away. His Lordship and Her Ladyship are in Spain. I recall your letter arriving. I forwarded it to the master. If you'll come this way, I'll show you to your rooms."

"Thank you," Lady Portia replied archly. Her head high, she followed the debonair servant. Mariana followed, suppressing a giggle.

Sturbridge led them to two large suites overlooking the quaint side street, Wexford-on-the-Quay. With aplomb amd great gravity, Sturbridge bowed. "The maid will send tea up forthwith."

Portia flashed her most brilliant smile. "How very kind."

True to his word, a bountiful repast appeared in short time.

After tea, tiny sandwiches, and cake, Mariana went to the eastern facing window. Spillers Island Gaol lay in the bay some distance from the shore. This day being clear, she had a view of the distant stone building. Its grayness resembled an impenetrable head rock with the currents rushing around it. Mayhap, they'd been foolhardy coming here.

She turned as a knock sounded. The housekeeper came for the tray.

"The housekeeper is a vexing creature," Aunt Portia said after the woman departed. "I fear she's allowed Rosamunde and Algernon's absence to go to her head. Sturbridge is absolutely cowered. She relayed we're welcome to stay as long as we like, but she can't offer a carriage. We're expected to make our way about the city."

"At least we aren't in a common inn," Mariana said, selecting a dress for the evening which she placed across the bed, a gray gown with matching lace mutton sleeves and shawl.

She smiled at Portia. Her aunt was accustomed to having every wish granted at Thornywilde. The carriage brought around at her slightest whim. Visits to the dressmaker, her friends in the village. Here, of necessity, they'd go into the street and take a hansom cab. It wasn't the end of the world, certainly not a disaster sufficient to cause the forlorn expression on Portia's face.

* * *

Dinner was announced. Aunt Portia and Mariana made their way downstairs. Sturbridge led them to the dining room. Candles burned on the sideboard and flickered from an elaborate silver candelabra in the center of the long table. Two places were set on lacy serviettes. "Your Ladyships," Sturbridge said, indicating the two chairs. A tall footman with a severe air brought in the first course of clear soup and fish in a delicate sauce. He then filled their thin goblets with a fragrant white vintage.

Their presence in this luxurious household troubled Mariana, despite her aunt's assurance that all was well. All didn't seem well. The servants, while solicitous, couldn't altogether mask their suspicions. Nor could Mariana blame them.

Baby lamb, beef cutlets smothered in a rich red wine sauce, ringed with fresh asparagus and assorted vegetables were served. Cheese and fruit arrived next. Iced sorbet, to cleanse the palate, concluded the dinner.

It was well past ten o'clock before Mariana and Portia retired to their rooms.

"I fear we're a ways from the livery," Mariana said as she dismissed the ladies maid and helped her aunt ready for bed. "Tomorrow, we'll ask Sturbridge to send a footman to order a carriage for us."

The following morning after a late breakfast, a smooth-faced boy called Rob appeared to escort them down to the waiting carriage. "And, you are a footman," Mariana said to the boy.

"Aye, Your Ladyship. I'm a footman-in-waiting. When the master and 'is wife be out of the country, and the others busy, I do the odd jobs."

Rob, wearing an expression of endearing importance, escorted them to the waiting carriage. He handed the ladies up the step with aplomb, bowed, and then waved heartily as only a youngster can, the freckles on his fair face standing out in the bright morning sun.

Mariana gave the coach driver instructions to take Aunt Portia to another residential house. The people there were distant kin and a message had been sent advising them of Lady Portia's visit, to which they'd received a cordial reply.

Her aunt safely deposited there, Mariana gave further instructions. "To King John's Street."

"Aye, madam."

"And, wait," she said to the coach driver, "I shouldn't be long."

Alighting, her heart in her throat, she walked briskly into the stone building that housed authorities in charge of prison passes. Surprisingly, she met with success, not only success, but success in record time with three prison passes in her pocket.

She called at the distant cousin's house, visited for the shortest time possible and appear civil, collected Aunt Portia, and set out for Algernon and Rosamunde's house.

"You have the passes," Aunt Portia said for the third time, an expression of incredulous wonder on her face. "I can't believe it was that easy."

"It's arranged," Mariana replied. "I've given Sturbridge notice we shan't expect dinner here. The passes are good for this evening only."

"And, a pass for the boy, too?" Aunt Portia said.

"Yes, Rob is amazingly resourceful for one so young. We may need him before we get back."

By late afternoon, Mariana, Aunt Portia, and Rob boarded the coach bound for the ferry to transport them out to the gaol. The ferry lay some great distance from the house. It seemed they'd gone no more than a few miles when the coach rumbled to a stop at an inn called the Shale and Whale. It had grown dark. The driver climbed down from the box and lit the carriage lamps.

Mariana opened the carriage curtains to view the countryside in the day's last light. They were in an isolated area with houses great distances apart. Purple haze ringed the far hills. The sea to the east had taken on an ominous cast as the tide rushed in. Black waves crowned with gray and white foam broke upon the rocks. Seabirds screamed, swooping downward, searching for the last morsel of the day.

The coach lamps successfully lit, the driver ascended the box and they continued. At a crossroads, the coach turned onto a road running parallel to the bay then rumbled to a stop at a crossroad. Looking out the window, Mariana saw a carved Celtic cross of great height. Surely, it was tenth century or perhaps earlier. What peril it represented as prisoners passed it and on to imprisonment. No, she thought. The Celtic cross gave hope to those unfortunate souls passing by it. Hope they'd live to escape the prison. With a lurch in her heart, she realized Thomas had viewed this ancient cross. She prayed it had brought him comfort.

Aunt Portia reached for her hand. "Don't worry, love. We'll see Thomas freed."

"I pray so," Mariana murmured. The coach rumbled on.

They'd worn heavy veils, which seemed suitable, since both wished to conceal their station as much as possible. Rob looked a regular sight. Aunt Portia insisted he wear a beaver hat and high collar to make him appear older. In Mariana's opinion, it made him look more like an ill-dressed gnome. Nevertheless, he carried a round stick beneath his great coat. Hardly fitting for protecting two ladies on their way to Ireland's most notorious prison, but uplifting to Rob's ego.

"Gaol off to your left," the coach driver called.

Flickering lights beamed across the span of black water. The stone fortress, some distance from shore, loomed misty and sprawling. In the meager moonlight, it was difficult to form a true picture of the structure. More difficult, imagining Thomas imprisoned there.

The road narrowed, its bumpy bed interspersed with deep pockets of sand, making the way treacherous for the horses. They reached the dock house where the ferry, tightly moored, bobbed in the foamy surf. No light emerged from the weathered structure.

The coach moved on and stopped before a small house of rough planking. Weak scrims of light threaded through its shuttered windows.

The coachman stepped down and opened the carriage door. Gesturing toward the ferry house they'd passed, he said. "They've shut 'er down. Ferry won't run 'til mornin'."

Aunt Portia poked her head forward. "Where's the oarsman?" she demanded militantly. "There should be an oarsman to take us out despite the hour."

Shrugging his neck into his collar against the wind, the driver pointed to a smaller hovel a-ways down from the ferry house. "If iny's to take ye, 'e'll be there."

"Drive on," Mariana ordered. Their passes were for this evening only. Though, she'd had an easy enough case of procuring the passes, she'd been aware of suspicious glances as the official viewed their letters of identity.

"Aye, madam." The coach rumbled forward, stopping before a crude abode of stone and thatch that more resembled a rookery than a house.

Opening her purse, Mariana handed coins to Rob. "Go inside, lad. Make arrangements. Don't give all the money in your hand. Not at first. Only if the man refuses or stalls."

"Aye, Your Ladyship," Rob scuttled out with an arch frown at the driver.

The boy returned, accompanied by a burly man in the process of pulling on a gray knit cap.

"Three passengers," the oarsman said.

"Aye, three," Rob answered importantly.

Mariana pressed extra coins into the coach driver's hand. "Two hours. I'll expect you back here then." She spoke sternly.

He scanned the overage in his palm. "Aye, madam . . . er . . . Your Ladyship. As you wish, Your Ladyship." He bowed.

They disembarked, aided by the coach driver. The oarsman stood aside, waiting.

Sand seeping into her boots between the laces, Mariana followed the oarsman down to his boat—a seaworthy craft outfitted with four oars. Aunt Portia trailed with Rob holding the older woman's hand. The oarsman saw them settled into the boat. He gave an impatient snort as Rob sprang aboard at the last. The oarsman nodded to Rob. "Pull your weight, young laddie. We'll do the work of four men."

With Rob's help, they gained quick access to the gaol. The oarsman disembarked first, securing the boat. "I'll wait for ye." He settled against the hull and took out a pipe.

They started forward toward the prison. A dim post lantern glowed over the prison entrance. They made their way there. A baby cried in the distance. Closer now, the scent of boiling cabbage carried on the wind.

Mariana rang the large bell at doorside. A man opened the door at once. A jailer, she assumed. He motioned them inside a high-arched, hallway with dim wall lights where he perused their passes. "Uumph," he muttered, then bade them follow to an anteroom where an inspector promptly removed Rob's stick.

"Wait here," the jailer said.

He returned with a short man, obviously a man of authority. "Jimson, Your Ladyship, under-warden at Spiller's Island," announced this person.

He perused their papers, then looked up. "These seem to be in order but our rules is only one visitor allowed in the halls at a time. The prisoner's sister may go in." He nodded at Mariana. "Send for the gaoler to escort the lady."

An older man, with a limp and an untidy mustache, came shortly. He bowed to Mariana. "Your Ladyship, if ye'll follow."

Her leather boots clicking on the stone floor, Mariana followed the man down the warren of halls. Spillers Island wasn't a pleasant place. The clinging scent of disinfectant did little to mask the odor of foul clothing, unwashed bodies, and the ever present scent of scorched cabbage. If the under-warden had seen fit to search her person as he had Rob, she would be behind these bars. She'd tucked flint and a small wad of wicking into her skirt hem. She also carried a packet of sandwiches inside her cloak.

The gaoler stopped before a darkened cell. The cot in the back of the cell held a dark form. "Mr. O'Geary, you 'ave a visitor."

Would Thomas think her insane coming here? A man emerged to the front of the neighboring cell. He stood at the bars, peering at her. She saw a bedraggled family inside this cell, the fellow of middle years, side-whiskers askew; a woman, his wife; a spindly boy about nine or ten and a soft-haired girl of tender years. The woman moved to a small table and distributed bread.

"O'Geary," the gaoler called again, striking his nightstick along the bars. "Ye've a visitor." The lump on the cot moved. Thomas hobbled up. He wore heavy leg irons. His wrist irons were affixed to heavy cuffs that bound his hands together in front of his body. He made a most uncomfortable picture.

"One 'alf hour, Your Ladyship," the gaoler announced. "Of which ten minutes has passed."

As he unlocked Thomas's cell, a second gaoler joined him. This man had cadaverous features and a receding hairline. What hair he had was coal black and slicked down to his ears from a middle part. He didn't appear an ominous fellow, though, despite his unusual features.

"Stand back a moment, Your Ladyship," the cadaverous man said, relieving the first jailer and pushing open the cell door. He went in alone. Leading Thomas to a table in the center of the cell, he chained the prisoner's legs to a metal stake driven into the stone floor. Enough room was allowed for Thomas to sit in a sturdy chair. The gaoler gave Mariana an oily smile as he emerged from the cell. "Your life is on your own 'ead should the prisoner resort to violence."

Thomas recognized her. An expression of explicit horror passed across his face. His stricken gaze followed her as the gaoler led her into the cell.

"Dearest brother," she said, taking the one chair across from Thomas.

The gaoler took up a position outside the cell door.

"What are you doing here?" Thomas whispered once they were reasonably alone.

She reached out, placing her hand atop his.

"There'll be nay physical contact, Your Ladyship," the officer ordered from his stance at the door.

With a swift glance at the man, she said. "I apologize, sir. Viewing my brother in this place distresses me sorely. God, help us," she said turning to Thomas. "Are you all right?"

"You managed to see me? How?"

She replied almost under her breath. "Aunt Portia knows people." Then, for the guard's ears. "Dear Aunt has accompanied me. She and your nephew wait in the under-warden's office."

The guard seemed preoccupied with jotting something in a small notebook. The man's attention diverted, Mariana drew the packet from her petticoat. "Flint. And, sandwiches."

"You shouldn't . . ." He'd barely secreted the items in his breeches before the guard rapped the bars. "I'll be escorting ye back, Your Ladyship. The 'alf hour is up."

She grasped Thomas's manacled hand. "Be brave, dear brother. The fight isn't over."

"God bless you, dear sister," Thomas said, bowing his head.

Lifting her chin, Mariana addressed the guard. "My brother is no murderer. His crime is being a famous painter sought by royalty and the English King. While we wait for his exoneration and release, our family will remember every kindness to him." As she spoke, she slipped a heavy purse of coins into the guard's hand.

His eyes lit. She'd judged him correctly. "Your Ladyship, I'll personally see to yere brother's safety. The best that come 'ere are nay more than common knaves. An artist, you say. . ."

She turned to Thomas as the guard unchained him from the table and led him back to the bunk. "You may contact your barrister on King John's Street." It was the best she could do to let him know where she was staying.

He gave her a puzzled look.

Chapter 27

homas listened to the muffled sounds of footfalls receding into the distance as Mariana walked away. Sound seemed to carry forever along the astute halls. Especially, now that night had fallen, those weary citizens suffering incarceration would settle for another period of troubled sleep. He tried easing the burning tension on his wrists by sliding the metal cuffs to different positons. Didn't help. Most prisoners weren't shackled while inside their cell. His atrocious murder required the most stringent restraint.

A short time later, the cadaverous guard returned. He lounged against the cell door, stroking his mustache. "So, ye're a painter o' the gentry, eh?"

Thomas, sitting up, rubbed his wrists where the chains chaffed. "Portraits are my specialty," he replied.

"Ye can paint a face, can ye?" the fellow asked as if coming alive.

"I most assuredly can. I say that without boasting."

"Ye could paint me?" Though the guard kept his voice low, excitement threaded the question.

"I haven't paints here but I could do a decent sketch if I had charcoal."

"Me sweetheart would fancy a picture," said the man, leaning against the cell door, so close his prominent nose poked through the bars. Sifting his mustache between thumb and forefinger, he stared at Thomas. "Ye wouldn't take liberties if I brought ye out a wee while. Long enough for a quick drawing. Ye work fast, as well, I pray. I saw an artist once in London's Hyde Park. 'E did the most marvelous pictures in nothing flat."

"Charcoal is a speedy medium," Thomas assured the guard.

"It's irregular, me takin' a man up for murder outta 'is cell."

Feigning a yawn, Thomas sensed the man's resolve weakening.

"It wouldna do to draw in 'ere, would it?" the guard asked, gesturing around the cell.

"Hardly," Thomas drawled, yawning. "Not enough light."

"Aye. I thought as much," the gaoler said. He turned to leave, frowning heavily.

As Thomas leaned back on the pallet, he watched the guard through half-closed eyes. He sensed the man fancied a free portrait in the worst way. "I'm not enticing you to do anything against regulations. It was my sister mentioned I'm an artist. I am. If you want a sketch, it's my pleasure to favor you. I admit drawing would break the tedium in here." Thomas turned his face to the cell wall.

"Aye. If I shoulda decide, I'll be back," said the gaoler.

A solid stone wall separated Thomas's cell from the adjoining one. However, he and Mr. Bunch, housed next door, spoke often as they stood at the front of their cells, and the guards were busy elsewhere. He could count on Mr. Bunch taking avid interest in the evening's occurrences. Thomas shuffled up from his bunk and made his way to the front of the cell.

He wasn't disappointed. Mr. Bunch rapped something metal softly across the bars, announcing his presence. "'E'll be back, that one, 'e's vain as a peacock."

Thomas chuckled, low in his throat. "If he were to let me out, I believe I could overpower him."

"Aye, if ye're wise, ye'll run the first chance ye git. There's nay justice 'ere. The wife, I, and the wee ones 'ave been 'ere goin' on six months. Nobody on the outside will raise the fee for our debts. Paltry sum, too. The Bunches' are a lost lot. A ship of lost souls. So," Mr. Bunch continued in a lighter tone. "Was the lady your wife or sweetheart?"

"Neither," Thomas replied. "A very dear friend."

"Aye. I knew she weren't your sister. You're fortunate. Friends forget you in this place."

Mariana hadn't forgotten him and he loved her more for it. Despite the veil shadowing her lovely face, he'd viewed her pain over his predicament. "You are right, my friend," Thomas whispered. "I am a fortunate man."

What irony, Thomas thought. Locked away in Spillers Island Gaol with murder hanging over his head, and likely a noose after his trial, if Jagger had his way. And he counted himself lucky.

Mr. Bunch continued. "That guard will return to have 'is picture drawn. 'E's not only a vain sort, but stupid to boot. What I'd do if I wasn't fettered with the wife and little ones, I'll tell ye, if ye're interested."

Thomas pressed nearer the corner of the cell. "What do you propose?"

"'E's waitin' til 'is superior goes below. 'Is superior sits at a table where the hall ells. When this man is finished with 'is reports, he leaves for pleasanter quarters. Behind the table is the guard's water closet and storeroom. They store their pitch flares there. Pitch on long staves, they are."

Thomas thought of the fire material secreted in his pockets. How novel of Mariana bringing such to him. But, then, he'd found her a most unusual young lady. Foolish to think he'd set fire to the gaol. If he did, innocent people could die, and probably, himself, as well. "I can't risk setting fire. Too dangerous for others."

"Ye don't understand," Mr. Bunch went on in his raspy whisper. "Me and the missus have a coal brazier in our cell. Before we retire, I make weak tea for my missus and toast a morsel 'o bread for the children. While ye're in the hall drawing the oaf's picture, I'll 'ave an accident. Catch the straw afire. The guards will come runnin'. In the confusion, ye run into the water closet, bolt the door on the inside. Break the window glass with the staves a'holdin' the flares. The sea is deep on the ocean side of the gaol. If you swim strong, keep north a mile or more, ye'll come to a low beach and a bog beyond. Ye'll be not far from KinKerry."

"Thank you, my friend," Thomas whispered. Slipping to his pallet, his heart beating furiously, he considered the risky plan. What other choice had he?

Perhaps an hour later, the soft rattle of keys sounded. The vain gaoler *had* returned. "The way's clear," the man whispered. "I've the charcoal and paper ye need." The guard unlocked the cell door and approached Thomas's bunk.

"Unlock my feet. I can scarce walk in these irons and if I do, I'll wake the dead."

"Ye must remain chained," the man insisted.

"Methinks," Thomas said, raising his head. "The noise of me dragging chains will likely wake the under-warden below or the dead. We cannot risk that. If someone hears me out of the cell, they'll come to investigate. It'll not go well for you. I'll not be able to draw your likeness." After a moment's silence while the guard considered Thomas's words, Thomas said, "I admit you have a most interesting face."

The guard stared, perplexed, dull wit evident in the man. Finally, he asked, "Ye vow as an artist to the gentry, ye'll not try to run."

"My word is my bond."

The gaoler bent, unfettering Thomas's feet. Thomas followed him out of the cell.

Mr. Bunch, in the adjoining cell, stood over his brazier fanning a weak charcoal fire to life. "Evenin' guv'ner," he called, smiling at the guard.

"See ye have no accidents with that stove," snapped the guard. To Thomas, the guard said loud enough for Mr. Bunch to hear, "These debtors swarm our 'alls like vermin. I daresay few in Dublin 'ave paid a bill in their lifetime."

At the end of the hall stood the table Mr. Bunch spoke of. An oil lantern burned on the table. Chunks of charcoal and white paper waited there. The water closet door stood about three feet behind the desk.

"What light makes for the best picture," the guard asked, taking the lantern, jockeying it about in various positions, bringing Thomas's thoughts to the portrait and not his possible escape.

"That'll never do," Thomas mused, settling down on the chair behind the desk. "The light must be higher. Mayhap that shelf above you. Shadows from the lantern glow will cast striking emphasis on your features. Your face will be somewhat silhouetted giving you a touch of mystery."

The guard grinned. He was missing several front teeth. "Aye. Tricks of the trade, eh? Ye are a gentleman's painter," he said, lifting the lantern to the overhead shelf. Thomas pretended to study the lantern glow. He saw no locks fastening the water closet's heavy brass latch.

"Ye 'aven't all night," warned the gaoler. "Begin at once."

"Perhaps this isn't a good idea after all," Thomas said. "I cannot ask you to bend more rules. But, I haven't the dexterity I need in my wrists with chained hands. It's impossible to do you justice. You may as well take me back to my cell."

"Aye. That's all ye're waitin' for? Why didn't ye say so?" The gaoler fished a key from the chain about his waist, and unlocked Thomas's cuffs. "Ye're not to tell the warden about this, ye understand?"

Thomas nodded, seizing the charcoal, sketching rapidly.

Noises sounded from Mr. Bunch's cell. "Blast it, love!" Mr. Bunch bellowed. "Fire. *FIRE!*" he screamed. Thick white smoke billowed from the burning straw. "Me wife, me bairns, they'll perish!"

The gaoler sprang to the opposite wall, sounded a warning bell. Taking a pail of water that Thomas hadn't noticed from the floor beside the table, the man ran to assist the Bunches.

Seizing the split second of opportunity, Thomas hurled himself into the water closet, bolted the door on the inside. He grabbed a heavy pole affixed with a flare, beating the glass window. It refused to break.

Pounding footsteps drummed outside the door as more guards rushed to put out the fire. With a final thrust of the pole, the window splintered. Quickly, Thomas pushed out the remaining glass leaving an opening large enough for him to bail through.

God help him if Bunch hadn't been right about the deep ocean surrounding this east side of the gaol. Without looking back, he leaped outward into total darkness.

Chapter 28

"*I* cannot believe Thomas drowned," Mariana whispered to her aunt as they sat in Rosamunde's dining room over morning tea. Sturbridge had served, brought breakfast, and withdrawn. Mariana kept her voice low lest the butler overhear their conversation. He'd become increasingly suspicious. Indeed, he had barely answered when Aunt Portia inquired if a letter had arrived from either Rosamude or Algernon.

"I fear we must leave," Aunt Portia replied, under her breath. "Even the housekeeper seems suspicious."

"I know," Mariana said, a tremor in her voice. She rose, went to the window, and looked out. She'd mentioned King John's Street to Thomas in an obscure way. And, in return, she'd noted his fleeting quizzical glance. If Thomas hadn't drowned, they must remain in Dublin until he had a chance to contact them. He was now a fugitive running for his life, with every Dublin policeman looking for him.

Earlier this very morning, she'd observed Sturbridge listening at the door when she was talking to her aunt. The past few mornings, she'd hired a coach and ridden for hours throughout the city on the odd chance she might recognize Thomas on the street.

She turned to her aunt, indecision plaguing her. "Meet me in the garden. We can speak freely there."

In the front hall, Mariana pulled her cape about her shoulders. Rob sprang up from a bench in the receiving room off the hall.

Startled, she gasped. "You frightened the life from me. Why are you lurking there?" She motioned to the receiving room door.

The lad blushed. "I didna mean to scare ye m'lady. I was waiting for ye, "ere's a bag o' crumbs. 'Er ladyship asked me to bring 'em to feed the pidgeons."

Aunt Portia had taken a fancy to the pigeons. "Very well." She took the greasy bag of crumbs and walked to the garden where Aunt Portia was sitting near a concrete balustrade.

"Good," her aunt said, eyeing the bag. "Rob didn't forget the crumbs." Portia removed the glove from her right hand and began spreading the crumbs to the clutch of pigeons crowding her feet. Their stout bodies on short legs waddling about amused Mariana. "They're really beautiful," she said, admiring their colorful plumage.

"There're of the dove family," her aunt said. "These are quite tame, though some live in a feral state."

The novelty of admiring the birds worn off, Mariana said to her aunt. "You're a swift one. I expected to see you in the hall."

"I came out the back way." Portia tossed more crumbs to the foraging pigeons. After casting a guarded glance back at the house, Aunt Portia removed a letter from the folds of her shawl. "I hadn't time to give this to you with Sturbridge and the housekeeper so close. It came by special courier early this morning from the magistrate who issued our prison passes. He's much disturbed about Thomas's escape. He wishes to see you immediately. Before you were up, I sent word by Rob that you were fevered and couldn't be disturbed."

"I daresay Rob was surprised by my remarkable recovery when I saw him in the hall just now," Mariana said dryly.

"So be it," Aunt Portia said dismissively. She continued. "I also sent a substantial purse. That should silence the magistrate for a time. I understand he's not an ethical man." She passed the letter to Mariana.

Mariana scanned the document. It was as her aunt reported.

Aunt Portia continued. "We must leave at once for Thornywilde. This house is being watched. The police were here earlier. They asked to see you. I told them the same story, and begged them to leave because of your delicate health. At this moment, two of the forces stand across the square. Don't look in their direction." Aunt Portia shuddered. "They must suspect we're someway responsible for Thomas's escape."

"How? That's impossible. We merely lied that Thomas was our kinsman."

"My dear, Thomas's escape has started a manhunt like no other in this century. Carriage drivers are an easy mark for bribes. A coach driver could easily confirm to the police that a lady from this house visited the magistrate's office. The police may think Thomas will come here to make contact with us. Even if my suspicions are only that . . . suspicions, we can't risk such an encounter."

"But. . ."

Putting up her hand to silence Mariana, Aunt Portia continued. "I haven't had a chance to talk to you with these curious servants about, but I've instructed the lady's maid to pack our things. Rob stands ready to secure a coach for the country."

"I can't leave. Not until I know Thomas's fate."

"Don't be foolish. We must go home at once. He jumped into the sea, Mariana. He'll be miles and miles from Dublin now—washed up shore to the north, or to the south. Or..."

Aunt Portia didn't say it, *or, he's drowned.*

"I can't leave. For a time, at least. I'll go to the registry and get a woman to travel with you, aunt. You can go on to Thornywilde."

Aunt Portia bristled. "Do you think I'm an invalid? I've traveled the length and breadth of Ireland, England and Wales, even France, without a lady's maid. Our world isn't a wilderness, you know."

"Maybe not a lady's maid, but you had assistants."

Aunt Portia sniffed. "What of you? I can't leave you here."

Mariana lowered her head and rubbed her temples as if contending with pain—all for the benefit of the watching policemen she spied across the square. "I can better serve Thomas here in Dublin."

Aunt Portia shook her head vehemently. "You'll do no such thing. Staying here is too risky. It isn't to be done, Mariana."

Mariana pressed the older woman's hands between her own. "I know the risk. What if Thomas is found? We cannot allow an innocent man to hang. You and I both know he didn't kill Ian Cluny. I've thought about what Thomas might do and I've decided he may risk contacting us here in Dublin."

"You don't know that."

"No, not as an absolute fact. However, I think it likely."

With a deep sigh, Portia nodded.

As they sat in the garden, a police coach drew up across the thoroughfare, stopping where the two officers stood. A third policeman emerged from the coach and the three stood talking, often glancing over at the Carlisle mansion. Mariana knew she and Aunt Portia must act quickly. Thank God the Carlisles remained out of the country and not embroiled in this mess.

Portia saw the police coach, too.

"No time to dawdle," Mariana said. "Before you leave, pack a change of men's clothing for me, a high collar, a voluminous coat, and discreet breeches. Leave the things in my room. I can dress as a highwayman if I must. Rob will help you."

"A highwayman!" Aunt Portia shrieked. "Have you taken leave of your senses?"

"Sssh. Would you have your voice carry across to the police? I haven't time to explain now. I assure you I know what I'm doing." If only she truly believed her own words, for the germ of an idea had this moment popped into her head. "Now, do as I bid. Gather the things I need."

"I'm not helpless, Mariana," Aunt Portia snapped, with a shrewish look. She glanced across the square. "No. I won't allow this. It's too dangerous. You must come with me to Thornywilde."

Mariana, seeing quick movement, beckoned to Rob, who'd entered the garden. He stopped, bowed, his wide mouth in a grin, his red curls bouncing. "Your Ladyships."

Mariana, fond of the boy, especially his forthright nature, beckoned him closer. "Have Sturbridge summon a coach for my aunt within the quarter-hour. It's desperately important."

"Yes, Lady Mariana."

"First, though, go to the registry and secure a gentlewoman to travel with my aunt."

Rob bowed again and scrambled up the incline to the house in record time.

Some hours later, Aunt Portia and a traveling companion departed for the country, leaving the Carlisle house even more dismal for Mariana without her aunt's presence. No time for reflections, she must act quickly. Mariana sought the housekeeper. The woman, a Russian, frowned deeply.

"I should like to borrow Rob for a time from his duties."

The housekeeper's eyes narrowed. "You may as well, Your Ladyship. He's the laziest cellar boy we've had here."

"I may need him for a day or two."

The woman shrugged one shoulder. "Yes."

The haughty housekeeper summoned Rob, said a few words sharply in Russian that the boy evidently understood, and turned leaving Mariana in the hall with the lad. "You're to dress in your Sunday best," she said, noting the adventurous gleam in his green eyes.

A short time later, Rob rejoined her, well turned out in tan linen breeches, a short, gray woolen jacket with large brass buttons and a white hat with a round brim. The hat was too small and gave the appearance of floating above his auburn curls.

Chapter 29

*R*ob in tow, Mariana hailed a hansom to the magistrate's office. The office where she'd gotten the prison passes. "Wait here," she instructed the boy, leaving him outside the building. Inside, Mariana asked for the gentleman in question.

"I'm afraid he's unavailable, miss," an assistant said. An assistant who sought to impress her with a beguiling smile. "He left a short time ago for a fortnight's trip. If you like, you may leave a message. He does send a courier for his mail."

"How unfortunate," Mariana said, thinking fast. Odd, that the magistrate had summoned her, then left town for an extended length of time—no doubt with Aunt Portia's generous purse. "I shan't leave a message. The matter can wait until he returns. Good day to you." She turned on her heel.

Outside, she took a careful look at the building and its several entrances. A small neat courtyard to the west of the front entrance had a large door where several young men, obviously clerks, stood enjoying the sun, and smoking. That courtyard and door proved interesting. Not easily viewed from the street.

"Rob," she said. "Fetch a cab."

Once boarded, she sank back against the seat wondering if she'd lost her mind for the desperate thoughts troubling her. She must help Thomas. If only she knew he were alive. Had he started a fire in the prison with the flint and wadding she'd smuggled inside? God forbid. Why had she brought the flint? She'd heard prisoners were allowed to cook simple meals. Not in Thomas's case, she thought ruefully. He'd been bound like a dangerous wild beast.

"Where are we goin', m'lady?"

"What? Oh." She'd forgotten about Rob, until he spoke. He looked over at her, a frown line between his eyes.

"My father's townhouse. Dismiss the coach and wait in the garden."

They reached the familiar square. The solid mansion appeared little changed from the day she'd arrived, eager to study languages. How naïve she'd been, thinking her life lay before her like a familiar path. A school girl's dream now. Study, then after receiving her mother's inheritance, opening a girls' school. Dreams, all dreams—wishful fantasies.

With trepidation in each step, she made her way up the walk and onto the steps where she'd first seen Thomas.

The garden appeared tidied and more inviting than when she'd first viewed it. However, the pair of life-size, stone lions still stood forebodingly. She knocked. At the first rap, a maid answered the door. After a quick glance at Mariana's stylish blue silk, the maid ushered her inside the familiar vestibule.

"Whom do ye seek, miss?" The girl was polite, but frankly curious.

"I'm Lady Mariana Belmont, His Lordship, Charles Belmont's daughter. He is the owner of this townhouse. I understand it's let. Who's in residence?"

The girl bobbed a curtsey. "The tenants, Your Ladyship?" Blinking rapidly before answering, she finally said. "Mr. and Miss Durrett, brother and sister. Neither is 'ome. Mr. Durrett is in trade and can be found at the grain exchange. Miss Durrett is with her family in the country." The maid peered at Mariana from under her pleated cap.

"That's unfortunate," Mariana said, producing a calling card from her reticule, handing it to the girl. "There are papers here in the house belonging to my father. I must secure them. We closed the house rather quickly due to my father's . . . illness."

"But, miss, uh . . . Lady Belmont, I 'in't allowed to give ye leave to go through the Durrett's rooms."

"No need to disturb their quarters. My father's private papers are stored on the third floor in his studio. He had that section sealed. Besides, I take full responsibility."

Mariana walked past the maid and up the stairs. The maid didn't follow. At the former artist studio, a small, heavy commode blocked the door. With some effort, Mariana pushed it aside. Surprisingly, the door wasn't locked. However, the noticable coating of dust in the entryway suggested no one had visited it.

Inside, the studio remained as she remembered it—worktables cluttered with Thomas's paints and brushes.

The model's costumes still hung behind the screen. All seemed as they'd left it.

Closing the door, she made her way to her father's private office, a large airy room behind the studio. White canvas dust covers shrouded his desk and tables. She opened the windows and began removing dust covers.

A quick search of the desk yielded nothing of importance—a few ledgers pertaining to Thornywilde's piggeries and a list of the farmland tenants with their crop yields in years past. There was no record of Ian Cluny other than a birth record. His exile to Australia nor his return to Ireland had been noted.

She had no idea what she sought. However, dark mysteries shrouded her father's activities and Thornywilde.

There must be something here, she thought desperately. The maid may grow edgy and demand she leave. Wooden file cabinets lined the far wall. She opened the top drawer of the first cabinet, her fingers sweeping methodically through miscellaneous trade bills, most dating years before.

On the brink of giving up the search for anything of importance, she spied a square box of Chinese design in the last cabinet's bottom drawer.

The Chinese box was tucked behind an open box of seashells. Nostalgia washed over her. Her father had loved the sea—painted it magnificently when he was a young man. Had he kept the beautiful shells to remember happier times? Pushing the box of shells aside, she lifted the Chinese box from the drawer.

It was fashioned of black lacquer, inlaid with red and gold dragons. She pried at it, and discovered an easy spring that opened the lid when she pressed the dragon's left green eye.

A packet lay inside—a sheaf of ledger sheets, bound in brown velvet ribbon, dating back some twenty years to the present. The sheets listed sums of money disbursed to E.G. over the years. Could that be the woman, Ena Guthre, the infamous distant cousin who'd accompanied Mariana's mother, Lady Catherine, to Thornywilde after Catherine's marriage? Aunt Portia had told her about this woman.

After each payment, her father had jotted a brief description of the transaction. The notations were confusing. Barely able to decipher her father's handwriting, she read. E.G., *surly and demanding. Warned her. E.G. ill-needs funds. Sent. E.G. delivered damaged parcel to T.O.*

On and on, the curious listings and notations continued. Her hands trembling, she folded the notes, pressing them into her reticule.

Why had her father continued to pay this woman these many years? Was the woman her mother, and not Lady Catherine?

After a quick search of the other tables and cupboards, Mariana found nothing of interest. She hurried out, closing the door, and pushed the commode against it as she'd found it.

The maid met her at the foot of the stairs, a crease of worry across her plain face. "Shall I tell the master that Lady Mariana Belmont has called?"

"By all means," Mariana returned crisply. "You may also relay that I visited my father's office and retrieved some personal correspondence. We will see to closing the studio at our earliest convenience."

Upon Mariana's return to King John's Street, the Carlisle mansion appeared more unwelcoming than ever, though the policemen across the square were no longer on survelliance. "Wait with the carriage," she bade Rob, who nodded enthusiastically.

Sturbridge met her at the door. Upstairs, she found the tapestry bag of gentleman's clothing her aunt had packed. With a grim smile, Mariana wondered what servant's wardrobe now lacked a few items.

The butler met her in the hall, glancing at her valise. "Lady Mariana, shall I see about a coach?"

"I've secured one. You may inform the housekeeper I'll send Rob back as soon as possible. It may be a day or so."

"Yes, m'lady."

"Where are we off to, m'lady?" Rob asked when she joined him in the coach.

"Never you worry. Just do as I say."

He nodded.

Mariana said to the driver, "The coachhouse, if you will."

"Aye, madam."

The coach rumbled across town, with Mariana wondering about Thomas. Had he survived? Where would he go? Where *could* he go? It was much too risky to send inquiries to the gaol. The magistrate who'd issued the prison passes would return to the city in a fortnight. *I mustn't be here then.*

They arrived at the coach house in record time, a whitewashed, stone building with a black door that stood at the end of a narrow street. It was surrounded on the far side by a small paddock where a number of horses grazed.

Leaving Rob in charge of her baggage, Mariana entered the coach house. She had no idea why she'd come to the coachhouse, except she must do something or go mad. A number of travelers stood at the high counter waiting their turn with the clerk. She settled on a round horsehair settee, her brain awhirl. London? Perhaps. Had Thomas made his way there? The letter from Mr. Canady summoned him to London.

The line at the counter hadn't dispersed. She could hire a coach to the Dublin docks, and take the ferry to Holyhead, and on by coach to London. Not a good idea. It would be approximately six days, traveling day and night before reaching London. A formidable trip, at best.

A foolish thought. Thomas had broken a window, plunged into the sea with nothing on his person and no money. He couldn't pay for passage.

The name Martin Canady occurred often in her father's ledger sheets, the ones now in her valise. With luck, Thomas may have contacted Mr. Canady to send money. If she went to London, perhaps Mr. Canady could give her some idea of where Thomas might have gone. She sighed. Canady, himself, may very well be in prison if unable to refund the people who'd purchased Italia's paintings.

Chapter 30

Dublin

*T*he sea churned unmercifully, rough and cold as ice. Thomas lay in a sheltered crevice between two massive stones. Noisy screeching gulls and terns swooped and fished, mostly near shore. Irksome as they were, he welcomed the company. They were living creatures. His arms ached and his legs had gone numb. He'd lain all night in wet clothing. Thankfully, his linen shirt had dried, but his breeks clung to his legs, clammy and damp.

Now what, he wondered? After plunging from the gaol window, he'd swum past the first headland that jutted out into the Irish Sea. Fearing the prison would send boats looking for him, he'd made for shore among the jagged rocks. He feared risking swimming north to the shore near KinKerry that Mr. Bunch had told him about.

His stomach rumbled. No need to entertain thoughts of hunger. He lay back against a flat stone and thanked God for a warm day—warmest this February. The stone reminded him of a grave slab, and very well may be, if the authorities found him. He laughed, ruefully admiring the colorful early spring flowers cropping up amongst the rocks. God's handiwork. No gardener could grow prettier posies and in such an unlikely place.

Boats from the prison had passed earlier. Thus far, no land search among the rocks. He couldn't count on that for long. At dark, he'd leave. What had Mariana meant, *your barrister on King John's Street?* Perhaps she'd taken rooms there. A puzzle.

A horn sounded across the water. A faint cry sounded closer. More police boats. "Allo, allo, ye bloody murderer, may your killin' body bloat in the deep, and your clean-picked bones bleach in 'ell."

Thomas flipped onto his stomach, crouching lower. The police boat came near to shore, then continued southward.

He closed his eyes. A sixth sense had him on his feet in seconds as a shadow moved between him and the sun. He seized a woman's bare foot as she stooped over him. Screaming, she dropped her basket scattering seashells and spilling flowers. Her kerchief slipped over her face and her gnarled hands clutched at her apron. He pushed her over and lay crushing her frail body against the flat stone. Once he knew the police boat was out of earshot, he released his hold on the woman. She seemed very old, her skin slack on her bony arms as pushed back the kerchief from her face. She gaped, her toothless mouth wide open. "As the saints preserve me, Thomas O'Geary."

"Old Madge?"

He lay back against the rocks and laughed until his sides ached. "Of all people in God's green world—it's you. What in heaven's name are you doing in Dublin?" For a moment, he forgot his predicament and helped his elderly friend to her feet. She brushed off her skirt, and chose a smooth rock and sat down. He began gathering her spilled shells.

"Leave them be," she said without irritation. "The rarest are marred." She seemed as awed by his presence as he with hers.

"So, Madge," he began. "What brings you south to Dublin?"

Her wrinkled face crinkled more and her pale-blue, Celtic eyes took on a misty, faraway look. "'E came. That one from Thornywilde. The one with white hair and black eyes. 'E and his mam come once before 'Is Lordship took sick and died. They bought mushrooms. This time, I'd come from gathering me 'shrooms. I saw 'im with the white hair. I hid among the crags and watched for I feared 'im. The spirit of evil rests on 'im." Old Madge brushed tears from her eyes. "'E burned me cottage. All is lost. 'tis ash and charred stone. A-feared 'e'd kill me, I stayed hid 'til nightfall and then caught one of me ponies. Gentle beast, she thought I 'ad food for her." The old woman threw her head back and closed her eyes. She shuddered as memories overwhelmed her. "I come 'ere to me widow sister to sell shells and flowers on the street."

"Sir John Desmond!" The man's name left a bitter taste in Thomas's mouth.

Old Madge began rocking back and forth, her arms clutched around her body. ". . . It's as if 'ell's demons reared up on the earth. 'Er, from long ago who hated Lady Catherine. She was there. Watching from the hills.

She's evil, that one, her 'eart's as black as doom," she whispered, her gaze myopic in recalled horror.

"Ena Guthre?" Thomas questioned. "She was with Sir John?"

The old woman slowly opened her eyes and squinted against the sun. "She come first. Then, 'e come."

Thomas frowned, his brain a maelstrom. Why would Ena return to face His Lordship's wrath since she'd not delivered the paintings? She must know Sir Charles was dead, or she'd be running from him. "How did she travel?" he asked Old Madge. "On foot?"

Madge shook her head. "She rode a horse. A sorrel. She 'ad a wee boy with 'er."

Thomas's heart softened at the kindly soul with her worn basket and tattered skirts. The old woman had experienced much the same loss as he now suffered—the end of her world as she knew it. "You could go to prison for speaking to me," he warned her. "I'm escaped from Spiller's Island. The police are searching for me."

"Aye. I heard about ye on the street. They say ye died in the sea. I seen policemen lined up the beach for miles before KinKerry."

He'd made the right decision after all. If he'd taken Mr. Bunch's advice and swum north, he'd be locked deeper in Spiller's Gaol.

Shaking her head and stroking her basket, Madge blurted, "The Cluny lad's a wicked lad. 'Is dues is paid in 'ell now. Due, they was, and overdue."

"Madge, I didn't kill the man."

"I know ye didn't. It 'in't in ye."

Standing and lifting her empty basket onto her hip, Old Madge lowered her voice. "I'll fetch clothes for ye." She motioned toward the restless, gray-green sea. "'Tis too dangerous to stay here by the water. Go to that copse where the rocks cut through. Stay there 'til I bring food and clothes."

She returned late in the afternoon as the sun dipped low over Dublin Mountains. "Women's clothes," he said, laughing, as she untied the bundle and dropped the clothing at his feet.

* * *

Mariana ordered a cup of stout tea from the stall by the door. Instead of taking her place at the the coach ticket counter, she sat, sipping the fragrant beverage as one daring decision after another flitted through her fevered brain. She reviewed the nebulous thought that had occurred when she'd asked Aunt Portia for gentlemen's clothes.

She'd stay in Dublin. She'd seek out a discreet lodging. A popular inn was out of the question. She needed a secluded area. A place away from main thoroughfares. She hurried outside where Rob waited with her baggage. "Secure a coach." Once boarded, she called up to the coach driver, "A street with modest rooming houses, please."

What seemed miles later, the coach stopped. "Shepherd's Manor, madam. 'Ere's as good a street for the like you ask."

She and Rob began walking. Linden trees spread early green leaves, and birds sang among the branches. There were cross streets as well, with *For Let* signs in the window.

One house appealed to her. It was an old-fashioned white stone with green shutters. It also had two outdoor staircases. A white placard in the front window announcing a vacancy caught her eye.

She marched up to the door and knocked. A woman past middle age opened the door. She had a number of pins in her mouth. Removing the pins and carefully sticking them into a mushroom cushion at her wrist, the woman spoke. "Aye, afternoon to ye."

"We're looking for lodging," Mariana said—nodding to Rob standing some distance behind her. "My servant in training."

"Aye, lass. 'Ow long would you be needin' lodging?"

"A very short time. Perhaps two or three nights, perhaps less. I'm come to the city from the country and my kin are away."

"Where do these kin live, if I may ask," the woman said.

"King John's Street."

"Aye, there you say. 'Tis a lovely swank part of Dublin. Do come in my dearie." The landlady showed her a suite of rooms off the eastern set of outside stairs. "'Tis a room we often let to gentlemen," the woman explained, bustling around opening windows and straightening curtains. "The private staircase is a feature they fancy." The woman smirked and rolled her eyes. "Gentlemen without a wife bein' what they are, you know. As for the lad, I have a tiny room over the stable."

"So, miss, your kin are out of the country, aye?"

"Yes."

"King John's Street is as fine a street in Dublin as there is. Quality folk there, to be sure."

The landlady paused from her constant chatter and handed a key to Mariana. However, her willingness to linger in the room longer than necessary suggested she might be one who thrived on minding others' business. No doubt with a penchant for repeating everything she gleaned to anyone who would listen.

She told Mariana that she and her two unmarried daughters occupied rooms on the far side of the rambling structure, as did the other tenants.

"Dinner is at eight sharp. We're working class. None of the fancy late dinners. Afterwards my daughters and I retire to the drawing room." The woman paused speaking and clasped her hands over her bosom dramatically. "We save our most delicate stitching until the evenings. We find it relaxing to sew and chat. A wee drop of sherry and time to catch up on the day's events. Dublin can be quite notorious," the woman said. "We even have an escaped prisoner from Spiller's Island gaol in our midst—a terribly bloodthirsty killer. Murdered an innocent farmer in the country. Chopped his head off with an axe." The woman's eyes lit. "Perhaps you'd join us later in the drawing room?"

"I should love to, but I'm afraid this evening I'm much too tired. I need to rest."

"Of course, miss. It's every evening we spend so. Another evening is as well as tonight." The woman departed with Rob.

The suite seemed comfortable, with decent furniture. The elaborate iron bed and its companion commode stood in the deep ell behind a curtain. An adjoining dressing room opened off the bedroom with blue basin and pitcher. Mariana unbuttoned her boots, replaced the boot-hook on the commode, sank down upon the bed and closed her eyes.

She awoke at the sound of a tinkling bell sounding from the hall. A knock sounded at the door. "Who is it?"

"The maid, miss, your dinner." She'd overslept the dinner hour.

The maid, a young girl with dark hair pulled into an untidy bun, opened the door and placed a laden tray upon the small table by the window. When the girl left, Mariana lifted the napkin and examined the meal. Adaquate enough, she thought. A stew of beef and a ramekin of baked vegetables, along with warm bread and tea.

After she'd eaten, she placed the tray in the hall outside the door. No one moved in the hallway. The parlor where the landlady and her daughters sat to sew was on the other side of the house.

Such a clandestine plan, Mariana thought, her hands trembling as she unlatched the valise Aunt Portia had packed. She stifled a giggle at her aunt's selections. Blue breeches, too long, but she could tuck them into her boots, a ruffled shirt with a high celluloid collar, dark gray topcoat and a large beaver hat. She'd be the grandest dandy in Dublin. If a little outdated.

After the lights were extinguished below, and the three women long retired for the night, Mariana wound her hair into a knot on top of her head. She flattened the topknot, securing it with a silver clip. The hat was large enough to pull low over her forehead and hopefully hide her eyes. She needed a mustache. Seizing a piece of coal from the brass hopper on the hearth, she carefully drew a thin line across her upper lip. Standing back, she surveyed her appearance. In dim light, she'd easily pass for one of the many young clerks working in the city.

At last, Rob's candle went out in the room over the stable. The patch of light from the landlady's drawing room had long since darkened proving the ladies abed. The other tenants were on the far side of the house. Deciding the hour late enough for her departure, Mariana crept down the stairs and across the dew-wet grass to the gate. She paused in deep shadows to see if anyone followed. Nothing.

Lifting the gate latch, she hurried into the street. A lone gas lamp burned at the far corner, its light a creamy arc attracting a cluster of insects nattering around the dim glow. A few pedestrians walked about taking the evening air. Nodding at a couple who strolled arm-in-arm, she started toward the corner, her head down, the hat low, and her heart beating furiously at this new daring freedom.

Fog rolled in from the sea bringing patches of impenetrable vapor and giving the night a surreal aura. Her boot heels clicked on the paving stones. It seemed she'd walked miles and miles and passed many cross streets before she reached the corner leading toward the court chambers. The magistrate's offices.

The weathered old stone building looked very different after dark. It rose like a citadel in the mist, its main chambers facing the street. She knew from securing the prison passes that the honeycomb of private offices formed a loose quadrangle behind the central court, and all of these offices opened to the common courtyard she'd viewed. Junior clerks often worked late hours copying the endless reams of legal documents. Pulling the hat lower, she hurried along. Should she be stopped, she'd offer any excuse to get inside the building.

A quick glance behind assured her the street was empty. Ahead, a few lights burned in various court windows. Also, there appeared to be no one in the courtyard at this late hour. Easing off the paving stones and into the courtyard, she kept to shadows, grateful for the thick turf underfoot masking her footfalls.

She stopped under a spreading elm tree grateful for its cover, though it was not fully in leaf this early in the season. Her breath came ragged. Not that it appeared anyone was around to hear. She eased toward the large, exterior door that led into the building's main vestibule. Lifting the heavy latch, she pulled. Ancient hinges creaked as the door swung open.

Once inside, she stood in shadows, listening. The magistrate's offices were at the far end of the vestibule. She hurried down the hall in that direction. Outside the door to the magistrate's suite, she stopped. This door stood slightly ajar, faint light spilled from within onto the dark flooring beneath her feet. Someone coughed.

Darting into the shadow-drenched doorway across from this office, her heart hammering against her ribs, she peeked through the partially open door. A thick candle burned in a glass globe on the magistrate's desk. His chair was empty as well as the secretary's stool under the window. She couldn't see the wall of shelves and files on the left adjacent to the desk. The stale scent of moldy paper assaulting her nose, she pinched it in time to stop a sneeze. For what seemed an eternity, she crouched in the doorway until her feet grew numb from standing in one position.

There'd been no movement in the office. The cough could've originated elsewhere. Easing across the hall, she slipped inside the magistrate's office, closing the door behind her. Thank God no one occupied the office. Odd, however, the unattended candle left burning. She hurried to a row of storage cupboards where stacks of folios spilled from the shelves and the cabinet's broad top. Quickly, she thumbed through a few. The documents bore official seals and most were dated months before. Some, a year or more before. Where would a clerk file documents awaiting a superior's seal? Near his desk, of course. Such a cupboard stood in front of the clerk's high desk. Rifling through the documents, she found her prison pass application. Seizing it, she stuffed it into her greatcoat.

"Who goes there?"

She'd not heard the door open. Wheeling, she froze, and faced a young clerk standing in the doorway, his eyes round with surprise. He held a mug. "Man, what in damnation are you doing in the magistrate's office? You new lads haven't permission to come in here."

Mariana rushed toward him—lifted her hand, jostling the cup. The mug fell to the floor, shattered, splattering tea over the man's untidy cravat.

She fled the room.

"Dirty thief," he screamed, running after her.

At the greater door to the courtyard, she pushed and fumbled. The heavy oak stuck. The clerk almost upon her, she gave a heave, and the door swung free. Outside, she headed across the street, and into a dark alley. The darkness, her safest bet. The clerk followed into the street, his determined face silhouetted beneath a streetlamp. If she dared move or run farther, he'd see her. Pressing her trembling body against an overcroaching building, she waited. For a panic-stricken moment, she feared the pursuing clerk would follow. He'd stopped running. He advanced a few paces as though he meant to access the alley where she hovered. Instead, the clerk shrugged.

By the streetlamp's glow, he appeared very young, and at this moment, not too brave. Shrugging again, he retreated toward the court building from which he'd exited.

He'd likely judged his clerk's salary insufficient to endanger his life by chasing a thief who, pound to a penny, had accomplices waiting in the dark.

Her breathing returning to normal, Mariana started through the alley. Surely the alley wound to one of the crossroads leading to the Shepherd's Manor area.

Something rattled in the dark— like a coin or a key tumbling onto the cobbles. She froze. Rough hands grasped her throat. Her assailant slammed her against the wall. She gasped, her windpipe blocked.

"Come from the magistrate's offices, aye?" threaded a male voice against her ear. She heard her coat pocket rip. To her horror, the mugger grabbed the papers she'd risked her life to secure. "What have you here? Choice documents to sell, eh, lad? Don't you respect Ireland's law and the king across the sea?"

The hand around her throat loosened. Mariana wrenched around. She blinked in unbelief at the tallest woman she'd ever seen. The Amazon's kerchief hid her face. She wore peculiarly short skirts while wielding a man's strength.

Seizing the moment, Mariana raked her fingers down the woman's cheek, grabbed the documents and in a split-second raced toward the street.

The woman caught her leg easily, sending her sprawling across the cobblestones. "You've no right to take my papers," she cried, her voice strangled. "They mean nothing to you." The beaver hat rolled from her head. Her captor ripped her hair from its clasp. "A woman, aye! Well, I never -"

The man said incredulously, "Mariana?"

Dazed and out of breath from landing belly first on the stones, Mariana tried to focus. "You know me?"

The rude hands that had gripped her fiercely now gently raised her to a sitting position. The kerchief fluttered to the ground.

"Thomas?" Mariana couldn't believe her eyes.

"It's me, love, as cross-gendered as you."

Slipping his arms around her, he lifted her to her feet. "How I've worried about you, luv," he whispered against her hair.

"And, you!" Her voice broke on a sob. "I've feared you drowned in the wild sea. Thank God, you're safe."

Retrieving her hat, he pushed it onto her head. "Your bonny locks will draw attention even in the dark. We cannot stay here."

She laughed. "That's a fact. What are you doing here?"

Taking her arm, he steered her through the alley, and toward the waterfront.

"You're going in the wrong direction. My rooms are the other way."

He didn't slow his pace. His arm looped in hers, he led her along. "We must talk. It isn't safe here. There's a grassy slope a-ways where none are about at this hour."

She nodded, stumbling forward, past rows of houses crowded close. At last, the houses were farther apart. They were near the sea, for the wind carried the scent of salt.

Chapter 31

Dublin

*M*isty salt spray doused her cheeks as they hurried through the night. He stopped at last. "It'safe here," he said. The moonlight illuminated a high, grassy knoll, the sea roiling, and the rush of surf pounding the great rocks.

"A moment," he said, removing a flannel petticoat from beneath his skirt, spreading it on the grass for her. She dropped down onto it, catching her breath.

"Look at us," she said, with a mirthless laugh. "We're dressed ridiculous enough that we escaped detection."

"We pray so," he said. "Now, why are you in the court buildings at this hour?"

She explained. "I had to get our prison pass record from the magistrate's office. I was the last person to visit you before you escaped. My name is on the documents, along with Aunt Portia's. The police suspect I helped you. However, if they have no proof, they can't arrest me. And, you," she said, "how can you remain in Dublin when you're sought in every corner?"

He nodded, his dark hair spun with silver in the moonlight. "Old Madge is here in Dublin. She fled from the country to her sister. Sir John burned her cottage. Before John showed up and destroyed her house, Madge saw Ena Guthre in the hills. That woman means to harm you, Mariana. I don't know why. You must stay clear of her."

"Perhaps, I suspect why," she said, "though I don't know the whole of it."

Thomas didn't question her further, but said, "She threatened to kill Madge when she refused to tell her your whereabouts."

Mariana's breath caught. "I've heard that woman's name all my life. She means nothing to me, though rumors about her have followed me since childhood." She didn't say, *rumors about her birth, suspicions that she might be Ena Guthre's child, and not Lady Catherine's.* Instead, she looked up at Thomas, and into his eyes that gleamed with dark light. "I stayed in Dublin to see you . . . to . . . make certain you lived."

He caught her hand, drawing her close. She nestled against the rough bodice he wore. It carried the scent of wool and beeswax. "What are we to do?"

"For starters," he said, taking the prison pass applications from his pocket. "Destroy these. The magistrate can cry thief all he wants. His reputation is such no one will believe him. He's notorious for taking bribes."

"I shouldn't have taken them," she said folding the papers, stufffing them into her coat pocket. "I don't want to bring the man trouble even if he's dishonest." She truly didn't.

"You are a caring soul."

"My aunt paid a hefty sum to secure these passes. He was led to believe that you're my brother."

Thomas squeezed her hand. "Thank God, I'm not."

Her heart quickened. Would he kiss her?

Instead, he said. "You're in danger here in Dublin. Go to Thornywilde at once." He continued speaking. "If the magistrate is found to have taken a bribe from your aunt, he'll answer for his wrong. Now, you've removed proof of such proceedings, you've nothing else to do here."

"You're right," she whispered, feeling his body's warmth through the bodice. He slipped his arm around her shoulder, sheltering her from the damp wind off the sea. Little she could do with his head sought by the crown. She winced. Her knee ached from the fall on the cobblestones.

Thomas straightened. "May God forgive me if I was too rough back in the alley. I didn't know who you were."

"It's all right. I'll be fine." She looked at him. "Where were you going dressed like this?" She traced his muscled arm with her finger, and felt him tighten with tension.

"I was making my way to Old Madge when I saw you running into the street with the clerk on your heels." He laughed softly, drawing his thumb down the side of her face. "I thought to save a wayward lad from a life of crime. You are lovely in the moonlight-"

She didn't let him finish, but faced him squarely. "I don't know how to help you. How can the mushroom seller help you?"

He adopted her serious tone. "Old Madge and her sister have devised a way to get me out of the city."

"What will you do if you can escape Dublin?"

Shadowy light from the scudding clouds silhouetted his profile, his jaw firm. "I'm bound to Thornywilde to find Ian's killer."

"But-"

"Don't say it, Mariana. Jagger believes I'm guilty. He has no plans for investigating further. He has his man. My escape further escalates my guilt in the inspector's eyes. I can't risk a trial. Nor can I forget the gallows," he said with a rueful chuckle.

"Jagger's wrong," Mariana whispered vehemently. "Odious little man."

"We know that," Thomas said soothingly. "I . . . uh . . . feel like kissing you."

"Would you," she whispered, reaching and drawing his face to hers.

Chapter 32

*M*orning dawned in Shepherd's Manor with Mariana long awake. She'd packed her few belongings and sent word for Rob. Once on the street, she pressed coins into the boy's hand. "You're to go to the gaol and pay for a Mr. Bunch's release. His debts shouldn't exceed what's here. What remains is yours for your service."

The lad's excited expression spoke clearer than words. It was obvious the cellar boy had enjoyed his current adventures. Mariana liked to think that in the future, as Rob washed wine bottles, chased rats and went to the market, he'd remember her.

"Goodbye, Rob, you've been most helpful."

"I'll ne'er forget ye, miss." He followed her onto the green as she hailed a coach. He waved until she moved out of sight.

* * *

It was late night when Mariana arrived in Lough Glendelough. Rain threatened as a page led her to the stables to rouse a stablehand. The available coach was old and leaked. She had no choice except to board it and go home. Once at Thornywilde, she hurried up to her room. Minutes later, Abbie joined her. "M'lady, Gannett said you'd just come in." Abbie's eyes rounded in shock as she eyed her mistress. "You look a fright, m'lady. You've gone and gotten yerself ill, you 'ave." Abbie began helping Mariana out of the wet clothing. "You're blanched white as a ghost."

Once in her dressing gown, Mariana bent over from the vanity stool as Abbie dried her hair with rusk toweling. "Is Aunt Portia abed?"

"Aye, m'lady, and fast asleep."

Chapter 33

*T*he horse Mariana's purse provided proved ample, but not spirited. Old Madge had purchased the gelding from the livery. Now, the beast stumbled and swayed as the way grew steeper, stones and stubble underfoot. Ahead in what light starshine provided, Thomas saw he neared Old Madge's ruined cottage. Rain had begun over an hour before leaving him in a miserable state.

Wet, spent physically, and fearful of every furtive movement in the night, he stopped the animal near the remnants of one of the walls. As best he could judge in the dark, the crude paddock fencing remained. He dismounted, tethered the beast in the paddock where there was plenty of grass. He stretched out under what shelter the partial wall offered and went to sleep.

He woke cramped and filthy, the scent of wet ash strong in his nostrils.

After washing at a nearby stream, he donned the clothing Old Madge's sister had provided—a priest's garments. He learned the old woman's sister did mending for a theatre group. She'd added mustaches and whiskers. He prayed the actor's gum would bind the false hair.

This dreary morning after donning a floppy hat, he set out on horseback for the village. He needed stout tea and needed it badly. Disguised as a man of the cloth, he prayed he wouldn't be recognized, and the mustache and beard gave him an ecclesiastical appearance. As did the plain black tunic and coarse-weave trousers. News in the village of his escape wouldn't be as forthcoming as in Dublin.

Anger seethed within him against Sir John Desmond. Why had the man burned Old Madge's place? What could he have against a simple woman who owned so little of the world's goods? Had John believed Old Madge was inside the cottage and he wanted her dead? Again the troubling question - why?

Thomas had never liked the foppish young man, but he'd never considered him capable of arson. Nor of murder.

The horse cantered along the road leading into the village. Thomas, his head down, passed scattered cottages with wide yards between them. These soon gave way to narrower houses clustered closer together, separated only by stone fences.

Ian Cluny's murderer could be in the village. He had only to ask the right person. He wondered about Mr. Canady, the old jeweler. Had he been arrested for theft? Thomas had never trusted Ena Guthre, nor understood her ties to His Lordship. He knew of a certainty that normal restraints eluded the woman's brain.

As he approached the village's outlying shops, he slumped over his horse, pulling the broad-brimmed hat lower. He'd not lived in the village as a youngster, but merely visited temporarily during the summers. Unlikely anyone would recognize him except Inspector Jagger or Deputy Whitcomb. Lough Glendelough's main street led into a square where smaller lanes angled off into all directions.

A sense of genteel peace hovered over the village this early in the morning. An ancient church stood at the head of the main street, once Catholic, now Anglican. The livery, an inn, and the blacksmith occupied the north side of the cobblestone road. Across from these establishments were several larger stone houses with thatched roofs obviously very old, and immaculately kept. Their gardens graced his view.

The livery stood on the periphery of the shops. Past the livery, coach house, and adjoining inn stood a bakery, a butcher shop, and smaller places of business. Another inn with a pub lay beyond. Thomas alighted at the livery, boarded his horse, and started on foot toward the shops. Several early shoppers with baskets on their arms emerged from the bakery and the butcher.

"Mawning, father," said one man. A woman, squinting curiously at Thomas, accompanied the man.

Thomas touched his hat brim in greeting, nodded benignly to the woman.

His gut crying for hot food, he stopped at the inn farther into the village. He couldn't risk the larger inn adjoining the coach house. He'd gone there once or twice. Upon opening the broad oaken door, the scent of sizzling oil, spiced pork, and thick wafts of blue smoke greeted him. The room's low ceiling hovered black and dingy from ages of peat smoke.

The pleasant buzz of conversation carried around the walls. A maid of young years in a white cap and apron knelt before the huge hearth, tending sausages.

Choosing a corner table in the room's recesses, he soon had tea of the deepest brown color and the promise of hot sausages from a waiter running between the tables.

Customers continued to filter in for breakfast. Mostly men, though a few women. A look satisfied Thomas that Ena wasn't present.

His breakfast arrived. "So, my good man," he said to the waiter, a man of at least forty years. "Your service is admirable."

"Thankee, father."

Thomas felt his face redden beneath the beard. "Have you lived here a long while?" he asked the man.

The waiter shrugged. "I should say fifteen years, by count."

"Then you wouldn't recall a woman who lived at Thornywilde Castle? In service there, perhaps twenty years past."

The waiter laughed. "Thornywilde? The gentry don't favor nay inn for victuals, father. Nor their servants."

Thomas smiled up at the man. "Their regret for the food here is delicious." The waiter started to move away. Thomas spoke conversationally as if he spoke more to himself than the waiter. "The person I seek would have lived here some three and twenty years ago. I've heard she returned for a visit of late. She's tall, striking looking and often travels with a young boy—her grandson."

"None like that I've noticed." The waiter, eager to be off to his duties, for the place was filling quickly, turned.

"Very good, my son. Thank you."

Breakfast over, and not wishing to draw undue attention, Thomas deposited coins in the till basket and left the inn. He would call on the vicar next.

Chapter 34

*T*rusting his wits to supply some explanation for his unusual attire, Thomas arrived at the vicar's parsonage and rapped on the door. The vicar answered the door. A tall man with receding white hair, and a distracted air. He stared hard at Thomas. "The Roman Church is farther afield," he said.

"Thank you, kindly. I shall call there next," Thomas replied. "If it's no inconvenience I'd speak with you."

"No inconvenience atall. None atall," the vicar assured, leading Thomas inside. "I'm honored by your visit. This way to the parlor." The cheerful man then cast a confused gaze over Thomas's rumpled tunic and breeches. "Do I know your order?"

Thomas smiled, grateful for his hat's wide brim. "An exclusive sect— a splintering off from the main group."

"Well . . . yes, that does happen."

Once settled in the vicar's comfortable parlor, Thomas began at once. "I seek information about a relative of one of my parishioners." How easily he spun deception. However, the thought of Mariana in danger assuaged any guilt over his duplicity. Too, his own neck strayed not far from the noose.

"I see." The vicar frowned. "My housekeeper is on holiday today. I cannot offer refreshments." He spoke in a distracted tone.

"I seek no refreshments for I've had a wonderful breakfast at the inn down the way." Thomas paused. The vicar's preoccupation unnerved him. Did the man recognize him? He must engage the vicar's interest at once. "There's a small inheritance involved in my search. My parishioner wishes the proper person notified as one cannot be too careful with inheritances. Of course, there's a significant reward for information."

The vicar brightened. His high forehead wrinkled in thought, he said ponderously, "Careful is the watchword where money is concerned."

Tenting his fingers beneath his chin, he shook his head back and forth. "The love of money is the root of all evil. I admire your diligence on behalf of your parishioner."

Thomas smiled—ecclesiastically, he prayed, as the cleric sat beaming at him.

"Now, father," the vicar began. "Whom do you seek in my small corner of the world?" He managed to insert a great deal of interest into the simple question. Money was like that, Thomas thought, forever whetting the imagination and at times dulling the conscience.

"The lady in question is Mistress Ena Guthre, originally of Cork. She came here some three and twenty years ago to Thornywilde as lady's maid to Lady Catherine. She left after Lady Catherine's death. Rumors say she returned here a short time ago. I came the moment I heard. Unfortunately, I'm afraid her trail has grown cold."

The vicar, drumming his long fingers on his chair arm's carved wood, murmured. "Hmm. I'm unfamiliar with the name." Shifting, the man crossed his long legs. The sole of his slippers bore holes the size of robin's eggs.

"I'm originally from the north," the vicar continued. "I've served as vicar here going on twenty years. I will gladly check the rolls and contact you if I find such a name in past records. You understand this may take some time."

Thomas nodded.

Thomas rose, half-doffed his hat. "If I may, I will call on you in say a fortnight, if that's sufficient time for your search."

"Yes. I'll have my secretary look into our records."

The visit to the Roman Church produced the same results.

Thomas then walked about the village calling in at the shops. In each one, he met with the same disappointing results. No one remembered Ena Guthre from the past. None had seen an unfamiliar woman traveling with a young boy.

The last shop on the village square was a modiste's establishment. This shop stood apart from the others, and had the appearance of a private home except for a small sign over the door. Thomas shook the hand bell, which gave off a harsh, clanging sound. A woman's voice called out. "Enter, please."

He opened the door and stood in an anteroom. Ahead, a middle-aged woman sat near the window, bent over a sewing frame. She looked up when he entered the shop. Her gaze narrowed, and she frowned slightly, staring at his clothing. Thomas suspected her disappointed by his raiment identifying him as an ecclesiastic. Gentlemen often ordered gowns for their wives, daughters or mistresses, but not a priest.

"Good morning, Madame."

She pushed her needle into a heart-shaped cushion on her arm. "What can I do for you, father?" She got to her feet and curtsied.

"I wouldn't interrupt your work. I'm seeking information about one Ena Guthre who served at Thornywilde some three and twenty years ago. Perhaps of late, you recall seeing a tall woman of middle age in the village with her grandson."

The woman pursed her lips. "'Twould be a simple thing—noticing a stranger with a child." She spoke curtly. "We see few besides ourselves. Maybe the occasional tourists come across the Irish Sea. Why do you seek this . . . this Ena Guthre?"

"It's a personal matter relating to one of my parishioners." For some reason, Thomas didn't feel led to repeat the inheritance story. When the woman couldn't help him, he thanked her, bid her good day, and started toward the livery.

Collecting his horse from the stable, Thomas mounted the gelding and rode toward Thornywilde, choosing a less traveled route through the hills, on the offside chance he might meet Gannett or one of the others who'd recognize him. It was too soon to reveal his presence. There was a murder to solve, the art thief, Ena Guthre, to locate, and he needed to maintain his secrecy to avoid arrest and the rope.

The winding path through the hills and a strong east wind taxed him as he skirted Thornywilde, heading for higher slopes past the old castle. The spot he chose was well populated with trees, poplars, elms, and a few oaks. Dismounting, he staked the horse to the farthest tree where it could graze in the deep spring grass. Spreading his cloak on the ground, he settled into a vantage point overlooking Thornywilde below.

The familiar mail post rumbled up to the house from the direction of the Erin Rose. A short time later, Gannett emerged from the back, walking to the stables. He emerged driving the carriage. Lady Portia awaited him. From this distance, Thomas thought she looked like a finely dressed miniature doll. She and Gannett stood engaged in conversation. His eyes burned from watching the house. Activity continued, common to the estate. The dairymaids and the stablehands attended the animals.

The warm sun lulled him into a much needed nap. The long afternoon dragged past. After dark, he vowed to move nearer to the house and observe at the windows.

The moon had climbed high, and the castle's occupants had surely settled for the night when Thomas made his way down the hill and toward the house. He slipped around to the front of the building where he could view Mariana's rooms.

By standing at a distance within a thick hedge, he saw her at her dressing table.

* * *

That déjà vu feeling rippled over Mariana. The dark sense of impending trouble loomed. The unpleasant feeling left her frustrated and worried.

Abbie brushed her hair. "'Tis a bitter night, m'lady," Abbie commented softly. "The wind is up."

Mariana smiled to herself. Abbie saw the worst in every situation. "It's merely a thunderstorm moving in. One that'll likely pass quickly," she replied, rubbing pomade on her arms.

Wind rattled the windows and a driving rain drummed against the panes. Standing, Mariana slipped her peignoir onto her shoulders, making her way toward the bed.

"That'll be all, Abbie." Abbie scurried around, folding clothes into the press. She stopped. "I'll light the candles. I know the oil lamps bother you." Mariana didn't comment, though she loathed the heavy scent of burning oil.

The little maid stared at the darkened windows. She shuddered at a particularly loud thunder roll. "I can believe this were an evil place in the auld times."

"Abbie, calm yourself. It's a rainstorm. Not the end of the world."

"Yes, m'lady."

Once Abbie left the room, Mariana placed her book of sonnets onto the bedside table. She let the candle burn as she lay back, staring at the dancing shadows against the far wall displaying grotesque shapes. *Abbie was right,* she thought. The house often seemed invaded with a *present* evil—*not evil of old time.*

Perhaps she should ring the bell-cord for one of Mrs. Hooks's sleep potions. The hour must be very late. One blessing, she thought, Thomas lived and another blessing—Lady Vesta and Sir John had not returned from outings at another country estate.

* * *

The morning brought two unwelcome faces at the breakfast table— Lady Vesta and John sat there, heads bent in conversation that stopped the moment Mariana entered the room. Acknowledging them with a stiffly placed smile, Mariana bade them good morning. Aunt Portia, wearing a grim expression, walked to the head of the table with Abbie's assistance.

Her Ladyship, her dark eyes bright, said to Mariana, "John and I have visited your mother's Cork estate."

"Oh-" Mariana glanced at her aunt. Portia's expression revealed nothing.

"It's quite impressive," Her Ladyship continued with an arch stare.

"Indeed." Mariana sipped her tea. "Why are you interested in my mother's holdings?"

"No particular reason, my dear. Your father told me you will inherit when you marry."

Eyeing the mercenary woman, Mariana held her tongue.

"The very day you are married," added Lady Vesta smugly.

"If only she were willing," John said, making cow eyes.

Mariana recalled the day in Dublin when this odious woman had confronted her with this information.

"If you remain a spinster," Lady Vesta continued, "your mother's fortune will come to you on your thirtieth birthday. I see I shock you." Her Ladyship laughed—a brittle chuckle that didn't warm the coldness in her eyes or soften her stern features.

Chapter 35

*T*homas continued to watch the castle from the hill. This very morning a group of policemen had ridden up Cormac Hill where Jagger's men had been found murdered. The police presence in the area kept Thomas close to his camp site instead of riding back into the village.

He stared down into the copse where Ian Cluny's body had been discovered. The wood was so dense and dark, he couldn't fathom how the man's body had been found.

Thornywilde's servants went about their routines. He watched the dairymaids go to the house with cream and butter. They'd repeat this chore in the late afternoon. The dairymaids were young women of the cottagers. The stable hands moved around the paddock, tending the horses. Down the far vista to his left, pigs squealed as the tenant farmers fed them. Their stench reached him, even this far up the hill. One of the stablehands, acting as cellar boy, carried in armload after armload of firewood. The long day wore on.

Toward tea time, Gannett brought the gig around. Sir John took the reins and drove down to the Erin Rose. He returned several hours later. There was no sign of Her Ladyship.

Wasted time, Thomas muttered to himself. Trapped on this blasted hill and unable to move freely. How could he ever have the opportunity to solve Ian Cluny's murder? He must get word to Mariana that he was here in the hills.

Moving into deeper shade, Thomas ate a rough meal of brown bread and sausage he'd purchased from a street vendor before leaving the village. It had gone quite stale. Spreading his cloak, he closed his eyes and dozed.

When he woke, twilight was fast fading. Thornywilde lay below the hills, her windows glowing like dark glittering jewels in the fading light. As soon as full dark fell, he'd move nearer to the house.

He hadn't long to wait. Clambering down the rocky hill, he kept in shadows. The climb downward proved more difficult than it appeared from the hilltop. His foot struck a loose boulder. Rocks showered downward. He stopped, his breathing labored. A horse sensing danger neighed in the paddock. Thomas waited long moments before starting downward again. At last he reached the back paddock behind the carriage house.

From within the stables, voices of the stablehands wafted on the still, night air. The air was nippier this night after the rain the night before. He debated how best to approach the house. It was dark enough that with luck, he should be able to slip into the house through the series of ancient, unused corridors off the old sculleries. This warren of rooms led to the castle kitchen.

Unfortunately, there were no shrubs or trees to shield him once he left the shadows. He must sprint across the lawns toward the house. It wouldn't do for one of the stablehands, or even Gannett, to see him. Their surprise would set off alarm.

If he managed getting inside the house, he'd seek out Mrs. Hooks. She'd always been kind to him. She'd see he had food. Too, she'd get word to Mariana. The better way to access the house lay to the east through the wood, with its bridle paths and heavy cover. It would take him longer, but at this point, safety trumped speed.

A good hour later, he slipped forward from the woods, easing onto the dining room terrace. The family should be eating dinner just now. Normally, the terrace doors stood open. Fortune moved with him. Indeed, the terrace doors were ajar. The silken drapery panels were pushed slightly apart, affording him a perfect view. They sat at the table, Lady Portia, Lady Vesta, Sir John, and Mariana.

Lady Vesta, her lorgnette lifted, glared at Lady Portia. "You say you believe Thomas has a sister. I have my suspicions. To my knowledge Thomas O'Geary has no sisters." She pushed the lorgnette nearer her face, regarding Lady Portia as if she observed some distasteful filth. She continued. "How convenient you and Mariana chose the exact time of

Thomas's incarceration to visit your Dublin friends. Of whom, I have since heard, were out of the country."

Lady Portia paled.

"You don't suggest my aunt or I had a part in Thomas's unfortunate predicament," Mariana intervened haughtily.

The lorgnette dropped to Lady Vesta's bosom, spinning on its golden chain. She laughed brittlely, wielding her knife delicately as she cut her steak. "Perhaps not his predicament, but his escape," she said slyly, "Chief Inspector Jagger was here again this morning," she continued. "He, too, believes your and your aunt's visit to Dublin most opportune."

Thomas caught his breath. He'd not seen the police coach at the house.

Sir John looked up. "Maman, tell her the rest." John's pinched face repulsed Thomas.

The noblewoman's glacial gaze silenced her son. "I am coming to it."

"Tell me what?" Mariana asked.

"It seems no prison pass for the mysterious sister, aunt, and nephew could be located at the magistrate's office; which is highly irregular. That gentleman is out of the country on an extended vacation. A clerk reported a break-in at the magistrate's office. It seems a thief disguised as a young clerk overpowered him, which after some thought he believes was a woman disguised as a man."

Portia stared, her face contorted with shock. "You are suggesting Mariana or I am responsible."

"I suggest, my dear Lady Portia, that perhaps you and your niece stand on shaky ground."

Thomas barely restrained himself from rushing in and confronting Lady Vesta. He stilled his rage by logically admitting that the woman spoke the truth. She had a network of spies everywhere.

Mariana, her voice taut, admonished the woman. "You repeat idle gossip, and it's uncalled for."

"You believe so, my dear."

Sir John started laughing. "What are you waiting for?" His goading annoyed his mother.

"Quiet," she ordered.

"Yes," Mariana said, scowling thoughtfully. "What are you trying to say?"

"Very well, it's time you knew. Within a few days I shall be Thornywilde's mistress. Sir Charles made his will over to me. I am the true heir. My word counts here—not either of yours. You," she said, addressing Portia, "are no more than an interloper—a poor relation who came here to care for a child reputed to be a bastard and you have remained to sponge off Charles until this day. I'm not asking you to leave the premises, mind you, but you will do well to remember your place."

Trembling, Mariana stood, flinging back her chair. "How dare you!"

Lady Portia stumbled to her feet, pale as death. Mariana rushed to her, taking her aunt's arm. "You mustn't allow her to bully you," she whispered. She helped her aunt back down into her chair at the table. Crossing the room, Mariana pulled the bellcord. Abbie came at once. "Lady Portia must go to her room immediately. See she has whatever comfort she needs."

"Yes, m'lady."

Livid with rage, Mariana turned to Lady Vesta. "If my father had overhead your speech just now, you'd be the one to remember your place."

Her Ladyship laughed. "Unfortunate you can't visit the hereafter and inform him."

"Yes," laughed John. "Visit him in the hereafter." He lumbered up, angled toward the sideboard, and grasped the brandy decanter, sloshing amber liquid onto the polished mahogany. He lifted the snifter in a mock toast. "Yes, go to him, daughter of the manse."

Thomas watched and listened, sickened. Ignoring the mother and son, Mariana lifted her head, looped her gown's train over her arm and left the room.

Her Ladyship stood and made her way to the sideboard, where she poured an unladylike amount of brandy into a sparkling snifter.

Slumping forward, his mouth twisted in an intoxicated snarl, Sir John bleated, "What am I to do? One minute you want me wed to Mariana, the next minute I fall from your grace. I swear, mother, you are mercurial." John downed his remaining whiskey in one long gulp, splintering the glass onto the polished mahogany table.

"Temper, temper, my wayward boy. You'll indulge your conjugal passions yet for I want Mariana both wed and dead." She offered her hand to her son. "If you'll assist me, I shall go upstairs."

After Her Ladyship left the room, Sir John tottered up from the table. He reeled toward the doors leading to the terrace. Thomas longed to reach out and grasp the scoundrel by his throat. Instead, he flattened his body against the terrace wall, and waited until John moved away. After a short interval, Thomas circled the house, crouching in shadows, scanning the upper floors of the bedchambers.

A light burned in both Mariana's and Lady Portia's rooms. A gnarled cypress tree grew beside the balcony beneath Mariana's bedroom window. The old tree appeared sturdy enough to bear his weight. Moving under its thick canopy, Thomas hurled himself onto the lower branches. With ease, he scaled upward, and with some effort, vaulted over onto the balcony.

He peered inside the window. He couldn't believe his eyes. Abbie stood in the middle of the room, candlelight flickering off the wicked blade of a large knife she held threateningly before Mariana.

Had the girl taken leave of her senses?

"I'll kill her, m'lady. I don't care if I hang by my neck 'til I'm dead. She 'as no right to talk to you and Lady Portia as she just did. It's . . . it's . . . unholy."

Mariana, her face deathly pale, still wearing the satin gown she'd worn at dinner stood in a pool of light near her bed." Put the knife away, Abbie, I mean it."

"But, m'lady…."

"Do as I say."

A tense few seconds passed.

Abbie dropped her head, sobbing. She handed the knife to Mariana, who buried it amongst fabric in a workbasket. Thomas breathed a sigh of relief. What if he'd jumped through the closed window and in shock Abbie had stabbed Mariana?

Mariana took the workbasket and placed it in the armoire. Abbie, her head down, her slight body racking with sobs, continued to stand in the center of the room like a lost waif in a sea of nothingness.

Mariana moved to her side. "You're a good girl," Mariana soothed. "Sit there on the stool and compose yourself."

Abbie sank to her knees in front of her mistress. "I don't know what come over me. I don't . . ."

"Look at me," Mariana commanded.

Slowly, Abbie raised her head.

"As evil as Her Ladyship seems, she's within her rights as Charles's legal heir to order Thornywilde's affairs as she pleases. If my presence or my aunt's presence disturbs her, I'm not the first relative in Ireland to be banished to the upstairs. In fact, I'm relieved not to face her or her son at meals."

Thomas noted a harsh light filling Mariana's eyes—like a yellow sunset before a violent storm.

"I'm sure my aunt feels the same way," Mariana continued.

Abbie, struggling to smile through tears, managed. "It 'in't fair, m'lady. The like of her below is witch's works. E'en, if I speak out of me place."

"We'll discuss it no more."

"Yes, m'lady."

Thomas grew impatient. Would the girl never leave Mariana's room? Though he could scarcely blame her for lingering. Who'd want to risk the company and commands of the two hellions below?

Abbie moved to the armoire and pulled out Mariana's dressing gown.

"Leave it," Mariana said dismissively. "Have Mrs. Hooks send up a pot of tea. I've a great deal of thinking to do. Tea may help clear my brain," she said wearily.

"Yes m'lady."

After Abbie's departure, Mariana locked her bedroom door, tucking the key beneath the bed pillow.

Hovering on the balcony, Thomas debated his next move. Should he call out to Mariana? Perhaps rap on the window. Either act may elicit alarm. If she screamed, John or Lady Vesta may respond. Little choice, though. He couldn't risk standing on the balcony. Surprise, his only option. Pushing his hat lower, he tested the window. Unlocked. Springing forward, his boots struck Mariana's bedroom floor with a bound.

Chapter 36

agger, slumped in the swivel chair in his new office, toying with a quill pen. The police station had relocated to a new building. He didn't approve of the present location. He preferred the former offices nearer the inn where he had the advantage of observing the village's activities from his window. Not here. Irritated, he cast the pen aside.

There'd been no progress locating Thomas O'Geary. Common belief - O'Geary had escaped to the countryside, likely the Thornywilde estate.

Jagger thumbed a letter. Lady Vesta had informed London's High Court of Jagger's derelict of duty in bringing the renegade to justice. She hinted broadly at his incompetence and conflict of interest since O'Geary had ties to the baron's estate, the county baron under whom Jagger served. The same baron from whom Jagger often obtained favors - His Lordship, the deceased Lord Charles Belmont. Only now, the man's former fiancée inherited ownership of Thornywilde.

The High Court Commissioner had forwarded Her Ladyship's letter to Jagger's Dublin superior. The implied charges burned in this man's flesh like a canker. He'd sent the scathing letter Jagger held. *Find Thomas O'Geary at once or be removed from the post of Chief Constable.*

Swearing under his breath, Jagger took up the O'Geary folio. How many times had he read the report? Hundreds.

A woman masquerading as O'Geary's sister visited him the night he escaped Spiller's Island. An older woman and a boy accompanied the sister. Shortly after the visitors departed, a suspicious fire occurred in the inmate, Bunch's cell. The cell adjacent to O'Geary's. Water closet window broken. O'Geary plunged into the sea from the water closet window. No body had washed ashore.

Bunch's debt mysteriously paid the following day by a boy. Bunch released. Bunch's whereabouts unknown.

A suspicious burglar entered the official chambers and stole permission slips admitting the threesome to the gaol. The burglar was not apprehended. A clerk in the magistate's offices suspected the thief had been in disguise, and possibly a female.

Had O'Geary drowned? Jagger doubted that. He recalled the artist's powerful arms - arms capable of swimming the fiercest surf. As his men put irons on O'Geary that day at Thornywilde, he had noted O'Geary's long fingers and discolored nails. He'd seen nails like that before. He couldn't recall on whom.

Slamming his fist on his desk, Jagger scattered the notes onto the floor. He was not suited for the position of Chief Constable dealing with the criminal world. People of ill-repute. He should be an academic in comfortable surroundings, writing essays on the ways of the world, and education in particular. Often, he found himself daydreaming of another life—a life that had slipped through his fingers to the bottom of the Indian Ocean.

To compensate for this lost life, he dealt harsher with criminals. In his heart, he believed anyone afoul of the law should swing from the end of a rope. Sitting back, he closed his eyes, visualizing O'Geary's hooded body as it dropped from the gallows into the pit below.

Politics. Politics and money. Jagger's world revolved around both. Too much of one and not enough of the other. Being Chief Constable, he appointed the jury and judge in criminal cases. The next criminal court assize convened in Dublin 2nd July. He meant to have O'Geary in custody by then, condemned.

How he hated this Godforsaken Ireland. A country divided by religion and politics. An Anglican, he favored the ancient Gothic cathedral he occasionally attended. The great church was sparsely peopled with the few landed gentry who remained in this wretched country. He felt at home in the cathedrals' cloistered hallows. The fact that in ages past, the Catholics erected the magnificent structure, mattered not.

Most of the gentry, like Lord Charles Belmont, spent the majority of their time in England or abroad on the continent.

Jagger hated the Catholics, their masses of poor—starving in mud huts—yet faithful to their Archbishops, Bishops, and Priests. False hope in an ageless deliverance that never came.

He meted justice fairly, with half the Irish barristers being Catholic and half Protestant. He, being the person with supreme authority, however, chose the juries and judges. Never had he taken a bribe to sway jury or judge.

The O'Geary case infuriated him. He itched to see Thomas O'Geary dead.

Taking up the pen, he dipped it into the inkwell. A letter to the Lord Lieutenant representing King William. The Lord Lieutenant, a puppet of a man with no real power, but influence, could demand the death penalty from the crown. Jagger carefully worded his plea, giving reasons for the crown to supersede Ireland's lower courts in case the assize favored O'Geary.

As he wrote the petition, Jagger knew real power rested in England's ministers. Mostly men without consciences - most of whom could be bought. He paused in his writing, a chilling thought skittering through his mind. The Lord Lieutenant *could* also issue pardons.

Unlikely in this instance. Thomas O'Geary had no influence. Or did he? He was known and respected in royal circles for his artistic talent. It was rumored he had ties to the elusive genius calling himself Italia.

The petition completed, Jagger sat back in his chair.

Melancholy filled him, unnamed longings, a sense of great loss. Closing his eyes, he wondered what life would be if he'd been able to go to university as planned - and for which he'd studied long and hard.

His father had placed the family's life savings, including his wife's inheritance, into a partnership in a merchant line. The venture proved lucrative. For several years, the family enjoyed exalted status. They had the luxuries and influence that money could buy.

Mishaps began to occur. Several ships went down in the North Sea. The firm's chief accountant absconded with a large sum of money. It was rumored he was in Australia. Two more freighters bound for America lost in the North Atlantic.The sinking of the largest ship in the Indian Ocean left the family penniless.

Jagger's education halted abruptly. He likened his future to a ship sinking beneath icy black water to an untimely grave.

His education suffered. Not Oxford, he was forced by circumstances to attend a Catholic religious college in Portugal known for educating both religious and secular students.

Shrugging, Jagger took a deep breath, exhaling slowly. That was old history. Rising, he pulled a law book down from the case behind his chair, thumbing through it idly. Never had he wanted anything to do with the law. A barrister shuffling papers in dusty rooms, visiting dingy prison cells, seeking to sift through lies to defend a client. Daily facing the arrogance of England's courts.

He snapped the law book closed. He should be grateful his father's few connections, political connections, had landed his son this job in Ireland. Especially after the damnable actress affair. Chief Constable of an Irish county far surpassed peddling bootblack. For that was his occupation during the years he attended the university. Selling bootblack on Portugal's sun-baked streets. A common drummer. A penniless youth with an uncertain future.

How dare he go soft-sop with mercy for criminals, for no mercy had been shown to him.

As a youth, he'd watched people in Portugal's streets. He'd come to know the furtive glances of thieves, spot those with daggers beneath their cloaks. He had learned the banter and manipulations of the swindler, and viewed those with lust seeking the brothels. Those possessed of demons too terrible to recall.

This scrutiny of strangers intrigued him still, and served him well in his present occupation. Several days before he'd watched a priest walk into town from the direction of the livery. An oddly garbed priest. The man's clothing reminded Jagger of some of the priests in Portugal's poorer parishes. This man walked past the police station to the Protestant parson's house alongside the Anglican cathedral.

Odd that a Roman priest would call on an Anglican cleric. Jagger had meant to inquire of this stranger's business. Strangers in Lough Glendelough evoked curiosity, since not many came their way. Yes, he'd call on the cleric this very day.

He decided against appearing at the parsonage outright. Better to pave the way first. Taking up a new nib, he inserted it into the pen and hurriedly dashed off a note informing the cleric that the police would call shortly about a serious matter. Given time to stew over an *official visit,* the vicar would be in a nervous state—more advantageous to interrogate. An excitable man—the vicar.

Taking up the quill again after dispatching the note to the vicar and the letter to the Lord Lieutenant, Jagger made notations on a leaflet.

Priest.

Peculiar habit.

Large hat—possibly Italian woolen.

On foot.

Calls on Anglican vicar.

After the notations, he filled the remainder of the page with question marks. *???????????*

Where questions existed, answers lurked.

"Bring the coach around," Jagger ordered a deputy. "I'm going to my house for lunch. "Fetch me in an hour."

After eating the fish pie his housekeeper prepared, Jagger boarded the waiting carriage. "To the Anglican vicar's house."

Jagger, especially fond of the gold-inscribed official emblem on the carriage door, enjoyed driving through the village and the countryside as the citizenry viewed him, supposing him to be about important police business. He kept a stern countenance, looked neither to the right nor the left as the coach sped through the streets and lanes.

"You may call for me in three-quarters of an hour."

The deputy nodded.

The vicar answered the door. "Ah, Chief Constable Jagger. Do come in." The man led Jagger through to the comfortable parlor with dark paneled walls, and three arched windows of medieval design. The windows faced onto a charming garden. A silver tea service that had served many visitors judging from the squat pot's dents and dull finish stood on a round table before the windows.

"I am delighted to see you," the vicar said, indicating a soft leather chair. "I was having a light repast. May I offer you tea—a biscuit."

"Thank, you, no."

"I admit I'm somewhat intrigued by your earlier note. You wish to see me about a *serious* matter?"

"It's kind of you to see me on such short notice." Jagger ignored the man's eagerness to get at the meat of the visit. In police work, he found playing the cat with a doomed mouse, ignoring his victim's nervous anxiety to get it over with, often produced the effect he desired. Nervous anxiety often led to blurting out facts.

Jagger nodded at the china platter displaying various biscuits and tiny sandwiches. "On second thought, that appears a delectable type of biscuit." Obviously, the vicar had gone to a great deal of trouble in a short time for the Chief Constable's visit.

"Has it an apricot filling?"

"Yes, yes, yes it does."

The vicar beamed as he rang a bell-cord. A portly middle-aged woman with untidy hair appeared. "More tea and biscuits for the Chief Constable. Those with the apricots." A catch threaded the parson's voice as if he rushed to speak before he had oxygen enough to form words.

The woman curtsied, went to the table, poured out, and placed several of the dainty apricot biscuits onto a floral china plate. "Sugar or lemon, sir?" she said with a kindly smile for the Chief Constable.

"Neither." Jagger smiled magnanimously. He sniffed the tea. "Ah, a wonderful blend, a superb blend."

The vicar looked on anxiously as Jagger sipped the tea and nibbled at the biscuits. "More tea? Another biscuit?" The parson's urgings bore a hint of hysteria.

"No. Thank you."

"About the serious matter. I can't imagine. . ."

The simple note had disturbed the poor man. Instead of relieving the man's angst and curiosity at once, Jagger played the cat a while longer. "I am from England, you know."

The vicar nodded, a frown between his grizzled brows.

Jagger crossed his legs, continuing lazily. "I am amazed by Ireland's moist winds, but I find the climate most agreeable."

"It *is* a delightful climate," the vicar replied. "A blessed country."

Jagger spoke suddenly. "I apologize if my message alarmed you."

"No, no, no . . . nothing of the sort." The vicar's long head bobbed vigorously.

"Good," Jagger continued, his expression bland. "Some days past a priest came to the village. Did he by chance call on you?"

"He did." The cleric paused. From Jagger's years of investigative work, he suspected the cleric weighed exactly what information to share, and what to withhold—if there was anything to withhold. In an attempt to put the man somewhat at ease, Jagger leaned forward, lowering his voice. "You know we are seeking Thomas O'Geary for Ian Cluny's murder."

The vicar blinked. He seemed startled as if he'd come from a dark cave into the harsh sun. Jagger continued. "Ian Cluny was a Catholic. I understand he could've been involved with the Ribbonmen. As an outlaw, he'd have many enemies."

"I should think so," said the Vicar.

"Perhaps," Jagger agreed. "His murder was unfortunate as is all murder. The taking of another's life is against the law. Both God's and man's."

"Of course. Of course." Rattled, the vicar stared at the empty contents of his cup. He looked up at Jagger.

"We arrested Thomas O'Geary for Cluny's murder. You have no doubt heard that O'Geary has escaped from the gaol. He's in a foolhardy situation—a fugitive from the law."

Th vicar slid up straighter in his chair. "I agree. And, a dangerous situation for everyone, with an escaped man about."

"Where do you think O'Geary might go?" Jagger asked suddenly.

The vicar's lips moved inaudibly as he searched for a response. "Why, sir, I have no idea where he might go. It's rumored he drowned since he wasn't discovered north toward sandy shores. If he didn't drown, perhaps London." The cleric appeared to clutch at straws.

"Perhaps," Jagger agreed, tenting his fingers beneath his chin." Swim the Irish Sea to Wales. Impossible. A boat? None went out that night. None was reported stolen. My good man, what does that suggest to you?"

The vicar's eyes bugged. "Why, he's still in Ireland. Dublin, I'd wager. No," the man recanted as though some mist cleared in his head. "He'd be a hunted man there. Do you think he could be here in the village?"

"Do you?"

The vicar jumped.

"Is there more tea?" Jagger asked.

"Of course. Let me call the housekeeper." Ignoring the bell-cord, the vicar bolted from his chair, hurried toward the back of the house as though stalked by the angel of death.

He returned a short time later more composed. His housekeeper followed with a fresh pot of tea.

Jagger smiled at the housekeeper. "I've admired the rectory flower garden and have meant to compliment you," he said to the vicar.

The vicar seemed surprised. Casting a bewildered gaze out the mullioned windows, he murmured. "Thank you. Working the earth is a joy. I won the garden show's grand prize last year with my dahlias."

"Tell me about the priest," said Jagger, changing the subject abruptly.

The man strove to answer. "There seemed something . . . uh . . . familiar about him. I couldn't put my finger on what." Jagger noted the vicar's hands trembled.

"He didn't name his order—some fringe group—some splinter from the main church. I know how disgruntlement grows. These Catholics are such a . . . a controversial group. Fervent beyond reason at times. Their people become outraged over the smallest matters. It depends on the presiding bishop and priest for things to go smoothly." The vicar cleared his throat. "These upsets aren't only among the Catholics. Some of our members are disturbed over recent changes in the common prayer book. These things happen. Though I confess, I'm not at all privy to happenings with the Catholics. . ."

Jagger smiled benignly. "Ah, trouble in Christendom. We creatures of clay resist change. What did this familiar not so familiar priest want with you?"

"Information," the vicar spewed at once. "About a woman who lived at Thornywilde years back. Ena Guthre. He said he'd heard she was in the village recently."

"Did he tell you why he sought her?"

The vicar nodded. "One of his parishioners left her an inheritance. I believe he mentioned a small reward. If the woman attended church here in the village, it occured before my time. I told him I'd check the roles. I suggested the Roman Church since he appeared to be one of theirs."

"Tell me, did you by chance notice the priest's hands?"

His brows together, the vicar thought. "Of course, I mean . . . now that you mention it, he must lead one of the pastoral orders those who farm with their hands for his nails were stained. Yes, I noticed that. Why do you ask?"

"No reason, my good man. You've been most helpful. I hope I haven't disturbed your routine."

* * *

Back at headquarters, Officer Whitcomb met Jagger. "A note, Chief, some lad delivered it."

"A lad, you say? You saw the boy?"

"No sir. When I come from lunch, the duty deputy said a boy brought it."

The note read:

Come to Thornywilde at once. Thomas O'Geary whom you seek is nearby. The unsigned note was printed on rough paper, though the penmanship reflected a person adept at writing. Someone with skills beyond a village's primary schools—an educated person. He didn't like the sound of it. Nor did he believe it to be truth.

Once Whitcomb left the office, Jagger studied the note. He began to suspect it bore a ring of truth. Attitudes of late at Thornywilde had puzzled him. The maid practically pushed him out of the house when he last called on Lady Portia. Her Ladyship had seemed incredibly dense that same afternoon. Unusual for the sharp intuitive person he knew her to be. Perhaps she'd written the note.

The day being fine and sunny, almost unseasonably warm for February, Jagger forewent the carriage and ordered his horse.

Avoiding the main road out of the village, he chose to approach Thornywilde from the north through the hills, If O'Geary had returned to the village and lurked nearby as the note indicated, he'd likely hide somewhere in the hills. The way led over Cormac Hill where the policemen had been found murdered and mutilated.

The path proved steeper and rougher than he'd thought. After the better part of an hour later, he stopped at a small lough, allowing his horse to drink. Dismounting, he stretched his back. Something white upon a nearby rock caught his attention. He picked it up. A child's shirt—not old and weather-worn—but of fine cloth, well made, and quite new. What tenant owned such a garment?

Perhaps a tenant like Ian Cluny, who'd rob and steal. Tucking the shirt into his pocket, Jagger tethered his horse to a sapling tree, and started up the steep incline before him. Thornywilde Castle lay a good distance away in the valley below.

The scent of smoke jolted him, acrid and closeby. At the jagged apex of an outcropping of rock, he leaned over and looked directly below. Startled, he leaped back. Dropping onto his belly, he scooted forward for a better view. The smoke curled upward from a campfire beneath the ledge. A sorrel nibbled grass. A woman lay in the grass, a boy beside her.

Easing back before the twosome saw him, he made his way to his horse and mounted. Best to ride in upon them at full gallop.

The woman bolted up, staring hard. Clasping the boy to her skirts, she squinted up at him, pushing strands of untidy hair from her face. Her fine-boned face appeared hard, her clear eyes glinted as cold as polished metal. "Good day, officer. What do you want of me?"

"Your name and your business, Madam?"

"Molly." She said after a swift glance at boy by her side.

"So, *Molly,*" Jagger said, stressing Molly. "What brings you to Thornywilde's far meadow?"

She said nothing, her expression glacial.

"It's a pity, Molly," he continued. "That you're not Ena Guthre, for the village vicar told me that a priest came here seeking Ena Guthre to give her an inheritance. She traveled with a lad, her grandson."

The boy twisted the woman's skirt between his fingers.

"Speak up, Molly," Jagger demanded. "Where are you from? What seek you on private land?"

"I'm from across the Irish Sea," she said. "England, south of London."

He laughed. "With that brogue? You're Irish born." He'd had enough of her gaff.

"You're Ena Guthre and the boy is your grandson. You once lived at Thornywilde."

Her eyes narrowed, her fists clenched and the pulse at the base of her throat throbbed. Jagger saw violence in her. Maybe madness.

Chapter 37

he shock of Thomas in her bedchamber near frightened
Mariana into a fainting spell. He rushed and caught her before
she slumped onto the floor. "No," she protested. "I . . .
thought you were a vision?"

"No vision."

Trembling, she pushed her hand over his mouth. "You're not safe
here. Jagger came this very day. He saw Aunt Portia yesterday. He suspects
you're near Thornywilde . . ." *God's saints,* she'd sent Abbie for tea! What if
Abbie found him here?

"Abbie will come any minute."

"I have only seconds with you," he said. "Jagger may think I'm
hereabouts, but he doesn't know for certain. I could be anywhere."

"But, how can you-"

"I need food and clothing. I trust Gannett. He's my friend. Have him
bring provisions to the hill behind the estate."

Mariana nodded frantically. "But-"

"I wish Her Ladyship, the Lady Portia to know."

"But-"

Within a twinkling, he slipped out the window, onto the balcony and
away into the dark. She stood looking through the impenetrable darkness
for a last sight of him.

There seemed wisdom about Thomas's decision. With Gannett's help,
Thomas would have freedom to go about his search for Ian Cluny's killer.

Chapter 38

he morning dawned misty and hazy on the mountain. Stretching his knotted limbs, Thomas made his way to the stream where he washed, sluicing the ice-cold water onto his face. There had been riders on the mountain the night before. Policemen.

Not risking a fire, he ate cold bread and drank water from the burn. *Riders!* Cursing, he dropped to his belly; he should've stayed back among the trees. Two horses approached from below, too far away to identify, but he suspected the lead rider was Gannett. He recognized the big bay as the mount the handyman favored. A roan with rider followed.

Saints be with him! It was Gannett and Abbie.

He stood. "Hallo! Here."

Gannett drew up, dismounted, and helped Abbie down. The girl went to the saddlebags and produced a basket of fresh scones with two pots of jam. She laid the food on a cloth. Next, she brought out a rasher of cooked bacon tied in a cloth, along with a cold joint of beef. She also produced a bottle of ale. "This is for later, sir," she said, with an awkward curtsey.

Thomas smiled at her attempted etiquette. "You're both a welcome sight." "Is a pipe safe?" Gannett asked, reaching for his leather tobacco pouch.

Nodding, Thomas said. "We're downwind." He ate most of the bacon, stowing the scones and jam for his dinner. "Is Lady Mariana well?" he asked, wiping bacon grease on the thick grass.

"Aye, sir," Gannett replied, a wreath of blue smoke enveloping his long, bony head. "She's well, but in fear for you. The Chief Constable was at the house again yesterday."

"I know. I saw his coach. Did you overhear anything?"

"I did," Abbie piped up.

"Speak up, lass, what did you hear?"

"Lady Portia said she fears you're dead," Abbie reported. "Most distraught, she looked. Told the Chief Constable, ye didn't kill no Ian Cluny. Said it brave-like, e'en though Lady Chasteen and Sir John were in the room."

"They're back, then," Thomas mused. He'd watched the infamous pair drive off the day before. He hadn't seen them return.

"Aye." Gannett slid his pipe to the corner of his mouth. "They were to Paddy's, Patrick Stephenson."

Abbie plopped down on a smooth stone, her little face red under her frilled white cap. "Something ain't right at the house."

Thomas, alarmed, turned to her. "What do you mean?"

The girl hugged her arms around her upper body. "It 'appened in the night. I were in the scullery. I 'eard noises—from the back of the house. That old turret room. I crept up there. The door was unlocked. It 'in't never been unlocked. Least not as long as I can remember."

When excited, Abbie forgot her fine diction.

Gannett nodded. "She's telling the truth. The wife and I heard noises, too. I went up there. It's sure unlocked. I went to Lady Portia. She don't recall it ever being unlocked."

Abbie, her eyes round with fright, crossed herself. "'Er Ladyship says it's best locked for it 'arbors evil memories," She inched closer to Gannett. "We 'eard spirits of the long dead."

Thomas wanted to say *nonsense,* but thought better of it. Abbie, a superstitious little soul, had her own beliefs on the matter of spirits. He wondered if taking her into confidence had been a good idea.

Thomas gazed down at the house. The room in question jutted from the back of the house, seemingly clinging onto the stone wall by unseen claws. Its slit windows were boarded. Something turned in the dark corners of his mind. He faced Gannett. "You say Lady Portia has no idea who unlocked the room."

"Aye," Gannett replied.

Abbie, flinching, darted a shuddering gaze at the house. "Lady Portia thinks Lady Vesta and Sir John have a evil scheme." The little maid began to cry softly, rocking her slight body back and forth.

"What do you mean?" Alarm threaded through him. "A scheme? What sort of scheme?"

Abbie bolted up from her rock perch and rolled back her sleeve, displaying angry bruises. "I seen Sir John listening at Lady Portia's door. He saw me, caught my arm and near squeezed off the flesh." Abbie wept louder.

"Hush, gel, would you have the law down on us?" Gannett warned.

Not to be squelched, Abbie continued. "We dare not step foot downstairs. Not like we once did, but creep about like mice. Even lady Mariana and Lady Portia."

"'Tis true," Gannett confirmed, his honest face creased with concern. "The fact, sir, we have no position atall. I would go, save for Lady Portia and Lady Mariana. Miz Hooks would sooner enter her grave than leave them two alone in that place."

The scene at the dining table the night Lady Vesta upbraided Lady Portia burned in Thomas's mind.

God's teeth! What a state of affairs. The two servants returned down the hill. After Gannett and Abby left, Thomas studied the ill-reputed tower room. He knew it led to an ancient dungeon. Its peak spiraled above the main roof's highest point. One couldn't enter it from the outside.

Fury flashed in his heart that John Desmond had crushed the maid's frail arm. If the man ever touched Mariana, he swore he'd kill him. Perhaps Abbie had exaggerated about hearing noises, she being a superstitious little creature. But Mrs. Hooks had heard noises, too. She'd sent Gannett to investigate. Why unlock a barred door to an unused chamber holding nothing more than pigeon droppings and vermin?

The food satisfied his hunger. Lying back, he enjoyed the warm sun. After dark, he'd go again to the Cluny cottage. Cluny's father, Gildun, an influential farmer on the estate, had many tenants under him. Unrest stirred in men like Gildun, who worked in uncertain times with tillable land being turned into leas for His Lordship's more lucrative enterprise, cattle and sheep.

* * *

Toward mid-afternoon, Thomas roused and moved to watch the house. Sir John walked to the stable, and then emerged, riding his horse. The silver fittings on John's steed flashed in the bright sunlight as he rode into the wooded park where Ian Cluny's body had been discovered. Approximately two hours later, judging by the sun's descent, John rode back into the paddock. Afterwards, he lingered in the stables.

A short time later, Gannett brought the carriage around, and Lady Vesta boarded. The carriage sped off in the direction of the village. No sight of Mariana or Lady Portia.

As night drew on, Thomas watched the turret room with a new thread of interest to see if a light burned there. Nothing.

After nightfall, he donned the beard, the tunic and the hat. He started toward Gildun's cottage. "I would speak with Master Gildun," he said to the frazzled woman who answered the door.

"Father," she said, surprised. "I don know ye. Where is Father Francis?"

"Don't be alarmed, daughter," Thomas said. "I'm from another parish. It's Gildun I would speak with."

The woman's black eyes narrowed. "He 'in't 'ere. What parish, Father?"

"The north," Thomas said. "When do you expect Gildun?"

"Aye, not this long night," the woman said suspiciously, peering hard at Thomas.

"Be at peace, daughter. God be with you." Thomas couldn't hurry away fast enough.

Fog roiled into the low places from the east, and rough grasses slapped his breeches, as he hurried through the swirling mist toward Thornywilde. He was well out of breath. Silence shrouded the place when he reached the castle. He froze. A furtive sound - like crunching pebbles - ominous.

He stared hard. The damnable fog. He saw something - a shadow's glide, someone - a boy. The youngster didn't see him. The boy kept glancing behind as though someone followed. Waiting until the lad came abreast, Thomas reached out, seizing the lad's arm. The boy's free arm swung, rounding on Thomas like a lion, fighting and clawing.

"Ye wee fool!"

Thomas knew that voice. *Ena Guthre.*

Clapping his hands over the lad's mouth, Thomas pulled him down. Pinning the lad with his body, Thomas held him fast. Snaking out his free hand, he caught the woman's ankles. Tripped, she stumbled forward. He couldn't hold them both. The boy broke free and ran.

Wriggling free, Ena jumped to her feet, the shimmer of steel in her hand. She held a long knife. Swinging viciously, the blade barely missed Thomas's head. He ducked, squatting in the tall grass. Lying still, not daring to breathe, he waited for her to come closer.

"Aye, who are you would dare harm a poor lad?"

Lying still, Thomas waited. She swept through the grass, closer and closer. The dim moon highlighted the blade. He waited for the perfect moment. Sprinting up, he seized her hand holding the weapon, pushed her back and pinned her to the balustrade. He thrust her other arm behind her back, twisting wickedly. She groaned. He could break her arm easily. The boy returned in the dark, and began kicking Thomas's legs.

"Call off your hellion, or I'll slice your head from your shoulders," he hissed against her neck, so close, he smelled her fear.

"It's enough," Ena cried to the boy. "Do as he says."

Thomas dared not move the blade from her neck. "Send the boy on his way. I have business with you."

"Do as he says," she ordered the lad. He remarked her coolness as she spoke to the boy.

The tall grass swayed with whisking sounds. Seconds later, a horse whickered, then thudding hooves sounded in the night's stillness as the beast galloped away.

Thomas pulled Ena around to face him. She was a strong woman, but she didn't resist.

"A priest! What do you want of me?" Her eyes, over-bright behind a harlequin's mask in the misty light, narrowed.

For answer, he jerked the mask from her face. "You lurk in darkness, dressed in black. Why?"

His slouch hat fell.

Arching her neck, she faced him. "You, Thomas O'Geary! I thought you'd swung from the rope." She spat at his feet. "Thomas O'Geary." She laughed, more a sneer. "No one will admit you into the house. You—a hunted man, and you accuse me!"

Pushing the knife against her throat, he hissed. "Why are you here?" He twisted the sharp blade against her throat until she cried out.

"You corrupt, filthy man. You are like all the rest—trying to frighten me. I have done nothing wrong. It's no crime to visit a house I once called home."

Tightening his grasp on her arms, he slid the knife across her throat, its blade scraping skin. "The truth or I draw blood."

She managed a mangled sound. "You've dealt with me over the years, Thomas O'Geary. I'm not your enemy." Her voice took on a cajoling tone. "I lived here once when my cousin came to Sir Charles as his bride." Ena lowered her voice.

He strained to hear her words. "Catherine bore no child." Lowering her voice still more, she rasped. "Mariana is a harlot's babe. A common wench bore her. The babe was brought to appease a dying woman."

For the briefest moment, her lies tempted him. Coming to his senses, he matched the venom in Ena's voice. "You lie. Mariana isn't a harlot's child."

Ena grunted.

"Where are the paintings you stole from Canady?"

She laughed. "For a price, I'll tell you . . . only if you release me, and take the knife away." Her voice throbbed with malice.

The darkness of the night, holding her with a knife angered Thomas. He felt the fool, and felt still, this woman mustn't best him. What could he do with her? Kill her? He was no murderer. He slid the knife against her throat, gently this time. "I repeat, where are the paintings you stole from Canady?"

"The paintings," she began. "Thomas, let me go. I'm no threat to you."

He released his hold. "The knife is mine," he said. She didn't move away, but stood before him, rubbing her wrists. "What are you really doing here?"

She laughed again. "One question at a time."

"The paintings, then."

From the darkness, stinging powder laced his face.

"Aaaaaaaaagh!"

He'd fallen for the oldest trick in the book.

Chapter 39

*C*riminals, Jagger mused. How stealthily they moved, like vermin among the populace, ever vigilant, ever ready to deceive, ever ahead of their captors. Thomas O'Geary, the worst of the lot. Playing the good artist, then murdering Cluny.

Cluny, he laughed wryly. The man needed murdering for the men he'd massacred on Cormac Hill. A great puzzle, though, the ties that bound the artist and the Ribbonman. If he knew that, he'd know where to find O'Geary.

Today, he played a hunch. He'd ordered the police coach for investigative work. Drawing on his jacket, he stepped outside. "To the Norris Registry," he called to the driver.

The coach rumbled over the cobbles, drawing to a stop before the modest, whitewashed house that served as the local domestic registry. You needed a domestic, you called upon Mrs. Norris. You needed a gardener, you called upon Mrs. Norris.

Today, he needed answers.

Mrs. Norris opened the door. A florid flush washed over the woman's face. She blurted. "Inspector Jagger, is there a problem with your housekeeper?"

"None," he replied blandly.

The woman's heavy bosom and broad forehead seemed to fill the narrow entryway.

"I'm forgetting my manners, I am," she blathered. "Leaving you on the stoop. Do come in." Bustling ahead into the low-ceiling, cluttered room, she pushed aside a number of pillows on the brocade sofa, disturbing a large yellow cat. The cat arched its back, yawned, and settled again.

"Would you like tea?"

"Thank you, no. I'm here about one of your domestics."

She frowned. "My word, these people aren't *mine*, you know. I simply try to match them with employers."

Apparently coming to her senses that he was the county Chief Constable, the highest police official in Lough Glendelough, she coughed nervously, and lowered her voice. "Is there a police problem with someone I've recommended? I can only rely on what they tell me," she said defensively.

She'd not invited him to sit down. They both stood awkwardly staring at the reclining cat.

"It's difficult to know a person's complete background," he said with confidence, for he doubted any in Lough Glendelough knew of his own past troubles with the actress. "Where can I find Harriet Blackwell, the domestic who goes up occasionally to Thornywilde?"

Flustered, Mrs. Norris reddened. "Oh, dear, I am remiss. Please, sit here Chief Constable Jagger." She indicated a chintz-covered chair with bulging cushions, obviously the cat's bed. Comfortably settled across from him on the sofa, Mrs. Norris cleared her throat and began speaking hurriedly.

"When Mrs. Blackwell is in the village, she stays at various houses letting rooms, nothing fancy, you understand, and seldom at one place long." Mrs. Norris reached, stroking the cat snuggled beside her. It retaliated by latching a claw onto her bombazine sleeve. She jerked her arm back. "Naughty puss."

"About Harriet Blackwell," he prompted.

Mrs. Norris's brows angled in concentration. "She's a very hard worker, I assure you."

Jagger sighed. His job weighed heavily at times. He should be above this cat and mouse questioning best left to those on the beat. He'd once held the administrative position better suited to his training and experience. With an inward curse at fate's ill hand, he faced the woman before him, fixing an unpleasant frown at both Mrs. Norris and the cat.

"Precisely which house letting rooms did Mrs. Blackwell last occupy?"

"It were on King's Row East. But it'll do you no good to go there. Mrs. Blackwell came by two days ago, said her daughter was ill and needed help...." Mrs. Norris' voice trailed.

"Where can I find the daughter?"

Her bosom heaving, the woman gestured. "Somewhere north, maybe near KinKerry. I haven't a firm idea. The daughter is none of the registry affair."

Further questions yielded nothing of importance. Jagger stood, astonished at the number of golden cat hairs attached to his dark trousers.

Mrs. Norris followed him to the door and out onto the stoop, nattering all the way that she'd contact him the moment she heard anything from Harriet Blackwell.

An hour later, his feet burning from a tour of rooming houses along the bayside, he'd found little of importance about Harriet Blackwell. True, she'd been a tenant at several rooming houses, yes, she always paid her bill before leaving.

One proprietor denounced her as reckless with his property for smashing a valuable lamp. Other than that, Harriet Blackwell seemed a sprite lost in the night.

Since it was coming on noon, Jagger met the coach at the corner and rode back to the station to let Whitcomb off for lunch. Leaving an underling deputy in charge, Jagger took the police coach to his house for luncheon.

He arrived back at headquarters before Whitcomb. When the man returned, Jagger sent him to the other side of the bay to inquire further after Harriet Blackwell.

It was going on four o'clock before Whitcomb returned to headquarters. His boots were dusty, his expression weary.

Jagger looked up over a cup of stout tea. "What did you learn?"

"The Blackwell woman is well known along the back streets, sir. Not a pleasant sort, I can assure you. But those of her acquaintance knew that Mrs. Hooks, the cook at Thornyilde, preferred Mrs. Blackwell for extra domestic work when the need arose."

Jagger nodded. "And?"

"None seems to know her present whereabouts, sir. It's been her way to come to the village at times, work for a while, and then disappear to where ever she comes from."

Jagger settled his cup onto its saucer. "The Blackwell woman has a daughter. Did you learn where I can reach this daughter?"

Whitcomb nodded negatively. "I was most discreet, sir, when I asked about the daughter. None had heard of her, but one house did remember that Mrs. Blackwell has a grandson, for she brought him to the village on occasion. This would have been three or four years back if the proprietor's memory served him right."

"That will be all, Whitcomb."

"Thankee, sir."

After Whitcomb left Garda Headquarters, Jagger slammed his fist against the desk. The tea in the fat glazed pot still hot, he poured a cup. The Blackwell woman had served at Thornywilde the night Lord Charles Belmont took gravely ill. Perhaps important, perhaps not. Bad mushrooms. Bad mushrooms thought to have been brought to the house by O'Geary.

Did a link exist tying the poisoning to Ian Cluny's murder?

Baffling.

One fact glared. Thomas O'Geary's personal knife had been discovered beneath Ian Cluny's lifeless body. A knife matching the set Whitcomb discovered in the artist studio.

Sipping tea, he shuffled papers aside rapidly, choosing one particular letter—the official response from Home Office. He scanned the official order from his superior giving him permission to arrest Thomas O'Geary for the murder of Ian Cluny. An arrest to hopefully placate the black hearts of other Ribbonmen ready to take up arms to avenge Ian's savage murder. A nasty murder. Knifed like a stuck pig.

But Cluny had been an evil man, surely responsible for the three dead policemen on Cormac Hill, even though Lady Mariana had not identified him. Her Ladyship's involvement remained guarded. No public announcement at this time. Home Office's strict orders.

Jagger smiled to himself. He'd draw Lady Mariana forth at the trial. There were rumors she and O'Geary had a strong friendship. Likely, they were lovers. What better ploy—pit her testimony against her lover. Lovers shared confidences. O'Geary had motive to kill Cluny if he thought the man a threat against his beloved.

Jagger withdrew Cluny's autopsy report. The victim had been stabbed in the back, either by surprise or by someone he trusted. A chunk of roasted beef had lodged in Ian's throat, possibly choking him, or causing him to gasp for breath as he was attacked, likely rendering him unable to defend himself. While in panic from near choking to death, the unknown assailant then plunged the broad blade into the man's back piercing his heart. If that were not enough, the killer then slit Cluny's throat.

After cutting the man's throat, the king's coroner reported the knife then inflicted six vicious stab wounds. After the blood bath, the knife had been removed then placed beneath the torso.

From the crime scene in the wood, Ian had poached one of Thornywilde's beefs, dressed it and cooked it over a makeshift spit a good distance from the mansion. An act of utter treason and disregard for those in the great house. Also, an act devoid of any fear of discovery. Why? This in particular disturbed Jagger—the blatant woodland feast. Had the man no fear of being caught? The man's last meal spread on a strip of homespun coverlet.

Whitcomb had gone to all the estate's tenants and farmers, questioning everyone carefully. None would admit to owning the strip of coverlet. In fact, it was very much like all such hand-loomed textiles in many of the cottages.

Home Office had demanded a speedy arrest. Jagger had complied. Only O'Geary escaped. Escaped with the court poised to bring in a guilty verdict. The farmers and tenants wanted vengeance. They wanted O'Geary found guilty of murder, and hung.

Chapter 40

peculiar day dawned. Scant sky peeked between heavy clouds that turned a curious yellowish hue as the morning wore on. This unnatural light hovered over the apple trees casting the gnarled branches a sharp lime color.

Otherworldly, Mariana thought, looking at the peculiarly colored sky. Fat raindrops pelted the mullioned parlor windows. She put her book aside at the click of footsteps in the hall. Her pent breath expelled quickly. It was only Abbie.

"We're taking a cold lunch," Abbie said. "Mrs. Hooks is to bed with a furious toothache. It come on 'er sudden. The rain, she said."

"Where's Her Ladyship and John?"

Abbie shook her head. "I don't know. They went out."

* * *

"Damn the rain!" Thomas, soaked to the skin, pulled the slouch hat lower, water sluicing in a steady stream from the sodden brim as he ran for the narrow cave he'd discovered up the mountain. He settled on the cave's dusty floor, his breeches wet, sticking to his body. Mayhap, the rain wouldn't last long. His thoughts as dismal as the weather, he sat there, his back against cold stone.

He'd learned nothing during his vigil in these lonely hills. Not even why Ena Guthre and her son lurked at Thornywilde that night. Too, he feared someone would see Gannett during his sporadic visits to the mountain. For safety, they no longer met in person. Gannett left supplies in the cave. He'd been this day, for there was fresh bread and two bottles of ale.

The long afternoon passed with him wet, cold, and miserable. The rain had stopped and a striking rainbow stretched from glen to glen. He started down from his vantage point when a carriage drew up before the Erin Rose. Blast! The Garda Siochana. The police. Jagger emerged from the police coach and hurried inside the inn. Inspector Whitcomb alighted last, pacing beneath the inn's deep eaves.

Thomas swore. Too dangerous to fetch his horse. *Bless heaven!* Charging down the road from Thornywilde, a chaise sloshed across ruts throwing muddy spray as it rounded the bend toward the village. Gannett, swathed in a flapping black slicker sat upon the box. Who from Thornywilde traveled this foul day, and at such reckless speed?

Jagger emerged from the inn. Both police officers scrambled into the coach, setting off at a rapid pace following Thornywilde's coach.

The immediate area safe, Thomas sloshed to the lea above his cave, and mounted the borrowed gelding from Thornywilde's paddock. Urging the animal forward, he kept distance behind both coaches.

Ahead, Gannett reined before the vicar's cottage. Mariana stepped down from the chaise, popped open an umbrella as large as a black cloud and hurried to the parsonage door. Perhaps she needed spiritual counseling. Thomas's gut told him differently.

The Gardai continued on to police headquarters.

To keep out of sight, Thomas rode down the embankment beneath Lower Kelly Street Bridge, stopping the horse in the deep gorge where he had a clearer view of the vicar's house. The wet priest's clothing chafed. Turning back toward the hills, he rode to the ruins of Old Madge's cottage. He'd seen activity there some days past. Perhaps she'd returned from Dublin.

An air of heaviness hung about the place as Thomas's mount cantered into the yard. The cottage stones supported a thin overhead thatch, as though someone had fashioned a temporary shelter. Old Madge was nowhere about. He mustn't tarry here—too dangerous. Back at his camp, he waited until dark.

The night drew on, foggy and misty from the recent rain. He threaded his way down the hill to the great house, using caution, should Ena lurk in the dark. She'd foiled him once. He vowed she'd never do so again. He passed the stables without mishap. Voices from within told him the groomsmen were inside.

Ahead, light fanned outward in a thin arc from the kitchen windows. Someone approached. Catching his breath, Thomas slunk against the stone wall, then expelled a sigh of relief. Gannett, a lantern in his hand, made his way toward the sculleries. He stopped, stamping mud from his boots.

"Gannett, it's I, Thomas. Make no sound."

"Aye, sir, where are you?"

"Here." Thomas inched from his place of concealment.

"Aye, sir, if you've come for supper, it's cold from the larder."

"Food would be welcome," Thomas said, "but it's information I seek."

"Come inside," Gannett said. "My missus suffers a toothache. I'll set out meat crocks."

Thomas nodded, following Gannett into the older part of the house, the warren of unused rooms from ancient days.

Thomas waited. Gannett returned with food "Where's Sir John?" Thomas asked once he'd satisfied his hunger.

"In the village, sir. A ball at one of the estates."

"His mother and Mariana are with him?"

"Aye, both."

Thomas's heart clutched. Surely, Mariana harbored no tender feelings for the dandy. Yet who truly knew a woman's heart? Desmond was handsome, polished, and titled—a catch for any woman. No matter that he lived under his mother's roof and thumb. Willing the jealous stab away, he said, "Jagger and Whitcomb were at the Erin Rose earlier."

"Aye, sir, they believe you're hereabouts. They ride through the hills."

"I know. I see them."

Gannett had been at Thornywilde many years. However, Thomas was unsure if the man's tenure went as far back as Lady Catherine's marriage, and Ena Guthre's presence.

"Do you know the woman who served Lady Catherine, one Ena Guthre?"

Gannett appeared puzzled. "Nay, that was before me time here."

"I want to warn you, and the others in the house," Thomas whispered. "The woman was here, she and her grandson. She attacked me on the grounds. I don't know what she wants, but I fear it's harm she means, especially to Lady Mariana. You will keep a sharp eye."

"Aye, sir," Gannett said, his eyes wide in alarm.

Thomas left for the cave, weary of hiding and clandestine searches that turned up nothing about Ian Cluny's killer. Ena Guthre was no fool. She realized that, with the right word to the right person, he'd be arrested. However, the right word from him, and she'd go up for art theft. He wondered about Mr. Canady. Was the man in prison? His thoughts rambled as he trekked upward through the rock and damp gorse. Mariana had asked him about Italia. Bound by an oath, he couldn't tell her what he knew. Her father was Italia. His Lordship had demanded secrecy. Thomas knew His Lordship's gambling debts took the estate's profits. The enormous sums of money selling the popular paintings, his *dabblings,* His Lordship had called them, kept the place fractionally solvent.

To protect his identity from his creditors, His Lordship had devised the brilliant idea of selling his paintings through his old art teacher, Martin Canady.

The completed paintings were passed to Ena Guthrie, who brought them to London to Thomas. How the Guthre woman figured into this complicated plot, Thomas didn't know. There must be an attachment to Ena in His Lordship's past. Was she a former lover? Or, perhaps the mother of a child born on the other side of the blanket. Was that child Mariana?

His Lordship had been a dapper dresser, a brilliant conversationalist with quick wit, welcomed in every great house, who hid his weakness with the bottle, and with cards. His rakish escapades masked his God-given artistic talents. His work sang. Once one viewed Italia's work, the viewer became astounded, the imagery so magnificent one could almost hear the rush of surf, view the turn of a bird's wing in flight, or become lost in the brilliant clouds. He'd demanded perfection. He was a genius. And now, he lay dead in the churchyard. And Lady Vesta inherited Thornywilde. It should be time Mariana knew the truth about her father.

Had Lady Vesta Chasteen played the sly fox that night at dinner, and poisoned His Lordship under everyone's nose? Lady Vesta, an ambitious woman, who lived above her means, had a reputation for leaving bills unpaid until forced to settle. She owned extensive lands north of Thornywilde's estate. With Thornywilde added to her properties, her rents would double.

Thomas straightened his shoulders, knelt, and then crawled into his cramped cave.

Chapter 41

homas spent the deep hours of dark listening at the cottages. He heard rumors and threats aplenty, but no evidence to who murdered Ian Cluny. It appeared the tenants had no idea who had killed one of their own. He listened to threats and grumblings against His Lordship. The man's death had put his tenants in a problematic position—they had no one to blame.

He made his way back to his hill long before the men working the estate rose from their straw beds and went about their jobs. A light caught his attention. Light in the west tower. His heart quickened. Who'd venture into that infamous chamber at such a dead hour?

He had time to investigate before daybreak. He turned and started toward the house, his priest's robes flapping. He neared the paddock. No lights yet in the stables. Stumbling, he crashed into a water trough. *"Saints preserve me!"* he roared as two groomsmen and a sleepy stableboy rushed outside.

The trough held freezing cold water. Thomas sat up, leaves in his hair and dripping wet. Quickly, he pulled the soggy hat low over his eyes.

The head groomsman, hands on his hips, leaned so close over the trough that Thomas saw the whites of the man's eyes. "Aye, too much drink, Father, ye bloody fool. Get your hide from my beast's water and go sleep it off. And, ye a priest, ye bloody hypocrite."

Back on the hill, he stripped off the wet breeches and linen shirt, draping them on a rock just inside the cave entrance. He settled on the cave's dirt floor for what remained of the night. How could he endure? He'd learned nothing, and saw no favorable end to his exile. He'd give himself up to Jagger if it weren't for the rope. God's teeth, he couldn't die for a murder he didn't commit. He slapped at something crawling across his leg. Listless and tired, he didn't move to examine what crawled, maybe a lizard, a harmless gray spider, or a fallen bat. The cave was full of them.

Damn Ian Cluny and his murderer. In the eyes of the estate's simple people, Cluny had taken on the persona of a saint.

Chapter 42

*E*na found the boy at Lough Conor by the red gate as they'd planned. "Grandmama," he cried running to her, burying his face in her skirts. "I didna do good, did I?"

She looked at him with distaste. The blood of cowards flowed in his veins. A weak lad, like Sirabell, his mother and like Lady Catherine. No amount of hard tasks or harsh words toughened him.

"Did you bring bread?" she asked.

He nodded.

"Go wash in the lough, and I'll fix our breakfast."

The lad walked away, dragging his feet, his thin shoulders slumped forward.

She struck flint to the small tower of dry grasses and twigs. The flame caught up, and in minutes a merry fire blazed. She set the iron griddle on carefully stacked stones.

When they'd eaten, she ordered the lad, "Take the horses higher where the grass is deep."

He lingered, fingering a jacket button. "I'm afeared, Grandmama, when you go away at night."

"Ye must be brave, lad," she said, annoyed. "Ye want to go back to the bottle shop?"

He winced as though struck. "Nay, I'd die first. 'E beat me everyday."

"Then, see to the horses." She thought a moment. "See who hides on the other hill." She'd seen a horse and it wasn't the policeman.

Timothy's thin face brightened. "It's 'im, the guvnor, he is, 'im that buys our supper in London town."

"Bosh, boy, do as I bid or I'll take the cane to ye."

Thomas O'Geary! Ena mused, lying back in the grass, lighting her pipe. A stroke of pure luck. O'Geary with a price on his head. He'd get the gallows. That left only Martin Canady, the milk-livered worm who handled His Lordship's paintings. He must die, too. Debtors gaol was too good for Canady. He needed a knife between his shoulders.

"Lady Catherine!" Ena sneered. Catherine—the interfering witch. Charles Belmont had wanted her, Ena, until Catherine had invited both Charles and Martin to one of her summer balls. Charles became besotted with the witless Catherine.

Too, he'd paid for his unfaithfulness to her through the years. Paid, and paid dearly.

His money had kept Ena. A loyal man - only a loyal man would honor her financially for the duties rendered to Catheine.

Only, the foolish weak wasteling had fallen to gambling. He had no talent for cards. He was a hapless dreamer at business, too. His talent was his eye for color, form, and scale as he dabbled with his paints. With her hand to guide him, they could've lived regally.

But even with Catherine long dead, the fool had continued to shun her. When he hid his talent from the world, she assisted him. Italia, the fanciful name. Charles grew smug when his painting brought in fortunes. Fortunes he had squandered.

Then, he'd become betrothed to that maggot of a woman, Lady Vesta Chasteen. He'd died before Ena could take his life.

Reaching for a twig, Ena held it to the fire and relit her dead pipe. How had their halcyon youthful days come to this? Ena flung the pipe to the ground, beating its dead ashes into the earth. Disjointed thoughts threatened her sanity. She closed her eyes. How dare Charles! How dare he take feckless scheming Lady Vesta to wife. He had died before Lady Vesta landed him at the altar. She must die, and that churlish son of hers. Thomas, too.

This day before the sun set, Ena vowed to take Timothy to the almshouse. She'd leave him there.

Sirabell taking to her sickbed had burdened her with the boy long enough. If Sirabell wanted him, let her fetch him.

Tonight, Ena vowed to spill Vesta Chasteen's blood—then, Mariana Alice Belmont. And Thomas. Yes, Thomas. Only he must die after Mariana. The way it must be - the only way to lay the past to rest. If

O'Geary were fool enough to interfere, hunted like a jackal, as he was, he'd not escape the dagger in her stocking. He'd die before the others.

Chapter 43

"*W*here's Sir John?"

Abbie flinched under the force of Lady Vesta's gaze. "'E left, Your Ladyship."

"He should've told me," Her Ladyship muttered, pulling on her gloves and checking her bonnet's angle in the hall mirror. "Don't stand there, you, lack-a-day. Get to your chores. Get busy."

Abbie turned to scuttle away.

Lady Portia called to Abbie.

Lady Vesta barked out an order. "Bring my velvet bonnet and gray gloves. I'm going for a drive."

Abbie, her eyes wide, her bottom lip trembling, didn't know whom to obey. "Aye, Your Ladyship," she said to Lady Vesta. "The carriage is out. Gannett drove Lady Mariana into the village."

"Quit whining like a ninny. I can handle a horse as well as the next person. Have one of the stable drones saddle a suitable mount. You, Portia, I was looking for you. Come take the air with me."

"But-"

"I insist," Lady Vesta demanded. "I don't expect you to ride a horse. We'll take the cabriolet. I won't take no for an answer."

Proper instructions were sent to the stables. Shortly, a groomsman brought around the cabriolet, hitched with Lady Portia's favorite mare, Dimples. The man held the reins, standing beside the seat.

"Your services aren't needed," Lady Vesta said to him. "We're merely taking a short run to the Erin Rose. I'm sure Lady Portia can manage her favorite steed. You'd like to drive her, wouldn't you?" the woman said to Portia.

"Well . . . I usually sit; I don't stand."

"Of course, you may sit."

Portia, muffled in blue wool, nodded.

They reached the Erin Rose without mishap. Lady Portia wondered what the invitation was all about. She felt extremely uneasy, following Lady Vesta into the inn. "Have your tea," Lady Vesta said, pausing in the inn door.

"But-"

"I'll ride a bit," Vesta said, cutting across Portia's words. "Wait here for me."

Unceremoniously dismissed, the older woman sat at a comfortable table overlooking the hills. She smiled when the young serving girl placed a pot of stout tea, and a generous plate of seed cake before her. Really charming being here, she thought. The dining hall, warm from a great fire, the surrounding buzz of conversation companiable, even though she wasn't a part of it. She prayed Lady Vesta wouldn't drive Dimples too hard. She looked up as a woman entered the inn. The woman, dressed in country attire, draped in a long shawl and wearing a felt bonnet pulled low, looked around the room, spotted Portia, and then approached the table.

Portia blinked, looking up at the gaunt woman. There seemed something familiar about her. Startlingly, it came to her at once. *"Ena Guthre?"*

"You're surprised, Lady Portia," Ena said, pulling out a chair, and sitting down.

Portia, trembling, felt as doomed as a mouse in one of Mrs. Hooks's larder traps. "Why are you here?" she whispered.

"You aren't pleased to see me?" Ena chuckled, a disarming sound.

"W. . . would . . . you like some . . . er, tea?" Portia said, her hands fluttering. She pressed both hands to her bosom, her breath coming in constricted gasps.

"We haven't time." Ena motioned toward the door. "My grandson, Timothy, is waiting. There are things you and I must discuss that aren't suitable for his tender ears."

"I don't understand." The cold cast in Ena's eyes frightened Portia. She knew Ena possessed a vile temperament. Portia had experienced that temper when this far-removed cousin had attended Catherine. Best to remain calm. Whatever could Ena possibly want? She hadn't long to wonder.

"You and I shall take a ride in your fancy cabriolet," Ena said, standing and drawing the cloak over her shabby gown.

"But . . . uh . . . that's impossible. Lady Vesta has the cabriolet." She didn't trust the look on Ena's face. "What of your . . . your grandson?"

"Ah, dear Timothy. I shall buy his dinner as we leave. He can take his time eating. You and I shan't be gone long."

"But," Lady Portia protested, "I've not finished my tea."

Ena's eyes narrowed. "We shall order fresh when we return."

"But-"

Portia's protests fell on deaf ears. Casting a desperate glance about the dining room, and not seeing Mr. Fitzwilliam, the smiling serving girl, or anyone she knew, Portia said, "I can't leave; Lady Vesta is to meet me here."

"You await Lady Vesta?" Ena scoffed. "I daresay that willful person hasn't given you another thought once she rode off."

"Rode off?" Portia blinked, and took a good look at Ena. She didn't appear particularly dangerous—paler, somewhat pathetic.

"I have news of Mariana," Ena said, lowering her voice.

"Mariana?" Gannett had driven her niece into the village. "What news? Has there been an accident?" Portia clutched the ruffle at her throat.

"She's safe. We'll discuss her." Ena took Portia's arm, helping her up from her chair.

Portia cast a desperate glance about the dining room. "I don't see Mr. Fitzwilliam. I must settle my bill."

"It shall be taken care of," said Ena, taking Lady Portia's cloak and draping it around the older woman's shoulders.

Outside, Portia looked around. "Where's your grandson?" she blathered in a high-pitched voice. The cabriolet stood ready. Dimples tossed her head, neighing cheerfully at Portia, awaiting the usual carrot.

At that moment, three Garda policemen rode into the inn yard. The men dismounted, giving cursory nods to Ena and Portia.

Ena released Portia's arm. "A minute, luv," she said hurriedly, starting toward the paddock at a rapid trot. She did not return.

Chapter 44

*T*homas had settled against a lichen-covered rock to survey Thornywilde. Strange goings on at the castle this day. Lady Vesta and Lady Portia had taken the cabriolet to the Erin Rose. They went inside. Vesta emerged moments later, and got into a hired coach with John Desmond. Thomas would know that white head from any distance. He recognized Ena Guthre's tall form leaving the inn with Lady Portia. Ena had left abruptly when three mounted policemen arrived at the inn. Most confusing.

Why was Ena here? Her flimsy excuse of returning to the estate for nostalgic reasons made no sense. Damn the sneaky woman—she was a thief. She'd stolen valuable artwork that may have Martin Canady in the gaol.

Shifting, Thomas straightened his legs. He'd crouched for what seemed hours. It appeared nothing untoward was going on at the old mansion. He stood, shaking grass and leaves from his breeches. The breeches were going threadbare from constant wear. All of this had to end soon or he'd go mad. He trekked up the hill to the glen where he'd left the horse.

Later that night, he rode near the castle and tethered the horse in the wood. He slipped past the paddocks and barns, making his way toward the kitchen, where dim lights shone from within. The windows were too high to allow a view. Mrs. Hooks should be alone, if not abed. Oftentimes Gannett sat with her until the late hours. Taking a chance the scullery maid was fast asleep, he rapped softly at the kitchen door.

After a long interval, the sound of shuffling footsteps approached. Mrs. Hooks opened the door. Her mouth flew open. "Mr. O'Geary! Ye startled me so. Gannett said ye'd be wearing priest's robes. And, none so fine, eh?" she said looking at the holes in the knees of the breeks.

He hurried inside. "When do you expect Her Ladyship and Sir John?" he asked. "Where have they gone?"

"To Squire Stephenson's. They'll be home late. Sir John wished to stay over the night, but 'Er Ladyship refused." Doubt crossed Mrs. Hook's broad face. "Ye'll be hungry, sir."

"I haven't time. Gather some things. I'll take with me. You must fetch the key to the turret room."

She shuddered. "Why ever, sir? There's nothing there 'ceptin' the wind and dust. 'Tis an evil place. No God-fearing soul climbs them stairs. The auld 'uns tortured enemies there. Ye hear their cries on a windy night. Besides, Gannett nailed it shut. No key I'd fetch could help."

Thomas persisted, masking his impatience, "I need a crowbar, then. Where are Gannett's tools?"

Reluctantly, Mrs. Hooks lit a candle, and bade him follow. They wound their way through the storeroom corridors off the kitchen. In a room that appeared to have been used for a laundry, Mrs. Hooks opened a creaking door below the room's slit windows—windows cut in stone for arrows. Even these sculleries were fortified once. The cook removed two heavy, iron-prying bars from the cabinet. She stood, her arms folded over her chest.

"Lead me there."

"Ye mean I'm to go with ye?"

Back in the kitchen, she lit another candle, and started down a drafty passageway. She stopped before a steep set of stone steps leading upward.

"Go on," Thomas urged. Would the woman lose her nerve? She started up the stairs. He followed. Their footfalls disturbed roosting birds overhead. Squawks and anxious fluttering wings sounded. A nuisance being disturbed from rest, he thought. "Bring the light closer, Mrs. Hooks," he said, kneeling. Gannett had not only secured the door with iron nails, he'd wrapped the ancient hardware in massive chains set with a number of rusty locks.

Thomas pried at the locks. Surprisingly, they fell away easily. The heavy door swung inward.

Mrs. Hooks, candle aloft, exclaimed, "Declare and mercy, there be a bed on the floor."

Chapter 45

Two weeks later

"John is drinking constantly," Mariana complained to her aunt as they stood in the kitchen—practically prisoners after LadyVesta's orders. "He's forcing himself on me," Mariana whispered, lifting the kettle to pour over the fragrant tea leaves. The scullery maid stood over the wooden sink peeling potatoes. *Best, the servants heard little,* Mariana thought, keeping her voice low. "Her Ladyship wishes me to marry him for my inheritance from my mother. Despicable of them, since they have Thornywilde and all its holdings after my father willed it to her." Taking the tray with the tea things, Mariana bade Portia follow her into the dining room.

Aunt Portia sighed, looking around the room furtively as Mariana poured out. "You will never marry Sir John Desmond, conveniently or inconveniently," Portia said heatedly.

"I would die first."

"Don't fret, girl," Aunt Portia said "Let them have Thornywilde. Since the day your father wed Catherine, it's brought nothing but unhappiness."

* * *

February sped into March, with situations in the house unchanged. Mariana and Portia kept to their rooms as much as possible to avoid Vesta and John. Thomas hid on the hill, his position more dangerous each day.

The latter part of the week, Chief Constable Jagger made a surprise visit to the house, asking for Mariana.

"Lady Mariana," he began, closing the library door. "It's known Thomas O'Geary is in the hills. He's been seen. You've seen him, as well.

We'll catch him. It won't go well for him, should we surprise him, and he foolishly resists."

What did the inspector expect her to say—expose Thomas? A bead of perspiration pooled between Mariana's breasts, running down, dampening her shift. "I've told you time after time, I've no idea where Mr. O'Geary could be."

"Very good, m'lady." He gave her a false smile and an exaggerated bow.

After Jagger left the house, Mariana paced the floor. She'd have no peace until later, when Gannett would return from the hills with news of Thomas.

A rap sounded at the door. Startled, Mariana cried out.

Abbie entered and curtsied.

"What is it?"

"You have a visitor."

"Not Chief Constable Jagger again."

"No, m'lady. A lovely surprise. Ye're to go to the drawing room and close your eyes."

"What foolishness," Mariana muttered, straightening her skirts, then pinching her wan cheeks for color. She looked a wreck. She *was* a wreck. A hopeless wreck.

At the drawing room door, she closed her eyes at Abby's promptings. Not Thomas, she thought. Even he wouldn't come to the house in broad daylight.

She opened her eyes. "Kathleen!" Kathleen Stephenson, her dearest friend from the old days, stood in the center of the room.

Mariana ran into Kathleen's outstretched arms. "How dare you play tricks on me," she chided, once she'd drawn back from the fond embrace. Kathleen still held her hands at arm's length, gazing at her.

"How long have you been at Shannon Hall?"

"I arrived this morning," Kathleen said, releasing Mariana's hands, and clasping her around the waist as they moved toward the settee.

Joy flooded Mariana. "How I've missed you. And, how positively radiant you look."

Kathleen beamed, happy and adorable in her green riding habit and little hat, with its perky yellow feather.

Mariana burst into tears.

"My dear, whatever is wrong?" Kathleen knelt before the settee, taking Mariana's hands in her own. Leaning forward, Mariana sobbed on Kathleen's shoulder.

"You must tell me whatever's wrong," Kathleen began, once Mariana's tears stopped. "I'm so sorry about your dear father's death. Everything . . . uh . . . is all right?" Kathleen asked.

Mariana wondered how to tell Kathleen all that had happened. For the moment, she filled in the merest details. "There was a bad dish with mushrooms. He fell very ill. More so than the rest of us, for he'd been sick and away at Lady Vesta's estate." Mariana paused. She didn't know how much gossip had circulated about the troubles at Thornywilde. "There was a murder here in Thornywilde wood. Mr. O'Geary stands accused."

"How horrible," Kathleen sympathized, her countenance innocent. "Who was murdered?"

"Ian Cluny, one of the cottager's sons. A dreadful man, I've heard."

"How could Mr. O'Geary be involved?"

"One of his knives was found beneath the man's body. Tho' Mr. O'Geary swears the knife was stolen from his studio in the old summer house."

Kathleen's brows met over her short nose. Her green eyes wide, she confessed. "I've heard about the murder. My father-in-law told me. He told me, as well, that Mr. O'Geary escaped from Spillers Island."

"It's true. He's a fugitive. You're so kind to come," Mariana said, changing the subject.

"How could I stay away, my dear girl," Kathleen said, her bright eyes damp and threatening tears, "when my dearest friend in all the world is troubled. You must take heart. You mustn't allow any of this to trouble you unduly. Mr. O'Geary will be brought to justice, and found innocent."

"If only I could believe your rosy pronouncement," Mariana said, trying to appear hopeful.

"Now, tell me, you are in love?" Kathleen said. "I just know it."

"Perhaps I might be." Mariana blurted before giving the answer the question deserved.

"Sir John, is it! Sir John intimated as much to my father."

"Heavens, no!" Mariana spoke so forcefully Kathleen drew back.

"I'm glad," Kathleen replied once she found her voice. "Father isn't too impressed with him. Is he over his gunshot?"

"I think he was over it the moment it happened. But he was terribly wrong telling Patrick I'm in love with him. That's . . . that's . . . unforgivable."

"Sometimes men are foolish about such things," Kathleen said sagely. "I'm sure you'll set him straight. Just don't include my name."

"You needn't worry there," Mariana assured her friend. Taking a deep breath, she exhaled on a long sigh, smiling at Kathleen. How lovely it would be to lean her head on Kathleen's shoulder and tell her everything—about meeting Thomas in Dublin at her father's townhouse, about finding the murdered policemen and the likelihood that Ian Cluny had been the Ribbonman who'd slit the policemen's throats, about her escapades in Dublin, about Thomas hiding in the hills. She couldn't. Too dangerous. It was best to speak of superficial things. When the proper time came, she'd tell Kathleen everything.

"The baby?" Mariana demanded happily. "How old is he now?"

Kathleen laughed. "It's a she. And, she's two months old. I have named her Marileen after the two of us."

"How sweet. Why, it's a lovely name. Oh, Kathleen, I've missed you so." Mariana fought back another crying spell. How ironic it seemed. In the past, she'd been the strong one and Kathleen the weepy, dependent one. Now, their roles were reversed.

"Now, fess up," Kathleen urged playfully. "Who's the lucky man you *might* be in love with?"

"It's too soon to name him. Besides, he might not love me in return." That was a falsehood. Mariana knew Thomas loved her dearly. At least, he'd told her as much. But it would never work. It was all too complicated. Still, it felt divine being cherished by Thomas. What could she say for herself? She loved a man, a commoner, a commoner accused of murder. A commoner, at this moment, lurking in the hills above the estate.

"I can't stay," Kathleen said, glancing at the ormolu mantel clock. "I've only popped over to ensure father you're all right, you and Lady Portia. Father hasn't seen much of you or your aunt."

"I know," Mariana said, mindful of Thornywilde's awkward situation, where she and Lady Portia were relegated to the upper regions of the house.

If Kathleen had further questions, she masked them well. Instead, she pulled on her gloves. "My husband and I are going on holiday. When I return, I expect to find you ready to tell me all about your mysterious lover. I promise I'll badger you until you do."

Mariana moved to the bellcord. "Forgive me, I haven't ordered tea."

"No, I haven't time. My carriage is waiting. Do give me a kiss, sweet friend, and promise to see me soon. We shan't be on holiday long, then I'll be here at Shannon Hall."

"I promise, Kathleen." They made their good-byes with hugs and kisses.

The house seemed incredibly desolate after Kathleen left.

Mariana took lunch up to Aunt Portia and sat with her afterwards. Her aunt's thin face appeared thinner and much paler. Portia seldom stirred from her rooms other than to join Mariana in the kitchen at odd times. It was a fine day, warm for early March, with the riotous wind at bay. "Let's go for a walk. It'll do you good."

Aunt Portia shook her head. "I want to, but not today, perhaps, tomorrow." Aunt Portia seemed diminished from the daring woman who'd accompanied Mariana to the Dublin gaol.

"Tell me more about Kathleen."

Mariana proceeded to do so.

"So, she has a new baby."

"Yes. A girl this time."

Mariana talked until her aunt grew sleepy, then she called for Abbie to help Portia into bed.

Kathleen's visit inspired Mariana to write a note to Thomas. Gannett could deliver it the next time he saw Thomas. Perhaps she did truly love him, she mused, penning the letter. The letter written, she slipped it in into her sleeve and went down to the kitchen to look for Gannett.

Mrs. Hooks wasn't alone as Mariana had hoped. The cook and her helper were putting the finishing touches on a dessert tray. "Oh, m'lady, how can I help you?" Mrs. Hooks wiped her hands on her apron and led Mariana into the small workroom off the kitchen.

"Where is Gannett?"

"Aye, I'd best not say, Your Ladyship."

Of course, he'd not returned from the hills. Often times, he couldn't find Thomas and returned later, often after dark. "Have Gannett take this to Mr. O'Geary."

Mariana handed the letter to Mrs. Hooks. A noise sounded behind them. Mariana whirled. *John.*

He strode forward, planting himself between Mariana and the cook. "Give me that letter," he demanded of Mrs. Hooks.

"How dare you interfere with my correspondence," Mariana said, seething. Before Mrs. Hooks could hand the letter to Mariana, John wrenched it from her. Leaning against the worktable, he glanced at the letter with bleary eyes. After a snide glance at Mariana, he began to read aloud.

My friend,

I fear for your life. I know you are helpless in your present situation. Lift up a prayer for all of us. The days drag, as I know they do for you. Will this ever end and our lives return to normal? I risk your safety writing this, but I feel at times, I will lose my mind.

Yours Affectionately,

Mariana

"Whose safety do you risk?" John Desmond demanded.

Mariana cringed at the venom in his voice.

"How dare you read a private correspondence? Give the letter to me."

"And, signed, yours affectionately." John sneered, waving the thin sheet over her head, "You, the ice maiden, bear affection for someone. Whom I beg to know? Or, do I already know!"

"John, you are being unspeakably rude. I demand you return my letter."

He began reading the letter aloud again. Mariana lunged, tearing it from his hands. Darting forward, she ripped the page from his hand and cast it into the kitchen fireplace where it shriveled, shot up a bright yellow flame, and then disintegrated.

John stumbled forward, awkwardly grasping her, pulling her into his arms. She gasped, looking around. The larder door stood open. The kitchen maid, obviously inside. Mrs. Hooks stood, hands over her mouth, a horrified expression in her eyes.

"Follow your maid, woman. Your betters have the kitchen."

Mrs. Hooks fled into the larder, closing the door after her.

John squeezed Mariana tighter against his chest, so tight she felt her breath stop.

"You are a choice bit of flesh, my love." He ran his finger down the side of her face. His breath reeked of whiskey.

Lunging forward, Mariana planted her hands against his chest, pushing him back with all her strength. Unsteady, he lost his balance, toppled over, and struck his head on the corner of the kitchen worktable.

Stunned, and bent half over, he straightened, grabbing Mariana's arm, pulling her closer. An enormous bump emerged on John's forehead, blood trickling down his face. "See what you've done," he slurred, drawing his finger through the seeping blood.

Breathing hard, she pitched backward. John's erratic behavior terrified her. He gripped her harder still. Lady Vesta stepped into the kitchen and stopped, looking from John to Mariana. "Why is my luncheon late?" Realizing a struggle was in progress, a horrified expression spread across her face. "You're bleeding," she rasped, rushing to John's side. "Release him at once," she cried at Mariana. "What have you done to him?"

John weaved back from Mariana.

"An accident. Maman, don't treat me like a ninny," John whined.

"I demand to know what's going on." Her Ladyship's voice rose to a piercing shriek.

For a charged moment, Mariana thought John would turn on his mother. His expression reminded her of a cornered animal uncertain whether to attack or retreat. Unsteady on his feet, he hovered closer to Mariana, forcing her backward. She glanced upward. A heavy vase stood on the shelf above John's head. Lady Vesta pushed Mariana aside, reached up and touched her son's forehead. "You're bleeding. We must call-"

"Uh," Her Ladyship blinked. Gannett appeared in the doorway followed by Chief Constable Jagger.

Lady Vesta, silk skirts billowing, whirled to Jagger. "My son has been attacked!"

John lumbered forward, clutched her arm. "Enough, Maman!"

For once Her Ladyship obeyed him. Bewildered, and on a sob, she prattled. "That is, I regret, Chief Inspector, we cannot offer you luncheon." She gave Mrs. Hooks a cutting stare. "Our cook is behind schedule. Come to the library."

"What of me, Maman, my wound?"

"Have Mrs. Hooks attend to you until I can send for the doctor." Turning to Gannett, she ordered imperially. "Go for the doctor. My son has had an accident."

Jagger, hat in his hand, advanced. "Your Ladyship, this isn't a social call. Thomas O'Geary is in the area. If he should come to the house, get word to me immediately. He's a dangerous man."

"Of course, we'll contact you," Lady Vesta flung back at the inspector. "Do you think we'd harbor a dangerous killer?"

Mariana caught her breath. *Thomas, a dangerous man!* The dangerous people stood before her—*Her Ladyship and Sir John.* Mrs. Hooks set to work at once. She brought a basin of warm water and soft cloths. She bade John sit at the kitchen work table.

The inspector bowed to Mariana. "Your Ladyship."

Pivoting, Inspectator Jagger started toward the front of the house. Lady Vesta, her hands at her temples, her hair escaping her chignon, followed. *Saints' souls, I pray she follows Jagger to the village,* Mariana thought. Bending quickly, she salvaged the part of her letter John had dropped in the skirmish. She cast it into the fire, where it curled into ash as Mrs. Hooks bathed and bandaged John's wound.

John, subdued, left the kitchen. "Madam," he called to Mrs. Hooks, "have your man send the doctor to me."

"Aye."

The moment John moved out of sight, Mariana rounded on Mrs. Hooks. "We must warn Thomas."

Chapter 46

Mariana sat by the window with her embroidery, her gaze sweeping to the hills. A sharp wind came up during the afternoon. Poor Thomas, left to the elements. She caught her breath when a group of policemen thundered past, their horse's hooves flying. Inspector Jagger made good his threat that he intended searching more diligently for Thomas.

Lady Vesta, beside herself with hysterics after the altercation in the kitchen, kept to her room.

A Godsend, Mariana thought. She'd not seen John since the doctor had called and attended him. Hopefully, he slept. Close on tea time, Mariana started downstairs. She stopped, her hand going to her throat.

John, his head bandaged, stood at the foot of the stairs. Slamming his foot on the first riser, he blocked her path. "That letter was to Thomas O'Geary, wasn't it?"

"Don't be ridiculous." She tried to push past him.

He laughed crudely. "Imagine, our dear Lady Mariana playing the tart for a commoner?"

"You're drunk. Get out of my way." He closed the space between them. Losing her balance, she grappled for the banister. Her foot slipped. John caught her before she fell. Leering at her, a dangerous glint in his eye, he husked. "Don't be frightened, my sweet. Relax. You're safe with me."

"Get out of my way."

His eyes bright, his touch probing, he grasped her arms, his eyes level with her breasts. "A pity the letter isn't in your bodice, my love, or I should be forced to retrieve it." Drool pooled on her bare skin.

"If you touch me, I swear I'll kill you."

Fumbling, he lifted his head, trying to pull her forward to kiss her. She brought her leather boot up and kicked him against his shin. She'd have aimed higher for his more vulnerable parts, but hadn't time.

Cursing, he lunged back. "You'll pay for that."

Seizing the moment's freedom, she ran upstairs, shut herself in her room and locked the door. She stood against the door, heaving to catch her breath. He didn't follow. It was becoming impossible to remain at Thornywilde. Yet, how could she leave? Where could she go? She couldn't leave Aunt Portia at Lady Vesta's mercy. Nor could she abandon Thomas in the hills. Two people she loved best. Both needed her now.

This night, she was glad she and Aunt Portia were expected to take supper in their rooms. Abbie readied Mariana for bed. Mrs. Hooks had sent up one of her potions—a heady tea, sweet with spices. Mariana found her eyes closing, her limbs relaxing, and she felt herself drifting. A knock rudely brought her to consciousness. Taking the candle, she slipped to the door. Surely, John wouldn't continue his pursuit. "Who's there?"

"Abbie, m'lady."

The maid entered, closing the door. "M'lady, Gannett said to tell you that Mr. O'Geary is gone from the hill."

"Gone? Where?"

"He didn't say, m'lady."

Chapter 47

*M*ariana assisted Mrs. Hooks making nut cakes. "Where is the sugar hammer?"

"In the dry larder, Your Ladyship. I'll fetch it."

"No need." Mariana pushed her hand through her hair against the kitchen's humidity. "Your lovely sauce will stick." Going to the larder, Mariana found the hammer. She had proceeded to break apart the hard sugar loaf, when loud voices sounded from the front of the house.

Where was Abbie? She should be finished with the bedrooms by now. Securing her straying tendrils of hair, Mariana pulled off her apron and made her way to the the door. She stopped short, her hand flying to her opened mouth. The front door gaped open. A crazed woman stood inside, the sun a halo behind her, her face cast in dark relief.

"Who-?" The startled question had barely left her lips when Lady Vesta and John emerged from the drawing room. Seeing the woman, Lady Vesta stopped, grasping John's arm.

The strange woman proceeded toward Mariana.

"What do you want?" Mariana's voice wavered. The woman seemed not to hear her. "Who are-? Stop, I say!"

The stranger, her expression bespeaking madness, lunged forward. She held a long heavy object like some sort of iron bar in her hand. In an instant, she crashed the weapon across Sir John's head. The blow sounded like splintering wood. Fresh blood ran freely, staining John's bandage. He fell to the floor in a dead faint.

Lady Vesta screamed, dropped to her knees over her son. "You've killed him! You've killed him!" The woman jumped over Sir John's prone body, scrambling toward Mariana. "Stop!" Mariana screamed.

Her Ladyship rolled over and over in a tangle of silk skirts and petticoats, then wobbled up on all fours like a dog. Blood smeared across her face, her hands, and her lace bodice. She stared open-mouthed at Mariana as if in a stupor. The interloper, distracted by Lady Vesta's panic, paused before wrenching a dagger from her pocket.

"Run," Mariana shrieked to Her Ladyship.

The dagger raised, the woman turned from Vesta, then pivoted to plunge the glinting blade into Mariana. Launching around, Mariana pushed the madwoman back—the dagger blade above her like a hangman's axe poised to fall. Struggling, her foot struck the discarded iron bar and she fell onto her knees before the maniac.

A shot rang out. The woman fell.

Wheeling, Mariana looked up. Thomas, wearing priest's clothing, stood, a derringer in his hand. "Saint's souls!" she cried. "It's you, Thomas." Scrambling up, she limped into his arms.

"My love," he whispered, burying his face in her hair.

Chief Constable Jagger pushed inside the door—two deputies following.

"Seize the priest!"

The deputies acted on Jagger's orders. "Only, you aren't a priest, are you, Mr. O'Geary. Hardly, with two murders to your credit."

Chapter 48

*A*t his desk in Garda headquarters, Jagger reveled in his good fortune. He'd captured the fugitive, Thomas O'Geary, with little effort. He visualized his job as secured, his Dublin superior pleased. A promotion in sight. Perhaps, even a commendation from London Home Office.

"Whitcomb, my good man. Bring Mr. O'Geary to my office." Jagger couldn't resist toying with his mouse once it lay impaled upon its trap. At the sound of chains rattling along the hallway, Jagger sat up straighter. He tented his hands like a man in penitent prayer. He eyed O'Geary coldly as Whitcomb led the man inside. Not cowed, certainly not beaten, O'Geary stood before him. *Damn the wretch,* Jagger thought, taking in the man's stalwart form, his arrière-pensée - his mastery of mental reservation.

"There is a severe law against masquerading as a priest and taking unsuspecting people into your confidence."

O'Geary sat down on the stool the deputy indicated, stretching his long limbs as though he lounged in a drawing room. He appeared thinner than Jagger remembered. As any fox would who'd run about the hills without a den. "Have you nothing to say?"

"Sir, I did not realize your comment required a response."

A harsh snort of indignation. "An explanation, then."

Thomas, with eyes both clear and blue, looked at the Chief Constable. "I have killed no one, save a maniac woman intent on killing Lady Mariana." He paused, then bent his neck for a brief moment. He looked up. "I want to see justice done as well as you."

The sun shining through headquarter's high window showed the stubble of the man's fair beard. In that light, too, Jagger saw the shadow of dark hollows beneath O'Geary's eyes.

"Justice?" Jagger sneered. "Fleeing prison and taking to the countryside, putting decent citizens in mortal fear. Bursting in on those at Thorndywilde. You call that justice?"

"From another's perspective, hardly so. But that isn't the truth of the matter."

Damn the man's arrogance, Jagger thought. He watched O'Geary closely. The criminal mind had long fascinated him. O'Geary represented an unusual criminal, a skilled artist, a man whose work was sought on the continent by the rich and famous. A man who'd duped a simple gaoler into believing he was to have a portrait sketched. A sketch by one who painted royalty. The man before him was clever. Jagger couldn't deny that.

"Suppose you tell me your version of justice," Jagger taunted.

O'Geary didn't hesitate. "Find Ian Cluny's killer."

"I have," Jagger said smugly.

Ignoring him, O'Geary continued. "There's much you don't know. For starters, Sir John Desmond and his mother, Lady Vesta Chasteen wanted His Lordship, Sir Charles Belmont of Thornywilde, dead. They tampered with mushrooms from Old Madge."

Jagger held up his hand. "Do you refer to Old Madge, the imbecile?"

"She's hardly an imbecile, sir."

"Your opinion. Continue."

"Sir John purchased mushrooms. He asked for poisonous ones. An experiment, he said. Old Madge was smart enough to give him spoiled mushrooms, not poisonous ones. They made His Lordship sick—very sick. He couldn't recover. He was murdered."

"A vicious rumor," Jagger said. "Go on. The mushroom woman likely wanted His Lordship dead."

"Hardly," Thomas said. "Sir John burned her cottage. He meant to kill her."

"Ridculous," Jagger hooted. "Besides, the old hag's no longer in the hills."

"No, she isn't," O'Geary said softly. "She fled to Dublin."

"She aided you there?" Jagger demanded, sitting up straighter. "She'll go to gaol for helping a murderer."

"The poor woman feared for her life. Not only at Sir John's hands, but at Ena Guthre's, who tried to kill Lady Mariana."

"Who is this Ena Guthre you murdered at Thornywilde?" Jagger had viewed the woman in the local surgery—a tall creature, emaciated from rough living. How she clung to life defied everyone.

"It's a long story, this story of Ena Guthre," Thomas began. "She was a distant cousin of Lady Catherine Belmont. She came to Thornywilde to serve as lady-in-waiting when Lady Catherine wed His Lordship. They had a parting of the ways and Ena left Thornywilde. She was known by His Lordship in his youth at Cork. She also knew Martin Canady, His Lordship's art teacher."

Thomas paused, inhaling slowly.

To get his lie straight in his mind, Jagger thought.

Thomas continued. "I don't know the full connection between Ena Guthre and His Lordship. I do know that he trusted her to transact some business dealings. Business dealings that involved Mr. Canady. Business dealings that involved a great deal of money. It's believed that Mrs. Guthre stole some valuable property belonging to a man His Lordship represented. His Lordship's illness kept him from resolving the matter before he died."

Thomas paused.

Jagger found the story fascinating. A fabrication, but fascinating. As much as he hated the aristocracy, he admitted an interest in their privileged world. "Go on."

"Over time, Mrs. Guthre became unhinged, or, mentally incompetent, or mad. In her warped way of thinking, she believed Lady Mariana responsible for her bad fortune. She plotted revenge for these imagined wrongs. She came to Thornywilde, slipped into the castle and occupied the tower room where she spied on the household."

Thomas paused again.

"Go on, or I shall have you returned to your cell."

"Mrs. Guthre learned that His Lordship was engaged to marry Lady Vesta Chasteen. Ena . . . Mrs. Guthre, believed herself in love with His

Lordship. She believed that His Lordship should have married her and not Lady Catherine. I'm certain she meant to kill both Mariana and Lady Vesta." Jagger frowned. "She seemed more intent on killing Lady Mariana."

"It would appear so," Thomas agreed. "Yet, who knows the mind of a mad woman? Perhaps she thought Lady Vesta was dead. The woman was on the floor near her son when I came into the hall."

Jagger pointed his silver letter opener at O'Geary. "Tell me, O'Geary, why *were* you at Thornywilde that day? You didn't know the Guthre woman was there. Don't tell me it was to protect Lady Mariana. Your tales of chivalrous intentions ring false."

Thomas shrugged, drew one long leg up, massaging his chafed knee. "I'd thought on it for some days. I'd had no luck finding Cluny's killer." He met Jagger's gaze. "Frankly, I was tired of running and hiding. I meant to turn myself over to you, but, first, I wanted to tell Lady Portia and Lady Mariana my intentions. They are . . . they are my friends. I didn't get the chance. Ena burst into the house. I did what I had to do to stop her. She was too crazed to listen to reason."

Jagger stood. "I must say you have spun quite an entertaining story. *Whitcomb!*" Jagger called.

The large policeman loomed in the doorway. "See O'Geary back to his cell."

"Yessir."

After O'Geary's departure, Jagger drew out paper and dipped his pen into the inkwell. He paused. He'd not yet sent reports of O'Geary's capture to his superiors. Perhaps he should delay a day or more on caution's side. If the Guthre woman died as a result of O'Geary's shot, he could charge two murders against the charlatan. Keeping silent for the moment was a risk, but one Jagger felt he must take.

Should word leak to Dublin about O'Geary's incarceration at Lough Glendelough, he could always claim failed mails. "Whitcomb," Jagger barked.

"Yes, Chief Inspector."

"Go to O'Geary. Demand Old Madge's Dublin whereabouts. Threaten him."

Whitcomb returned minutes later. "Lower Glannery Street below the River Liffey."

JONNI RICH

Chapter 49

ariana knew emerald green was Kathleen's favorite color. *Lovely bracelet,* she mused, emeralds glittering on Kathleen's arm as her friend pushed a velvet jewel cask to Mariana.

"You may choose any trinket you fancy."

"Trinkets?" Mariana sorted through the expensive baubles. "You jest," she exclaimed, taking a sapphire bracelet set in yellow gold, "these are costly and exquisite. Hardly trinkets."

"Nothing is too good for you." Kathleen looked on eagerly as Mariana plundered the small treasures.

Slipping the sapphire bracelet onto her arm, Mariana held it up, admiring it. "The sapphires," she said. "If you insist on favoring me with a gift, though I don't know why." Frowning hesitantly, she unlatched the bracelet and plopped it back into the cask. "I really can't take it."

"I absolutely will not take no for an answer." Kathleen retrieved the bracelet and snapped it on Mariana's wrist. "The bracelet is to remember me by. Now, promise you'll come and visit. It's been ages since we've been together."

Mariana sensed her smile fading. She tried appearing cheerful. "I'll come . . . when I can. Aunt Portia . . . and..." Her voice trailed.

"I understand. Of course, you must take care of your aunt. But she cannot need you forever," Kathleen said. Bustling up and closing the jewel cask, she shouldered her cloak. "I really must hurry or Harry will send the servants after me. I wanted to see you to say goodbye."

Once Kathleen left, Mariana carried the tea tray to the kitchen, the sapphire bracelet sparkling on her wrist. Abbie hadn't returned for the tray, which was unlike her.

Mrs. Hooks stood over the worktable chopping vegetables. She turned and looked up. "M'lady, you put a fright in me when your shadow fell across the table."

"We're all jumpy," Mariana said, placing the tray on the worktable. "Where is Abbie?"

Frowning, Mrs. Hooks wiped her hands on her apron. "I don't rightly know." She paused. "She went—ye know—up to him. Sir John didn't come down to breakfast. He rang for a tray."

"Have you seen her since?"

Mrs. Hooks squinted. "Let me think. She took in the kitchen wash. Then, she was to bring in the turnips. I can't say as I've seen her since. Believe me, I will have a harsh word with her when I do. Leaving me to do everything. Thornywilde ain't no fancy house with a queen's staff."

* * *

Whitcomb led Thomas back to his cell, from the stark windowless block on the prison's far side, from the small room reserved for punishment and torture. His leg ached from the chain's weight, and the walk. Whitcomb had only questioned him. The man hadn't appeared threatening, but demanded to know where to find Old Madge. He'd betrayed Old Madge's whereabouts, praying the while the old soul would conquer her mistrust of the village people and return to tell her story.

Despite what many thought of her, many more held her in high regard, for she knew every plant that grew in the hills, every remedy for plaguing ailments. Not only the unlearned trekked to her cottage for help, but many a fine coach and carriage traveled there, as well.

Chapter 50

*J*agger couldn't explain why he vacillated and hadn't forwarded news of O'Geary's capture to his superiors. Each day he delayed, he further chanced ending his career in disgrace. He knew if he lost the village Chief Inspector's post, he'd return to England in shame. He walked a tightrope.

He'd sent Whitcomb to Dublin to locate Old Madge. If O'Geary had told the truth about the mushroom poisoning, he could build a case against the arrogant Lady Chasteen and her son. Thomas O'Geary would hang for murder, and the woman and son could fight their way through the courts for murder.

The next morning, Jagger woke with a thundering headache. He dressed, set out for his office. There, he couldn't concentrate, either. For discipline, he took out a book of Latin poetry. The Latin made him less mindful of his aching head. Most of the passages he knew from memory, except here and there, when an unfamiliar word stopped him. Now, after three cups of strong tea, he felt somewhat better.

A knock sounded at the door. "One moment, please." Closing the book, he slipped it into his desk drawer. "Come in."

Whitcomb stepped inside, his broad flat face wreathed in a smile. An old woman accompanied him.

Jagger gawked. The creature with Whitcomb resembled a gnome more than a woman. *Old Madge,* he thought. She looked very different today from the infrequent times he'd seen her. Her appearance bordered respectable. She wore a dark brown frock that sharpened her intelligent blue eyes.

Whitcomb closed the door looking as pleased as if he'd returned some rare escaped animal to its keeper. "It's her ye were asking for, sir."

Old Madge walked to his desk, curtsied, and came directly to the point. "I came with your man since ye were seeking me."

"Have a seat."

"Thankee, sir. Thankee." Old Madge lowered her small frame into the chair at the desk's corner. Her short legs prevented her feet reaching the floor. He understood why many thought she was one of the wee people. Personally, he didn't believe in such rubbish.

"State you name, madam," Jagger said, assuming an authoritative tone.

"Madge Greevy, widow of Simon Greevy, fisherman, lost in the Irish Sea the second year of our marriage."

"What do you know about the death of Ian Cluny?"

Madge faced him squarely. "Her, Ena Guthre knifed him in his back, sir. She bragged about it and said she'd get a reward, that he was one of the Ribbonmen. She said Thomas O'Geary would hang for the crime since she stole his knife from the artist studio."

"How do you know this for a fact?"

"For a fact, sir, she bragged to some of the tenants what she knew."

"Can you name these tenants?"

Madge shook her head. "I could name them, sir, but they donna come in. Too fearful, the tenants are. Too fearful of the Ribbonmen. Too fearful of the Garda."

Jagger would come back to Cluny's murder. To his righteous mind, the man had needed murdering for what he did to the policemen on Cormac Hill. That sentiment would never find its way into any official report.

"What do you know about the mushrooms that killed Sir Charles Belmont?"

Old Madge bristled "I sent me 'shrooms to Thornywilde with Mr. O'Geary. Me 'shrooms are good ones, as fine as the lush meadows, sweet rain and the good God produces. But, 'im from Thornywilde wanted poison 'shrooms."

"Who from Thornywilde?"

"'Im, Sir John."

After her daring statement, Old Madge sat back, her large head tucked into her shoulders. The only sound in the room was the ticking clock and Whitcomb's sudden intake of breath.

Jagger's blood rushed. He tightened his lips. Madge Greevy trod on dangerous ground.

"Do you think you can toy with His Majesty's law?"

"I canna tell ye in so many words what is His Majesty's law, sir. I can tell ye the truth, which I've done."

"Madam, consider your station," he said harshly.

"I can prove what I know if ye will let me have me way for the space of one day."

Jagger frowned. Women hadn't the same rights as men and this old hag lacked common respect. She was less than a village wife.

She looked at him, sunken eyes clear, a slight smile playing about the corners of her wide mouth. "A woman is no different from a man, Chief Inspector, sir. Among us, there's good alongside the evil. In nature, too." Her bright eyes sparkling, she continued. "The bitter grass springs up beside the sweet. The false vine beside the fruitful . . . the devil's spores beside the true 'shrooms."

Jagger was on the verge of dismissing her when she leaned forward, her blue eyes riveted on him. "Sir, I'm no the fool though many take me for such. You didna bring me from Dublin just to ask what I believe about Sir Charles's death." She cackled. "Thomas O'Geary spoke truth when he said he didna kill Ian Cluny. He didna kill His Lordship, neither."

"And, you know who did?" Jagger taunted, pushing his chair back. He went to the window. Let the old witch dig a pit for herself. Later, he'd see her sent to an asylum. "What do you propose?" he said, turning.

Madge Greevy replied. "'Tis on this wise, sir . . ."

Chapter 51

Spring fast approached, the mornings dawning clear but still cold with a nip in the air as though winter regretted its passing. Mariana opened the deeply recessed bedroom window, inhaling the southern breeze, still cold with the hint of salt. She began to dress.

She shuddered, pulling on her stockings, pink silk with moss green rosettes. John had resumed his amourous overtures, forcing her to avoid him. She was grateful he'd recovered from the terrible blow he'd sustained the day Ena Guthre attacked them all. But not grateful enough to encourage his attentions.

Her Ladyship and John had left the house early to visit one of Her Ladyship's village acquaintances. The mother and son weren't expected until late evening. Their absence lent a cheerful air to the house. Pulling her light shawl about her shoulders, she started downstairs. Her step fell light on the stairs and down through the hall. In the kitchen, Mrs. Hooks stood over the rumbling stove, browning strips of pork for a meat pie.

"Morning, Your Ladyship."

Mariana acknowledged the cook.

The stove glowed from all its chambers, emitting cozy warmth. Mariana put the kettle on for tea. "Has there been word from Abbie?" It had now been thirty-six hours since they'd seen Abbie.

Mrs. Hooks shook her head. "Most odd," she said. "She musta run off with a lover, the poor dearie."

Not like Abbie, Mariana thought, measuring tea leaves into the pot, the leaves emitting an aromatic scent. The kettle whistled. Mrs. Hooks hurriedly added the boiling water to the teapot.

Settled at the dining room table with a jar of plum jam, and toast from the warming rack, Mariana frowned in thought. *Abbie would never leave without telling us,* she brooded, slathering jam across the toast.

Still puzzled, she went back into the kitchen. Mrs. Hooks slid the browned pork onto a sizzling warming plate. Turning, she wiped her hands on her apron, her face beet red from the hot stove. "Oh, m'lady. It's something I can be helping ye with?"

"I'm not satisfied about Abbie." She found it difficult expressing her anxiety about the little maid. Granted, Abbie could be excitable at times. However, loyalty endured as the girl's truest characteristic. Mariana's vague unrest about Abbie's absence had now burgeoned to alarm.

"As I've told ye, afore, the last I saw of Abbie was the day after Mr. O'Geary shot Mrs. Guthre. She brought in the kitchen wash. I sent her for turnips. I never saw her no-more after that. 'Tis most odd, I admit."

"Indeed." Mariana poured a cup of stout brown tea, swirling fresh cream into it. "Try to remember the day of the shooting. There must be something more. Something we can't remember."

Mrs. Hooks sighed sympathetically. "I miss the wee lass as much as any." The cook's scant ginger brows met over her wide nose, her thin lips sucked inward in thought. "She brought in the kitchen wash. I sent 'er to the root cellar for turnips. I neer saw her no more." Mrs. Hooks shrugged. "Gannett's asked about the village. None's seen 'er."

"There must be some logical explanation," Mariana said. "Tell me, what did Abbie do after she brought the turnips to you?"

Frowning, Mrs. Hooks replied. "She ne'er brought no turnips. I ne'er saw her again. You don't suppose the wee people stole her away. They'll do so if you disturb 'em in the hills after dark. All white-faced, they are, waiting to take a mortal beneath the ground. Abbie was fierce on believin' in the wee people."

"That's silly superstition. There's an explanation for her disappearance." The girl wouldn't have left with a lover from the root cellar. Not that dusty, dank place with its hard-packed soil and stone floor. No place for Abbie to contemplate meeting a lover. She'd have come up from the cellar with dirt on her face and gown, and cobwebs in her hair. Too, she was dressed in her roughest, most unflattering gown, her grubby work dress. However, many a domestic ran away with a lover rather than face their employers. A not uncommon occurrence among domestics, especially the young pretty ones. And, Abbie was a pretty girl.

Mrs. Hooks was speaking.

"What did you say?"

"Now, 'Er Ladyship says I needs a day helper besides the scullery girl, Sally. One from the village, she says. With all the cookin' and them to be waited on, it's moren' these old knees can manage." Mrs. Hooks voiced her last remark under her breath.

"Of course, you may send for help," Mariana said. "When you find such a person, send them to me for examination." She didn't care if she defied Lady Vesta's wishes.

She met Gannett. "Tell me, the day Abbie disappeared, how did she seem to you?"

"Seem, m'lady?"

"You know. Was she excited . . . er, had she a new gown or hat, maybe?"

"Oh, no, m'lady. She was the same as always. That's it, m'lady, the same as always."

Mariana suppressed a wry chuckle. You could rely on Gannett for an understatement.

The morning and afternoon passed, with still no word from Abbie. Mariana considered seeing Chief Inspector Jagger about the missing maid. Perhaps she could learn something of Thomas's condition at the gaol.

After lunch, she was busy with the ledgers when Mrs. Hooks popped into the library, a tiny woman in tow. *What's this,* Mariana wondered? The woman appeared too old for a domestic. Though the woman wore a voluminous black bonnet hiding most of her face, there was something familiar about her.

A chuckle rumbled softly beneath the bonnet. "Ye don't recognize me in me finery."

That voice! It couldn't be! "You're Old Madge!"

"Aye, m'lady, 'tis true."

Old Madge had aided Thomas in Dublin. Mariana owed the woman a debt of gratitude. "Please have a seat."

"Thankee, Lady Mariana. A fine ride I had up from Dublin. In a carriage all the way, thanks to Chief Constable Jagger. Changed coaches twice, and each time I enjoyed a fine meal at the inns."

Mrs. Hooks rolled her eyes, then left them alone. Old Madge leaned forward. "I'm 'ere about Thomas. There's work to be done and quick."

"I don't understand."

"'Tis on this wise. There's some that say I go to the hills at night and talk to the wee people and that I'm to be feared. It's foolishness, but to them that believe it, it's truth. Truth can be like that, how you make it."

"What has that to do with Mr. O'Geary?"

Old Madge closed her eyes and began rocking back and forth in the chair. A tug of fear washed over Mariana, viewing the woman's trance. The same feeling she'd experienced all the years before, when she and Kathleen had gone into the wood, spying on the old woman. Old Madge's voice barely audible, she whispered, "There was two. There was two. Me knows there was two." The old woman's eyes snapped open. "In time ye'll know. There was two."

"What are you talking about?"

"Ye mustn't follow when I leave this room. 'Tis a wee bit of work must be done. Secret like. When the time's ready, I'll show you."

Surely the odd creature wasn't mad. No, cunning intelligence shone from the clear dim eyes. An odd request, though.

"You mean to hide in the house?" Mariana asked incredulously.

* * *

At seven o'clock sharp that evening, Mrs. Hooks and the new domestic, Lilly, a rawboned girl of sixteen with an overbite and large ears, served supper in the dining room. Her Ladyship and John had returned early from the village and presided at the table.

"What has become of the regular girl?" Her Ladyship snapped as Lilly followed around after Mrs. Hooks.

Mariana overheard this as she prepared to take trays up to her aunt.

"Abbie is away," she said to Lady Chasteen as she passed through the dining room.

"There're always away when you need them," John slurred. He pushed his chair back, staggering to the sideboard where he poured a stout whiskey, sloshing a bit onto the lace runner. With an unsteady gait, he veered away from the table, cutting Mariana off from the hall. He leaned forward, lips pursed, to plant a kiss on Mariana's cheek. "Dearest, you look peaked," he said, instead.

Recoiling, Mariana frowned as he shuffled back, and slid into his chair. If his mother thought his behavior odd, she kept it to herself. His eyes were red-streaked. Thus far, Mariana had kept him at bay, though his attentions grew more shocking and disturbing with each day. He was a dangerous man beneath his lackadaisical façade.

Glaring, Her Ladyship threw up her hands. "Are there no vegetables? Can this bourgeois not produce a decent parsnip?"

"I'll bring in the vegetables, ma'am." Wheeling, Mrs. Hooks started toward the kitchen. Her Ladyship pointed to Lilly. "Gel, go with her and quit ogling your betters."

Disgraceful exhibition, Mariana thought. Upbraiding the servants rudely. Her father would never have allowed such behavior. Shaking with anger, Mariana tarried in the hall.

Lilly returned within minutes, bringing an oval platter covered with a silver lid. She set it before Her Ladyship. Her Ladyship lifted the cover, screamed, clutched her throat, and dropped the cover to the floor where it rolled near Lilly's feet. Lilly stared at the lid as if it had a life of its own. Her Ladyship pointed to the dish as though it were a serpent. "Who is responsible for this? Charles died eating this horrid mushroom pastry. It's never to be served in this house again."

Mrs. Hooks dashed into the dining room wielding a pork pie. "Your Ladyship, what's wrong?"

Her Ladyship, eyes bulging with anger, her face a chortled red, began to scream. "You dare serve mushroom pastry and have the gall to ask me what's wrong!"

After an anxious glance at Lilly, Mrs. Hooks retrieved the lid from the floor and set it on the sideboard. Confused, she wrung her hands. "I've made no mushroom pastry. I don't understand." She turned to Lilly. "Where did ye get this dish?"

Lilly could barely speak for weeping. "Her, the maid in the passage." She gestured to the butler's pantry. "She gave it to me."

Her Ladyship sputtered. "There's no other maid at Thornywilde."

Lilly howled louder.

"Take this insufferable dish away."

"No." Sir John reached for the pastry, dishing a large portion onto his plate, and taking a generous bite. He leered at his mother. "Divine pastry. So light, it fairly floats."

Speechless, Her Ladyship stared at him as if some sick realization occurred to her and the horror of that knowledge silenced her. The surreal moment stretched.

Sir John continued eating the pastry like a petulant child. "Dear Maman. Do have some. It's delicious. I'm as fond of mushroom pastry as my dear, dead father-to-be was."

Her Ladyship scowled. "Perhaps, you'll succumb to the same illness as your dead father."

Lilly appeared from the kitchen. "Dessert is served." Mrs. Hooks marched in with seed cake and hard sauce.

The candles flickered. Mariana jumped in the hallway. The dinner trays in her hand rattled. She slipped the trays on a hall table. Were the terrace doors ajar?

Her Ladyship gestured to the pastry. "My witless son enjoys a practical joke," she said to Mrs. Hooks. "Carry this disgusting dish to the kitchen." Lilly scurried forward, picked up the dish, and dropped it. Pastry and shards of glass lay in a sticky knot.

"Stupid girl!" Her Ladyship hissed.

Sir John laughed.

As Lilly cleaned the floor, the candles sputtered and went out. Her Ladyship beat the table with her fork. "Light the tapers."

Mrs. Hooks came with the tinder "'Tis a draft from the terrace."

"Who gave you permission to open the terrace doors?" Her Ladyship seemed in acute distress.

"I'm sure Gannett left them locked tight," Mrs. Hooks said. She went and closed the doors.

What was Old Madge up to?

Sir John refilled his whiskey glass.

The floor swept clean, Mrs. Hooks announced she was serving coffee in the drawing room in twenty minutes.

"I would have more hard sauce, first," Her Ladyship said.

Mrs. Hooks brought the sauceboat around and poured a liberal amount over the cake. Her Ladyship began eating the sticky topping. Moments later, she dropped her fork, lurched forward, and fell face first into the hard sauce. It splattered down the front of her silk gown

John weaved up from his chair as if his feet couldn't locate the floor. He started toward his mother. Staggering, he fell against the door, and slipped onto the floor. Pushing up, he tried to sit. "What's happening?" he slurred, his arms akimbo, his hair an untidy white mass.

Mariana watched in horror as he scooted around like a maimed crab. She hurried into the dining room and tried to assist him. He was too heavy. She managed to drag him against the sideboard, his legs splayed in front of him like a scarecrow's.

Her Ladyship stirred. Her face wobbled in the sauce. She mumbled incoherently.

"Lilly, Mrs. Hooks." Mariana screamed. Mariana kept trying to lift Her Ladyship's head. The woman kept pushing her hands away. Mrs. Hooks came running into the dining room.

She looked from Sir John on the floor to Her Ladyship in the sauce. "My soul, what mischief is this?" The cook pried Her Ladyship's face up and mopped her forehead with a napkin.

"She's dying!" Sir John screeched, trying to stand, but instead slumped down, a perplexed expression etched across his face.

Mariana sent Lilly to fetch Gannett. With his help, they got both victims seated at the table. As if unsure what to do, Lilly stood fanning the both of them with her apron.

Coming to her senses somewhat, Her Ladyship pointed a finger at Mariana. "What have you done to us?"

The curtains beside the French doors rippled. Old Madge stepped into the room.

Sir John screamed—an unholy sound coming from a man. "You," he cried, pointing to Old Madge.

Old Madge laughed. Her strange cackle seemed to bounce against the dining room's dark walls. She pointed her finger at John. "Ye lied to me. Ye didna want the tainted 'shrooms to do away with a hunting dog gone bad. Ye wanted to kill his lordship. I sensed evil in ye from the first. Weakness and evil. I made a grave mistake." Old Madge advanced toward John as she spoke. "I laid your greatest folly to weakness, not evil, and for that His Lordship died."

John's eyes rolled. He went white. "It was Maman."

Her Ladyship drew back her hand as if to strike him. "What are you saying?"

Sir John threw a wad of soggy cake at his mother. Lilly and Mrs. Hooks sprang to aid the shocked woman.

"Get it off me," Her Ladyship screamed, staring at the gooey cake and sauce lumped on her pearl brooch. Mariana swabbed the brooch, trying to calm the hysterical woman.

Old Madge advanced to stand in front of Sir John. "The woman did not wish 'Is Lordship to die. It was ye. While 'Is Lordship lived, it would not be long before he would know you for what you are. He would have kept Lady Mariana from you."

Her Ladyship pointed a sticky finger at Mariana. "You have caused this, you horrible little witch!"

Old Madge sighed. "Perhaps I've done a worse crime than the two of you. I've poisoned two with my 'shrooms rather than one."

John struggled to sit upright. "Poisoned? You poisoned the pastry?"

"You're lying," Her Ladyship shouted. "We're not dying."

Old Madge laughed, the eerie sound like tinkling sheep's bells in distant meadows. "The poison was not in the pastry, but the hard sauce. It's deadly. If ye have last words, speak now for soon ye'll speak before your maker in eternity."

Her Ladyship clutched her throat.

Sir John gave his mother a quick glance, then screamed. "I killed him."

She gasped. "John, you couldn't."

"I did," he leered. "Your son!" He spat. "You've made sport of me since the day I was born. You've made me your lackey, your buffoon, a foil for your devious schemes. I killed your precious fiancé. I might add the fiancé you never loved, but wished to marry to get you out of debt. Only you inherited more debt from this cursed Thornywilde . . . this . . . this blighted place from the dark ages."

Throwing back his head, John began laughing hysterically. "I'm a killer, mother. For once I did something on my own, for my purposes without dancing like a puppet as you pulled the strings."

The terrace doors sprang open. Chief Constable Jagger and three deputies stepped into the room. "An interesting confession, Sir John. I'm arresting you for the murder of His Lordship, Sir Charles of Thornywilde."

John laughed even louder. "Arrest me . . . . arrest me . . . you idiot. Why bother arresting a man dying from this old hag's poisons."

Chapter 52

*J*ohn's wild laughter rang around the room.

They all stared at him, mesmerized, too stunned to interrupt, lest his corruptness somehow wash over them.

Jagger broke the spell. "Mrs. Greevy, what drug went into that hard sauce?"

"Sir, Chief Constable, a harmless gift from our Roman invaders. The Valerian root. I mix it with a secret ingredient which brings confusion. Later, they will sleep . . . soundly."

Sir John stared slack-jawed at Old Madge. His eyes bugged and his tongue protruded as though he couldn't control its contortions. Long moments passed before her words sunk into his consciousness. When he understood he'd been tricked, he lunged toward Old Madge.

The deputies subdued him after a fierce scuffle. Her Ladyship sat speechless as she struggled to focus her eyes.

* * *

Chief Constable Neal Jagger sat behind his desk long after normal hours. The old woman had spoken the truth. She got a confession. A confession Jagger wished he could conceal. Murder of Lord Belmont. The charges would never stick. Not with Lady Chasteen's connections. However, it did Jagger good for Sir John to sit in the village gaol until their solicitor in London made arrangements. It was a serious matter, arresting a person of peerage, even for murder.

Sir John would deny his confession, swear it was drug induced by Old Madge's hard sauce.

Jagger heard from Whitcomb, whom he'd left at Thornywilde after they brought Sir John in, that once Her Ladyship recovered from the sauce, she ordered a carriage and left. She'd told Whitcomb she was going to the village to see her son. That was not the case.

Jagger knew he couldn't afford facing Lady Chasteen and whomever high ranking official she would bring to influence her son's release. Even as much as Jagger was not a friend to the gentry, he would need to release Sir John and spirit him away from the village at once.

It was past time he wrote his Dublin superior about O'Geary's capture. With pen in hand, he wrote two letters, one to his superior and a duplicate to King George.

Sir,

Thomas O'Geary, fugitive from Spiller's Island Gaol, is incarcerated in the village gaol. I took the liberty of delaying this important information as a complication arose with a second party's confession to the poisoning of His Lordship, Sir Charles Belmont of Thornywilde. The matter is delicate, since a member of the gentry confessed. I have dispatched a letter to our vested sovereign's court and await further instructions.

Yours most respectfully,

Chief Constable Neal Jagger

He sent a rider on horseback with the letter to Dublin.

The one to King George, he crumpled in his pocket.

Chapter 53

*M*ariana sat with Aunt Portia in the drawing room the evening following Sir John's arrest. Mrs. Hooks served coffee as Gannett stoked the fire. Outside, a soft spring rain pattered against the windows. Mariana gripped her cup with icy fingers. Her eyes were red from crying.

She hated what Sir John had done to her father. She'd sensed the evil in John Desmond all along. "It isn't true justice that he'll never answer for what he did," Mariana said to Aunt Portia.

"My dear, we mustn't be bitter. He's been found out. He and his mother will never show their faces in Lough Glendelough."

"Is that true justice?" Mariana said as Mrs. Hooks rushed in.

"Ye won't believe it. Come with me."

"Whatever is wrong?" Lady Portia demanded, reaching for her cane. Mariana helped her aunt to her feet. They all ran to the kitchen. Abbie sat on one of the worktable stools, her heart-shaped face filthy. Lilly was busy sponging Abbie's face and arms.

"Oh, m'lady," Abbie wailed the moment she saw Mariana. "It's been ever so dark in the root cellar. 'E shut me in there and I couldn't get out. I'd have starved if I hadn't eaten turnips and carrots."

"Who shut you in the root cellar?" Mariana demanded.

"Sir John. He was drunk. He attacked me. When I ran outside to get away from him, he . . . grabbed me arm, dragged me into the cellar. Then he closed the door and fastened it."

"He didn't . . . didn't violate you?" Mariana said.

"No, m'lady, he merely left me to die with the likes of rats and such."

Abbie snuffled tears of joy. "It come about this way. He said I was listening by the carriage when he talked to Her Ladyship. I wasn't. I was on my way to close the root cellar for I'd left its door open. I thought him and Lady Chasteen were gone in the carriage but 'e'd slipped behind me. He shoved me in the root cellar, said I'd wake up on the other side in Hades."

Abbie began blubbering like a baby. Aunt Portia tried to soothe the distraught girl.

In the process of attending to Abbie's needs, Mariana discovered Old Madge had slipped away.

Chapter 54

*T*homas was no longer in the village gaol - Mariana had heard rumors that he'd been released. She must know for certain.

Later in the week, she stood in the drawing room watching the post coach speed toward the house. She clasped her hands and breathed a prayer. *Let Thomas be on the coach.*

He was not.

She jumped at every sound. She couldn't sleep. She'd sent note after note to Chief Constable Jagger requesting information about Mr. O'Geary. She couldn't stay in the house. She made her way to the stable where Gannett saddled Hera.

"Ye ride to the village, Your Ladyship?"

"Perhaps," Mariana said.

Gannett looked worried "I'll take ye in the coach. It could rain more. Ye'll be wet through and through. Lady Portia said I'm to look after you."

Gannett could be bothersome where their welfare was concerned . . . hers and Aunt Portia's. Still, she wanted to be alone. She needed to be alone.

She climbed onto the mounting box, slipped her boot into the stirrup, swung her other leg around the saddle horn. The mare danced, eager for a run.

"Tell you, what, Gannett," Mariana said. "If it starts to rain harder, you may drive the coach to the village. I'll wait for you at the livery."

With that, she gave the mare a tap and the horse cantered down the long path to the road.

Within the hour, Mariana stood outside Chief Constable Jagger's office in the company of Deputy Whitcomb. She asked to see the Chief Constable alone.

Whitcomb nodded and grinned. He tapped on the inspector's door, and opened it after a muffled voice called. "Come in."

"Lady Mariana," Chief Constable Jagger said, pushing aside a sheaf of papers on his desk. He stood and escorted her to a chair near his desk. "It's a pleasure to see you. What can I do for you?"

She came to the point. "Where is Mr. O'Geary? We've heard he's been released. You know that Ena Guthre killed Ian Cluny. Sir John confessed to poisoning my father. There's no reason to hold Mr. O'Geary in any prison any longer." She thought about Spiller's Island goal and shuddered.

Jagger tented his fingers. They were startlingly white against his dark blue uniform. He seemed indifferent. "My dear Lady Mariana. I'm doing everything I can. Lady Chasteen appealed to His Majesty on behalf of Sir John. Her barristers insist we detain Mr. O'Geary awhile longer. I had to have him moved for his safety." Jagger shook his head, smiling balefully as though he meant his words to sound sympathetic. "Until all the facts are in. This remains a highly complicated case."

"Still, Mr. O'Geary is an innocent man," Mariana countered, sensing Jagger's indifference.

"That may be true," Jagger continued. "His Majesty and advisors are embroiled in intense political intrigue, fighting to keep the Whigs in power. While His Majesty is attempting to form the government his subjects want, he is also trying to be true to his friends and their needs. The court has read Lady Chasteen's petition. A decision will be rendered, when I cannot say."

"The English Courts! Hasn't Ireland courts?"

"Her Ladyship has created a stalemate that we're unable to address. Our hands are tied."

"Where is Mr. O'Geary?"

"That is confidential information." Mariana knew the interview was over. Outside, the rain held off, though low sodden clouds blanketed the sky. She walked toward the livery where she'd left her mare. What could she do? Go to England and request an audience with the king? That might take months, if ever.

She passed the vicarage. The vicar was outside tending his flowers. "Lady Mariana," he said tipping his floppy hat. "So good to see you."

"You, as well," she replied. "Your flowers are lovely."

"Thank you. The flower show charter is important . . . an honor. I take it seriously. As do my parishioners." He looked at her keenly. "My dear, you are troubled. How can I help you?"

There was the possibility the Reverend believed Thomas O'Geary deserved to be in prison. Would he understand her concern?

"It's about Mr. O'Geary, isn't it?" The vicar said.

How perceptive of him. "I can't find out anything," Mariana said on the verge of tears. "I fear they've taken him to England to await a trial there."

"My dear, you must come inside. We'll talk about this."

Once seated in the vicar's cozy parlor, and served tea and cookies by the man's housekeeper, the vicar bade the housekeeper close the door.

"This is hearsay," he began. Before she could ask what he meant, he continued.

"I was at the livery some days back. It was a busy morning there. Our little coach needed wheel work. While I couldn't hear everything, mind you. And, I'm not given to listening out of turn, but I really couldn't prevent overhearing the wheelwright talking to one of the chief constable's deputies. The deputy speaking to the wheelwright, is, I believe a relative of the wheelwright. He said that the police coach left the gaol the night before bound for Harberst Castle."

"Harberst Castle," Mariana gasped. "I fear it's a worse place than Spiller's Island."

The Reverend sweetened his tea with four sugar lumps. "No, my dear, I understand the castle is a much more genteel gaol than what we have in the village, and certainly superior to Dublin's Spillers Island."

Back at Thornywilde, Mariana wrote to the authorities at Harberst Castle.

* * *

No reply arrived from Harberst Castle. However, a letter arrived from Lady Chasteen's solicitors, stating that Lady Chasteen meant to take possession of Thornywilde in the near future to settle Lord Belmont's debts that she had covered.

"We have less than two weeks to vacate," Mariana lamented to Aunt Portia. "How can that odious woman do this to us?"

"Be patient, dear Mariana. Think how your father loathed this place. He never cared for the country, nor this place or the farms."

"Where are you going?"

"To the library. There are books I must pack."

"It's lovely in Cork. You'll love it there. We will live in the little house your mother left you until you come into your inheritance."

"That won't be until I'm thirty. Quite a long time."

"Never the less," Portia said. "The little house is charming. It rests near a lovely lake. There are hedges, garden paths, fountains. Your mother loved that house. She and your father spent a great deal of time there after they were married."

Life was not a fairy tale, Mariana thought after Aunt Portia left the room. Life was a series of losses, gains, trust, distrust, and decisions. She sighed. She prayed the move to Cork was the right decision. Yet, she had no choice. The Dublin townhouse must be sold to satisfy her father's creditors. Thornywilde went to his scheming former fiancée.

Mariana went down to the library and continued her packing. Abbie brought tea. The dark steaming brew smelled wonderful as Mariana poured it into a cup. As she settled at the table near the window, the cabriolet drew to a stop on the gravel path in front of the house.

Old Madge sat beside Gannett. Mariana had not seen the woman since the night of Sir John's arrest. Strange, she thought, with a sense of foreboding. "We have a visitor," she said to Abbie. "Have Aunt Portia come to the library. Tell her that Old Madge is here."

A short time later, both Aunt Portia and Mariana greeted Old Madge. The old mushroom gatherer seemed to have reverted to her former odd self, and without the confidence she'd exhibited the night she tricked Sir John into confessing.

"She was a pretty one, like you," Old Madge said, nodding at Mariana.

At first, Mariana thought she spoke of her mother, Lady Catherine, but something in Old Madge's manner told her differently. Her heart pounded. "I don't understand."

Aunt Portia gave her a warning look.

Old Madge continued. "My husband, Greevy, had a good sister, a midwife of great skill. The biggest houses sent for her here in the village and beyond. She came to Thornywilde one night in a raging storm. She rode her pony. It stormed fierce that night. Greevy's sister came on—it was her calling—she said afterwards. Two babes came into the world that night—two girl babes."

Mariana gasped. Did the old woman speak of her? Had Ena Guthre delivered a baby that night, as well? Was the old gossip true? Was she a bastard?

"But-"

Aunt Portia urged Mariana to keep quiet.

Old Madge continued. "Lady Catherine was dying." She stopped speaking, staring hard at Mariana. "You come first, then the other one. As Lady Catherine lay on her death bed, she cried, 'Bring me my babes.' Ena took one, the last one born, away. She put ye, m'lady, in your mother's arms. She put her knife to Greevy's sister's throat. 'Ye speak a word of this night, ye'll die by my hand.' She lied to Sir Charles and said the other babe had died. Then, she brought a babe from a loose girl and placed it in your dying mother's arm, and you in the other. That way Lady Catherine died in peace with her two babes. There was two. Ena Guthre took one for her own. Your father never knew different."

The old woman looked hard at Mariana, a strange expression fixed on her wrinkled face. In half shadow, she appeared otherworldly. "Ena Guthre burned Greevy's sister's cottage over her. She killed her. And, she would have killed me, too. And, you."

Long after Old Madge left, Mariana sat trying to make sense of the horror the night she and her twin were born. *A sister! A twin sister!* Where was her sister reared as Ena's daughter? *Thomas,* she thought. He would know. He had dealings with Ena when they helped transport her father's paintings.

Chapter 55

*H*arberst Castle lay to the north along a ridge of rocky hills. The oldest section, constructed in Roman times stood ruined, sullen and dark against the evening sky as Gannett skillfully drew the coach up near the castle entrance. A lonely outpost in a forgotten part of the world.

Gannett stepped down from the box, marched to the castle door. Mariana followed.

A jailer met them at the door. "What seek ye, here?" the man demanded.

Mariana stepped forward. "One, Thomas O'Geary. We are relatives of the man. We must see him."

"Ye're too late, relatives," the man said. "Hims gone to England on answer to the king. There's no more here to do with Thomas O'Geary." The man slammed the door in their faces.

* * *

The last day at Thornywilde before Lady Chasteen took possession, a coach drew up. Mariana peered through the library window, then squealed in delight. "Aunt Portia. He's here! He's here."

"Who, dear? Who's here?"

"Thomas! Thomas is here!"

Thomas's step sounded in the hall. Mariana flew to meet him. How haggard he looked. Poor Thomas. "Thomas! You're really here."

He moved toward her, holding out his arms. She flew into them, leaning her head against his chest where she felt his heart beat as rapidly as hers. "My love," he whispered, caressing her hair.

"Oh, Thomas, how horrible this has all been." She clung to him tighter, her tears staining the front of his rough jacket.

He lifted her chin. "You mustn't cry. It's over. We are free from Her Ladyship and Sir John. Don't be sad."

They went into the library where Aunt Portia joined them. "You must tell us everything," Mariana pressed.

The story progressed. He'd indeed been sent from Harbrest Castle to London on order of the king. In London, there were meetings with Lady Chasteen's solicitors. Thomas had been held in private apartments, not a jail cell. He had guards and couldn't come and go at will. After weeks of this confinement, he'd been informed by messenger that he was free to go. "It came as a great surprise," he admitted to Mariana and Lady Portia. "I expected a long imprisonment, and an unfair trial. I doubted I'd ever see freedom again."

"We've worried so about you," Lady Portia said.

"It's over," he said. "I have word from Martin Canady."

"What of Mr. Canady?" Mariana asked. "I know about the stolen paintings. Is he in jail?"

"No. It seems other friends were able to secure funds to cover Ena's theft. I never trusted the woman. And, I admit, I never understood His Lordship's loyalty to the woman. I assumed his and hers was a long, complicated relation."

"It was both long, and very complicated," Aunt Portia agreed. "They knew each other as young people in Cork. Before Charles married Lady Catherine. I always felt that Ena loved Charles and hoped to marry him. She was a peculiar girl, but I never dreamed the depth of her wild fancies."

"Nor did you know that my father and she carried on a business relationship."

"No, I didn't know that," Portia admitted. "However, I can visualize his concern for Ena if for no other reason than that she was once a close friend of Catherine's."

Lady Portia pulled the bellcord for Abbie. "I've hardly let the poor girl out of my sight since her ordeal in the root cellar. Mariana, you must tell Thomas about that."

Abbie came into the room. "We shan't have more tea," Aunt Portia said. "You may take the things. We'll leave Thomas and Mariana to celebrate his return."

"Lady Chasteen is to take possession of Thornywilde in order to repay his debts to her. In fact, today is our last day here."

"I didn't know that," Thomas said. "The last I heard Lady Chasteen was in Paris. She and Sir John. I understand they plan to make Paris their permanent home."

"Good riddance for Ireland," Mariana said, somewhat heated.

"Are you sad to leave Thornywilde?" Thomas asked.

"I'm not truly sad. Of course, there are things about the old place that I'll miss. In fact, I'm happier than I deserve," she said, looking up into Thomas's blue eyes. Eyes that held so much emotion.

He shifted from the chair by the fire to the spot beside her on the settee. "You must forgive me," he said, "if I stare at you, but you must know that I feared I'd never see you again."

"Would that have been so terrible?"

"More terrible than you can imagine."

"For me, as well," she said barely above a whisper.

He drew closer. "May I speak freely?"

"Would you?"

"I have loved you for so long. I think from that first day in Dublin when you alighted from the carriage with your trunk of books."

She smiled. "Can you ever forgive me for the awful trick I played on you?"

"You mean impersonating a model?"

"Exactly."

"Perhaps I could, with persuasion."

"This persuasion, you speak of?"

"Perhaps we speak too much," he suggested, slipping his arm around her shoulder.

"Perhaps so."

He leaned forward, his hand caressing her face as he lifted her lips to his. It was a long moment before he drew back. "There's naught to forgive, heart's dearest. There never has been."

"I do love you, Thomas O'Geary," she said.

"If you'd not loved me back," he whispered, "I think my life would be over. It will always be you, Mariana, and only you."

How blind she'd been. And, foolish, as well, to think she'd never love a man. "My school!" she exclaimed.

Thomas' brows furrowed. "Your what?"

As secure as she felt in his arms, she pushed him aside, and sat up straight. "I've always dreamed of opening a school for young ladies. I knew when I either married, or came of age, I'd have my mother's inheritance."

He looked long and steadily at her. "What are you trying to say?"

"Only that someday - someday soon, I can open my school."

"You mean not waiting until you're the ripe old age of thirty to inherit? You mean something else?"

"Something else, entirely, Thomas O'Geary."

"You mean to marry in the near future?"

"I am considering it."

"It will be a spectacle," Thomas said. "You the loveliest bride in Christendom."

"And, the groom?" he began, practically under his breath. "Who is this luckiest of mortal men, I pray."

"Why, Thomas, I thought you'd never ask."

The next long moments were lost in the oblivion of their passionate kiss.

"Thomas," Mariana began, once they drew slightly apart. "You must know there has been a question about my birth. It has followed me all my life like a dark shadow. The question of whether I am Sir Charles and Lady Catherine's legitimate daughter. Or, a baby substituted when the true infant died at birth. Ena Guthre told me I was a harlot's babe sent to my mother on her deathbed to ease her dying pain, and to give my father an heir. None knew the true story. The midwife who delivered me is dead. My mother is dead. My father was not admitted into the birthing room until I was there.

Thomas, I have a twin sister. A sister Ena Guthre kidnapped that night and reared as her daughter. I am my father's true heir. And, so is my sister. Nannies and lady's helpers cared for me until I was about three or four when Aunt Portia came here. I never knew any of this until Old Madge revealed the truth."

"Sssssssh." Thomas placed a finger on her lips. "Don't continue, Mariana. The past is the past. Let it lie dead with the dead."

"You don't understand. I *am* the daughter of Lady Catherine and Charles Belmont. I'm no imposter. No by-blow brought in. And, I have a flesh and blood sister."

Chapter 56

homas left for Dublin the following morning with plans to meet with Mr. Canady, who'd traveled from London.

A sense of forboding troubled Mariana all day. She hated that Thomas left so soon after they declared their love for each other.

A rough wind tore at the budding trees. After the evening meal, Mariana and Aunt Portia withdrew to the library with their coffee. Neither felt much like conversation. Gannett had laid a warm fire.

"If it's as well with you, Mariana, I'll take myself off to bed."

"Shall I ring for Abbie?"

"Yes, my dear. Do send the dear girl to me."

"Will ye be wantin' a log or two more in here?" Gannett asked after Lady Portia went upstairs.

"No. Let the fire burn itself out."

Mariana lay back in the comfortable chair, her eyes closed, her mind spinning wonderful dreams of wedding gowns. June, she must wed in June. The weather would be lovely then. Of course, Kathleen must be there.

She must have dozed, for when she opened her eyes, the fire had become ash, and the room had grown cold.

Her fingers chilled, she hurried to the kitchen. She'd take hot milk up with her. If Mrs. Hooks was abed, she'd make it herself.

The cook wasn't in the kitchen. No matter. Mariana fetched a saucepan and milk. The outside door opened. Mariana looked up, expecting to see Gannett in the passageway. Sir John stood there. He held a derringer, a dangerous weapon that he pointed at her. "No," she screamed.

Mrs. Hooks came rushing into the kitchen. She stopped, an expression of pure horror etched upon her face.

John swung the gun around at the older woman as one staring at an unbelievable apparition. He fired a shot. Mrs. Hooks fell to the floor.

"You monster!" Mariana screamed.

John seized her arms, pinning them behind her back. "No bullet for you, my lovely," he husked, his hot breath steaming her neck. Her face to the wall, she couldn't see Mrs. Hooks. "Think of what you're doing."

Ignoring her, John pushed her farther against the wall, the force of his body heavy against hers. "You'll die slowly with time to regret what could have been," he said spitefully, nipping the back of her earlobe with his teeth. She screamed.

"Who's to hear, lovely? I've taken care of the others. I locked that horrid little maid in the turret. Old Gannett is staring up at the sky after I put a beam across his head. The old woman here should have been in bed."

Mrs. Hooks moaned. John seemed not to have heard her. Thank God she wasn't dead.

"You murderer," Mariana shrieked. "Come to your senses."

Sir John bit her neck. She tried to kick him but he kept one knee pressed against the small of her back. If only she'd worn her hoops, her body wouldn't be so vulnerable. Instead, she donned a soft gown with only one petticoat, and that not horsehair. He jerked her hands back and jutted his knee deeper into her spine. "Always the do-gooder, aren't you? Seeing to everyone except me. You were to be my bride. Don't ask me why I still want you, but I do."

Instinct warned her to remain as calm as possible. She wasn't truly injured. Not yet. As she tried to breathe normally and keep her wits, he jammed her harder against the wall where the acrid scent of dust and varnish filled her nostrils. Either her bones would break or the wall, or she'd faint. She gasped for breath. Another wrench in the small of her back brought a spasm of pain. Pain so sharp her knees buckled.

She must distract him from his sadistic actions. "I'm glad you lived after the blow to your head. I feared you were dead when we didn't hear from you. From you, or your mother."

"Ah, lovey, you lie. You never cared a whit if I lived or died. Now, did you?" He sucked at her neck, then his teeth drew blood. She cringed in horror.

The next instant, he hissed like a viper, and slid down her back. He slumped onto the floor. She turned. John Desmond lay at her feet, the length of a carving knife buried to the hilt in his back. "Abbie!"

Abbie ran forward, crying hysterically. "He ain't fit to live, not after what he's done to all of us. Is he . . . is he . . . is he dead?" The little maid went ashen white, then collapsed alongside her victim. She sat on the floor next to Sir John staring at him as if he were the devil himself.

Mariana knelt over Mrs. Hooks. A trickle of blood trailed from the elderly woman's temple. Opening her eyes, she tried to sit up. Thank God, she was alive. Mariana helped her onto a chair.

Abbie still sat in a forlorn heap staring at the dead man. Mariana shook Abbie's shoulders. "Get up. He can't hurt us now. I'll see about Mrs. Hooks. You go outside and find Gannett." Abbie didn't move. Mariana pulled the maid to her feet. "Hurry."

Abbie tried to stand, but refused to look away from Sir John's body. She seemed transfixed in horror. Mariana wheeled the little maid around. "Go find Gannett."

At last, the instructions sank in, for Abbie started toward the kitchen door.

Mrs. Hooks's wounds weren't life threatening. The bullet barely grazed the woman's temple. She sat in a chair now breathing normally. She gave the still form on the floor a wary look. "Is 'e dead?"

Mariana shuddered. "He is." Not much blood spilled from the wound. Evidently, the knife had staunched most of the flow. Mariana pulled a tablecloth from the drying line beside the stove and draped it over Sir John's body. At one time, none of them had believed he was capable of murder.

Minutes later, Abbie came into the kitchen leading Gannett. Mariana gasped. The man had a lump the size of a goose egg on the back of his head and he was soaked from lying in the rain. Despite the wound and his wife fussing about him, Gannett would have none of their sympathy. "It's no need to pamper me like a baby, woman. I'm going for the chief constable."

"You'll do no such thing." Mariana meant it. Gannett had suffered a terrible blow. He could lose consciousness and fall off his horse. "Keep him here," she said to Mrs. Hooks.

She ran out to the stable, rousing a stablehand. "A man's been killed at Thornywilde. Bring the chief constable and the doctor."

A nightmare followed. Jagger and Whitcomb arrived along with the village doctor. The policeman examined Sir John's body. The two men questioned Abbie and Mariana until Abbie dissolved in a flood of tears.

When Mariana could no longer tolerate more of Jagger's badgering questions, she took control. "We did not see Abbie with the knife, but it happened as she told you."

"That's right," Abbie said with a sudden flash of courage. "Sir John had Lady Mariana against the wall. I saw she were in terrible pain. Then, I saw Mrs. Hooks on the floor. I took her for dead. I didn't think, I just ran and stabbed the knife in 'is back."

"You didn't hear a shot beforehand?" Jagger asked.

Abbie nodded. "I heard a sound. I thought it was thunder or the shutter banging."

Chapter 57

Three months later
Cork

*M*ariana and Thomas had set their wedding date for the first week in August.

"Do you like this little house?" Aunt Portia asked as she sorted through the boxes of linens Kathleen had sent as a wedding gift.

Mariana sighed, looking around the morning room. It was perfect. The house was perfect. No majestic staircases, no turret rooms like Thornywilde, but a great deal of light from the many windows and a charming walled garden. "I love it here. I love being near the sea. And, a lake of my very own just outside my door." She clasped her arms around herself and smiled. "Thomas and I will never have a cross moment here. His studio is perfect, too."

"Your mother grew up in this house," Aunt Portia said. "Later on, your grandparents moved into the manor house that's now let. Someday you may want to live there. It's much grander." Aunt Portia grimaced. "You certainly have linens enough to outfit a large house."

"Thomas and I will take the large house one day. It will be my girls' school. And dear Kathleen will have to send even more linens."

"Did I hear my name?"

Mariana wheeled. She'd not heard the door. Kathleen stood in the hall. Mariana ran and embraced her dearest friend. "How did you find me?" Mariana demanded once they drew apart.

"Aren't you going to ask me to sit down or remove my bonnet and cloak?"

"Oh, Kathleen, it's so good to see you."

Kathleen sat on the chintz settle near the window where a soft summer's breeze lifted her stylishly-curled, red tendrils around her cheeks.

Mariana followed Aunt Portia's gaze to the Italia painting over the mantel. There was no reason to deny the artist now. "It's a lovely picture, isn't it? My father painted that seascape under his pseudonym, Italia."

Aunt Portia looked startled at first, then shrugged and took up the conversation. "Our dear Charles led a double life. He would have been happier if left to his paintings without the care of Thornywilde. He was never cut out for business."

Kathleen turned towards Mariana. "I saw Thomas in Dublin," she said. "He told me you were here. And, about the wedding. It'll work so wonderfully well. I'm going north to my husband's lodge to entertain some of his friends. I begged Thomas to let me surprise you. He's such a dear, Mariana. I couldn't have chosen better for you myself."

Kathleen stayed the remainder of the afternoon, then insisted she must leave. Mariana walked her out to the waiting carriage. "I'll miss you," she said.

Kathleen smiled. She'd grown so sophisticated and capable, it was difficult imagining her as the quiet, somewhat withdrawn girl she'd been. "You are my dearest friend, and once you and Thomas are married and settled, I insist you come and stay at least a month with us."

"Of course, we will."

"My dear." Kathleen's manner changed and she appeared solemn, almost troubled.

"What is it?"

"Perhaps Thomas should tell you. He left it up to me. I shouldn't have spoken."

"You have spoken, and you seem so troubled until you've set my curiosity ablaze."

"He has found your sister in London. She is very frail. Her name is Sirabell, and she has a son that Ena left in an orphanage north of the village. He means to bring Sirabell and her son here when he comes to Cork. I think he secretly wanted me to tell you before they arrived on your doorstep. It would be such a shock. He was troubled that you may not want to meet this woman."

"Is that all? Not meet my twin sister! How could I refuse?"

That evening Mariana wrote to Thomas telling him that Kathleen had shared his news. He was not to worry. She'd welcome her sister and her nephew.

Chapter 58

July

Sirabell and her son, Timothy, had been with Mariana in the little house in Cork for several weeks.

A week after Sirabell and Timothy had settled in, word had come that Ena Guthre had died. Mariana had seen to it that the troubled woman would have a decent burial.

Mariana still found it strange looking at the sickly woman who resembled herself. Their hair was the same dark color and their eyes, the same blue, but a difference existed around their mouths. Sirabell's lips were thinner and wider. Also, she was a bit shorter and much, much thinner.

"She's had a hard life," Aunt Portia confided. "She told me that her husband, a seaman, deserted them. She has no idea if he's dead or alive."

"How sad," Mariana said, feeling slightly hurt that Sirabell hadn't confided in her. They were sisters after all. "She hasn't come to me with anything about her former life," Mariana said to her aunt.

"It will take time, my dear. This is very new to Sirabell."

"She's new to me, as well," Mariana said.

"That's true, but you didn't have such a person as Ena Guthre for your mother."

The morning before Thomas was expected to return, Mariana and Sirabell sat in the morning room sewing the hems in Mariana's lingerie.

"You will make a lovely bride," her sister said, looking up and pushing her needle in the cushion at her wrist.

"You are very kind." Sirabell often displayed a mercurial disposition and Mariana found herself choosing her words carefully.

Her sister's composure crumbled. "No, I'm not kind. I'm weary and heartsick at what my mother . . . I mean what Ena has done to both of us.

To all of us." Sirabell gestured outside the window to Timothy, who was brushing a downy pony. Dropping her head, she covered her eyes with her hands. Sobs shook her frail frame.

"You mustn't cry," Mariana said, going to her sister's side. "Things will come 'round. You'll see. We must give it time."

"How can we ever be normal people?" Sirabell said sadly, looking up quickly, her eyes red-rimmed. "Timothy and I cannot stay here and accept your kindness. It's . . . it's unnatural." She spoke almost fiercely. "You and Mr. O'Geary will soon be married. You don't need strangers underfoot."

"You're not a stranger," Mariana said firmly.

"I am, and you know it." Sirabell slipped to the front of her chair. "I want us to be friends and in time, I think we shall. But this is too soon."

Of course, Sirabell was right. Mariana felt much the same way, but her sister's needs overshadowed any awkwardness and inconvenience her presence presented. "I can't allow you to go away. Not now, that I know you exist. This is a transition time. We must both be patient."

"Don't think I'm ungrateful. I'm not. Lady Portia has told me about a little cottage not far from here. It's part of Lady Catherine . . . I mean our mother's holdings. If Timothy and I could move there and I can rest and try to regain my health, I'd be most thankful."

"Of course, you can have the cottage. It's as much yours as mine."

* * *

August

The wedding day arrived. Mariana insisted the ceremony take place in the garden with the sea as a background. Gannett escorted her to the canopy, where she met Thomas at the altar, and they exchanged their vows. Her heart so filled with happiness, she wanted to laugh and cry at the same time.

"I do," she repeated after the vicar.

"You may kiss the bride."

Thomas lifted her veil and pushed it aside gently. He took her in his arms and touched his lips to hers. "We will have a wonderful life," he promised.

"I know," she whispered.

The End

www.ingramcontent.com/pod-product-compliance
Lightning Source LLC
Chambersburg PA
CBHW020210260626
47156CB00002B/321